From The Women's Press Ltd
34 Great Sutton Street, London EC1V 0DX

Nina Sibal holds BA and MA degrees in English literature; from 1969 to 1972 she taught English at Delhi University. She joined the Indian Foreign Service in 1972, and was First Secretary in India's Permanent Mission to the United Nations in New York between 1976 and 1980. She chaired the UN group which drafted the Convention on the Elimination of Discrimination against Women. From 1983 to 1986 she studied law, and received her LL.B in 1986. She is currently at work on another novel.

NINA SIBAL

Yatra

(The Journey)

 The Women's Press

First published by The Women's Press Limited
A member of the Namara Group
34 Great Sutton Street, London EC1V 0DX

Sibal, Nina
   Yatra.
   I. Title
   823[F] PR9499.3.S/

   ISBN 0-7043-5009-2
   ISBN 0-7043-4019-4 Pbk

Typeset by Reprotype Ltd, Peterborough
Printed and bound in Great Britain
by Hazell Watson & Viney Ltd, Aylesbury, Bucks

Contents

Principal Characters

The Chahals of Kohat

Swaranjit Kaur, a young girl from a family of metal workers from the village of Kotli Loharan near Sialkot

Manmohan Singh, her brother

Garkal the *dacoit*, her grandson

Sucha Singh, known as the Miser, son of Manmohan Singh

Makhan Singh, son of Sucha Singh, a businessman

Gopal Singh, his other son, a barrister

Prabhjot Kaur, wife of Gopal Singh

Kailash Kaur, daughter of Sucha Singh, favourite of Swaranjit Kaur

Sobha Singh Palji, her husband

Bhagwana, their servant

Gulshan, their slightly crazed daughter, alias Maitreyi Phillips, assistant to Dr Zimbabwe, the Magician

Prakash, nephew of Sobha Singh Palji, lover of Kailash Kaur

A green-eyed musician, the unnamed love-child of Prakash and Kailash Kaur, a Junior Commissioned Officer

Lajwanti, daughter of Gopal Singh and Prabhjot Kaur

Satinder, elder son of Gopal Singh and Prabhjot Kaur, also known as Sardarji

Poonam, his beloved first wife

Meera, his second wife

Anita, their daughter

Sudershan Chawla, Anita's husband

Paramjit, younger son of Gopal Singh and Prabhjot Kaur, an army doctor

Sonia, his wife, a Greek woman from the island of Paros

Krishna, their daughter, a teacher and social worker

Anu Whig, her husband, a lawyer

Sohail, their son

Gola, son of Paramjit and Sonia
Shalini, his wife

Dhiraj Kumari, Paramjit's lover
Mrs Kapur, her sister, mother of Dhiren Kapur
Michael Stavros, a Greek shipping owner, Sonia's first lover
Surjit Markand, director of a refugee camp near Jullundur, Sonia's
  lover
Anjali, his wife, friend of Sonia Chahal
Mona, their daughter, in love with Dhiren Kapur
Ranjit Dhawan, a doctor, Krishna's lover

Dr Hassanwalia, Chief Medical Officer at the Military Hospital,
  Secunderabad
Susan, his Anglo-Indian wife
Pritam Lal Whig, a bankrupt
Bhim Lal Whig, his son, editor of the *Punjabi Tej* and father of Anu
  Whig
Chaman Bajaj, his friend
Sampuran, later Baba Sampuran, Poonam's brother, member of the
  Babbar Akali movement, a terrorist
Bhaskar, another activist in the Babbar Akali movement
Bhai Dhian Singh, an old man from the village of Gyani Basantpur,
  sympathiser of the Babbar Akalis
Mr Ajit, bureaucrat stationed in Calcutta, handling relief operations
  along the Bangladesh border
B.L. Choudry, a politician active in Kalidiggi
Father Serifis, missionary, local head of the HART organisation osten-
  sibly providing medical relief to refugees in the Kalidiggi area
Pratibha Anand, head of the Red Cross, a political figure from the
  Independence Movement
Bibi Chinti, a sinister figure present during violence and betrayal
Ram Adhikari, servant of Satinder and Meera
Malik ⎫
Trikha ⎬ political adventurers
Gurmukh Singh Sharifa ⎭

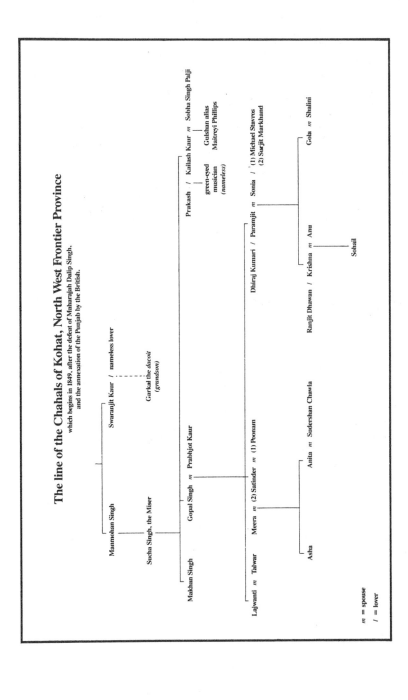

The line of the Chahals of Kohat, North West Frontier Province

which begins in 1849, after the defeat of Maharajah Dalip Singh,
and the annexation of the Punjab by the British.

Manmohan Singh

Sucha Singh, the Miser

Makhan Singh

Swaranjit Kaur / nameless lover

Garkal the *dacoit*
(grandson)

Gopal Singh *m* Prabhjot Kaur

Prakash / Kailash Kaur *m* Sobha Singh Palji

green-eyed
musician
(nameless)

Gulshan alias
Maitreyi Phillips

Lajwanti *m* Talwar   Meera *m* (2) Satinder *m* (1) Poonam

Dhiraj Kumari / Paramjit *m* Sonia / (1) Michael Stavros
(2) Surjit Markhand

Asha

Anita *m* Sudershan Chawla

Ranjit Dhawan / Krishna *m* Anu

Gola *m* Shalini

Sohail

m = spouse
l = lover

Based upon Survey of India map with the permission of the Surveyor General of India.   vide letter NO. 62A-3/AI SI® Vol XI
© Government of India Copyright 1987.

Based upon Survey of India map with the permission of the Surveyor General of India.   vide letter NO. 62A-3   SI® Vol XI
© Government of India Copyright 1987.

□□□□□   Krishna's *Padyatra*
■■■■■■   journey of Sardarji and Gola
oooooo   journey of Manmohan Singh and Swaranjit Kaur

1
Krishna and Family, 1984

Krishna's arrival in Delhi was heavy with the loss of fathers.

Anu, her ex-husband, was waiting for her beyond the customs barrier at the airport. She was surprised and pleased to see him. London had been lonely. Her short visit had been useful in terms of the contact she had made in the Forestry Commission. And an international environment foundation had committed funds for an important river project in the Gharwal Hills. But it was good to be back in Delhi, and find Anu there to receive her. His manner was deeply disturbed, as if the usual protective layers had been stripped away.

'Krishna,' he said. 'My father's been murdered. Shot dead in Jullundur, three days ago.'

She had last met her father-in-law, Bhim Lal Whig, ten years ago, during the divorce proceedings. So much had happened since then. His photograph in the newspapers sprang to her mind as she stood there. He had been an active politician, aspiring to be Chief Minister, always with his alter ego, his friend Chaman Bajaj, who had wanted to destroy Krishna.

'Oh, my poor Anu!' She held him right there, an island in the stream of busy passengers and moving luggage trolleys, his large, plump body fading into her shoulder for a moment. 'Why did you bother to receive me? There must be hundreds of things for you to do. Your mother...'

'I just wanted to. You were returning from your first visit abroad.' They drove in silence. The murder hung as a deep area of gloom above them, waiting to be touched. After London, the sudden grip of Delhi's summer was savage on her back.

Arriving at her house in Delhi she had stepped across a telegram slipped under her door. 'Father had a massive heart attack. Come immediately.' Its message was pasted in typed, uneven patches of letters on pink paper. Anu calculated that it was already fifteen

1

days old. Hysteria spread through her. Her father might be dead already, swollen and convulsed, blue from his heart attack. 'There's a night train to Dagra,' she said, her voice tight in her ears.

Soft darkness hung between the eucalyptus trees on Ring Road as Anu drove her to the railway station. There was hardly any traffic until they got to the crossing at the Indraprastha Power Station. Then they were flung into the sky by the new Asian Games flyover, and cars and trucks whizzed past them at great speed. Her much-loved city of Delhi, which had given her such an unkind welcome, lay spread out below. A grey, octagonal stadium, one of Delhi's new monuments, a huge yellow crane, and ladders from construction work still drawn up beside it.

'Come back with me tonight, Krishna,' Anu said softly. 'I'll take you to Dagra tomorrow.' How safe, to let herself into the long channel of his affection, to be gathered in by his arms from the hard loneliness of waiting for Ranjit, from the need for making herself, piecing together each moment, the edges of the one before dimming as she came to the next, formal constructions like this cold, modern stadium.

'Come with me,' he said.

A harsh sky behind the stadium was lit by three huge chimneys from the power station. They threw up shapeless ghosts of luminescent smoke, spotted with iron grit, like tall angels of death. She could not talk about death, not yet.

'How is Chaman Bajaj?' she said.

'I know you never liked him, don't let that put you off. Now that my father is dead, he won't come to the house. And I've given him my father's dogs, those Great Danes which terrified you. The outhouse is empty.'

'Anu, I must go to Dagra tonight.' She thought of their son, Sohail, at school near Dagra. Perhaps he was with his grandparents. 'I'll bring Sohail back with me.'

'No seat,' the man at the ticket counter said when Anu asked for a ticket for Dagra. His bush shirt was crushed from the day's work, and patches of sweat spread under his arms. The fan above his head circled slowly, its ancient blades black with soot from the trains.

Anu drew her away from the queue and waited until the others had got their tickets. Then he took the reservation form, carefully clipped a fifty-rupee note to it and pushed it through, under the booking clerk's watchful eyes. The crisp banknote scraped on

2

wood, was loosened and put away. A big register was pulled out, columns were consulted. Then the clerk said tonelessly: 'There is recent cancellation. Berth in ladies' section is available.' Carefully, he wrote out her details: Krishna Chahal, Female, age 36.

She took out the telegram again, on the railway platform after Anu had left. Her hands were dark and thin against its pink paper, even faintly blue in the neon light. The dark colour of her skin was the most unusual thing about her, a colour which had deepened and got darker over the years, sometimes suddenly. Like a barometer it registered the changes in her life.

Once her skin had been pink and white. Born of a Greek mother, and who knows what father. The skin was no help at all with that question, though she had been anxious to zero in on fathers, before she had learned the hard way to take the whole world as parent. It had responded with its colour to magical events and people. Until recently, she had not affected those people and events, just watched them, her skin darkening in response. But now she had begun to claim a high-priced freedom from her skin, to get out and actually reach what was happening, to shape events, to assume the quality of leadership.

The remarkable change in her skin's colour had not been gradual, like a baby's grey eyes deepening naturally to brown. It had happened in waves and patches, as she nosed out personal and national events, flushing and darkening from them.

She had been eight years old, the year her brother Gola was born, when she had seen a patch for the first time. Still pale, like a fresh wound, spreading over her thin thigh, gathering up the fine blonde hairs as it went along, clearly visible in the light from the street lamp across the road.

Her father, who till then had loved her completely, had picked up a black shoe, to beat her for shouting rudely at him. He had chased her slowly in his socks. Her parents had thought she had run out of the house. As she sat on the bathroom steps, breathing in the fragrance of an ancient banyan tree, slowly falling asleep, she had heard them sending out search parties to her friends.

When she had woken up, the skin on her face papery with dried tears, she had noticed the patch, and had run back into the dining room. Her father had taken her into his arms, his cropped moustache harsh against her forehead, his skin smelling faintly of shaving cream.

From then on, the darkening nature of her skin had belonged to

3

her, as her secret. Only she had understood it. And Ranjit, who had entered into her life later, and had known of her pain. Others had noticed only the darkening evidence, especially her mother who had been increasingly agitated as she examined her from day to day.

Sonia Chahal had had her favourite theories. 'There must be someone on your father's side, some black crow whom one of his ancestors married, which brings on this odd colouring.'

'Or maybe your mother went to bed with a Turk.' Her father's reply had been humourless, intended to destroy. Anything would serve her parents to hit out at each other and this included the increasing pigmentation in their daughter's skin.

'Anyway, why worry,' her father had continued. 'It is the colour of most Indians. And she's very beautiful. Have you seen her eyes? Large and brown, with a double row of black lashes. And such good features: a graceful body, her neçk rising like a gazelle's. So what if she's dark? I named her well. Krishna. Lord Krishna was dark, and beautiful.'

But there had been a desperation about Sonia Chahal as she had taken her daughter from one doctor to another. 'Who will marry a dark girl?' she kept on repeating. The European woman had quickly discerned the market prejudices of her new land.

Army doctors had examined Brigadier Paramjit Singh's daughter with care, and had pronounced it a mysterious ailment. Only Krishna knew about her skin's disease. India was hurting her, making her a dark, glowing bruise. Her skin was a sounding board, a large, hollow shell, through which she heard the distant beating of a sea and listened to her mother's heart.

'She was such a beautiful baby, lying there in the crib. I had her in the Military Hospital in Secunderabad. Her little arms were pretty and white. In fact, the nurse commented on how fast she lost the redness of birth. Now look at her. I just can't understand it.'

It wasn't the pain of childbirth that Sonia remembered principally. Like a flash, her brain had lost hold of the pain, with no residue, only a long lethargy and weakness, as her breasts had flowed with milk.

There had been no one to talk to, no friends, no family. Her husband had been away on field exercises in Sholapur. But the baby had been white, that was important. She had thought it was Michael's. She would have been able to go back to Paros with it,

4

and nobody would have remembered her Indian marriage. She would have been the reigning belle again, blonde and beautiful.

The walls of her hospital room had been clean and white, newly washed, with knobs of prefabricated structure showing through beneath. The clean sheets had smelled faintly of starch. She had lain there quietly, her body loosening and relaxing, expanding back into its old shape, settling back after the recent trauma of birth. A nurse had brought in a covered tray with her first meal. For a long moment Sonia had stared at the food: a dish of *daal*, watery curds, two black, tough-looking pieces of meat in the centre of the plate and a pile of dry *chappatis*. At home in Paros, straight after childbirth, her mother would have brought her newly-baked bread, chicken soup with a whole egg in it, steamed fish smelling fresh and salty from the sea and a white napkin wrapped in the aroma of cinnamon. She had burst into loud tears, crying into the *daal* which had moistened the *chappatis* and had made a small pool in the centre of the chipped plate. Through the heat of a Hyderabad summer, Sonia's thoughts had whistled and shaken, heavy with tenderness for her distant mother and her deserted Paros. It was now a small, shining island, set firmly as a jewel in a wedding necklace, the blue and dreaming sea.

Almost all of Paros had come to see her off. Friends and family had filled her cabin with flowers. A bell had rung the first warning, starting the long farewells. Finally the third bell had gone, and she had stood alone on deck, and watched the long tongue of Lacci quay fade, the new double-storeyed houses and the cross of the Catholic Church added by the Italian occupation army. She had hitched her fortunes to an Indian officer in the British army and he had drawn her away. Slowly the outline of Paros had disappeared and only the dark-grey heavy water of the sea, silvered by a faint light, had stayed with her on the boat.

She had seen Piraeus for the first time next morning and had formed no attachment to its war-ravaged dock buildings, its jungle of masts and hulls and its road side vendors of crisp doughnuts. A cousin had been there to receive her. They had played together as children, but now he had seemed distant, as if already, in Lacci, she had parted from everything Greek, to go to a handsome, brown-skinned foreigner with a small moustache and brilliant black hair. But she had not yet reached him. She wondered if she would ever reach him, if his hands would enter the vast empty spaces around her heart and hold her close.

She had concentrated again on the white-washed wall of the hospital room, trying to see it, hoping her beautiful child would wake and demand to be fed, demand something, anything that would bring love from her and fill up the emptiness inside. But the baby had been quiet, sleeping like an angel.

All through her childhood and growing up Sonia had been possessed by a feeling of the sea hemming her in. She had longed to get away. Having been bred on an island had prepared her to go far abroad. But not so far that the walls should swim around her.

Sonia's mother had proffered threats. 'Perhaps I'll never see you again,' she had said, sitting on a narrow bed under the window, her black dress frayed at the wrists. Pale blue eyes had filled with tears, which spilled over and spread in a fine glaze over her cheeks. Fear and loss were in the air between them. 'Why must you go so far? Couldn't you find anybody here to marry you?'

Sonia was already twenty-five years old, and she had not been able to bear the prospect of spending the rest of her life in Paros, tending grape vines, goats and children. But it had not been for lack of suitors, of that she was quite certain.

'My sister is the most beautiful girl in Paros; be sure you look after her well,' her beloved brother Yannis had said to Paramjit. His luminous grey-blue eyes, exactly the colour of hers though not so staring and greedy, had been filled with love. He had died soon after she left Paros, killed in a sponge-diving accident, his lungs choked with water, his beautiful blonde hair floating to the surface like sea weed.

Which was the real Sonia? The most beautiful girl in Paros, a tall, fair, sinuous woman, with the strong, easy torso of a swimmer, a straight Greek nose, quite unbelievably perfect, bright eyes and masses of blonde hair, or Paramjit Chahal's wife in late middle age, shortened by spondilitis, her face and heart like a savage circus tent of wrinkles? The two women were rolled into one, knocking casually together.

Paramjit had written to her saying that the British were pulling out of India and that the Raj was coming to an end. Perhaps it had been like that when the Italian Army was pushed out of Paros by the British, and they had bundled up all their belongings, leaving behind only the shell of their new church with its gilt cross. But, of course, India was a large country, and the British had been there for two hundred years, so they must have had a lot to pack up.

She had always been able to see the sea from their small house in

Paros, at the end of a narrow path. The lagoon was tiny, a clear blue and empty, since no one came to this poor part of the island. She had looked at it from the window while her mother had cried, a desolate sight, bidding her goodbye. Then they had gone up the bright green hillside to a magenta-coloured shrine dedicated to St Anna, where she and Yannis had been baptised.

She had come gradually out of her long silence as the ship had approached Bombay. Her first view of Bombay harbour had been framed by the windows of the dining room. She had rushed up to the deck and had stood against the guard rail, her palms sweating with excitement and fear, a nameless mixture of hope and desire. It was with her whole life extended that she had approached India. There had been nothing behind her.

That was the only way to approach India. Slowly, by sea, so that you had a sense of land coming to you with its arms held out, reaching for your life. There was no point touching down quickly, in an aeroplane, coping with the pressure of passing air and a heart lurching backwards as a jet speeded to a stop.

It had been early morning, serene, washed clear by rains. Ship hulls and masts had been sharp clumps against the blue of sea and sky. The distant hills of the mainland had been still green, the edge of a continent shadowy in the waving fronds of palm trees. She had seen an occasional country boat in full, white sail, its high prow swinging up and down. Then a fleet of fishing boats, about forty to fifty of them, had set sail on the morning tide, spreading through the ships like minnows, then going on past them. The sea and the wooden hulls of the boats and their sails had been a rose pink and had gradually turned to mauve.

Sonia had been completely bewildered and stupefied by what she had learned to recognise later as typical Indian chaos, passengers and porters rushing in all directions, seemingly without objective. There had been no time for Sonia to register the fact of Paramjit's presence. Everything was in a flurry before they had left for Delhi and the wedding. Only the name of their hotel, Wilson House, where she had left her heavy luggage, had emerged from the welter of English names and uncertain explanations in Greek with which Paramjit had assailed her.

And there had been time for a visit to the Caves cut into the rock at Elephanta Island, eleven kilometres across the Bombay Harbour. They had boarded a launch crowded with passengers, climbing off the bottom step of a flight leading down from

Bombay, the Gateway of India. Once again they had been moving slowly across the sea which she had left so recently. Her silence and loneliness had returned in a great rush, and she had hid her face in Paramjit's shoulder. He had worn his khaki uniform and for a while the old romantic magic from Paros was back. Everything else had flown away from her with speed. Paramjit had reached across and had taken her hand, fondled her arm, put his strong, muscled shoulder firmly against hers. She had sensed a pride and possession in this. Then she had begun to notice the disapproving glances of white married couples and single white men. Some of them had turned away and lapsed into indifference when they realised she was white but not British and spoke a strange European tongue with the Indian man who dared to touch her in public.

Climbing the steep steps which led up to the caves, the slow process had begun. They had begun by admiring her beauty and she had gloried in the interest which washed over her large, easy limbs, clad in dark loose trousers and white blouse. Then the interest had become a cool disdain as they had seen that she was accompanied by an Indian, who had posed her on the steps, or against the bole of a banana tree, or beside a grinning boy selling guide pamphlets to the caves. Paramjit had taken photograph after photograph, as if to put his triumphant association with a white skin firmly on paper. That he had been an officer in uniform made the white tourists' disdain covert and silent, but it had been there, a tangible presence. Sonia had begun to see that in India her whiteness gave her an automatic advantage. In Paros she had been aware only of his splendid battledress, the handsome Sam Browne belt that swung across his chest on army parades, his courteous chivalry and the large amounts of money which had mattered a lot in the dire, war-stricken state of her mother's kitchen.

Ugly idols had emerged from the rock face inside the caves. Paramjit had tried to capture her wandering attention with explanations translated from the guide; he had made her feel bullet marks on one of the walls. Then she had ambled off towards the exit, wiping sweat from her face. His voice had followed her, saying that the British shooting range had destroyed Shiva caught in the Dance of Creation. She had stood under a silk-cotton tree at the edge of a high drop, gathered balls of fluff that floated down from overhead branches and had folded them into her handkerchief. She wondered what she was doing there, under a large leafy tree in a strange land, with a man with whom she had no

8

connection. Then Paramjit had caught up with her, and had drawn her away from the edge of the hillside.

He had not made love to her in Wilson House; he had been waiting for the wedding. She had crossed the seas to him; there was no going back. Nevertheless, he had been in his own way a conventional man and she had lain alone in her bed at night during the short period before they took the train to Delhi. The window had been open to let in a cool breeze from the Arabian Sea, which seemed to lap against her head although it lay beyond the curving face of Marine Drive, gay and glittering with lights. The whisper of coconut palms and mangoes in bloom, the smell of tube-roses and jasmine had come in. Every smell in Bombay, sweet or foul, had been strong, like unstopped scent bottles. Sewage, sandalwood, spices, a dead pariah dog, burning gnats, and fish manure under the *toddy* groves. She had been alone with the smells. In the morning, when she had looked from her window she had seen a line of bare female bottoms defecating at the edge of a drain, their owners anonymous and impersonal, faces wrapped firmly in flowing robes of modesty.

When she had descended to the dining-room she and Paramjit had been escorted to the Indian section, much smaller than the British section. Scores of British officers and their families had been billeted in the hotel, waiting for ships to take them home. India had been about to become independent. The hotel staff had been unfailingly courteous to Paramjit; they had been offered both kinds of cuisine available, Indian and European. But she could not miss the startled turn of pale blue British eyes as they had spotted her, a treacherous patch of white among a sea of brown faces. An edge of irritation had attached itself to Sonia's voice. Maybe Sonia's mother had been right; maybe she hadn't made such a good deal after all.

The heat of the Delhi wedding had almost suffocated Sonia, dressed in an orange satin *salwar-kameez* which had belonged first to Paramjit's sister, Lajwanti, who had pulled it out from an old trunk, showing off the thin waist of the shirt and beautiful gold embroidery on its sleeves and on the ankles of the *salwar*. But Lajwanti had been six inches shorter than Sonia and the hem of the shirt had come half-way down her thighs instead of below her knees, which didn't bother Sonia at all. She considered that she had too much covering anyway, especially with the three yards of prickly chiffon set with sequins in which they wrapped her head.

9

What had bothered her was wearing second-hand clothes for her wedding. She had trailed behind Paramjit, tied to him with a piece of cloth, making circles round the Holy Book which Paramjit's mother had carried all the way from Kohat. This was the last time the family had assembled in the presence of the holy heirloom acquired a century ago by an ancestor, an orphaned boy of eleven, who had arrived in Kohat with his young sister, Swaranjit Kaur.

The old lady had stepped out grandly at the end of the fourth circle, and had embraced her new daughter-in-law. But the hands passing over Sonia's hair had been hard, and the chest and arms against which she pressed stiff and bony.

It might have helped if Sonia had been less beautiful. Only Meera Aunty, vague, wrapped up in the future of her own two daughters, had not resented the good looks of the new blonde goddess. But it was Meera's husband whom Sonia had noticed. Sardar Satinder Singh Chahal, Paramjit's elder brother, head of the family. He had looked out from the wedding photograph above the head of the bride in his long black *khaddar achkan*, white *churidars*, and saffron turban, a red rose twirling jauntily in his button-hole.

'He is dressed like a politician,' Paramjit had whispered to her, seeing her look towards him. 'A typical politician.' Then the family pride had won through. 'He is very well known in the Freedom Movement, especially for his non-violence. He is Minister in the North West Frontier Province government.'

Sonia was happy enough to join in admiring his brother, who had said very little. Everyone had listened to him when he did speak. He had addressed her always as 'Madam'. That, combined with the old filigree necklace set with tiny precious stones which Paramjit's mother had put around her neck, had made her feel like a queen.

After the wedding, she and Paramjit had been tourists in the city of Delhi. He had taken her to Kingsway, the widest avenue in the world, past King George's statue, through the beautiful arch which commemorated the Indian soldiers who had died fighting for the British Empire in a war that had taken place before she was born, to the huge spread and splendour of the Vice-Regal Lodge with its two massive arms of the Secretariats reaching out on either side, and, lower down, the gracious rotunda of the Houses of Parliament where, Paramjit had insisted, his brother Satinder would enter as a member soon. When Satinder was not around Paramjit spoke admiringly of his brother. In his presence, however, he became

10

belligerent and chafing, like an injured bull, as if he carried a long-standing grudge of neglect against him.

Paramjit's albums were full of photos of those ten days. The bridal couple had posed on either side of a cannon outside the Vice-Regal Lodge, in Connaught Place, in nameless gardens against fountains and fruit trees that appeared to be in bloom. Her preference in clothes was evident in the photos. She had worn suits with padded shoulders and pocket flaps at the top, taken in at the waist, with trousers or fitted skirts below. One V-necked dress had tended to recur. It had two black sprays of flowers on either side, running down from just below the breasts to the stomach, with a narrow belt holding in her delicate waist. Another favourite had been a dress with small, puffed sleeves, buttons down to the waist, which had showed the entire length of her firm legs below, running down to black, perforated sandals open at the toes.

There had been no picture of the only time she had worn a sari during that period. They had arrived for a stroll in Connaught Place, where all the fashionable new shops were. Meera Aunty had tied the sari, in her usual inefficient manner. It had come undone and had trailed after Sonia. She had been walking almost in her petticoat, peering into the glittering windows, when Paramjit had seen her. She had not been able to understand his fury and deep embarrassment, since even her legs were still covered, as they were not in the dresses he liked so much. The muscles in his body had been tense and hard and she feared he would strike her. 'But there's nobody here who knows us,' she had said, her voice rising even higher than his. The pain of the first night he had climbed her, mixed with the heat in the stifling room which Lajwanti had given them as their 'wedding chamber', had risen in her mind. She had stood there still as a rock, hating him with all the fury in her heart, as he had gathered six yards of cotton cloth from the floor of the B block verandah and had somehow bunched it around her.

'Why don't you move a finger to help?' He was trying at the same time to locate a taxi.

'I don't know about these things,' she had said stonily, as the pain had risen again from the times he had rubbed dryly inside her. The pain had closed around her heart. He had pushed higher and higher, yet so tentatively, into her, his hand and his mouth like individual creatures which could not touch her, and must stay forever outside her.

11

'Well, it's time you learned,' he had muttered. 'You're Indian now; you have to wear saris.'

'I'm not Indian, you can see that. I look different from you and your family, and I always will be. I'm Greek. Do you hear me, Greek!' Her voice had been rising in hysteria, but he had not seemed to hear that, or care. Besides, he had managed to flag down a taxi. 'Oh, so you're saying that you are white and we are brown! It doesn't matter. You can be as white as you like, but you belong here now. The moment you married me you automatically became an Indian citizen. That is the law. In a few months we will be Independent. Next time you go to Greece, you will carry an Indian passport, a nice, hard blue book with three gold lions on top. No more British crowns for us.' He had been bundling her into the taxi; having recovered his poise he could afford to be loquacious.

'You didn't tell me!' she said. She had felt betrayed. A vast, empty loneliness had opened inside her and was spreading rapidly, like something sick.

'What do you understand about passports and citizenship, anyway, with your education. You don't even speak English!' His voice had been cheerful and sneering. It had driven her crazy.

She had been trapped. 'I don't care! You should have told me. I want a Greek passport. I don't want to be Indian. Dirty, bloody Indians!'

The back of Param's hand had come across in a swift arc and had hit her squarely on the mouth. She had screamed; blood from her lip was salty-sweet in her mouth. Then she had been silent. The taxi driver had been watching them in his rear-view mirror, his shoulders hunched thin with caution. There was no reason why he had to interfere in a quarrel between a white memsahib and an Indian officer in a smart belted jacket.

Paramjit and Sonia had returned by train to Bombay, a couple settling into married life. At the end of the journey Bombay had received them like a queen, drawing them to her cold, impersonal bosom in a manner which had soothed Sonia. She began to find out about streets and places of interest. She had delighted in the string of Bombay's names, released like a tune into her brain. Wilson House stood on J.T. Road, close to the junction of Churchgate Street and Queen's Road. On the other side was Chamb Street and then Madame Cama Road. She had sat at the centre of a web of tarmac strips, whose names she began increasingly to recognise.

But what could she do with them? There was no one she could repeat them to, or share their magic with. Paramjit was now away in the evening as well; he had been doing a crash course in surgery at the Naval Hospital in Colaba. She knew no one else who spoke Greek, or even Italian, which she had learned at school. That is, until she had met Michael.

The manager of the hotel had been at hand to introduce him to the beautiful Greek woman and her Indian husband, an honourable doctor in the Army, who had done him the great honour of living in his hotel. As for Madam, she had been the only Greek in the great city of Bombay, apart from Mr Michael (whose last name he could not pronounce) and some Greek sailors. Naturally, Mr Michael was not able to talk to sailors on account of being an important shipowner, one of the wealthiest, who spent a lot of time in Bombay. In fact, he had a permanent suite in the Regent Hotel, very close to his offices in Dougal Road.

For Sonia, who had not been able to understand the manager's introductory patter, it had been enough that Michael had smiled at her warmly, had come all the way in his emerald green American car to meet a fellow Greek, and especially that he had spoken the language. It had been the Greek of the mainland, quite different in style and pronunciation from the island Greek she knew, and she had been quite abashed by its sophistication. Paramjit had needed a little more convincing to start the friendship. Michael had taken him to his fancy offices in Dougal Building on Ballard Estate. It had been in the European business quarter, adjoining Ballard Pier, where the mail steamers came in and not too far from the Victoria docks where his own huge oil tankers tied up. A square, four-storeyed building of grey stone, in which Michael's 'Stavros Shipping Co' had occupied a whole floor. Paramjit had taken in the exaggerated respect shown to the small, almost bald, Greek with twinkling blue eyes. Sonia, trailing after the men and stopping to look from the windows at the traffic piling up below, had wondered whether she had come all the way from Paros, crossing the heavy seas, to meet an ageing rich Greek from the mainland.

He had been sufficiently old and short, standing a good six inches below Sonia, for Paramjit to have had no qualms about Sonia's going out with him. Bombay had been in a state of flux because of the changing government, full of British waiting to embark for home. He had had no special circle among the other army officers, billeted closer to the hospital, or with the Punjabi

Community far away in Dadar and Matunga. No one would notice or gossip about his wife's wanderings. And it had kept Sonia off his back, leaving him in peace to pursue his medical course which seemed to require more effort from him than from most people.

Michael and his emerald-green Pontiac had taken Sonia all over Bombay. The Gateway of India, the Prince of Wales Museum, Flora Fountain, the core of Bombay's busy, jostling existence. She had seen the city's big banks and offices and its fancy shopping centres, the Mahalakshmi Racecourse, a beautiful expanse of green beside the sea, Juhu Beach in north Bombay, clean and palm-fringed, where she had been able to swim at last and the water had lapped her body gently towards Michael's eyes.

She had gone everywhere with Michael, refusing only when he had suggested a day's trip to the Elephanta Caves. 'I've already been there,' she had said, vaguely. He had brought her slowly into the folds of India, which he seemed to love, perhaps because he remained a foreigner.

'I return here year after year,' he said, 'and now I have an additional reason, a beautiful Greek woman in India.'

'I am not Greek any more,' she had said sadly. 'Paramjit says I became Indian on the day I married him.' Michael had not been really interested in such talk, but he had always been deft and tactful, in the way of a man who knows a lot of women and has been generous with them. He had been enormously courteous to her body. He had caressed her to peaks of pleasure with his hands and lips and tongue, opened her to a passion she had never imagined. She had no longer been dry and sore, as she had been with Paramjit. She had flowed like a river into the sheets of the Regent Hotel, yet she had felt it had been she who had brought Michael unspecified treasures.

Cascades of purple and red bougainvillea had come in through the window. Except for minor differences in colour and prints on the walls, their suite in Wilson House had been exactly like Michael's in the Regent Hotel. In the attached bathroom, a zinc tub, an enamel basin and jug, water buckets, the thunder-box and, alongside, on a wooden stool, a china receptacle with a lid. In the bedroom, an iron spring bed with a cotton mattress, a chair with two protruding flat arms, a dressing table and a massive cupboard with old newspapers on the shelves. In the outer room, a set of sofas, including an ancient love-seat, all facing the window.

Michael had been in familiar surroundings the first time he had been invited up to their suite in Wilson House for a drink. The special occasion had been India's first Independence Day, 15 August 1947.

'You can have a ring-side view of the celebrations from here,' Paramjit had said. 'No need to go out into the crowds.' Though that was exactly what Sonia had wanted to do. 'This is the only hotel from which you can see the Oval Maidan so clearly, right up to the clock tower and the palm trees.'

The procession in the Oval had just started. Soon it had been a moving mass, a sea of people, parked cars and high buildings. Sonia had wanted to go out and be among them, to forget in their noise and gaiety the new fact in her life. Paramjit had brought Michael a drink. 'We are celebrating two things today, Michael. Independence Day and Sonia expecting a baby.'

Just then Paramjit had been called down to move his jeep off the road; a procession was passing. 'It could be yours, Michael,' she had said.

He nodded. 'True,' he had said. 'But how will you know?'

'Surely from the colour of its skin?'

'Let's wait and see, then,' he had said. She had not been able to tell what he felt.

She had shaken her head slowly. Her hair had recently been permed and the curls were still stiff. A centre parting had gone up from her widow's peak. 'No,' she had said. 'We're leaving next month. Paramjit has been transferred to Hyderabad. There's some trouble there.'

'But the baby?' Now he had been concerned, upset.

'Paramjit will father it.'

'But what if it's my baby?'

'Even so. And I want it to be your baby.'

Michael's baby, even with the camouflage of another name, would still have left her floating as she was now, free somehow to leave one day. She had felt separate and far from the flag-waving outside. An Indian baby, Paramjit's, would have been like a stake driving her firmly and forever into the soil of India.

'Will you let me know?' Michael had asked.

He had given her the address of his lawyers – Malgin Brothers, in Radnor Place, London. The chambers had been there for two hundred years, they were bound to last at least till the end of his life.

There had been only one month left for Paramjit to finish his course in surgery. It had drawn all his energy and time, sucking him like a vacuum from Sonia's side. Slowly she had said goodbye to Bombay. And to Michael. He had sucked her two nipples so that they had risen high and crimson from her milky white skin; he had hidden his face in her wide, spreading hips and had nibbled the soft insides of her thighs. His tongue had gone over her body with infinite passion, licking off the salt of Bombay, stopping at the pool of her navel and then again at the other pool, thrusting into her the last send-off which his love could give her.

What had it all meant then? These months of visiting and love-making, while India grappled Sonia willy-nilly to its dark bosom? That now it should have gone like this, in these gentle, swelling lights and darks of farewell. She had longed to make patterns, to string together the Elephanta Caves, Malabar Hill, the Gateway of India, wide stretches of Arabian sea, Michael's offices, the loose muscles of his arms, his thin, oft-frequented thighs, as if these together could have made a necklace that would have lasted for ever, which Sonia Chahal and her lost, unwanted daughter Krishna could have grabbed when the waters of the Bay of Bengal closed over their heads. As if events could ever be a rosary on which you said prayers in despair.

Michael and Sonia had listened to a heartbeat growing inside Sonia's stomach. Little blue veins had sprung up on it, like a screen on which flowers would climb, but the belly itself had been small, only just beginning to round itself. When it was time to leave for Hyderabad Michael had not come to the railway station to see them off. He had sent a huge basket of fruit and a bouquet of flowers. They had nestled inside the first-class compartment, sending his presence with her for a short part of the way.

2

Mother and Child

Paramjit had been posted at the Military Hospital, Secunderabad, at the eastern edge of the Cantonment area on

Entrenchment Road, where the Chahals had shared a small house with Param's Commanding Officer, Major Verma.

The Chahals had turned for company to Dr Hassanwalia, Chief Medical Officer. Mrs Hassanwalia had been Anglo-Indian, Susan White before she had got married. They had lived in the heart of Hyderabad city, in the Pattargatti area around Char Minar, just behind the Lal Darwaza.

'She's probably been a nurse,' Paramjit had explained to Sonia. His mocking, superior tone educated her in social differences. 'That's the best these Anglo-Indian nurses could hope for, to get an Indian doctor to marry them.'

Nevertheless, Mrs Hassanwalia had looked almost European, and Paramjit had quite clearly liked to look at her. There had only been a faintly sallow tinge behind her fair skin; she had been delightfully petite, wore long, slinky dresses and had masses of curly brown hair. Sonia's interest had been directed towards Ely, their plump, pretty two-year-old daughter, whose hair had been black like her father's and had fallen in tight ringlets to her shoulders. Though she was, if anything, fairer than her mother, the watchful Sonia had spotted a brown tinge to the rosy blush which came often to the little girl's cheeks. What colour would the occupant of her own, as yet small, belly have? It was now beginning to push out the *salwar-kameez* she had taken to wearing. A brown blush like Ely's would have made it Paramjit's child, an Indian child. The colour of that skin would pull Sonia firmly to the earth of India; she would never be able to leave, to return to Paros. But the child might be Michael's. Then it would have a clear, rosy complexion, no burnishing from centuries of Indian sun. She would not have minded even if it took Michael's brown, instead of her own blue, eyes. There were plenty of dark-eyed, dark-haired Greeks in Paros. But it had been the colour of the child's skin that mattered. Sonia's chance of one day getting away from India, her slim hope of freedom, had been tied to that.

The first formal call had been from Captain and Mrs Chahal on the Chief Medical Officer at his residence. Paramjit had been very particular about Army protocol which required this visit. The Hassanwalias had lived in a spacious house, with a wide verandah in front, a large garden running around it, crowded with banana trees at the back and neat rows of fragrant white flowers in front. A sentry from Hyderabad State Force had kept guard at the front gate.

But Dr Hassanwalia had not encouraged them to visit his house and had entertained them instead at the Secunderabad Club.

'The atmosphere is not so good in that area,' he had explained. He had been anxious to keep their friendship. 'Ever since the Nizam decided that Hyderabad would become an independent sovereign state after the British leave, the situation has been getting increasingly tense for the Hindus here. Especially after he asked that Muslim fanatic, Qasim Razvi, to organise a private army. It is called the *Ittehadul-e-Mussalmeen*,' he had said. 'It has a shock brigade known as the *Razakars*. They have done nothing but terrorise Hindus and stockpile arms. You have no idea what it's like; you live in the wide open spaces of the Cantonment, with Army barracks and Cavalry Lines to protect you. We are surrounded by warrens of whispering streets, crowded with mosques, saboteurs and Muslim subversives. Meanwhile Mountbatten has given the Nizam two months to negotiate the fate of Hyderabad with the representatives of the Indian Government. Walter Monckton is negotiating on the Nizam's behalf.

'You should have seen what it was like here on 15 August, Independence Day in the rest of the country. Here it was quiet and as dead as a tomb. No flags could be unfurled. I saw a group of little boys, who had stuck the tricolour in their coat pockets, molested right in front of my house – and I could not do a thing.'

So here was a bit of patchwork which had clearly threatened to get loose, to break away altogether. But Dr Hassanwalia had believed in needle and thread, in repair jobs, in keeping the pieces sewn up together.

'I suppose I could leave but I don't want to do that, to run away. I believe Hyderabad will join India; it's just a matter of sticking out the next few months. The Nizam's all right, as far as I am concerned.

'It's Razvi who is a complete fanatic. He stares with eyes that bore holes into you. He would strike terror into the hearts of his friends and enemies if it were not that you could immediately see a streak of absurdity and charlatanism in him. He is slight and dapper and sports a fez at a rakish angle.

'Razvi was suffering from appendicitis, and he must have been in great pain, but he refused to see me. I heard him muttering from inside that he did not want to see Hindus, alive or dead. Then he yelled "Tell him to get me *Char Minar* cigarettes". You understand the emphasis was on Char Minar? He wants to take Hyderabad, to

18

have the Asaf Jahi flag fly always over the Nizam's palace and the Char Minar, the monument here. This Razvi has made up a song which the *Razakars*, his storm-troopers, sing; about how the waters of Cape Comorin will one day lap at their Sovereign's feet. And the Nizam rests on all this flattery like a nesting bird, waiting for it to hatch.'

The friendship between them had barely got started when Paramjit had left for Srinagar.

On 21 October the first batch of about 15,000 North West Frontier Province tribesmen, led by Pakistani army officers, had entered Kashmir. They had been supplied with modern weapons and lorries and had quickly penetrated deep into Kashmir, looting houses, abducting women, burning villages and massacring both Hindu and Muslim men, women and children. There had been three columns of raiders, one each starting from Poonch, Kohola and Muzzsafarabad. They had joined near Uri and attacked it. Brigadier Ramendra Singh, Chief of Staff of the Kashmir State Force, had had fifteen men with him at Uri. They had fought to the last man, trying to defend it. The raiders had occupied Baramulla and turned it into their headquarters. One day the raiders had sacked St Joseph's Hospital, smashed the hospital equipment, wounded the Mother Superior and violated and shot a number of nuns.

A tall, bulky man with a roughly tied turban and bushy beard, who wore the same type of *salwar* and loose shirt as the Pathan tribesmen, had been seen at various points in the hospital grounds during the attack. He had saved lives and, better still, the chastity of many women. Because of his appearance, the raiders had not shot at him, mistaking him for one of their own people. Only a small, green-eyed boy, who watched everything from a corner near the wall, had known that this was no tribesman but a true Sikh of the Guru fallen on difficult times. Sardar Sobha Singh Palji, a very important landowner of Bhimbar district in Kashmir, who had left his beloved wife Kailash Kaur and daughter Gulshan in Bhimbar in the care of his nephew Prakash, and had been overtaken first by Independence then by the raiders en route to his orchards in Poonch and Srinagar. He had been accompanied by his young son, who had watched the fight in a rain of bullets and bayonets which glanced off the boy's head as if from an invisible screen.

Loot and women had been the raiders' chief prizes. If they had not been preoccupied with these they might have overrun the whole of Kashmir before the Indian troops arrived. As it was, the raiders had been only a few kilometres from Srinagar. They had destroyed the electric power house and had plunged the city into darkness, when Indian troops, with Captain Paramjit Chahal among them, had landed at Srinagar airstrip. After a few engagements the raiders had been on the run. Baramulla, Uri and Poonch had been reoccupied by advancing Indian troops.

Since Paramjit had had to leave suddenly he had tried to telephone Dr Hassanwalia to keep an eye on his pregnant wife. 'Something wrong with the phone. Can't get through,' he had muttered. 'These civilian telephones. They don't know how to maintain their services. No discipline, not like the army. If you have any problems with that,' he had patted her belly affectionately, 'you can contact him.'

More than the telephones had been affected; Hyderabad had been in ferment. A delegation had returned from Delhi on 22 October, to obtain the Nizam's approval for a draft Standstill Agreement and a collateral letter produced by V. P. Menon on behalf of the Indian government. For three days the Executive Council had discussed the drafts.

Representatives of Qasim Razvi's *Ittehadul-e-Mussalmeen* had voted against them. Nevertheless, the Council had decided by six votes to three to advise the Nizam to accept the Agreement. On the evening of the 25 October a delegation had conveyed the Council's decision to the Nizam, who had formally approved it that same night but had postponed signing the Agreement till the morning. The delegation had been due to leave for Delhi with the signed documents, to clinch the Agreement, to bring the patch firmly into the fabric of India.

At about 3 am on 26 October, a crowd estimated at about twenty-five to thirty thousand had surrounded the houses of Sir Walter Monckton, the Nawab of Chhatari, and Sir Sultan Ahmed, members of the delegation. For good measure, and because of the feelings which Qasim Razvi had harboured against him, a detachment had ambled down the road and surrounded the house of Dr Hassanwalia, Chief Medical Officer.

There had been no sign of the Hyderabad police. At about 5 am the Nawab of Chhatari had managed to contact the State army authorities. Dr Hassanwalia and his family had been taken to the home of his friend Captain Chahal, in Secunderabad. He had not known that Paramjit was with the Indian troops who had been flown in to Srinagar on 26 October to counter the tribal invasion of Kashmir, a needle sewing the patchwork together with furious speed. Only Qasim Razvi, the scissors, who had been seeking his time to cut and cut, had been fully aware of the situation and was ready to make a hole of the middle of the new stitching. He had said, 'As the hands of the Indian Union are fully occupied with their troubles elsewhere, they will be in no position to do anything to us or to refuse our demands, if we insist.'

The Nizam had granted Dr Hassanwalia a meeting on 31 October. The previous day he had despatched Sir Sultan Ahmed to Delhi with a letter to Mountbatten, in which there had been threats to enter into an agreement with Pakistan in case negotiations with India broke down. It had put him in good spirits, enough to hear criticism of Qasim Razvi, if necessary.

Sonia had gone with Dr Hassanwalia, Susan and Ely to the Nizam's palace. They said he used precious stones as large as eggs for paperweights. She had entered a room crowded with furniture. They had looked amongst glass, heavy curtains, elaborate metalwork and had finally caught sight of a thin, slight man on a large settee with a featureless grey tapestry behind him. He had been dressed in a frayed cotton dressing gown, white trousers, caramel-coloured slippers, with light brown cotton socks lying loosely about his ankles and a brown fez perched on the back of his head. His mouth had hung loose over blackened teeth, some of which were stumps in his mouth.

He had listened while Dr Hassanwalia had related the whole fearsome business of his house being surrounded by a shouting, hostile crowd. His shoulders had been hunched forward in a pronounced stoop, his knees had knocked together, his whole body had been suspended, with an intense expression on his face. The vehemence of his high-pitched voice had startled Sonia. 'How do you know it was Qasim Razvi?' he had barked like a sharp, fierce terrier.

Dr Hassanwalia had spread his hands respectfully, 'Who could it be then, Your Excellency?'

'It must be that nest of Indian devils up north in Delhi, with whom Monckton has been dealing.'

Sonia's womb had been suddenly agitated, as if the baby growing there had hit out with all its passion against this insult, making Sonia breathless with surprise. 'Who knows what lies they are feeding to Mountbatten? But he must remember with whom he is dealing. I am a faithful ally of the British Monarch, not one of those petty princes to whom that wily politician Patel has been feeding his castor oil.'

'We are staying in the house of Captain Chahal who is away at present. This is his wife. His Exalted Highness will see that it is difficult for us to stay there indefinitely,' Dr Hassanwalia had continued.

A servant brought in a large, silver tray on which tea in four pale-blue china cups sat smoking gently. Sonia had sipped the spiced, milky tea resolutely. Its sweetness had seemed to go directly to the recently protesting creature inside her stomach. Now it lay still and quiet.

'I know where this lady's husband has gone,' the Nizam had said, his voice even sharper than before. 'To the Army Action in Kashmir. I do not care about Kashmir. Let them do what they like. Keep it or lose it. But I care about Hyderabad. I will never give it to them.'

Sonia stood up. 'I am sorry, I have to go,' she had whispered to Dr Hassanwalia, pointing to her stomach. She could not have sat still any more, the baby had been pushing and shoving against her as if struggling to get out. The front of her dress had been a flurry of moving bumps; she could not understand it. As if something the Nizam said had brought on the sudden movement.

The Nizam had called Dr Hassanwalia back from the door. 'You can move to the annexe of the Gol Kothi near Hussain Sagar. You will be perfectly safe there.'

The moment they were out of the room the baby had quietened. Dr Hassanwalia had been slightly vexed at the abrupt way in which his party had had to leave the presence of the Nizam. 'The baby is only four months,' he had said. 'I cannot understand why it is so active.'

'It is the Nizam who set it off,' Sonia had decided.

Paramjit returned to Secunderabad on 29 November, the day the Nizam had signed the Standstill Agreement with the Indian Union. She had thrown the door open to his knock. 'I was expecting Dr Hassanwalia and Susan,' she said, picking up one of his bags from the doorstep.

'Oh? Have they been coming over a lot?' His tone had been careful.

'They were staying here until a week ago. Then they moved to the annexe in the Gol Kothi. This morning they moved the last of

22

their stuff from the old house near Lal Darwaza. They have had such adventures!' Her usually lethargic tone had been alive and excited. 'Their house was surrounded by crowds. It is that fellow Razvi, Dr Hassanwalia says.'

'Don't you want to know what happened in Kashmir?'

'Oh yes,' she had said, pouring him some tea.

'There was a lot of fighting,' he had said. 'But we managed to get most of these raiders out. How is the baby?'

'Very active,' she said, although at that point the baby had seemed contented, humming in a dream of peace since Paramjit had entered. As if news of his success, the evidence he had brought with him, that some part of the patchwork was securely sewn, had been a soothing influence on the monster that had begun to jump and jiggle in the Nizam's presence a month previously, and had been restless and erratic ever since. Sonia had seemed to be sunk within herself, listening to some secret sounds inside her. Paramjit had tried to gather her attention to himself.

'I met a relative in Baramulla,' he had said. 'Palji. An uncle, really. He is married to my father's younger sister, but I had seen very little of him. I was a little boy when my father died, and then we moved from Kohat to Lahore during the first communal riots. Very strange. I met him quite by accident. I saw this huge, hefty man whom the locals were proclaiming hero of the action at St Joseph's Convent. He had saved a lot of nuns from the raiders. And he turned out to be my uncle. He knew my brother Satinder well. He told how he had taken him into the hills to get guns with which to fight the British. I do not know all that much about Satinder. We always think of him as a great supporter of non-violence. Also, all the time there was this little green-eyed boy, like a small crab, watching us; Palji's son.'

His description had not brought Sonia out of the slow golden haze in which she was wrapped, listening to a deep humming sound drawing closer and closer. She heard Dr Hassanwalia's knock before Paramjit did, and had been there to open the door. She looked at the empty space behind him. 'Susan, and Ely?'

'She is busy putting the house in order. We've just managed to get all our things together. I have brought you these from our new garden.'

He had held out a huge bunch of flowers, a riot of mauve, pink and deep red. She had had no time to make out the shapes of the separate flowers. Paramjit had been in the room, taking the

23

flowers. There had been a moment of silence, of acute embarrassment between the two men. Sonia had seen in a flash, in that
moment, the destruction of her warm, easy companionship with
the Hassanwalias, of the casual gaiety of the last month which had
been her defence against the brooding, hostile continent around
her. 'Oh. I did not know you were back, Paramjit.' There had been
another, short awkward silence. 'Well, when did you get back?'
'Today,' Paramjit had said. 'Sonia said you had some problems
with the crowds in Hyderabad.' His tone had been stiff.
'Yes. I am very grateful to her. She kept us here until Susan got
over her fear. She had refused to go back to Hyderabad. I came
today actually...'
'Sonia was waiting for you.' Nobody had known what to do with
Paramjit's sentence, it had leaped out fiercely at them.
Dr Hassanwalia had continued, '... to invite you both to a
reception which Mr K. M. Munshi will be giving next month. He's
been appointed Agent-General in Hyderabad. Sardar Patel's man.
The Nizam made all kinds of difficulties, would not give him a
house to live in, insisted on treating him as a mere trade agent.
Finally he's allotted him the Gol Kothi. We live in the annexe. The
house is not very grand, not by Hyderabad standards. You've seen
some of the mansions of the princelings. But the garden's nice and
I'm sure you will enjoy the party.'
It had been the end of his speech. Sonia had dreaded his
departure. Paramjit had waited only for the sound of his car pulling
away. He had picked up the flowers, had torn at their stalks and
petals and had thrown them across the room at her in clumps.
'How dare another man bring my wife flowers! She waits
anxiously for him to arrive; she can't stay on her chair. I come back
from war after a month and she can't listen to a word I'm saying; all
her attention is directed to the itch between her legs and a knock
on the door.'
'Listen. It's not like that.' She had not been able to bear the ugly,
senseless words.
But his words had created their own fury. 'It's not like what?
Why wasn't his wife with him when he came with the flowers?'
He had leaped across the room, hitting her very hard across the
face, pushing at her. She had felt herself toppling over, falling to
the floor. She had turned her body sideways, like a fish, to protect
her stomach. The thud of impact, all that extra weight landing on
the floor, had made her bones shake. She had cried, her body

curled over the quiet monster in her stomach.

'I'm a pregnant woman, I'm carrying a child. How can you think such things about another man?' Paramjit had helped her up and had wiped her face, but she couldn't stop crying. He had caressed her head, he had been infinitely tender with the cannonball which was her stomach.

Then Paramjit had begun to take her sightseeing, as if to make up to her. Now, however, the photographs in their album had not included the Hassanwalias as they had done earlier. Now the photos had been of Golconda Fort, tombs of the Kutab Shahi Kings, with Paramjit and Sonia posed formally under a tree in the garden of the High Court, or in front of shallow arches and small cupolas of Osmania University.

Sonia had found herself in a long tunnel of space where the ruins and buildings had entered one by one, evidence of India, that it really existed, in the age and strength of its stones. This had been the process which Michael had begun in Bombay, of drawing Sonia into the intestines of India. And what mixture was the child, watching already from Sonia's womb? From what bastard lineage, from Alexander the Great to the Pathans of Kohat and refugees of Sialkot, to green-eyed, wandering children, had it come, creating itself even before it was born? What words had been carved on the thin walls of Sonia's womb?

Pregnant women develop strange tastes. Sonia, the blonde, round-limbed goddess of Paros, had been drawn to the wild country around Golconda Fort, arid and bare, strewn with gigantic boulders of fantastic sizes and shapes, and to the Fort itself, whose strong, granite walls were of great thickness and ran four miles in circumference. Of the eight huge gateways and drawbridges, four were still in use, studded with sharp-pointed iron spikes to prevent elephants from battering them down. It had really consisted of four distinct forts joined to each other, and covered with mansions of the nobles, as well as bazaars, temples, mosques, soldiers' barracks, powder magazines, stables and even cultivated fields. Here, the whole population of Hyderabad could have lived in times of danger. Within the walls of her stomach, Sonia housed a whole world already busy forming itself.

Paramjit had not refused the invitation Dr Hassanwalia sent for Mr K. M. Munshi's garden party. It had arrived as a thick, ivory-coloured card embossed in gold, with the clear-cut crest of the Indian Union at the top, three Ashoka lions, steady and beautiful on a pillar, and the wheel of life just below them.

Gol Kothi had been bedecked for the occasion. It had been the Agent-General's first official reception in Hyderabad. Sonia had entered with Paramjit, clad in one of her bright wedding saris, which had folded gently and comfortably over her bulging stomach. Her ears had been bright with jewellery and she had flashed her head towards the official photographer who had stepped forward just then to capture a beautiful pregnant woman being greeted by the Agent-General. He had recorded also the slightly cruel curl in her nostril and her lips which had grown increasingly fine and thin.

Mr Munshi's clothes had consisted of a long white *achkan* and had reminded her of Satinder, her brother-in-law, on her wedding day. She had moved as far from this day as from her own childhood. Sonia had looked around, first towards Mrs Munshi who had worn a sari draped differently, the *pallav* coming over the left shoulder, covering her head, with its end, including a wide gold border, tucked into the waist. Then she had looked beyond her, searching through the groups of guests who had arrived before them. Already waiters in starched uniforms with red and gold waist bands, and green turbans had been beginning to thread their way between the guests and the tables, carrying trays with brown teapots and plates of food.

She had spotted Susan and Ely, and had moved immediately towards them; she had not seen them now for over a month. Ely had greeted her joyously and clung to her knees. Sonia had embraced Susan, who kissed her on both cheeks, but she had sensed a coldness in the touch of her shoulders. Dr Hassanwalia, standing near by, had nodded pleasantly in greeting, then continued his conversation with Major Khanna, Colonel Nanda and Mrs de Mellow, as had been recorded by the official photographer who was still trailing the beautiful pregnant woman.

'Which is your house?' she had asked bravely.

Susan had pointed to a low, pleasant bungalow at the far edge of the lawn. Then she had asked about Sonia's health. She had not invited her to see their house. When they had got home, Sonia had cried profusely. Paramjit had been in good spirits, and showed concern. She had not dared to say that she hated him for the loss of a warm friendship.

The child inside her had been getting increasingly restless, as if growing tensions in the city had been dragging it away from its smooth, feeding peace. Hindus inside Hyderabad had been being terrorised. There had been several border incidents. Another informant had been General Simrit Sinhji, portly scion of the princely family of Nasik, who had vast business interests in Hyderabad.

General Simrit Sinhji had been a heart patient. Before he had left Bombay his friend, Michael Stavros of the Stavros Shipping Co, had given him the name of Captain Paramjit Chahal. Paramjit had visited him behind the high curtains, white façade, shallow arches and inverted lotus cupolas of the Osmania General Hospital. Each time, he had come away from General Simrit Sinhji's side with a list of units and their positions, which a Hindu nurse had collected from medical charts of *Razakars* and regular State Force patients admitted in the hospital.

After General Simrit Sinhji had been discharged from hospital, Paramjit had been posted out on a field exercise with a surgical unit in Sholapur. This time Sonia had been really alone, with the baby jogging to its full term in an increasingly murky atmosphere. The baby became definitely agitated. The time had come for Krishna to leave this troubled arena, to join those others who were the needle and thread patching the uneven quilt of India.

On the morning of 13 April 1948, *Baisakhi* Day, the holiday of the Sikhs, exactly one year after she had been married, Sonia's daughter had been born in the Secunderabad Military Hospital. As soon as the redness of birth had cleared from the baby's skin, Sonia, breathless with fear, had looked at its colour. The skin had been white, as white as Michael's, as white as her own. Paramjit, returning to Secunderabad, had gathered her and the baby in his arms and had taken them home.

The Government of Hyderabad had continued to break the Standstill Agreement. Encouraged by the Nawab, the *Razakars* became more aggressive than ever. By August, Paramjit had been called back to Sholapur. On 31 August the Nizam had been asked to ban the *Razakar* organisation and to invite India to station an adequate military force at Secunderabad.

The Nizam had declined. In the Central Assembly, Sardar Patel had declared, 'We cannot let our attachment to peace ruin the future of India or of those territories that fall by geographical connection within that description.' On 13 September Major General J. N. Chaudhri had entered Hyderabad with a small force from the east by the Bezwada-Hyderabad road and a larger force on the Sholapur-Hyderabad road. Captain Paramjit Singh Chahal's field surgical unit had marched in its vanguard. Opposition had ended on the third day. Paramjit had taken photographs on the way, of villagers, of his surgical unit, of *Razakar* prisoners and, finally, on 17 September, of Trimulgherry Prison, on the day the Nizam's forces had surrendered to General J. N. Chaudhri.

Paramjit had stopped for a while at the Military Hospital where his baby had been born six months previously and had then gone on. The baby would have to be given a name soon.

He had found Sonia strangely quiet when he entered the house. He was instantly reminded of his last return, from Srinagar, of how she had sat there listening for Dr Hassanwalia's arrival, while he told her of Kashmir and Poonch and the mass of stinking corpses they had passed on the way. But this time she seemed to be guarding some grief. He had passed hurriedly to his daughter's crib and noticed the change right away. The baby's eyes danced; she tugged at the long black hairs on his arm. But he saw that the baby's arm was a shade darker than he remembered.

Now Sonia was no longer sure who was the baby's father. With this change in skin colour she would never be sure; she would always hang suspended between heaven and earth, not knowing whether to leave India or to stay. Only one sperm could enter the egg and fertilise it. Michael and Paramjit could not both be fathers to this child. But how did a baby that was pink and white for six months suddenly begin to get darker? Did the child belong to India or to her? Or maybe it belonged nowhere.

'When did you begin to notice the change?'

'I don't know exactly,' she said slowly. 'The end of August. Definitely about the time the Police Action began. During those three to four days it changed a lot.'

Already the skin was acting up, not the dramatic patch which Krishna would notice at the age of eight, but enough to lose her her mother's love.

'Now I know what name to give her,' Paramjit suddenly said. 'Krishna. We'll call her Krishna. A Hindu god whose skin darkened and got blue when he swallowed poison from a huge overhanging snake. Lord Krishna was a lover and a philosopher; he was in touch with everything.'

Sonia had been bitten; the poison of India was entering the child's veins, the quality of homelessness travelling from mother to daughter. Let her be called Krishna then; what did it matter.

28

3

Sonia Takes a Lover

They were woken by the sound of Asha, Sardarji's eldest daughter, banging empty tins in the kitchen next door. Sonia and Paramjit were snuggled under a quilt. This January had been very cold, as if in special dispensation to the refugees gathered in Jullundur. She could feel the child curled behind her, into the hollow of her back, reaching for warmth.

'Do you know what the girl is doing?' she whispered to Paramjit. 'She's collecting all these tins for you to take back to Srinagar when you leave today. So that when you come back on your next vacation you will bring them filled with provisions from your army rations.' It reminded her that after today she would not see him for at least six months and she began to cry.

'I know it's difficult for you,' he said, caressing her head. It touched him to see her crying in this helpless fashion. 'But what can they do? They are refugees here; they have come over the border from Pakistan like thousands of others; they've left everything behind in Kohat during this great bloodbath of Partition. And there are so many mouths to feed: my brother's own family, my mother, that half-crazed cousin Gulshan whom Bhagwana brought from Bhimbar and those two other families that live at the other end of the *haveli*. But at least they have this house. Otherwise where could I have sent you during these long field postings?'

'This great windy tomb of a house, where you have to walk miles and miles to get from one room to another! One night I woke up and found rats nibbling at my toes! I am so afraid this child will fall sick. Did I come all the way from Greece for this, to sit here, along with your brother's family, my child and I eating watery lentils and *chappatis*? All the stuff you bring from Srinagar is used to feed hordes of political workers.'

'You know Sardarji is a politician.'

'So? I don't care if he is a politician, I just don't want to be alone

29

here. What will I do, Paramjit? I don't even speak their language. And that huge man, Bhagwana, who is a sort of servant here, with his moustache and large *salwar*, has been making rude noises to me ever since he picked me up from the station in Delhi, when we came in from Hyderabad.

'You went on in the train, sleeping comfortably till Pathankot, while I got off with a six-month baby in my arms and came to Jullundur. Have I told you about the journey from Jullundur? We reached it at night. I was to be dropped off on the way, my knees were under my chin and the child was wailing with hunger. Then it began to rain; a wheel of the *tonga* came off and when we finally reached this fantastic *haveli*, this palace, they were not expecting us so the gate was locked. Of course they could not hear our shouts inside the house.'

He had heard the description several times. He drew her close and caressed one of her firm, beautiful breasts. The nipple rose under his palm and she turned towards him to rub the other against his chest. Then Asha was at the door, piling up the empty tins. He said, 'Would you like to visit Mrs Markand, whom we met in the Officers' Mess? Her husband is commandant of the refugee camp, just outside Jullundur. I can speak to Sardarji if you like; he will make the arrangements for you to go. She seemed nice, an educated woman. They say she took part in several *morchas* in Delhi with Miss Pratibha Anand, a leader in the Freedom Movement. Actually, Mr Markand has invited us to their Republic Day celebrations on the 26th. That's the day our new Constitution is to be adopted. India becomes a Republic on 26 January, 1950. I won't be here, but maybe you could go.'

The only thing wrong with visiting the refugee camp was that each time she had to go with Bhagwana. He sat in front with the driver and Sonia and her daughter were put in the back of the *tonga*. The camp was on the road to Phagwara. A big board on the main road directed them to 'Refugee Camp No VIII' on a dirt road. Thin barbed wire encircled the camp. Hordes of orange-coloured tents struggled across in untidy rows. At least fifteen to twenty people huddled in and around each tent. They had put up sheets, shawls and sometimes even saris to keep out the cold night winds which blew down from the north and the thin layer of hoar frost. The tents had moved gradually, getting out of line into smaller and smaller circles. At the very centre was the camp's single water tap. Queues and fights around it made for vital activity in the camp. When the water supply was switched off it sank back into a coma.

Today promised a break in routine, the celebration of the first Republic Day. The residents collected, curious and hesitant, near a silver-coloured flagstaff erected hastily at the centre of the camp. A short line of chairs were ranged behind it for the guests: a Maharajah who lived near by, and his favourite wife in good silk and fine *pashmina* shawl, the Deputy Commissioner from Jullundur anxious to start the ceremony and move on to his next official engagement, a landlord from Pathankot who yearned already for his orange orchards, and Anjali Markand's new friend, Sonia, with her little girl beside her. Anjali's bird-like figure, even with its weight of dark hair, seemed insubstantial beside Sonia, who bloomed like a village queen in a blue satin suit which her sister-in-law had insisted she wear for the occasion.

Sonia was disturbed by the ragged people massing before her. They looked hungry and there was bound to be infectious disease amongst them. Maybe it was not safe for the child. There was slush on the ground from the rain last night; her white boots would get dirty. She settled Krishna firmly on her blue satin lap.

The crowd shifted around, drew close, while Mr Surjit Markand the Commandant was speaking. Now packets of sweets were laid out on trestle tables covered with sheets, and it surged forward. The Deputy Commissioner's wife rose hurriedly, to thrust the packets at a sea of reaching hands.

'Ranjit!' Mr Markand called out in the mêlée, 'Come and help.' A young boy had fought his way to the front of the crowd and had then sauntered off towards the tents, his head turned disdainfully away from the packets of sweets. He went back to help with distribution. A plump fair girl on a blue satin lap peered at him from among the guests. Krishna was seeing Ranjit for the first time.

It had been a long, desolate journey to the refugee camp. More than a hundred years ago, in 1839, the British had annexed the Punjab, and another young boy, Manmohan Singh, and his sister, Swaranjit Kaur, had left Sialkot to travel across the plains and up the mountains to Kohat, near the Frontier. Then it was 1948. The British had withdrawn from their Indian Empire and, as their reluctant fingers raked back across the body of Punjab, they prised out millions of people, like easily resting insects, and sent them scurrying from pockets of their own land.

One day, more than two years ago, Ranjit's father had returned early from his factory on the edge of Sialkot. He was an engineer trained in Roorkee University, speaking with the careful weight and confidence which come from fifteen years of manufacturing perfect cricket bats and hockey sticks. Now there was panic in his factory. Men who had worked there for so many years that he had forgotten their religion rose against him in the name of Pakistan and told him they were Muslim. They looted everything in his factory but spared his life. Clearly it was time to leave, to join the convoy setting off under the protection of army trucks. His wife had packed two suitcases and all her jewellery and they had arrived in Markand's Refugee Camp in Jullundur. For a year now, Ranjit's father had been trying to get places for them on the overcrowded trains which chugged off from Jullundur station to Bombay and he had finally managed to do so. They would leave soon.

There was news only of tragedy in the refugee camp. That morning Ranjit had overheard his mother talking to a friend as they both waited in line for water. 'We travelled to Lahore with an old lady, the mother of Sobha Singh Palji of Bhimbar, who offered us a ride in her *tonga*. I was sick at the time, she probably saved my life, she let me ride on a pile of suitcases up in front. I will never forget her kindness. Someone brought news of her this morning. The old lady and her son had taken the train from Lahore. I kept telling her to stay with us. We were put into the compound of the DAV degree college in Lahore, but the old lady did not want to stay there; she said it made her think too much of her beloved grandson, Prakash, who had studied there. Then we lost track of them. It seems now that everyone on that train was killed. We heard that a train full of dead people arrived in Amritsar.'

Her friend turned to fill her bucket at the tap. Stories of people killed on trains to Amritsar had been common in the last two years.

His mother caught sight of Ranjit and called him to take her place in the water line. He drew lines in the wet ground around the water tap and thought of the old woman's grandson, Prakash. She had talked constantly about him on the journey, about his good looks, his intelligence, his devotion to his grandmother and his attachment to Kailash Kaur, wife of her elder son, who was a very important man in Bhimbar in the state of Kashmir.

'Prakash is in Bhimbar,' the old lady had said. 'He goes there each time my son Palji travels on business, to look after his property. There is a whisper that Prakash is a bit too attached to his aunt Kailash Kaur, but who am I to say anything? He has done so well in his father's business. We sent him out of Gujarat to study, because the boys in the college there are not of good character. Prakash is so beautiful, you see, with blue-green eyes like the people from the hills and a fair skin. So we sent him away to Lahore. But he came up to Gujarat for the holidays. I would not have been able to live without seeing him. I do not know when I will see him next. God knows when these troubles will end.'

'I am sure it won't be long.' Ranjit's mother had tried to reassure her by carefully selecting truths in which she herself believed. 'We Hindus have lived with Muslims, I am sure they will call us back; they cannot do without us. It has happened before, and we can start from scratch once again.'

The old lady was not to be comforted. 'I will not live that long,'' she had said. 'When the *tonga* reached the base of the hill, and I looked back through the *shisham* trees beside the road, at the city rising like a flat-topped cone, I knew it was my last view of Gujarat. Which is why I was talking of Prakash and Kailash Kaur to you. I have never talked about all this to anyone before, but you and I might never meet again.' The old lady had said nothing more about Prakash as the convoy went on through Gujranwala and crossed over into Lahore. Ranjit believed that the old lady was fleeing, finally, from her own disclosure.

Even with their own section of the convoy protected by several army trucks and jeeps, it had been touch and go. They had just passed a grey, desolate tomb, of the beautiful Noor Jehan, on the right of the road. A group of angry Muslims burst out of the trees, waving guns, sticks and long iron rods. They surrounded the leading truck. More and more had seemed to spring up from nowhere. They spread like a flood of water around the bunched mass of the convoy. It had been a riot crowd devoted to major undertakings like destroying Hindus.

The Major in charge of the convoy had climbed on to the bonnet of his truck, equally fierce, possessed by his responsibility. 'Move at once, or I shall order my soldiers to fire and I shall personally run my truck over you.'

Something in his voice had made them believe him. His two-ton truck was hard and solid before their eyes. The crowd had dispersed, once more breaking up into human beings, and the convoy continued towards the newly established Wagah check-post.

Sweet packets were distributed, Republic Day celebrations at the refugee camp were at an end. The guests retired to Mr Surjit Markand's residence. It was a cottage taken over by the government when its Muslim owner fled to Pakistan and stood way behind the camp, hidden by rows of *peepul* and *shisham* trees.

Food was on the table, laid out on a white lace tablecloth. Here there was no trace of frantic hunger. Guests slowly circled the table and reached for chicken and cheese sandwiches, coconut cake, *kababs* and *pakoras*. Only Sonia, coming from the *haveli*'s meagre resources, filled her plate up time and time again. Surjit Markand did not want to interrupt her eating. She was a goddess standing under the window, her brown-gold hair lit by sunshine, her nose straight and beautiful, the sun falling away from it in two even sheaths. Most of all, her breasts were large and firm, pressed up against the satin suit. Sonia was a tall woman and later her head was level with the top of the *raat-ki-rani* bushes in the Markand garden. All the guests had gone out after tea. Anjali was still putting away the tea things. 'I'll be out soon, don't run away yet,' she whispered to Sonia, catching sight of the relentless Bhagwana with his *salwar* and *tonga* who had followed them from the camp. Both understood they would be friends. 'My husband will stay with you.'

'So Captain Chahal has gone back to Srinagar?' Surjit Markand asked.

Sonia nodded. 'Those people in the refugee camp seemed very hungry. My mother said things were bad in India and people were very poor, but I did not expect this. We were hungry, too, on my island during the war, but at least we had bread.'

'What you saw was nothing. These people are comfortable now, compared to what they have endured. They've lost their homes, their relatives, and have almost died themselves. All that death and tragedy. This morning was a pleasant diversion. But you have lost your home, too.'

'What do you mean?' She was worried. What had happened to her newly acquired goods in Sardarji's *haveli*?

'You left your home in Greece, to come all this way. We are very happy to have you here.'

This was elaborate talk and her command of the language poor, maybe she was missing something. She knew only that she liked looking at him, as she had liked to look at the half-naked boys, their bodies wet and glistening from swimming, who had sat on the rocks in Paros. Some forgotten happiness quickened inside her. 'Come away,' her mother used to say. 'Stop staring.' There was nobody here to tell her that, and the smell of the *raat-ki-rani* flowers wrapped her body in trembling, sensuous perfection.

'What about you? Why have you come all this way from Delhi to look after this disgusting place?'

'Perhaps I came because I knew I would meet you here.'

She was startled. His face was completely confident but soft and admiring. It filled her with tremendous excitement to be so admired. 'This is the first time we have met and you talk like that,' she said evenly.

'But there will be many more times,' he said.

'Hush,' she said, pointing to her child.

'She is too young to understand.' They had acknowledged their complicity.

Sonia left Krishna with her cousin Asha, Sardarji's teenage daughter, during future visits to the refugee camp. At the end of February the wheat was green and high in the fields and mustard plants were so bright yellow that she could hardly bear to look at the waves of colour they put out into the air. She did not tell Sardarji that Mrs Markand was no longer at the camp – she had left for Delhi to help Miss Pratibha Anand set up a unit of the Indian Red Cross. With a stroke of luck Bhagwana fell ill and a silent, happy *mundu*, who observed nothing, was sent instead to accompany her in the *tonga*.

She was indeed a goddess – his first thought had been correct. Surjit looked at her large, white body below his, pressing down the soft stalks of wheat. More stalks formed an endless screen on either side. He put his hands lightly under her buttocks, feeling them move. In that short space of consciousness he knew he had never felt pleasure like this; it would tie him to this woman for ever.

She was looking over his shoulder at the perfectly blue sky, not looking at him, only feeling him. She felt the sure movements of his hands, his body, the flat flash of his thighs coming down on her.

Never before had his life played so immediately on another. Her face changed, delighted him. Only her eyes were clear pictureless reflections of the blue sky, with no clouds and no punctuations.

She was aware of the sharp edges of eucalyptus trees planted between farms, blowing high above them, thin and elegant against blue space.

35

'What is that?' she asked softly. 'We do not have them on my island. In Paros we have only olive and cypress, the tree of life and the tree of death.'

Making love to Surjit was like arriving home at first and last, she was relieved and sure, how well he fitted just there, moving in long excited strokes inside her. At last this strange hot country was becoming familiar; she knew that it held some pleasure.

4

The Story of Kailash Kaur

Kailash Kaur did not travel as far as Sonia did. Not to Jullundur. Nor even back as far as Sialkot, whence her ancestor Manmohan Singh and his sister Swaranjit Kaur had once set off to reach Kohat. She made part of the journey back, up to Bhimbar and Gujarat. Then it was too late to go further; she was overtaken.

Some things Krishna could, of course, check out. Like information about Sonia her mother and Surjit Markand. But Kailash Kaur, her aunt, was dead, and so was her strong, silent, phenomenal poet-ancestor, Swaranjit Kaur. What remained from that line? What was her evidence? What did the past finally have to offer after it had jiggled and shaken all these Punjabi ancestors together in its magic bag of tricks, its homeless, rampant Jew-satchel painted with signs and deepening rapidly, like a sky darkening towards rain before your eyes?

First, some offspring. A man in the blue serge ceremonial uniform of a Junior Non-Commissioned Officer stands at the centre of the Indraprastha Stadium during the Asian Games. He waves a thin baton and the Combined Forces Band plays his music. When titles flash on the electronic scoreboard they do not add his name because nobody knows it. This green nameless nymph, born of one father and taken by another. A familiar confusion. Who knows him as the bastard son of Prakash and Kailash Kaur, child of love?

36

Or his half-sister, Gulshan, daughter of Kailash Kaur and Sardar Sobha Singh Palji, this is Miss Maitreyi Phillips who abandons her legitimacy and the name of her forefathers to join Professor Dr Zimbabwe, the Great Magician. His Assistant, clinging for years to flashing swords which cut her in half, balancing on her head apples devoured by worms, or, with gentle, beringed fingers, holding out cards to little children from which they select only the Queen of Hearts. Perhaps the first sister, Swaranjit Kaur, with her clever, massaging hands and eyes glowing with silence sustains Miss Maitreyi Phillips through four major operations on her stomach, burned by nitric acid and churned by grated glass. Now she is not afraid of anything. For one who loses the will to live, what are a few razor blades, a little nitric acid, she tells her admiring nephew Sohail, Krishna's son, at a magic show in his boarding school in Morenapur, twenty miles from Dagra.

Krishna went elsewhere into the past, straight into the arms of her aunt Kailash Kaur, everywhere that her green-eyed lover, Prakash, had gone. She nosed up under heavy breasts, sprang through the shoots of her pubic hair, blindly felt the tender skin and fair young flesh of the body which lay under Prakash and the final bliss of her wet cunt with a sudden leap and arch of recognition, which would have embarrassed him if he had not felt her strong fingers against his back, and her mouth swallowing his in a kiss of tenderness which promised a whole future.

Krishna sank and whirled flying through cracks and dark spaces peppered with cold stars, seen from a terrace in Gujarat, through doors opening in Bhimbar and one which finally closed in a wash of blood. She went over a deep, grey-coloured outcrop of rock salt eight miles long and one quarter mile broad at Bahadur Khel, shining and gleaming right in the centre of Kohat in the North West Frontier Province. The salt mine was a veritable jewel, which made the fortune of Manmohan Singh and his sister, Swaranjit Kaur, Krishna's ancestors who came all the way from Sialkot to Kohat to garner it.

The salt mine really belonged to Swaranjit Kaur and not to Manmohan Singh, as it had been given to her as reward for an act of bravery. But her brother's family had taken possession of it completely after she failed the virginity test and her marriage had stood dissolved. The test was as thorough and rigorous as the medical examination conducted by immigration officials on Indian fiancées wanting to enter Britain. She had no business to be an

Indian wife if she was not a virgin. Her new husband had flung the trembling bundle of Swaranjit Kaur, wrapped in fine red wedding silk, out of his room, returned her to her brother's house in a far corner of Kohat.

'Did I save you from the British soldiers for this?' Manmohan Singh screamed at her. 'How hard I worked for the money to get you married!'

She did not mention the salt mine. 'Brother, you waited too long. I saw a beautiful man in the wheat field behind the house. He knocked on my window one day and I let him in.'

'Keep quiet. How dare you talk to me like this! Have you no shame?'

Her husband's shame had not lasted long. Within a few months the betrayed man had married a girl from the nearby district of Bannu and forgotten the deflowered woman he had married. But Swaranjit Kaur retreated into silence, and never spoke to anyone again, except to Kailash Kaur, daughter of her nephew Sucha Singh, the Miser.

She sang to the child as she sat massaging her in the warm sun of the courtyard, or told her strange stories while she wove the beautiful *khes* and *phulkari* for which Sucha Singh's family became famous. Merchants came from as far as Dera Ismail Khan to purchase them for special customers and she became a source of income. After a while, that was her only way of signifying to the family that she existed. While her brother Manmohan Singh was alive, and before Kohat grew into a formal town, she left the house for long hours, going outside the walls of the city, walking to the civil lines where bungalows were large and beautiful, streets broad and lined with growing trees: mulberry, *bakain*, willow and *shisham*. At least once a week her brother went out shooting, usually past Bahadur Khel, to arid, barren tracts of land on low hills covered with *mazri* or dwarf palm and wild olives. In sheltered places she spotted *ilex*, walnut and scotch fir trees. Sometimes her brother went as far as Hazar in search of black bears and the red or brown bears occasionally found there. Only once had he taken her on this long trip. They had to carry food and provisions. He also went out to the western hills, looking out for ravine deer, for *markhor* and *urial*. Now and again they came across small patches of wild hog, from which she made a delicious pickle which lasted the family all through winter. Middle-class women from Kohat, or even those from more progressive Sikh families, did not go out on shoots; such fine fancies were reserved for families of chiefs and princes. But nobody thought of Swaranjit Kaur as a woman any more. She did not belong to any of the known categories of virgin, wife or widow. Moreover, because she was discreet and silent, she attained an anonymity which verged on invisibility. This facelessness was valuable, and she was careful to keep secret her passion for the countryside, as secret as the Kohat Toi, a stream to the Indus which went underground above Kohat and reappeared some miles lower.

One day her brother was badly mauled by a leopard. A doctor in the Civil Lines Hospital gave him heavy tetanus shots, the infected flesh, already green and smelly with gangrene, was cut away, but the wound took long to heal and the scars stayed red and painful. It brought his *shikar* to an end and there was no way in which his sister could go out alone. No one knew what hurt Swaranjit Kaur more: eviction from her husband's house, or the end of her forays into the Frontier countryside.

It was only fitting that Manmohan Singh finally died of random leopard wounds. One morning an old wound opened up as if impelled from within and flowed a whole day and night in a bright, clear red stream down his chest. It spread across the courtyard to the room where Swaranjit Kaur sat weaving her *khes*, which were not then as fine as they later became. Her beloved brother's blood soaked up a deep crimson dye into the *khes* which lay between her hands. She tried to wrap his dead body in the beautiful garment, a flag for the hero of many travels, but his son, Sucha Singh, who knew nothing of travelling, insisted on a white sheet.

After the death of her brother she moved to two rooms on the ground floor, leading off the verandah which ran around the courtyard where the *baoli* stood. She seldom emerged from these rooms. Once was when Kailash Kaur sat in the *deorhi*, dressed and ready for her wedding, waiting for the priest to arrive from the *gurudwara* at the other end of the town. Swaranjit Kaur, her great-aunt, walked out towards her. Everyone turned to watch; they had forgotten this tall, thin woman, with a folded *phulkari* in her arms. Some recalled the story of her wedding night.

She had everyone's full attention when she opened up the large, exquisite piece of embroidery. A wave of excitement enveloped the gathered crowd of relatives and friends. No one had ever seen such bright, beautiful colours, such marvellous stitching. The *phulkari* was almost magical. She laid it around the bride's shoulders, smiling with love. A sense of apprehension went through the bride's mother in the presence of this strangely perfect beauty. She moved to take the *phulkari*, but Kailash Kaur held on to it, burying her face in its soft threads.

Swaranjit Kaur occupied rooms on the ground floor where no one else lived. The other rooms around the courtyard were used to store wheat, *daal*, rice, *ghee*, washing soap and cotton for the family's annual needs. They led to the back entrance, but she rarely went out. Her only visitor was a little servant boy from Fauji Dwarka Nath Tandon's bookshop, a shabby, overflowing place strongly resented by its elegant neighbour, Seth Mathura Das, whose store displayed imported household goods. The Fauji, as he was generally known because of a short stint in the Kohat Brigade of the Northern Command, found Swaranjit Kaur his most regular customer. She had learned to read and write after she had been flung back unwanted to her brother's house. She was literate at a time when there were 85 girl students in Kohat town and a total of 153 Sikh girls receiving education in the entire Province.

The Fauji wondered whether he ran the small bookshop in the back purely as a favour to Swaranjit Kaur, and to acquire the beautiful *khes* and *phulkaris* she gave him in payment for books. He sent his boy to tell her whenever a new consignment arrived from Peshawar. Her only other visitor was her niece, Kailash Kaur. They sat together for long hours each time Kailash Kaur made the long trip from her husband's house in Bhimbar to Kohat, going through the three states of Kashmir, Punjab and North West Frontier Province to reach there. For Kailash Kaur it seemed easy and restful to tell Swaranjit Kaur about the crazy, unnatural urges which flowed through her body, her desire to reach out and hold the haze which was floating past her, somehow to push against the walls of her life and flow over them.

But her aunt seemed to recede farther and farther behind the household stores, until one day she finally disappeared. The room seemed to change position, like a clay pot full of gold coins buried as security under the floor of a room. The pot was never in the same place, when you dug up the floor a few years later at a wedding, to pay a moneylender, or make jewellery. Kailash Kaur could not believe it: her aunt was just not there. When she needed to talk to her most, to tell her about making love with her husband's glorious, green-eyed nephew, Prakash, she would burst with happiness if she did not let it out slowly, in a thin stream, to her aunt. The room was right there, with its piles of dusty books and a couple of tin trunks, but no aunt. Old Fauji came in, too, looking for his most faithful customer, and spotted a pile of red-gold dust beside the bed. It smelled of open countryside, of grass and trees. It could be the dye she had used to make up the magical colours of her *phulkaris*. Or her own life which had consumed her.

Fauji took his books back and helped Kailash Kaur drag the two tin trunks up to her room, before the rest of the family stirred from their afternoon sleep. A girl after she married had no right to anything in her parents' house. They would take from her immediately the rich, beautiful *phulkaris* and *khes* which were packed into one of the tin trunks, though each had her name, KAILASH, woven into a corner. The legacy of the other trunk, poems and songs, was even more valuable and her father would definitely burn these as he would consider them immoral. They were love songs of longing, despair and desire; they released the terrible things she found in her own heart. Her aunt had not let her down after all; there was no need to talk to her about Prakash. The outcast Swaranjit Kaur had arrived with all her baggage; she was still there in Kailash Kaur's life.

In 1947 the Kabaili raiders came into Bhimbar and killed Kailash Kaur and her lover, who were in each other's arms. They ransacked her house, took her *phulkaris* and *khes*, but flung out the trunk full of poems. It was picked up by a group of gypsies travelling to Lahore to celebrate the first year of Pakistan's Independence. Their star singer, Karishma, learned the song for a *Mushaira*. Her throaty, passionate voice, singing the haunting songs, made her instantly famous. She emerged from the gloom of anonymity like a flashing planet, burned the hearts of all who heard her, and made a bigger fortune than Swaranjit Kaur's saltmine. Then she disappeared for sixteen years, going off with a man in the irresponsible fashion of gypsies. When she came back to Lahore she brought back the tin trunk which had started her off. Then her songs were even better; she made more records and tapes; the agony in her voice was deeper.

But long before that, Kailash Kaur's dancing eyes peeped through the lattice of her black satin *burqa*. Before she got married her mother insisted that she wear it in the street. There were only a few Hindu and Sikh women in Kohat and they did not attract attention by going unveiled. Kailash's mother wanted to keep to all

41

the city conventions in bringing up her daughter. With her two sons it did not matter so much.

Gopal Singh was coming back in March after four years of studying law in England. Her husband Sucha Singh grumbled about money and time spent on his studies. 'Look at my elder son, Sawan Singh. He knows just enough about accounts and writing to run the salt business. That's all I want.'

'There's no one in Kohat who has studied to be a barrister in England. There's a lot of money in litigation; he'll make it up in no time. We must celebrate his return with our daughter's marriage. *Baisakhi* should be an auspicious time.'

It seemed too close. Sucha Singh the Miser was disturbed by the sudden prospect of feeding a *baraat* for three days, buying presents for the bridegroom, and dowry and jewellery for his daughter, Kailash Kaur. 'Why so early? The girl is still young.'

But his wife had already settled things in her mind. Meanwhile she thought about getting *bukharis* ready. They needed new ones and it was always such a problem, getting money from her husband. In another month the dreaded *Hangu* breeze, cold and dry, would blow down the Miranzal Valley, cutting through their flesh.

'You know what will happen if you delay her marriage. You have a living example before you.' She was referring to Swaranjit Kaur, her husband's silent aunt, who was slowly falling to pieces in the ground floor rooms, among sacks of provisions.

Sardar Sobha Singh Palji, merchant of *ghee* and fruit and luminary of Bhimbar, arrived in Kohat just in time to enter the programme for Kailash Kaur.

Palji had sat in Kohat, in the cold sunshine of late October, watching his relative *Seth* Dwarka Das Vohra eat breakfast. Sethji's daughter had married Palji's older brother who had died of a mysterious ailment. Their beautiful, green-eyed son, Prakash, a delightful boy, had been brought up by Palji's mother in Gujarat. The *Seth* had eagerly bought the entire consignment of *ghee* which Palji had brought quite by accident to Kohat from Srinagar.

His camels and short, hard-muscled ponies did not usually come to Kohat. They went from Bhimbar, during six months of the year when the passes were open, through Naoshera to Srinagar, carrying cotton piece goods, wheat, brass and tin, tea, sugar, salt and tobacco. At least once or twice a year he went with the caravan.

42

The slow pace suited him; he liked the changing countryside, the close smell of the animals and the views as the caravan descended the valley to Srinagar. Also, he would stop off to inspect his lands and houses in Poonch and a small orchard of almond trees in Srinagar. His main traders were in Poonch and Srinagar. He bought from them rice, *ghee*, fine walnut wood, oilseeds, woollen shawls, raw silk and dried fruits. Fresh fruits he got only from Poonch, off his own lands. He loved to see them on the trees, peaches collecting bloom from the air, and shining, red apples. There was nothing like them in or around Bhimbar, only patches of dry forest, growing in tracts of scanty rainfall, and poor, sandy, salt-impregnated soil with *kikar* and tamarisk trees. None of them seemed healthy or alive when he came down from the hills, haunted by the memory of fresh air, green leaves and hanging fruits.

This time a new customs official at the octroi post in Baramulla had insisted that he pay excise duty.

Palji refused. It was a matter of pride with him that he never paid taxes on goods he brought in and out of Bhimbar.

'Then you can't go by this route,' Bamzai, the customs official, had said pleasantly enough. So Palji took another route to Bhimbar, via Kohat, where his relatives lived. Looking from the Seth's window, he fell in love with a girl in the street below, who was struggling with a black *burqa*. He looked away, burned by the fire in her brown eyes, and then back. His soul flew down rays of sunlight while her fingers tied the black strings under her chin. Then her slim figure was fully covered, a latticework of beaded black was pulled down over her magical eyes, and his soul became solidly determined. As if in echo, a voice came up from the satin confines. 'Seth Ji! Mother says can we buy some *ghee* from you? She heard you had received fresh stock from Srinagar.'

'You know that girl?' he asked his relative. Such a wonder did not seem possible. A girl whose eyes grabbed a man's heart with open fire. *Ghee* should go to her in boxes of gold and silver or it would burst into flames. She was like a horse racing with flaring nostrils across the plains of Punjab. How would his ponderous camels catch up with her?

'Yes, of course, she's our neighbour's daughter. They're looking for a husband for her. If you're interested ...' Relatives are helpful in such matters.

Baisakhi day was fixed for the marriage; the girl's brother was coming back then from England. Sobha Singh chafed at having to wait so long after he had made up his mind. He had been head of household for many years, his mother had very early on relinquished decision-making to him, and he was accustomed to instantly acquiring objects of his desire. But for Kailash Kaur he was willing to wait for ever. And suddenly Bhimbar was the most attractive town in the world, now that he would take her there.

They told her she was lucky to be marrying into such a family, with few relatives and a mother-in-law who spent more than half the year in Gujarat. Bhimbar would be wide open for the new bride to conquer, if she was wise and continued to keep her husband's love. Everyone had heard of how Palji, who had appeared so formidable, with his tall figure, fine clothes and thick black beard, had looked out of Seth Dwarka Das' window and had fallen in love with Kailash Kaur. The story had reached her father, who had made appropriate reductions in the dowry. Even Kailash Kaur had heard it. She had thought of it as she sat in the *deorhi* all dressed up, surrounded by relatives, waiting to go out to the courtyard where the Holy Book had been laid out under a brocade cover. Swaranjit Kaur's voice interrupted her, a low, cracked voice which she recognised from her childhood, singing a song only she could hear. A *Baisakhi* song, which was later found in the tin trunk, her aunt's legacy. The others knew only silence from the recluse who came forward with a magical *phulkari* for the bride.

Kailash Kaur entered Bhimbar as if escaping through a crack in the Kohat wall. Most of the area round the small town was salty and infertile, but Sobha Singh Palji's land was irrigated by several masonry wells. White bullocks trod around the mouth, turning a wheel which poured water for her bath. He took her there early in the morning. Instructions had been issued to all his minions to keep out of the way. She had married a man of many instructions, but he gave none to her. She grew into her role of model housewife with no directions either from him or from his mother, who lived in Gujarat with her grandson, Prakash. Like ghosts she and Palji slipped through the morning mist. The smell of cotton plants was fresh in her nostrils as they went, and it was so in the evening, when he took her to the Bhimbar stream through a haze of fireflies. All through summer, except when there was occasional thunder or hailstorm, or when the dessicated, scorching west wind blew, they ate their evening meal beside the stream. Servants carried food before them, spread out a cloth on the green grass, and left them there alone.

44

He went everywhere with her, even during the day. She was wise, collecting her annual stocks of grain and rice, of washing soap, dried fruit and *ghee*. Palji went to the bazaar every morning to check out new arrivals. When anything came from particular fields or areas he had decided were the best source for the product, like lentils from West Punjab, he would buy the entire stock, a *tonga* would transport it to the house, and the merchant's man would carry it to one of the little rooms which faced the courtyard where she stored all her provisions. Then Palji would lie on his string *charpoy* near the front door, watching her.

He had given up his journeys to Poonch and Srinagar. Business fell off; he was cheated. Without personal supervision nothing worked right; that had been one of his own rules, but he didn't care.

Then there was religion. She didn't know much about religion; it was something that happened only at marriages and deaths. Her grandfather, Manmohan Singh, had somehow fallen out with God and, despite pressures from women coming into the family, God's status in the family had never been restored. But with Palji it was different. He had a curious, restless mind, and religion offered an opportunity to explore different realms. There was something vigorous in his approach which she liked and with which she agreed. He remained a faithful *guru ka Sikh* but talked for hours to different saints and Mahatmas. Kailash Kaur learned to read the *Guru Granth Sahib* every morning and enjoyed her daily trips to the *gurudwara*. Her passage was studded with deeply respectful greetings, which derived first from homage to her husband as the richest and most sternly powerful man in the city, and slowly became directed towards her, as seemly wife and partaker in his power. She learned all there was to be learned for her role, and then her mind became restless.

Her restlessness infected her husband who had not been out of Bhimbar for five years now. 'Let us go on a journey,' he said. It worried him that she did not come as readily as before to lie beside him and caress his body. He missed the tender, playful touch of her hands and the gay abandon of her shoulders. She was fitting too firmly into the mould of wife, and it did not please him. Perhaps a journey would do her good. 'My nephews live in a village near Moong Rasool, on the other side of the Jhelum. They are involved in a land dispute and they want me to come and help them. It's good land and will become very valuable once the dam at

Moong Rasool is built. Maybe we can buy some land there. We must start thinking of our children.' But there were no children. That was part of her restlessness, he thought; a woman needs children.

The journey was made on mule and camel-back. A pack train of *ghee* and fruits had just come down from Srinagar, and Palji decided to take some of his goods straight on to Moong Rasool to sell. It was a fairly big town, with many British officials, and a large number of skilled workers for the canal headworks; the goods could be sold at a good profit, even the cloth pieces which did not sell so well in Lalla Mussa. Kailash Kaur watched from the window. It was still before dawn, and though it was only October the men outside shivered as they went about loading provisions, cooking utensils, clothing for the big Sardar and his wife, and the goods to be sold. They went into huge packs slung across camels and mules. Then the sky began to lighten. She saw the large, square yellow teeth of the camels gleam as they chewed the fodder, and she felt a fluttering excitement inside her which surprised her with its intensity.

His nephews' village was farther from Moong Rasool than they expected. The goods were left behind with the city merchants, to be sold to the large, floating population of workers who lived in prefabricated houses close to the canal site. The party went on to Mian Bari, just beyond Rohtas.

The two brothers lived together in a comfortable house and owned practically all the land in the village. Some Muslim tenants had been agitating, asking for more of the produce than was their due share, quoting laws and settlements made by officers of the British Raj. Palji was an old hand at this game. He had a private discussion with the Kanungo, the land officer of the village, and the matter was settled. The Muslim tenants went away muttering and unhappy, but then some people were born to be unhappy with their lot.

Kailash and the second wife of the elder nephew became very good friends. She came from Peshawar and was familiar with the excitements of city life. They discussed how much they missed people, the sights and sounds of the bazaar, and the commotion in a businessman's family. Ram Piari's father dealt in provisions and his chief supplier of salt was Sucha Singh of Kohat. Ram Piari was young, inexperienced, very friendly and unable to cope with her husband's five children from his first wife who had died in childbirth. She and Kailash Kaur settled into happy friendship. Ram Piari was Kailash's first friend since her aunt Swaranjit Kaur had put a magical *phulkari* around her shoulders and set her off on the road to Bhimbar.

Meanwhile Sobha Singh Palji paced through his nephews' green fields. They grew wheat, maize and sugarcane in a profusion he had not seen in Bhimbar. Water was vital; the Jhelum river gave life to the fields. His nephews scratched the surface and a crop grew. He liked the two men; they were full of praise for what he had done to settle their tenants, but two months had passed and he wanted to return home. He was disturbed when the winter rains came at the beginning of December, more than a month early. The Jhelum and other streams between Mian Bari and Bhimbar became swollen and difficult to cross, especially with animals and family. He did not want to put Kailash Kaur to trouble or danger, and decided to stay on until after the north-east monsoon had passed and the waters had subsided to reasonable levels.

Temperatures dropped below freezing at night. Palji and his wife settled into Mian Bari for the winter, eating peanuts and candy studded with sesame seeds around a roaring fire. One morning a message arrived from Bhimbar, sent collectively by all the small landowners of the area. Ostensibly they gave him news of his property, left unprotected for months now, but they also wanted to tell him about Pritam Lal Whig, a bankrupt from Bannu. He had arrived in Bhimbar with four daughters and two sons, had found Palji's large tract of land unfrequented, and had settled on a plot which at one point had had a shop on it, destroyed by a fire many years ago. The intruder and his sons had cleared away the rubble and were preparing to build their own house on the old existing foundations. Palji said: 'They are worried for their own land. If one intruder goes unpunished, there will be others who will be even more daring. They want to use the power of my wrath to make an example of this man. I'll take care of him all right, but in my own time. I can't risk these swollen waters now. And you are comfortable here, aren't you?'

Kailash Kaur nodded. She remembered another bankrupt, an acquaintance of her father's, a cloth merchant in Kohat. Dressed in plain white, he had sat cross-legged in his absolutely bare shop, staring at the flame of a single lamp burning before him. An eerie felling had settled on her when she had looked in.

Now here was this bankrupt Pritam Lal Whig, grandfather of Anu Whig who later married Krishna.

The erstwhile owner of an ice factory who settles on alien land is bound to be involved in litigation, and this breeds its own children. One of Pritam Lal's sons was inevitably a lawyer and the profession was later to take him to Kohat in search of briefs. Anu's father, Rai Bahadur Bhim Lal Whig, practised law for fifteen years as the junior of Sardar Gopal Singh, an eminent barrister of Kohat, returned from England. He was Kailash Kaur's brother, and Palji never forgave him for taking on the son of his long standing enemy as junior in his successful office. 'It is your brother's money which pays for these disputes which bother me,' he fumed at Kailash, who offered in explanation her brother's western education.

Under relentless pressure from Palji, however, Anu's father was made to leave Gopal Singh's office. He arrived in greener pastures in Quetta, where an uncle needed help in his civil contracting business. This had swelled rapidly during the Second World War, when the demand for construction went up.

Whig Sahib managed to get most of his money out of Quetta and into Delhi banks before Partition, but he didn't insist on his son joining the hotel business which he then set up. Anu was chosen to pamper his nostalgia for intellectual pursuits, to become a lawyer and, later, Krishna's husband.

But in Bhimbar, Pritam Lal Whig was an intruder, a trespasser on Palji's land. His house was ready by the time Palji's long cavalcade reached the outskirts of Bhimbar, six months after it had left the town. Whig met them on the narrow track that came from Lalla Mussa, before the gossiping group of local landowners had had time to organise themselves. He knelt in the dust and put his turban at Palji's feet. The big Sardar did not say a word; he went straight on to his house, not bothering to even look at Whig's audacious construction on the way. The bankrupt's whole family was lined up outside like a family photograph, standing shoulder to shoulder with their hands folded as he passed.

Then his fearful neighbours went to work, lighting the fires of his wrath, preparing him to throw Whig out with violence. Kailash Kaur could see him only as sitting cross-legged between slabs of ice, and she restrained her husband.

'He has two daughters of marriageable age. He might lodge a charge of assault against you.' Palji considered these words of wisdom, for which his wife was already well known, and went instead to the *kanungo* himself. He lodged a case against Whig, a fateful first step. Thereafter began a long period of litigation which was to span almost his whole life. The laws, like everything else in the *riyasat* of Kashmir, were slower and more backward than they were next door in the British-administered areas of Punjab.

The case reached the District Headquarters at Mirpur. By then the big Sardar was already very weary of the case. He found the judge's questions bold and insulting and he abused him in choice Bhimbar slang. Unfortunately the judge understood, and convicted him for contempt of court. The one night he spent in prison changed his whole outlook on life a second time. He resumed his journeys out of Bhimbar, rising straight into the hills which began just beyond it, exposing himself to the splendour of the mountain passes. By the time his case reached the Srinagar courts years later and he was finally absolved of the contempt charge he found he was making these journeys at least once a year.

He made no journey the year his daughter Gulshan was born, two years after his conviction in Mirpur. It did much to lift his gloom. She brought him joy, as Kailash Kaur did. He loved to touch the peach-like bloom of her baby cheek and her soft, thick curls.

'She has the complexion of jasmine; her face is fair as the moon,' he murmured to his wife. Not like Krishna's skin, darkening rapidly as she learned, understood and remembered.

Palji's two nephews were attacked and looted by a huge crowd of Muslims the very year he resumed his journeys. Disgruntled tenants persuaded some 1,000 people to descend upon the brothers armed with knives, staves and sticks. They were noticed even by vultures and eagles, who rose from *kikar* trees along the way and circled above their heads. The nephews heard the news and packed off their wives and children, eleven members altogether, to Chakwal, which lay beyond the low range of adjoining hills, and was defended by a wall and a small detachment of native infantry commanded by a British officer. They buried their remaining valuables before they themselves escaped with their retainers. Gold and jewellery had already been buried by their respective wives. Ram Piari was too young at the game, and had not done her job well, putting it all in a single room. The wall cracked open when the looters set fire to the building and gold pieces came tumbling out. Some of the other brother's stuff was saved. Their crops, stored and standing, were burned, their animals either killed and eaten, or driven away. The rioters searched the jungle patches behind the house for the nephews, but they hid well, back-tracked, and reached Chakwal in a most miserable state, riddled with malaria and pneumonia.

Palji found them all camping in his house when he got back to Bhimbar that year. They had nowhere else to go and nothing with which to rebuild their destroyed lives. Their numbers swelled and seemed to fill his house. His wife and daughter disappeared into the happy riot. Finally, Palji gave the nephews enough money to rebuild their house and start their crops going again.

'We will never forget this as long as we live,' they said, and left behind one of their retainers called Bhagwana who had some Pathan blood in him. 'He will take good care of our aunt and the little girl while you are away on your long and important journeys.'

Palji got his nephews and their hangers-on out of his house, but could not rid himself of the fear of loot, rape and death which they had brought with them. It clung to the walls, springing out of corners when he climbed the stairs to the kitchen to eat, and lay like a long, sleeping animal under the bed when he made love to his wife. Towards the end it even began to follow them to the well in the morning for their baths, to the Bhimbar stream in the evening, and to sit under the *shisham* trees in the garden all day, chewing on grains of wheat.

He was glad that his wife at least did not notice this monstrous creature which his relatives had left behind. In fact she missed the nephews' presence and sent them presents of *ghee* with people going across the Jhelum. But Palji could not bear to leave Kailash Kaur and Gulshan alone in Bhimbar when he went off on his journeys. Perhaps he could see his daughter Gulshan of the rose-complexion standing one day as Miss Maitreyi Phillips, leather-faced in sequined cloak, while Professor Zimbabwe flashed a shining sword through her stomach.

Meanwhile it was Palji's urgent desire to protect his nephews during his long absences. While he was away they would go to live with his mother in Gujarat. It was the district headquarters, with a wall around it, no army, but with three British officials in the Civil Lines who would make sure of their own safety, and therefore that of the city. More than that it was in Punjab, under the Raj. In Kashmir, the Maharajah was a long way off from Bhimbar, too distant to protect it.

The location of Gujarat was on Sher Shah's Grand Trunk Road, between Peshawar and Lahore, thirty miles south of the Himalayas, thirty miles east of the Pabbi hills. To the south stretched the wide, flat dusty plains of the Punjab. Krishna had to go only thirty miles on her own, abandoning Kailash Kaur who did not get beyond Gujarat, reaching back to Sialkot where all the journeys began, Manmohan Singh's in 1849 and his sister Swaranjit Kaur's. Then Ranjit Dhawan's in 1947, Krishna's lover.

Gujarat was built on a right-angled hill and sloped down from its crown to a single gate. Each time she left to return to Bhimbar, Kailash Kaur, sitting in the back of a *tonga* on the one-mile drive to the railway station, saw the town as a squat, dark toad-like symbol of her grief at parting from Prakash. The *tonga* took Kailash Kaur and her daughter Gulshan and Bhagwana their servant to the Dhakki-darwaza, beyond which the town expanded right up to the Civil Lines. She went to the Hindu area, Mohalla Killa, flanked by Mohalla Gyanpura on one side and the Goldsmith's Bazaar on the other. Her shoulders rubbed against the walls of narrow streets, until she reached a square, white house three storeys high, with light blue windows, pink façade, and coloured patterned glass. Her mother-in-law drew the *erl* from the huge front door, wooden, fretted and chiselled, and it swung heavily aside to welcome her into the *deorhi*. To its left a door led up a steep staircase to the family rooms where Bhagwana settled the child and the luggage.

A fine view from the roof, of the city standing in a hump on the side of a citadel, sloping down to green, fertile fields below. In the distance, the peaks of the Himalayas above the tender ground haze.

Between the *deorhi* and the roof, as her foot turned to climb the bottom stair, from the darkness of the corner came Prakash. Only 17 years old, tall, with huge shoulders, his eyes large, slightly slanting, pale brown with deep flecks of green, sleepy as a lion's, and his mouth fresh as a rosebud, unbelievably perfect, curling like a bow at the corners. He stared back at her, drawn by her gaze which was captured by the complete perfection of his beauty. His smooth-skinned hands rose to greet her, but Mataji gestured, and he bent to touch his aunt's feet. She touched his straight, silky hair, that was all she was allowed for the time being, she knew that, but her hand longed to slip down and feel the back of his neck, the skin stretched tightly across those firm shoulders. Kailash Kaur was a tall woman but he was taller. He stood beside her, smiling down with easy, open confidence.

51

'We had to send Prakash off to Lahore to study,' Mataji, her mother-in-law, told her as they sat in the kitchen drinking hot milk, while Bhagwana put Gulshan to sleep and opened up the luggage. Kailash Kaur looked around for Prakash, the room was cold without him. 'We have a college here, but the boys there are not of good character. They chased him in an indecent manner and bothered him constantly. He is a very beautiful boy. I don't know whether you noticed?' Kailash nodded. Prakash's beauty had settled into her like a big stone, pressing her breath out, stifling her with the sharp ache of desire. The wonder of it made her soft and tender inside, and loving. She wanted to touch, caress, inform his skin, his eyes and his mouth of how beautiful they were. But she was also hard with knowledge, aching with despair. This was forbidden to her. She was more than ten years older than him: he would not even look at her except with respect. She speculated constantly about his life in Lahore. He was at the hostel of a big college: DAV. The splendours of the mean, sophisticated Lahoris were open to him, they must have already swallowed the beautiful boy.

Kailash Kaur went to the bazaar, vegetable shops, cloth shops, all over the town of Gujarat, wherever Mataji wished to go, who enjoyed the new pleasure of being accompanied by her daughter-in-law. Everything must stay normal on the surface but below, where she really lived, swam a haze of despair. Through its dim confines, looking out one day, she noticed that Prakash paid her special attention, tried often to be with her in the same room and said sadly to her, 'My holidays are ending soon. I will have to go back to Lahore.' She loved the unconscious petulance in his tone.

Horses were racing through Kailash Kaur's veins. They carried her outside the walled city, past the lawyers' houses, beyond the law courts where her brother Gopal Singh attended a case which had drawn him from Kohat, past the tree-lined shaded avenues of the Civil Lines which would have pleased Swaranjit Kaur's heart, to the wheat fields just beyond. The horses were racing across the earth now; they sent shudders through the wheat fields, connected Sonia Chahal's back, bedded by Surjit at the edge of the refugee camp in Jullundur, to Kailash Kaur, drawing Prakash her nephew down upon her, showing him how to enter, guiding the hard, urgent tensions of his body, being filled finally by his harsh fragrance, the shuddering release of his flesh coming slowly to a halt, and the swollen happiness of her own limbs.

It was different each time they made love. He was pulled slowly but inexorably between the tight leaves of her desire, until he was possessed by a vortex which absorbed them both. Bhimbar was a bad dream; it intervened to separate them. She left the going back as late as possible, but it was later in the year than usual by the time their child was conceived. Snows were beginning to fall in the mountains but Palji was not yet back and she was determined not to leave a day before she received news of his return. Gulshan and Bhagwana were anxious to get to Bhimbar, but she resisted their pressure. She wanted only to look at Prakash in the morning, feel his vibrant presence in the house.

Prakash no longer had to return to Lahore; he had settled into his father's business. Electricity had just reached Gujarat; light fittings and electric bulbs were imported from Lahore and shining pieces of crystal glass hung like miracles above Prakash's head as he sat in the shop selling them.

Piercing cold winds blew down from the north, ducking between the high mountain peaks to reach the town. A strong fire burned in the room where she and Gulshan slept. Everyone was away at a wedding when he came to her. She traced the warm glow on his naked flesh as he lay before the fire.

'Mataji speaks of getting you married, now that you are back here and working in the shop. There are many marriage proposals; you are such a beautiful boy.'

'I have told them that I don't want to get married yet. I will never marry.'

Her heart leaped with joy, like a Mahsher fish in the Bhimbar stream, but she said, 'Why not? You have to get married some time.'

'I love you too much. Your body has spoiled me for every other woman in the world. But if you insist, of course...'

'No, no, no,' she said, all her noble responses lost in the teasing delight of his love. 'It would break my heart.' She knew it was at that moment, as she pressed him between her legs, while the flames of the fire leaped and stretched her eyes, that their child was conceived.

It was the last time she was in Gujarat. Palji was delighted with the birth of a son with pale eyes like the morning sky. If Gulshan whispered small sentences to Bhagwana as she watched from behind the door while her new brother got all the attention, she said nothing to her father.

Palji would not let his small son be exposed to the rigours of the journey from Bhimbar to Gujarat. It was only twenty-eight miles by train but already the troubles with the Muslims were a definite reality, and you never knew about these things. 'You like my nephew Prakash, don't you?' he asked his beloved wife, who was distraught because Gujarat had been forbidden to her. 'I'll ask him to come here and stay while I'm away on my journeys.'

The green-eyed boy was six years old when he went on his first journey with the big, adoring Sardar. They had just reached Srinagar when Partition was announced, and state rulers were asked to accede either to India or to the new country of Pakistan. They waited in Srinagar while the Maharajah made up his mind, then set off hastily for home. They had passed Baramulla and had reached Poonch when the Kubaili raiders came into Bhimbar.

They entered with staves and axes, huge metal-topped sticks and spears used for piercing wild pigs. Only Gulshan saw them kill her mother, Kailash Kaur. Even their violent instruments could not tear the woman from her lover's arms, and they would not spare time from looting to carve her out of his flesh. Gulshan watched the joint murder from behind a door, her eyes stretched wide-open with terror, not daring to warn or save them or to close her eyes. But she spoke enough in a high fever delirium, while Bhagwana carried her off in his arms to Kohat, to arouse the special curiosity of Bhim Lal Whig, son of Palji's old enemy. He interrupted his own flight for a moment to peep into the ravaged house, and saw the two naked bodies pressed into each other, their lips still open with dying promises.

The snake took many months to reach Srinagar, crawling up mountain paths, dodging invaders, hiding out in deserted villages. Meanwhile, Sobha Singh Palji and his son with green eyes had reached Srinagar, escorted to safety by Kailash Kaur's nephew, Captain Paramjit Singh Chahal, son of her barrister brother Gopal Singh. He had been immensely grateful for the protection, especially for his son. How lucky to find a relative in a position of power.

Captain Chahal's regiment had been posted to Poonch during the Kashmir action. He had been in Hyderabad too, for the police action. 'From one scene of activity to another, always to keep moving. Well, that was the army life, and I loved it, although your mother complained about it all the time.' Krishna was already a young girl when her father first told her about the fields of skulls they had passed in Rajauri, on the way to Poonch. Her father was a

54

needle, stitching together torn pieces of the new fabric.

'Your daughter Gulshan is safe with my brother's family in Jullundur. She reached them in Kohat with Bhagwana, just as they were getting out of the city,' Captain Chahal the protector re-assured Palji. Neither of them saw Gulshan watching Sonia and the others in Jullundur from behind cracks in the doors and the difficulty they had getting her to comb her hair. In fact, Palji never got to see her again.

News reached him gradually that his wife had been killed by the Kubailis in Bhimbar, together with his nephew Prakash left to guard her. The messengers were too tired with their own griefs to tell him anything else. All except Rai Bahadur Bhim Lal Whig. The snake ambled up from Bhimbar to Srinagar. He was fresh and choice, as if he had eaten only fruit and nuts on the way. He arched his back, curved his head and brought it close to Palji's big ear. He whispered something into it which made the erstwhile doting Sardar look, first with suspicion, then with despair and finally with loathing, at the beautiful grey-green eyes of the beloved son. He could not live with him any longer and died of a broken heart shortly afterwards.

5

A Train Journey

Krishna recognised right away the dog being carried in its basket into the train compartment in front of her. It was years since she seen its rubbery, yellow body, sinuous face and mournful, ordinary brown eyes. The mongrel's hairless tail rubbed unpleas-antly against her arm like an obscene muscle as she negotiated a narrow, crowded corridor looking for her berth.

'Your dog hasn't changed at all, Aunty Anjali.' She was already settled in a lower berth, her small body curled round a cushion, like a quiet animal herself. Anjali's husband, Surjit Markand, lover of Sonia, Ranjit's saviour, had died in the intervening years but she had put him away well behind her wide mouth, uncreased and brightly painted as usual; had wrapped him up in her neat cotton sari and long blouse. Her fingernails were still polished but her grey hair, drawn softly back into a knot, had grown scanty since the days of her marriage photographs. Krishna remembered the photographs in heavy silver frames, always below a window, through the many years that Anjali had been Sonia's best friend. Her eyes had changed, too. Once they had been bright and shining as a bird's, like her daughter Mona's, which Krishna had seen only ten days before in London, absorbed and concentrating utterly on Dhiren Kapur. He and Mona had been Krishna's chief contacts with international organisations and the Indian community in London. The funding of her river project would never have been possible without them.

The two women talked of Mona and London as they waited for the train to start. The upper berths in the compartment seemed empty, except for some luggage which belonged to a marriage party. Mostly men, who joked and laughed a lot with a young man called Lambu, obviously the bridegroom. From time to time one of them would come through the curtains, pull down a suitcase or drag one out from under her seat, scramble for something inside, close and lock it neatly and put it back. The compartment was silent as the train settled into movement. Social protocols were separating out and falling away from Krishna, all her faces, even the basic one of a tired woman in her thirties. She was simply a creature travelling through the night towards another who might be dead already. People and events emerged like luminescent animals from dark foam, each with its outline complete and entirely visible. For example, Uncle Surjit's face, slightly concave, with its high, receding forehead, intelligent, pointed eyes and attractive mouth, urging her to persuade Ranjit to leave right away and take the first train to Bombay before he was arrested for murder.

'Are you lonely without him?' she asked.

Aunty Anjali was startled, and came out of the haze which had settled on her eyes with the motion of the train.

'Surjit?' She looked a little embarrassed. 'Yes. Especially since Mona is not here. She was away in London when he died, and she hasn't been able to come back.'

'She wants to come back.' Krishna wondered if Aunty Anjali knew about Dhiren.

'Did you know that your father made all the arrangements when Surjit died?'

The death of Surjit Markand lay under Krishna's skin, floating below the surface like her father's yellow lotus flowers waiting for the sun to rise. They bobbed up now to puncture her with sharp, rolled petals, to release to the surface some of the black pain inside her, spread a pall of mourning, envelop her in the deepening colour of her skin.

Surjit Markand had died in his bed without a sound, while his wife was feeding her dog in the kitchen and his special coffee was cooking on the stove. Brigadier Paramjit Singh Chahal had stood beside the bed with his head bent as a mark of respect to the corpse, and to the weeping, thin figure of Anjali Markand, clad temporarily in the splendour of grief. She had acknowledged need of his help. He had gone out to her in a generous heartfelt sweep of emotion. 'Don't worry, Mrs Markand, Sonia will stay with you and I'll organise everything.'

'Who will light the funeral pyre?' the priest had murmured later to the man with a hat under his arm.

He had gone across to the covered shed where the women waited, the widow Anjali and his own wife Sonia, who had been crying incontrollably. 'You do it please, Brigadier Sahib,' Anjali whispered. He had not thought to ask Sonia; there was no reason why he should. In any case, she had been crying so much he could barely see her face through the tears. Perhaps the June sun had released inside her her exile and loss. Perhaps it had been a memory of wheat fields outside Jullundur and her first knowledge of Surjit.

On the train journey with Krishna, Anjali Markand raised herself from a stupor which had seized her and the sleeping dog beside her. 'I have not seen much of Sonia lately,' she said. 'Your father doesn't like her to go out, even to visit me. He's very suspicious, and he shouts a lot. So, how are they, your parents?'

'I don't know; that's why I'm going to Dagra. He had a heart attack while I was away in London.' So now a member of the public had been informed that Brigadier Paramjit Singh Chahal had had a heart attack and maybe was dead. All other facts could begin to cluster around that, form a discernible pattern, one which she could tackle better than the frantic mass of anguish which filled her.

Aunty Anjali's face was alive with concern, her eyes once again like smooth, black raisins. She leaned across the space between the two berths to tap Krishna on the arm, knocking over a bottle of

57

boiled water from the shelf jutting between them. Krishna leaped to save the bottle, managing only to cushion its fall. Some water had spilled on the floor, collecting dust, dirt and pieces of fluff in a faintly oily film. Krishna watched the smooth, curving edges of the puddle and noted how slow her reactions had been in saving the bottle. There was an uncomfortable disorder in having that puddle on the floor, with its oily film swinging from side to side with the movement of the train. Aunty Anjali's next words seemed to come from the puddle.

'Krishna, do you remember your father's friend, Dhiraj Kumari? The lady doctor in the army, who died soon after your father retired? Wasn't she posted in Morenapur at that time?'

Krishna moved around in her thoughts carefully, afraid of stumbling. She began at Morenapur. Dhiraj Kumari had been posted at the Military Hospital there, when Krishna went to admit Sohail to All Saints' School. Of course she had not met her, but Paramjit Singh Chahal's family always knew where the lady was posted, especially if she was only twenty miles away. Their mother made sure of that, told them all the gory details, real and imagined, of the Brigadier's love affair. Krishna knew for sure only about the photographs which the Brigadier had brought down from Sikkim when he was posted there. Dhiraj Kumari had been in every one of them, her figure now carefully blackened out by the Brigadier after Sonia's accusations.

Krishna had met her once. She had gone from photographic knowledge of a solid body in thick saris, her crinkly hair drawn firmly back, to brief acquaintance with a broad face and faint pock-marks on high cheekbones.

'Yes,' Krishna said, returning carefully to Aunty Anjali. 'She was posted at Morenapur. You know that my son Sohail is at boarding school in Morenapur. It's only a few miles from Dagra, so he can be close to his grandparents.' It was clear that Sonia had informed not only her children but also her best friend about Dhiraj Kumari's existence.

'Well. You haven't asked why I'm on this train, Krishna.' Aunty Anjali was alive and bubbling, now, absorbed with the challenge of her new project, almost coy with importance. 'Mrs Kapur is Dhiraj Kumari's sister. I'm trying to arrange a marriage for Mona with her son, Dhiren. He is a professor of Law and lives in Chatham, which is fifteen miles out of London. Mona wrote to me from London about him.'

58

'I know Dhiren,' Krishna said. 'I met him about ten days ago, while I was in London.'

'His father died a few days ago. Mrs Kapur is bringing the ashes from London to Hardwar to float them down the Ganges. She's to get on this train tomorrow morning at Hardwar and come to Dagra; she has property there. I want to settle this business of Mona's marriage before Mrs Kapur goes back to London. With Surjit dead, it is my responsibility.' Gradually her animation died down, running out like a wound-up toy, with her thin limbs beginning to subside for the night.

Two men from the marriage party came into the compartment again, talking in loud tones. They pushed aside the limp curtain which Krishna had adjusted to shield herself and Aunty Anjali from the light outside and the gaze of people tramping to the bathroom. As the curtain snapped back, rasping on the rail, she had exactly one moment to decide whether or not to be angry. It was easier and less fatiguing to tolerate them and not to make a scene. But she owed it to herself not to take the easy way out, to restore some sense of orderliness in this tiny corner of the universe. The puddle on the ground jogged a little and decided her.

'Whose seats are these? Why don't you put your luggage somewhere else, instead of coming in again and again to disturb us? This is a ladies' compartment.'

It was Lambu who answered, the prospective bridegroom. He wore a maroon knit shirt with 'Pierre Cardin' in beige letters on the sleeve. His manners were pretty and his accent somewhat strange. Perhaps he had come home from Canada and had chosen a bride, through newspapers, friends or an anxious mother. Already Krishna was regretting her interjection because he looked pained and abashed.

'Madam,' he said, 'I never meant to disturb you. But these are our berths; the conductor assigned them to us.'

'But this is a ladies' compartment!' She could feel her voice trail off.

'If you like, we'll make sure.' He turned to his companion. 'You go and see if these really are our berths.' His voice was not quite sarcastic; his response was just very elaborate. She felt heavy, boorish and rude, without being able to apologise for it. The man came back and in silence they climbed up and settled into the top berths, their shadows thin and shrouded in covers. The train jogged below her stomach, its wheels repeating a rhythm of the

59

rails. She could smell the hard cotton of her pillow, and a faint wet smell from the evaporating puddle on the floor.

She could feel herself dreaming, almost hear loud sounds of her own panting as she dreamed, but there was no way to struggle back into wakefulness. A woman called Badami, her head covered with a sari *pallav* like a village woman's, her head rounded under it, her face indistinct, sat opposite her, on the other side of a huge bin, watching her. Krishna was handling huge gobbets of raw flesh, her arms red with it, dipping into the bin. Suddenly she knew it was human flesh, because it came up threaded with a pyjama string, which held up a jig-saw puzzle of fleshy thighs. She was retching and sobbing into her pillow but now she was awake. She did not know what to do with the dream. It hung black and heavy upon her.

Anu had suggested, beside the roaring chimneys of Indraprastha Estate on the way to the railway station, that she should go back to him once again, wake up beside him in the morning. She considered the matter; it steadied her mind in the fearful half-darkness before dawn. He had not remarried during the ten years since they had been divorced, and they had made love several times during those years. It had been good, warm and comfortable. She knew she excited him, much more so now than ever before. Her body was a glowing, viscous mass, rubbing against the solid formation of his, flowing into the short curve of his neck, the round punctuations of his chest, legs and feet. He made her come easily enough, the temporary release of orgasm shooting and jerking through her. Coming was simpler with him than it had been with Ranjit, Anu knew her body very well. Yet each time, in one way or another, she found herself crying inside from frustration and loss. With Ranjit she had known perfection. Each time she realized again that she could neither go ahead nor come back from that point. With Ranjit she had been skinless and whole, no burden of darkening skin, completely belonging. Only with him life overwhelmed her, coming upon her suddenly, in flashes and huge movements. Every other man renewed in her the physical knowledge of being in love with Ranjit, whom she had not seen for more than ten years.

Driving to the railway station, a pink telegram in her fist, going past the belching angels of death at the Indraprastha Power Station, Anu had suggested that she should marry him again.

Waking beside Anu from this terrible dream, which now filled the whole train compartment, she would have waited until he had

60

woken up. Then, moving casually to the bathroom, picking the pins out of her hair and brushing it, she would have said, 'You know, I had a bad dream last night.'

His legs firm and unmoving under the sheet, so comforting in the reality of their outline, he would have asked, 'What dream?'

She would have gone over it, the horror would have been reduced to words of description. 'Oh, what's wrong with that?' His voice would have been joyously hearty, warm with laughter and love-making from the night, completely uncomprehending.

The dream was a man-eating dream, it terrified her. She needed Anu's matter-of-fact, solid presence, untroubled by rootless anxieties. He had offered to return her to the steady bosom of his peace, and she could not accept. She drew her knees up under her chin, wrapped her arms around her legs and put her head down. A porcupine, rolled into a ball, trembling, sheltering from danger, going into itself. A wave of longing, fatigue, utter terror flowed over her. Then, gradually, she began to reach a small, warm point inside, like a red warning light for aeroplanes in the complete darkness of the sky. She could feel flashes of dark colour going through her skin, suffusing it. Like a lightning conductor, reaching up to the hard points of the storm. She didn't even question any more why it happened that way, why everything must clock up against the colour of her skin so directly. Gradually her body loosened and unwound itself. There was no question now of trying to sleep, but her skin had achieved some purpose. An entity had been returned to her; she could function again, carry out actions, plan her motions.

She reached below her berth, and pulled out a hairbrush from her bag. Her hair was silky soft. If she had nothing else, when they added up eyes, lips, ears, breasts, and other beautiful possessions, she had her hair. With her skin, it made a double curtain to hide her. She rubbed long, smooth strands of it against her arms, her cheeks and the nape of her neck. There was so much of it.

The sounds of Hardwar station were outside the window when she awoke, and her hairbrush, crushed under her arm, had left a slug-trail of faint puncture points against her skin.

Aunty Anjali was awake and spry, her wide sleeping berth lifted up and neatly bolted away, the seat ready and waiting. She smelled of talcum powder and *Hamam* soap, she had even managed to change her clothes, in the tiny, wet square of bathroom, with its gaping hole of a toilet through which one saw the gravelled tracks passing rapidly below the belly of the train. Krishna noted in her an expectation and right degree of subservience with which the 'girl's side' are supposed to greet the 'boy's side' in arranging a marriage.

She still felt vaguely guilty about her behaviour the previous night. She had been self-assertive and aggressive on principle. What were the principles anyhow? Nothing seemed clear, the daylight wasn't helping much after all.

She could see Lambu and his group of friends now. They had trickled together from various points of the long compartment and collected near a tea vendor's cart just outside her window. Their luggage was piled up, suitcases with bright, hard tops, bulky bedding rolls, tightly strapped and bulging dangerously on either side of leather thongs, high, mysterious baskets covered and sewn up with gunny sacking, tiffin carriers of food and two clay pitchers of water. The young men were talking and laughing; they seemed to have done nothing else since last night. She watched them in a state of suspended animation, pushed into a corner in the compartment by Aunty Anjali's attention, which had swollen and grown, and which was directed wholly towards the door, waiting for Mrs Kapur, Dhiraj Kumari's sister.

Aunty Anjali was calling out and clapping her hands to attract the attention of a tall lady who had almost passed the compartment, followed by three *coolies* laden with luggage. She stopped and directed them into the compartment with one wave of her hand. Her hair was drawn back; she wore a familiar thick, magenta-coloured nylon sari solidly draped around her. The woman made a small conciliatory motion with her left hand, the square, carefully tended nails requesting Krishna to leave her berth and sit beside Anjali. Not a request to be refused. The other hand almost simultaneously directed the scrawny *coolies* to pile suitcase after suitcase on the berth recently vacated, probably still warm from Krishna's body.

'They scratch so easily,' she said, in a firm, sweet voice, 'but the trunk can go down there.' It was slipped under the berth, and the three men left, brass tags on their arms gleaming in the early morning sunshine. The train was stationary; it was a long stop at Hardwar. Krishna's watch still showed London time. She peered out of the window at a large station clock suspended on a far wall, and set it to ten past eight. Then she looked at Lambu and his friends. Somehow she felt closer to him than to the distracted old lady beside her.

He was very intent on something frying in a deep, black vessel perched on a small stove. Oil bubbled and occasionally splashed against the high aluminium sides of the cart. The vendor was ladling out bread *pakoras*, one by one, hot oil draining off through holes in his spatula. He jerked it slightly to knock off the last, clinging drops and slid crisp, thick, mustard-coloured triangles into saucers, one beside each cup of tea. The fresh smell of frying was agonisingly delicious. Her stomach ached with hunger as she watched Lambu open his mouth wide to eat. His fragile dignity which had embarrassed her the previous evening was gone. She longed for a *pakora*.

6

Arrival in Dagra

The train was going through a tunnel now. Soon they would be at Dagra station. Darkness in the compartment was complete and she could not make out even the outline of the women's faces. Aunty Anjali and Mrs Kapur were silent, each entering into a vague sense of expectation.

This would be the first time she arrived in Dagra when her father would not be there to receive her. Always, whether it was at the railway station or the bus stop, he had been there waiting in his car, with his hat on if it was summer.

'You have a house in Dagra, Mrs Kapur?' she asked.

'Yes, and it's not very far from yours. We can share a taxi. Mrs Markand told me that you are Brigadier Chahal's daughter.' Had Aunty Anjali, in a flurry of zeal, laying out all her wares to woo the prospective mother-in-law, whispered to her also about Dhiraj Kumari, who had had no social shelters apart from her job? Or perhaps Mrs Kapur knew already about her dead sister's erstwhile connection with the Brigadier.

'I might need your father's help,' she said.

'He's not been so well,' Krishna murmured. 'But what is the problem?'

'Years ago, we rented out our house to some students from the local Government College. They handed it down from one generation of students to another, and they're still paying the same miserable rent fixed fifteen years ago. Somehow we've got to evict them, and you know how difficult that is with the present laws. I want to sell the house now that my husband has passed away.'

Mrs Kapur's face showed the shadow of an urn full of ashes carried all the way from London, and floated down the Holy River at Hardwar to the singing voices of priests.

She realised Mrs Kapur's house was the one down the road past the meat shop, its occupants the same students who had helped her at the end of her *padyatra* less than a year ago. If it hadn't been for them, the *padyatra* would have failed and trees on a huge tract of Himalayan land would have been felled and carried away.

Mrs Kapur was waiting for Krishna near the taxi stand. 'Can I give the taxi your address?' she whispered. 'No taxi or scooter will take me to my house; they're afraid. The students have given instructions at the bus stop and the railway station and everyone knows they're vicious; they will do anything, beat up people, use knives.'

Meanwhile Aunty Anjali, hovering at Mrs Kapur's elbow, had been cut out of the arrangements.

'Don't worry about me; I'll take the bus to Kotla. When will I see you, Mrs Kapur? Have dinner with me tonight, and if there is any problem please stay with me. I'll come in a taxi to fetch you.'

Mrs Kapur moved to the other side of the taxi, supervising her mountains of luggage. Aunty Anjali's hand on Krishna's shoulder was weightless as a leaf. 'I hope Brigadier Sahib gets better soon. He strains himself too much. Give my love to your mother. Tell her I'll come and see her as soon as this gets sorted out,' she nodded towards Mrs Kapur, now free to acknowledge links with the daughter of her oldest friend Sonia.

The main road went on to Kotla, where American missionaries used to stay. Their taxi turned off at Salma Chowk, and went past Kamani Bazaar. It was still early, with the sun barely out. Shops had not opened yet, but pushcarts emerged from the morning haze and the smell of ripe mangoes was already heavy in the air. The mango season was at its peak, absolutely the hottest part of the summer, the heat bringing an utter sweetness to the mango flesh. Their heavy, warm smell wrapped around her.

'What do you plan to do about the students?' she asked Mrs Kapur.

'Actually, Chaman Bajaj has promised to help.'

Krishna was startled, an evil ghost from her married life had suddenly burst into the morning calm of Dagra. 'You know Chaman Bajaj, don't you?' Mrs Kapur went on. 'He is a great friend of Anu's family. He and Anu's father have always been very close, and we have known Bhim Lal Whig since before Partition. Chaman Bajaj is keen for his daughter to marry Dhiren. She has led quite a secluded life in Ropar. I asked him how she would adjust to living in London. He said that with a woman it didn't matter, she could adjust to anything. They say he's a powerful politician. We'll see this evening. He's planning to do something today. If he's successful in getting the students out of my house I'll have time to go to Ropar to see his daughter. If not, Dhiren can go ahead and marry his Mona. Her mother seems a sweet old lady. But no money and no influence. My husband used to say that a man should marry into a family which would increase his number of arms, that's how things get done. You must have connections. It's very important, especially for Dhiren since he lives abroad. He needs a powerful father-in-law in India.'

Mona had no father at all. Surjit Markand, who had saved Ranjit, who had been Sonia's beloved, was dead. 'Have you asked Dhiren about marrying Chaman Bajaj's daughter?' Dhiren's will was the only hope.

'Dhiren's a good boy. He will listen to what I say.'

Krishna knew Chaman Bajaj. An evil king, determined to win a prince for his daughter. Dhiren, living in London, was the prince. He would use all his evil machinations. To turn out a bunch of students from an old house was child's play for him. This would ensure the mother's approval. But she, Krishna, would run the race with him. Even if his strides were a giant's, covering huge spaces, she would have to pitch her strength against his.

Mona was almost her sister, the daughter of her mother's lover, Surjit's child. Besides, Dhiren was a stream which, joining Mona, would come and go between India and London.

'They say the rains will be delayed this year.' Mrs Kapur turned to her. 'The heat in Hardwar was terrible.'

The taxi turned off Bazaar Road, past the *paan* shop and an old woman on the ground nearby selling *gram*, down Shankardass Road. Bushes crowded up on either side, and mango trees with black trunks, long dusty leaves, and fruit hanging heavy between them. Had her father sold the contract on his mango trees as he had done every season?

She sensed fear in Mrs Kapur; her new suitcases did not give her enough confidence. Krishna got off at the corner of the lane which led to her father's house. She felt the sun on her head as she walked the last, short stretch. It had not taken on yet the oppressive heat of day. A small breeze blew in her face, with the smell of eucalyptus trees. Three years ago her father had planted fifty of them, on the perimeter of his land. 'An investment,' he had said proudly. 'After ten years they will fetch a high price. I'm always thinking of how to improve.'

With his luck the trees would probably crack up in a storm before then, but he would find another scheme – if he was still alive. She found him in the garden, the house rearing up behind him, slabs of grey and pink concrete with a small, ridiculous balcony jutting out like a hand of benediction. His tall figure was bent over the roses. He shaded his eyes towards the sound of the opening gate.

He was straightening up painfully, supporting his calves with his hands, much thinner than when she had last seen him, his soiled shirt, missing many buttons, hanging loosely about him. But he was alive. A warm wave flooded through her; it held all the care and love he had given her as a child. She saw it with sudden clarity, and knew in that instant how fearful she had been of his dying.

'What have you been doing to yourself while I was away?' she said as they embraced. She could smell a sour, old man's sweat through his shirt. 'And what's all this?' She pulled out the rumpled, pink telegram from her handbag.

'Who sent you that? Your mother doesn't know how to send telegrams. But it's correct, I had a massive heart attack fifteen days ago.' There was a note of pride; a substantial fact had been added to his life.

'Then what are you doing out here?'

'I've been feeling very well, in fact never so fit. Today is an exception. I'm restless and uncomfortable. Cramps in my legs. But an old soldier never gives up.'

'But you should be in bed.' Her voice was stern, breaking the euphoria of their meeting. He reacted sharply, unable to tolerate criticism.

'I'm a doctor. I know more about myself than you do. You're

just like your mother, always criticising me.' She put her arms around him again, stemming his anger.

'Let's go inside,' she said.

'No, no. Once we get there you'll start talking to your mother. I want to talk to you first. You know why I'm in the garden? Because she's driven me out of the house with her shouting. I think she's dismissed the servant again. How can I bear it? How will we manage? And Sohail is here, too.'

'What is he doing out of school?'

'He wasn't well. He called two days ago, crying into the telephone. Your mother fetched him from school. Just a cold and a slight touch of fever, but he was talking about dreams and meeting an aunt who was a magician's assistant. Do we have a relative like that? I think he's all right today.'

He was obsessed with Sonia, and went on and on about her. It wearied Krishna to listen to him. But this morning she was careful not to argue at all, or ask questions. Each time she disturbed his flow, he went back and repeated the sentences. His tongue was sharper; he was even less tolerant of interruption. Now he was armed with the privilege of a heart attack.

Sohail was already running down the stairs, his body heavy on naked feet, his shorts hitched up almost under his armpits and his shirt billowing out. His cheeks were cool, fresh and loving under her lips. She kissed him again and again.

Her mother came in from the kitchen. As they embraced she saw clearly over her head into the dining-room. Sonia Chahal had once been very tall, but now she had shrunk, bending with spondilitis, an injured ankle, sciatica, no one was quite sure how many things were wrong with her except that she complained. Additional webs of fine wrinkles were laid out on her skin, still soft as down, as her hair. Once it had gone up in two huge waves, one on either side of her head. How comforting, the most secure thing on earth for a child to run her thumb slowly along a smooth billow of her mother's hair.

'Go up and wash. I'll make some tea for you. What will you eat, Krishna?'

'You'll make the tea? So you have no servant? What did you do with Ramu?'

'What do you mean, what did I do? Your father's been complaining to you already!' He had walked in just then, and she turned upon him. 'Why don't you leave this poor girl in peace sometimes? You begin loading her with all this the moment she enters.'

'Who else shall I tell?' he muttered as he hobbled slowly into the dining-room. Krishna watched him. Years and years of the sounds of quarrels and reconciliations, repeated patterns and new ones, came towards her out of the woodwork and the walls.

For example, his feud with Surjit Markand, who had settled near by. Surjit was more intelligent and had known exactly how to provoke him. 'You're not a Brigadier,' he had said to him, 'but a retired Brigadier. You should put "retired" behind your name. I know about such things.' Since Surjit had been right, 'Retd' had appeared promptly on the Brigadier's nameplate, but he had complained bitterly.

'Who does he think he is? Just because he had this hush-hush intelligence job in Delhi at one time! If you weren't so chummy with his wife, I wouldn't let him into my house. He's just jealous of it. Look at that dreadful hole he has built. Three tiny rooms.'

'But Anjali is happy there,' Sonia had said. 'That's the important thing.' Then her tone had been rough and complaining. 'Besides, she has less cleaning to do. Not like me, slaving all day.'

'That's what you want everyone to believe, that you became a slave in India. But look where you came from. I picked you out of the gutter. You didn't have enough to eat. No electricity and no education.'

'That was wartime,' she had said, but she was already vanquished. 'My family is well off now. Krishna must go and see them some time. And I speak more languages than you.'

'Who understands Italian? Who bothers about your Greek? You can't even go to the bank. I have to do everything. All you do is soil my reputation; you say that I go with other women, that I don't look after my family.'

'You imagine all that,' Sonia had said. 'I don't speak to anybody about you. Or my children, I swear that. Why should I? Nobody is interested; they're all busy in their own lives. But you're always suspicious; you fight with all the neighbours.'

'Because you've poisoned their minds against me.'

Krishna had shared his deep sense of social ignominy. For years she had stretched herself as a social front, to shield Sonia's indifference to protocol. She had opened and shut in smiles, gestured in hospitality, seating guests in the drawing-room who, after they had drunk coffee and had eaten cake, still looked around

68

and said, 'But, Krishna, where is your mother?'

'I'm afraid she's not feeling too well; she's lying down.'

'Oh, what is the problem? Last time it was, perhaps, the back?' Smirking, and barely polite, the more adventurous of the women would offer to go in and see her.

'No no,' Krishna had said, not daring to add that her mother was probably washing clothes at the time, or wandering around outside waiting for the guests to leave. Then she had stretched into stiff, grown-up conversation, writhing with embarrassment at the awkward movements of Paramjit Chahal. He talked too much and lost the thread of his interminable stories. No dialogue was possible, since he could not bear to hear the other person speak. An opinion even slightly different from his own was an assault on his already shattered dignity, a further emasculation. The unnatural social burden had chafed against her; she had longed for the steady, rocking motion of a happy family. Mother, father, children travelling together, no matter where. Until gradually she had realized that social disruption was Sonia's only weapon, for attack, defence and survival, now that she had abandoned the pursuit of happiness.

Her father had cajoled her into other tasks. She had put her arms out, so that when he fell he should not go all the way to the ground. She had accompanied him on social calls. When people were sick, when the Army Book had prescribed visits to cultural shows, Krishna had been there. She had felt herself to be charming and grown-up, with ballast from her own intelligent sentences, and a growing fund of her mother's animosity. She had listened to their quarrels, angry tears and words so ugly it made her soul spit and vomit. She had been there in the violence of flights into the garden under a misshapen moon, and a pleading to return to the pretended safety of a house. Her mother was an angry god who had to be humoured, who would take and take her love without remorse and with no return. But she had been able to afford to give, contemptuously secure in her father's enormous ocean of love. She had felt forever the warmth of her father's shoulder, arm and side as she slipped down gradually, lying beside him in the car half asleep, returning from an evening engagement where she had been the only child present, her father's social blanket, to cover his nakedness.

On *shikar* expeditions, however, her presence had been entirely voluntary. Paramjit Singh Chahal had not needed anyone with him when he went out into the jungle with his gun, stalking big game.

69

Escaping from his wife's arid withdrawal to the green spaces of the jungle, there was no need for measurement, no comparison, only the warmth of hunting, in which his clever, intuitive movements fused with the wary life of the animal and the final domination of the kill. But she had taken the jungle as his gift; it released her into childhood. She was young and she had gambolled beside her father's casual love. In the jungle she had not needed her darkening skin any more. Here, no ancestors had come towards her, flailing their arms to embrace her, offering a seductive love which her life denied. Here she had been single, complete, with no skin and no outline, going nowhere from nowhere, her soul fully absorbed by trees and air. The only other place she had been like this was with Ranjit. Without event or thought, without memory, drowned completely in the enormous moment of his love.

Once, in the Madhya Pradesh jungles near Khudriya, going alone from the *dak* bungalow down the fire-line, she had seen a laburnum tree in a small clearing. Its yellow radiance had been a distillation of light. No green, no blue of sky, no other colour in its yellowness. An utter presence which had dissolved and released her.

'No more *shikar*?' she asked her father.

'I haven't been for years, now. Even before I returned, it became tedious, with all the game restrictions. And to book a shooting block was too difficult. The last time we went to Cheela I managed, through the good influence of General Simrit Sinhji who was in Lucknow then. He's dead now, poor chap. He was very fat; he died of his last heart attack. He was my patient in Hyderabad years ago, before you were born. Your mother will remember him. She met him several times there. She used to go out with me then, in our old Hindustan 14. She sang Greek songs through the window. Lovely voice. I've almost forgotten what it's like. Haven't heard her sing for years now.'

Sonia smiled sarcastically. 'Don't try to flatter me,' she said. 'No one is impressed with your sweet words. And don't tell Krishna stories of your grand adventures. I have only to tell her about what you did yesterday.'

'What did he do?' Krishna asked, wondering if there was ever a moment's peace and happiness in her parents' house, yet forced to ask by her dogged concern for justice, which pleased nobody and achieved nothing.

'Why do you always speak to her? You should listen to me

70

instead. Your mother never lets me talk.' An old man's small and futile tears, the pale shadow of his fury in the passionate gardens of her childhood. She sat silent and helpless.

Sonia had not planned to go this far; there was hesitation in her voice, even regret. But the balloon was released.

'Yesterday,' she said, and her husband left, unable to bear the story. Krishna knew he was listening from his bedroom. 'It was just hours before you arrived. Outside, near the water-pump, he threw me to the ground, slapped me. He said I had stolen the brass fittings from the watertap in the garden, to kill his flowers. That I had poisoned the chickens. I ask you, why would I do that? Why?'

Sonia's eyes were dry with exhaustion. They twitched at Paramjit's loud voice, roaring from his bedroom. 'Lies! All lies! Why do you listen to this bitch, this liar!' He darted out with extraordinary speed, grabbed a pile of albums from the bookcase and called out to Krishna, 'Come with me, let's get out of here and talk in the garden. I'll show you my new lotus flower. It will be open now, before the sun comes out. This woman will kill me if I stay here.'

The lotus flower. It was the same yellow as the laburnum tree. She was only faintly aware of her father fumbling in the older albums. 'Here he is. I knew we had a photograph of him,' he said.

'Who?'

'General Simrit Sinhji, standing in front of the Osmania General Hospital in Hyderabad.' He was reading a faded ink-written label, under the photo of a huge, blurred man posed before a white building. He pulled the other albums from her lap, leafed through them and put them down. Soon the white-pebbled edge of the pond was littered with decaying black sheets of photographs. 'I'm looking for our Cheela photos. A stag and a panther! What more can one ask for?'

The sun was hot on her back, the lotus flower had long since sunk below the water, its surface was flat and closed.

'Ah! Here they are.'

One showed Krishna with bare feet, standing on a verandah, lips pouted in irritation, with a rope attached to a small goat firmly wrapped around her hand. Her skin in the photo was several shades lighter. It must have been long ago. 'Why do I look so bad tempered?'

'I don't know,' he said. 'You were bad tempered that day, just like your mother. But you managed to save that little goat. We had taken it along as bait for the panther.'

71

'Where is Cheela?'

'Across the river from Hardwar and into the jungle. We took the ferry.'

Their car had broken down on a slope up from the ferry. It had been summer, the time when the animals were most visible, flushed out from the undergrowth by the heat in search for water. Her own face had run with sweat. She had stood under the scanty shade of a *kikar* tree, while her father and two *shikaris*, none of whom had known anything about engines, had stood with their heads under the bonnet of the car. She strongly resented the heat; she had no faith that the engine would ever get started again. Her father had turned to her, as if he had sensed her intolerant anger, then had said, 'Oh, your neck.' She had been startled and had put her hand to it. 'It's like the neck of a doe, so long and elegant. Beautiful.'

She was flooded with happiness at this memory and her voice was tender. 'Our car broke down that day,' she said, taking the albums from him. 'Now I remember.'

'We didn't go by car at all. The road was too bad. A jeep was waiting for us in the *dak* bungalow at Cheela. We went by truck, having left our car in Hardwar.'

'I am sure we had a car.' She was assertive, pushing memory into his mind. His eyes were small slits in the bright sunlight.

'Don't interrupt me. Just listen if you want to, or go away.'

She was amazed at how rude and aggressive he had become. But she could let go of the memory for his sake.

'The river was dried up, there were two water holes in the river bed. We could not decide at which one to tie the goat. We were at one of them looking for footprints. Every one except me saw the panther; he was behind a bush watching us. "There. Don't you see it? Why don't you shoot?" you shouted. I turned, but the panther had disappeared.'

'Were you angry with me?' she asked.

'No. I was never angry with you. I was just disappointed to have missed the panther. We went back into the jungle, to get to the other water hole, about a mile away. The jungle was very thick, with trees growing close together. Suddenly a stag emerged from between the trees and began running alongside the jeep.'

'It wasn't a stag, Daddy, it was a doe. I still remember a half-grown fawn which ran with it.' A flash of legs, hoofs close together, neck stretched out, high bounding bodies, incredible grace. A playful and curious doe with a fawn.

But her father was not listening to her. 'It was not a doe, I never shoot does. It was a huge stag, a *bara-singha* with all his twelve antlers grown. I shot at him with the twelve-bore. He fell twice before he died. We carried him to the bungalow. Perhaps that was when I took your photograph; you were protesting about the goat.

'We took the *bara-singha* with us to the other water hole. The panther could scent the goat in the jeep and was tracking us. It ran to the edge of the water bed and stood there, watching us. This time you shook me silently, gripping my arm. I turned, and saw the panther's eyes, red and glowing behind a bush. My shot went straight through the eye. It dropped immediately.'

7

Krishna's Marriage

She thought she would stay forever in the lazy labyrinth of grace, that the hot indulgence of her father's love would always cover her without question. He wanted only that she should feel his pain, acknowledge his humanity and she did that with a huge contempt, in the same way as she accepted his love; she took it for granted.

The spiral carried through to her brother's birth. Gola was born because Prabhjot Kaur, her grandmother, wanted him. The old lady's will was a constant, nagging presence in the house. It combined with the assault which India had mounted on Sonia since the day she had arrived. She had resisted, through Michael, through the changing colour of Krishna's skin, through one abortion. But then, nine years after the birth of her first child, she drifted into pregnancy, and loved the son who was born to her, with a helpless, vulnerable passion which cut out Krishna completely. Till then Sonia had given love and care in measured doses, through the haze of a new, savage country. Sonia's love was to be obtained with difficulty, temporarily, through support, grovelling and a reduction of the receiver's self to the smallest possible area. Krishna was a harmonium, opening and closing to her mother.

Gola's birth indicated the enormous possibilities of Sonia's love, denied to Krishna.

But her father's love was the same full wave. She continued to be the pride of his heart. As she approached marriageable age, however, she began to separate from its flood, to take on the distinct identity of daughter. Up until then society had existed at some distance, a preying monster which waited to swallow him just beyond the edge of his wife's gossip. Now he had to deal with society on intimate terms, open his arms to it full of gifts. He had to arrange a daughter's marriage.

Passing through the proposals of several army officers, he arrived finally at Anu, the son of Bhim Lal Whig, whom he had known as a large, kindly young lawyer working in his father's busy office in Kohat.

'How could you choose Bhim Lal Whig for Krishna's father-in-law?' his brother Satinder had exploded. He had heard of the proposed marriage through their sister, Lajwanti. She was busy with arrangements, since Sonia knew nothing of these matters.

'What's wrong with him? I remember him from Kohat. He's a very nice man.'

'His father was the sworn enemy of Sardar Sobha Singh Palji of Bhimbar, who was married to our aunt Kailash Kaur.'

'But our father took him on as a junior lawyer. He didn't care about the enmity, quite obviously. Why should I care?'

'Our father cared nothing about keeping this family together. Then he died, when we were all so young. It's I who have kept this family as it is. You can't marry your daughter into the house of an enemy.'

'I met Palji in Poonch. He told me he had got you guns many years ago in Kohat. I didn't know you were in the habit of using guns. I thought you were a man of non-violence.'

Satinder was quiet, the flow of his passionate anger diffused by uncomfortable facts. Paramjit went on. 'I helped Palji. He was stranded in Poonch. I helped him go to Srinagar. You might even say I repaid your debt. But I met him some weeks later in Srinagar. He seemed a broken man. Someone had told him a terrible story. That the Pakistani raiders in Bhimbar had found his wife Kailash Kaur in the arms of his nephew, Prakash, had killed them both and had left them there, locked in shame.'

'Must have been Bhim Lal Whig who told him,' Satinder said. 'Apart from Palji's daughter and our faithful Bhagwana, only Whig escaped from Bhimbar when the raiders came. Do you know that Bhim Lal Whig is a staunch Hindu, an Arya Samaji? You want to marry Krishna to a Hindu?'

'Why should I insist that she marry a Sikh? I didn't marry one myself. I introduced Krishna to Anu some time ago. Now she wants to marry him.'

Krishna's ancestors were a strange lot. Sometimes they made themselves up from nothing, like Gulshan/Miss Phillips, the Magician's Assistant, erstwhile daughter of Palji, who had watched her mother, Kailash Kaur, being killed by the raiders in Bhimbar during Partition. This had turned Gulshan's wits a little, and had given her strange powers to astonish the sane. Just as Krishna's skin astonished her, darkening with events and loyalties, registering journeys, and connections.

Sometimes her skin was like an airline map, criss-crossed with straight lines connecting up distant, unlikely places. For a long time, until she began to act, she had been its simple audience, watching the effect of life upon her skin, how it had responded to the pain of exposure, slowly ripening like a berry, turning from the white of Greek statues to the purple midnight of India's gods. Krishna belonged to neither. Not even to her own skin, which watched her inside and registered the changes, her discomforts and bad temper, her grating irritations. Sometimes she wished it would just get out of the way and leave her alone in whatever she was feeling, silent, as she was in the jungle or with Ranjit. Sometimes, of course, it was useful to have around, a pair of pincers to pick up and hold whatever was happening to her, a shower curtain to wrap around her, airless and plastic against the rain.

Her skin shadowed the exact moment when her father's love became distanced from his daughter, the time when a halting trickle of water came from the tap in Lajwanti's house in Delhi. Her father's hot, summer-stricken face was bent over it. Behind it lay the world's whole surface, huge and endless, acres of grass, uncultivated riches, a dream in the sun.

The water supply was slow; he had barely a few drops of water on his face, slipping in channels through dust which the Delhi air had put on it. 'Where have you been since yesterday?' There was violence in his voice.

'Oh, here and there. Visiting a friend. I didn't know you were coming to Delhi. When did you leave Dagra?'

'I went to your hostel yesterday. Your roommate said you were out for the night. Then I went to Anu's flat this morning. Some little boys playing outside, the landlord's children, said that he and "Mrs Anu" had gone out. Everything's clear to me now; you're sleeping with him.' His voice thundered across the narrow bathroom, putting fear for the first time into her heart.

'My own bloody fault. I introduced you. But not for this. To shame me.'

'It is not that way at all,' she said. 'You've not understood it correctly.' But he had already turned away, having given up on the water which refused to increase its flow. He was wiping his face, listening to her.

Those wretched little boys. They swarmed over her and Anu, emerging from behind the chimney or the low dividing walls on the terrace, whistling in low, obscene tones, or making a steady click-click sound on tiny tin blowers to tease the lovers on the roof.

Somehow she did not think of herself and Anu as lovers, though they dragged his mattress out and made love on the roof during the summer nights she spent with him. The bricks were hot through the thin cotton and there was no breeze, but the open air was better than stifling heat in his long, narrow room.

'We'll get married when I establish some kind of law practice,' Anu said.

'But I have only one more year to go before I finish my MA. Then I can get a teaching job. We'll have enough to live on.'

'That's not the same thing,' he said. 'It's not really a question of money. I have to see how my parents would look at it.'

'But they know about me. My father has spoken to yours, and they know each other from Kohat.'

'That was different. Your grandfather was a wealthy lawyer; he was Mayor of Kohat. My father was just beginnning his life. But your family lost all that during Partition. What does your father have now?'

'He has me. I'm not bringing you a dowry. Is that it?'

'It's not dowry. But we have to see how the family look at this marriage. After all, I don't want to alienate them.'

'I don't want to alienate them either.' He was four years older, but that was not why she trusted him. She had put herself in his hands, which were sane and kind and did not smell of the passionate, burning chaos that she knew at home. No veils of terror hung about him; everything was open and gentle. If she stood very close to him the storm would pass her by. Slowly his roof would

76

grow over her and stone and cement would rise in standing columns. In the small, cosy spaces this would leave her, there was no room for the emptiness of loss. Her skin, the sharp, accurate spy with years of training, reflected the news. Paramjit Singh Chahal's love for his daughter was leaking away; soon she would marry and belong to another family. She registered dispossession with a straight thrust, the seed of anguish going into her ground and out of sight.

'How is it you're in Delhi?' she asked her father. Her voice was conciliatory and hesitant, wondering if he would reply or subject her to the public humiliation of having spoken into the air in front of her aunt and cousins. She had always been tyranical, self-assured or sulky. Now for the first time she used the same adult tones she employed with her mother. Paramjit adjusted to the new equation like an insect dropped on a new leaf to feed, who understood that the forest still rose above him, tall, fearful and independent.

'Some work,' he said, reluctantly. 'But really I wanted to take you back with me to Dagra. Delhi is so hot, and your university is almost closed. But I can see you have other plans; you will not want to come back with me.' His voice was rough and despising, she could see that really he did not want her near him just yet.

'Oh. I would love to come back with you,' she said hurriedly. 'In fact I was planning to go home anyway. When do you want to leave?'

Passing through Muzaffarnagar, she heard loud film music and the creaking of giant wheels. The area behind Kamla Nehru Park was busy with activity which lit the evening sky in a bright neon glow.

'Oh, look! a *Baisakhi mela*!' she said, exactly as she would have said before this thick, resinous layer of tension had dropped upon them, holding them stiff and silent. Her desire to go to the *mela* cracked the film, and her heart flowed through in relief. He had agreed, the habit of indulgence was still with him. Perhaps things would be all right between them again, perhaps they could go back to how it had been before. She was voluntary hostage to Anu for domestic bliss, but she still wanted the freedom of her father's love. The *Baisakhi mela* was a pastiche of light, colour and sound, wrapping and unrolling like a gay tapestry, patterns swirling without detail. Booths, eating places, jugglers, circus, merry-go-round and loud-mouthed vendors lost their outlines, merged, ran into each other like a child's painting in a competition. She bought a snarling mud tiger, striped in black and yellow, and stuffed him into a shoulder-bag. Then they stopped before a booth selling *kurtas* from Lucknow.

'I want to buy two,' she told the man who was holding them out and haggling over the price. She held a thin, peacock-blue embroidered *kurta* against her body, to see if it was long enough for her. Then she asked for a large white one in a man's size. Immediately a cold stiffness returned to her father. He moved off into himself, pushing her out. He knew who she was buying the *kurta* for. He turned and walked back to the car. She paid and followed him, wrapped again in the pall of mourning which never quite left them again.

Making love to Anu was almost always good, and it got better as the years passed. In fact their sexual life was just about at its peak when she left him. His hands and tongue had learned about her body, but by then her insistent, demanding soul had let go of him, and she floated in a vacuum, a spaceship that had strayed beyond the solar system, into the awful loneliness of being earth's artifact in space, with gold-plated lettering on her skin to recommend her.

They now seldom made love on the roof outside; the landlord's boys were waiting for it too heartily, and the houses around them were too close. But her father was right, they did make love. Again and again, inside the room. She could see the tops of *ashoka* trees coming up from the road. But still she did not think of Anu and herself as lovers. She remembered details like the heavy curve of Anu's body, the sweet, soft smile in his eyes when she pleased him greatly, and sometimes the dreadful straining to reach something else, as if to go beyond the skin. But it did not pass into her flesh, become a part of her being.

Other details leapt out with more clarity. Like the face of Chaman Bajaj, when he had walked into Anu's small room and had found her sitting there comfortably on the bed, reading, in a short shirt and *lungi*, while a pot of beans bubbled on a hot-plate on the floor. She had looked up suddenly into his face. Dark skin stretched over wide cheek bones, flat brown eyes which flickered for a moment with surprise, and fleshy lips. His eyes had registered her position in the room, her situation.

'I have come to see Anu,' he had announced.

'He's not here,' she had said, wondering why her voice rose with such belligerence as if he had assaulted her.

78

The next time she had seen his face it was as Chief Trustee on the interview board for Lala Bhajan Ram College, where she had applied for a lecturer's job. He had not said anything to her, had asked no questions, but had made many whispering remarks to other members of the Board. The Secretary told her later that she had got the job despite Chaman Bajaj, because the university representative, who did not know him, could think of no reason why they should not take a brilliant First Class student fresh out of college, who had answered all his questions.

'Chaman Bajaj is a very good friend of my father's. They've been friends for years, seeing each other almost every day. They even went on holidays together, in the early days,' Anu had said.

'My father tells a story, of how Bajaj came to him one day in Delhi just before Independence. He had finished his new hotel, with money made in Bhimbar. Bajaj had taken him aside. "I have a message for you from Sardar Patel." Patel was Home Minister then, and Mavalankar was Congress candidate for Speaker of the Central Assembly. "He wants you to use your influence with Yashpal Sethi of Bhiwani, to have him vote for Mavalankar." Because it was Chaman Bajaj who asked him, my father had set off immediately for Bhiwani and had reached there late at night. Sethi was just settling down to dinner, and invited them to join him. When they had eaten, he asked how they had happened to come, and exploded when he heard them requesting his vote for Mavalankar. He filled the whole house with loud sounds of cursing, using the filthiest abuse he knew. They had heard him through, and when he had finished, Chaman Bajaj had said, "Sardar Patel will make you Minister if you cast your vote correctly." Then Sethi had calmed down and listened to them. Mavalankar won by a margin of two votes.'

'Did Sethi get to be Minister?'

'Yes, Deputy Minister in one of the States. Chaman Bajaj is good about that sort of thing. So you see, I can't imagine he would ever work against you. He knows we are to get married.'

'Maybe he sees it as a distant, improbable event.' It had often seemed that way to her.

But the marriage finally did take place, and Chaman Bajaj arranged the festivities. Bhim Lal Whig's reception was to be held in his own hotel, its huge ballroom having been refurbished. Chaman Bajaj promised that the President would grace the auspicious occasion.

She stood beside Anu on a raised platform at one end of the room, below bright, heavy chandeliers on the ceiling, against delicate *fleur-de-lis* and Persian designs reproduced in beautiful ceramic panels on the walls.

Guests milled around between the tables, talking alternately of the complexion of the bride, the approaching dishes of food, guessing what time the covers would be lifted off, whispering that the bride was beautiful, her hair long and luxuriant, her eyes soft and large, but noting how dark her skin was.

She had a vantage point, raised above the heads of guests. A short Gurkha, gnarled with muscles, in green army uniform with yellow braid running under the epaulettes, and the President's crest of three Ashoka lions emblazoned on his crimson armband, cocked his head from side to side in an obvious survey. Then he left. She filled the gap by looking for her father. He seemed to have handed her over already, consigned her firmly to the Whigs. She found to her surprise that she resented this. She had waited so long to belong here, to this new family's love and sane wisdom, since she didn't belong anywhere else. But she minded when, like cold fingers touching her soul, her father had said, with tears in his eyes, 'Well, now you belong to another family, you are not mine any longer.'

She remembered the wedding ceremony. She and Anu had just finished the fourth round of the *Guru Granth Sahib*. Her uncle, Satinder, had brought the Holy Book all the way from Chandigarh to Dagra for the wedding. It was a family heirloom, brought from Kohat by her grandmother, Prabhjot Kaur. Satinder, as the eldest son, was its custodian. 'Your father got married around this Book,' he had said, 'and you're my favourite niece.' He had brought it to Dagra, along with a friend whom he had called Baba Sampuran.

Baba Sampuran's sermon had amused Anu so much that he was still laughing at the end of the wedding. The old man had described, in rousing, gory detail, the sacrifices which the Sikhs had made in the cause of India's Freedom, at Guru-ka-Bagh, at Nankana Sahib – and during the Babbar Akali Movement. Then he had said, 'This is our daughter, Krishna. She is a young sapling who until now was planted in her father's garden. She is being lifted out, with her roots exposed to wind and rain, and is being planted in the garden of her husband's family. She has been nurtured with all our love. We hand her now to you. Take care of her.'

Krishna's eyes had been spilling with tears at the reference to their love, but still she had wondered, through the low sounds of Anu's laughter, if there had been women taking part in the stirring actions that Baba Sampuran had described, and if these brave women had all been delicate saplings planted in someone else's garden. Then she had embraced Sonia, and had gone to her father's arms.

She could not locate her father for a while at the reception. Then she spotted him, in dark trousers and white shirt, sitting in a chair near the door like any other guest, an ordinary man, abstracted and diminished. Sonia stood near by, talking to Meera Aunty, her hands moving through the air; and the others who had come from Dagra for the reception, the bride's family, polite, slightly nervous at attending Bhim Lal Whig's grand reception, where the President was now at the door.

His figure was long and elegant in the spotlight in which the TV man held him, his turban arranged in smooth folds, light gleaming from his glasses. The face of Chaman Bajaj was beside him, splayed with light. A tight crowd collected around the President, pressing up to be photographed with him. Bhim Lal Whig had always been solid, dignified and self-contained. Now he gave a small skip, a jump, and raced with speed across the room, zig-zagging to avoid the guests, and dived into a narrow chink of space between anxious elbows, also intent on a photograph with the President.

By the time the group of honour had moved across and had arrived at the platform which held the bridal couple, Chaman Bajaj had retreated to his subsidiary position of friend. Bhim Lal Whig was in charge, restored to former splendour. But it was too late, Krishna had already entered through the thin crack in his personality.

Something in Chaman Bajaj was her very antithesis. Something in her scattered in fear and helpless loathing as she listened to his voice purring out in even tones beside her. 'This is the bride, Sir,' he was telling the President. 'I would like to mention that there has been no dowry at this wedding. A matter of principle. You know Bhim Lal Whig, Sir. He is a man of such status he could have got any bride he wanted for his son, a girl rich, fair and beautiful, from one of the best families in the country. Instead he chose to marry him to this educated lady you see before you. She is a teacher, Sir, one who contributes to the life of the country. And he has not taken an *anna* in dowry.' Newspapermen took down the information for the next day's columns.

8
Chaman Bajaj

Chaman Bajaj, of all the people she knew, most despised her skin for its blackness. Prejudice in favour of fair skins was everywhere. All those who advertised in newspaper matrimonial columns wanted, or offered, fair-skinned brides. The darker the bride, the larger the amount of dowry she had to bring. Krishna already felt the pressure of compensating for being a woman and dark. But the opposition of Chaman Bajaj was much more fundamental; it went to the very root of the skin, negated it and reduced it to non-existence.

He thought women were for breeding, and kept his own wife and daughter on his farm in Ropar, until he could find the girl a suitable match, to despatch her from his responsibility. Meanwhile, he moved everywhere himself, slowly seeping through the skin of India, entering its veins, clogging its rivers and stopping the journeys.

'I'm a woman. I'm not even rich or fair. And a working woman, a teacher in the law faculty. He considers law a male preserve; my intrusion worries him. He's trying to destroy me.' She had discussed it with Anu.

'You're imagining it,' he said. 'Anyway, why worry; he can't touch you. You're safe with me.' He had been curling up to go to sleep. Why had she lifted away from Anu and the security of his body?

'No, wait,' she said, agitated, shaking him awake. Large cartwheels of light had tumbled in from the eucalyptus trees outside her window. 'Chaman Bajaj is evil. I feel it strongly. And I've exposed myself to him; let him into my life. By marrying you.'

'We have an excellent marriage. You know how often we make love. And he's not such a bad man, after all. Look at this beautiful house. It was Chaman Bajaj who got it for us. He's a real friend of the family. I can't understand what you have against him. He hasn't done anything to you. Maybe you're embarrassed because he saw you in my room that day, before we were married.'

'No, it's not that,' she said. It was one of the many things she could not explain to Anu.

'This huge plot of land and house on Akbar Road, right in the heart of the city,' he repeated. 'It was Chaman Bajaj who got it for my father, just after Independence. It belonged to a rich Marwari family who left to set up a motor-cycle factory in Canada. The new government was about to acquire the house for a museum.'

The house was old and beautiful, its floors paved with multi-coloured marbles, high ceilings and doors, with arches of stained glass panes above them. The walls had been hung with ancient pictures of gods and goddesses which Bhim Lal Whig, being a fierce Arya Samaji, had stacked in an outhouse, from whence Krishna unearthed them.

'But your father has hardly ever lived in this house. Why did he buy it?'

'It's a very valuable piece of property. It must cost 50 *lakhs* now. He didn't dare rent it out, because you can't get a tenant to leave these days. And he wanted to keep the house for me, for when I began my law practice.

'He had planned to live in Delhi. His hotel is here. But Chaman Bajaj has been building him up politically, as a future Chief Minister of the State. That's why he's been living in Naoshera Doaba, near his timber mills. And he's been running the newspaper *Punjabi Tej* for so many years now, from Jullundur.'

'My uncle Satinder speaks of the newspaper. It has often attacked him and his policies.'

Bhim Lal Whig hadn't done much to change the original structure of the house. He had added a small room that leaned against the outer wall, to house his dogs, Great Danes, which his wife refused to keep in Naoshera Doaba. There were four of them, huge beasts with heavy paws which padded silently, spreading on the tarmac of the driveway. Their lean, well-fed, sleek bodies were hurtling tunnels of energy. Shera, who had followed Bhim Lal Whig as a boy from Bhimbar to Srinagar, and from there to Delhi, looked after them. He and the dogs belonged together, guarding the house. They kept it safe for Bhim Lal Whig.

Krishna heard Shera's voice so often, calling out the dogs' names – Brutus, Shamim, Sitara and Bharti – that it passed like a storyteller's thoughts through her mind, running through again and

83

again without notice. But the dogs' barks were another thing, harsh and fierce, breaking the air into fearful pieces. They could not learn to recognise and acknowledge her scent; they received her entrance and exit into the house each time as though she were a fresh enemy, throwing their bodies in anger and attack against the screen doors of their room. Almost from the day she arrived in the house she began to plant trees and low bushes, build a driveway to the gate, erect a metal frame over which she stretched creepers and hung pots. She nurtured thick greenery, in the hope that this would absorb the dogs' sounds sufficiently, just until she reached the front door and disappeared behind the thick walls which let in nothing.

Once she even suggested to her mother-in-law that the dogs should be taken to Naoshera Doaba, to be near Bhim Lal Whig since he loved them so much. The woman took deep offence at the suggestion. Her large, round body, almost as tall as her husband's, drew itself out to its full proportions. Her voice, as always hard and aggressive, turned even stronger. Krishna had made the suggestion in front of other relatives. An elaborate exercise of power was played out more clearly for their benefit. Of course the dogs would stay in Delhi. Meanwhile she surveyed the house, asking questions about her possessions, quilts and stock of rice and tins of *ghee*, in a tone so offensive that Krishna turned her face away from the heavy, sweaty sound of the words.

Or she would slice a mango and bite into it. 'The mango's sour!' Her lips tilted back from her teeth, her voice turned, terrible and accusing, towards Krishna, as if she had some hand in the manufacture of sour mangoes.

Krishna wanted to refuse the house and every scrap it contained, to shove it back into the woman's hands. She had such a common attachment to things, planning, organising and purchasing them, as if you could capture life in them and manufacture an existence through their fabric.

But Anu's mother tried to time her visits to the house when Chaman Bajaj, a frequent visitor, was not there. In their feelings for Chaman Bajaj, Krishna and her mother-in-law found a meeting ground. The older woman feared and resented him. She felt the same strange anxiety, as if he were cutting at the very roots of her existence. He had taken her husband from her, had swallowed and regurgitated him, helping to create his wealth and political power as a front, behind which he moved all the pieces into patterns born from his own brain.

It was bad when Mataji and Chaman Bajaj happened to be in the house together. Anu was a non-combative, judicious presence; he did not enter into their games at all. But Krishna had to play them. Once her own mother arrived while the two were there and had added her presence to these deadly marathons. A wife's mother has no place in her daughter's home, but there she stood, outside the gate, with her blue, hard-bound suitcase, not daring to enter a driveway full of the dogs' fury. Shera quietened them and led her to the door.

'I can't stand Dagra for another moment,' Sonia said. 'Your father will kill me. I decided to come to you for a while. There was no time to tell you.' She had left Dagra before. They both knew she would go back, but meanwhile Krishna gathered Sonia into her arms. The tall, beautiful woman was shrunk, a bird from a storm. How did this fragile, old woman's flesh contain the strong, fiery demon that had burned Krishna's childhood, whose love, never given, had seemed the most precious thing on earth? Her spirit now retreated from conflict. Her father had said that she slept with the neighbours and that that was why they quarrelled with him. Maybe he even believed it, his thoughts came from years of sexual rejection and loneliness. He had assaulted his wife with his grief, and had crushed her. The goddess was now a small, smelly old woman, sexless and injured, held in her daughter's arms.

Krishna hated the fear which immediately entered her, trickling from the house behind her back, revealing itself to Sonia. 'Mataji and Chaman Bajaj are here,' she said.

'Oh, I'm sorry.' Sonia was still confused from the deep silence of being held in her daughter's arms. 'I know that a girl's relatives do not visit her husband's house. Your grandmother explained this to me several times.'

But she was lost and bewildered, entirely in Krishna's hands, just as Krishna had longed for years to be held in her mother's arms, slung in the hammock of her love. But she had been forced to stand alone, staring at the world from Anu's house. Krishna led her mother through an echoing entrance hall, a dining room with a polished teak table which gleamed in the evening light, to a small bedroom at the back, next to Sohail's. Maybe she could tuck her away for a while, like a special treasure.

But she had to be produced at the dinner table. Not all Krishna's love could protect her from that. Sonia was like a small pebble from the beach in Paros, sunk entirely within herself, within the stone walls of her anguish. Where now was the love of Michael and Surjit, the protecting care of an adoring brother? Where was the beautiful damsel, the most lovely of a dreaming isle? A lost, shrunken woman, connected only to Krishna, she ate slowly and with utter awkwardness. Krishna was embarrassed by Sonia's complete withdrawal, her face swathed in the white flag of surrender, her knobbled arthritic hands admitting defeat before the battle had even begun. Meanwhile Chaman Bajaj and Mataji sat at the table, girded as strong, independent warriors. They ignored Sonia, the beauty of Paros, assaulted by Indian custom, battered by her husband's despair. They cast cold, questioning glances at her. Krishna sat there struggling to eat, her body heavy with tension and insult, rocked by love.

Next morning Chaman Bajaj could not find his shirt. Krishna heard him questioning the maid-servant. 'A brand-new Terry-cotton shirt, white, with blue embroidery on the pocket,' he said. The woman murmured a reply. He repeated the description, his voice much louder this time.

Her reply was louder too. 'I put it in your room,' she said, 'with the other clothes.'

'Come with me, I will find this shirt,' his voice was hard and determined, 'if I have to turn the whole house over to look for it.'

Krishna left for the university, her classes began that week. She slid like a fish from the scene, wiggling its fins, going through cool water, leaving behind her the chaos of the house to sort itself out. The maid told her later what had happened. Her voice was still shrill with the outrage she had suppressed all day. He had stamped up to her quarters, turned all her poor possessions out on the floor, looking for his stolen shirt. Krishna went from the maid's fierce response to her mother's tears.'What happened?'

'I was in the bathroom,' Sonia said, 'having a bath, washing my clothes. There was loud knocking on the door. Mr Chaman Bajaj. But he didn't wait until I came out. He went straight to my suitcase, and turned all its contents out on to the floor. Shanti says he was looking for something she had washed that morning.'

'For his new shirt,' Krishna muttered, absorbing the enormity of his search.

'In my suitcase? What would I do with his shirt? He thinks I'm a thief, creeping out to get his clothes and hide them in my suitcase? It's my own fault, for coming here. Troubling you like this, embarrassing you. But what can I do? Where should I go?'

Futile acceptance of outrage by a woman who had been fighting India all her life. Krishna was furious. But both Chaman Bajaj and Mataji had left by then, in the same casual way in which they had arrived, taking the house, its rooms, her kitchen, her labour, the insult to her mother, for granted.

It was Shanti who found the shirt, in the cupboard which Mataji usually used. A neat hole had been burned into the shoulder. Krishna took it to the cupboard in the guest room downstairs, and found that this time Chaman Bajaj had locked it and had taken the key with him. As if he had now finally taken possession of her space. Krishna stood there, pounding and jerking at the door, hoping to get it open, gripped by fear and anger. She saw the area of his possession in the house slowly growing, taking over the premises, Anu and her own soul.

When Chaman Bajaj came the next time he brought Bhim Lal Whig with him. Some political meetings had been scheduled in Delhi. Krishna saw the two men come in through the front door. She bent to touch her father-in-law's feet in greeting. An electric current raced across her brain, picking up points as it went along. No conscious decision; there was just that slipping across her brain, her complete attention focusing on the issue.

It was a moral issue. She didn't quite know how, but it concerned her whole identity. So far her life had been too open to Anu and his family, they had gone through it like a knife through butter. A queer sense of unreality was spreading through her, as if she were somehow beginning not to exist.

She watched the two men as they sat opposite her, talking to each other and to Anu. She busied herself with feeding Sohail.

Chaman Bajaj said, pushing back his chair, 'I'll be leaving tomorrow. You could meet Pathak Sahib in the morning and follow later.'

'Before you go,' she said, looking straight into his face, 'leave the key to the cupboard with me.'

'What cupboard?'

She realised, with a small thrill of fear, that he was talking directly to her for the first time. 'The cupboard in the guest room. You took the key with you last time you were here.' Her voice was still even, she held it to the track like a railway engine, clinging to iron. It threatened to go off on either side at any moment. She and Chaman Bajaj were at the beaded eye of a storm, faces opened round them in ripples of horror. 'Sohail, why don't you eat, darling?' she asked casually.

'You have a duplicate key, surely?' Chaman Bajaj had been forced into a discussion. There was a trace of foolishness in his voice.

'Maybe. I haven't looked. But why do you want to take the key to this cupboard?'

He turned and walked down the stairs. Bhim Lal Whig followed soon after, a pillar of anger. That hurt her, because he had been gentle with her. Soon Anu trailed after them. Loud voices came from the bottom of the stairs. 'I will never come to this house again! I have never been so insulted in my life. And by a woman!'

A murmur of appeasing voices. Then she heard her father-in-law go out of the front door to the dogs. The yelling, excited bunch was gathered, and he took them out to the road for a walk. Their sound faded slowly. Anu came to her. His voice was unusually hard, heavy and strong. 'Go down to him and apologise,' he said.

'Why should I?' But his voice frightened her.

'If you had the duplicate, you didn't even need the key.'

'You knew why I did it. That's not the point.'

'You've made a big thing about nothing at all. The worst is, you've hurt my father. He loves Chaman Bajaj more than a brother. You should have left it to me. I would have done what I could, but quietly, not with this sudden violence. Now you have broken something.'

'Yes,' she said. 'What can I say to him now? You come with me.'

'No, you have to do this alone. Go down and say you are sorry.'

It was the physical violence in his voice which sent her down the stairs, and because there was still something left for her to do; she had to tell Chaman Bajaj why she had asked for the key.

'This house doesn't seem to be mine, I am like a ghost here,' she said.

'Oh, it's yours all right. It belongs to Anu.' Chaman Bajaj said, indifferent now, wanting her to leave.

'Not these walls.' Her hand hit hard against the whitewash. 'It's the question of a home. I hardly seem to exist here.'

'I don't know about all that. Why have you come here? Here's your key.' He flung the small piece of brass at her body. She bent deliberately and picked it up. She hated the tears which were pressing out of her eyes. 'You could have asked for it privately, I would have given it to you. There's nothing in the cupboard anyway. But you insulted me in front of everybody.'

'I'm sorry. I didn't mean to insult you, or to hurt my father-in-law. Just to tell you that I live here, too; that I exist.'

'I know what you want to tell me; that you are great; that you matter a great deal. What do you want people to do? Talk about what a wonderful person you are? Is that why you asked for the key?'

'Not that.'

'I know lots of women like you. Don't think you're unique. There's hundreds like you who don't recognise their long-term interests, who don't know how to look after their husbands or their husbands' families, which is the duty of a woman. It is the only thing which makes a woman's life worthwhile. But you don't know anything about that. You're selfish, pushing your own self forward. "See me! See me!" you cry out.'

She felt like a common street-walker.

'I would never have talked to you like this in public. It's because we are alone,' he said. 'Not like you, who have no idea when and how to talk.' The room was suddenly dark and sinister. She felt she had arrived very close to the furry surface of evil. Then he released her. 'Go now,' he said. 'I don't want to listen to your apologies; I do not accept them.'

His personality was firm and resolute once more, closed up, the crack she had established was hidden so carefully that she no longer knew if it existed. She turned and left the room, crying openly now. Her own being was suddenly full of webs, cracks radiating outwards.

Her skin was a dark tent around her, but it could not keep out Chaman Bajaj's voice which said, again and again, that she was not unique. What had she staked on this uniqueness, this individuality? Her skin had messed around so long with her outline, dimming it, rubbing out its sharpness, taking the impact of situations and people. She was shadowed with their passions, gathering their darkness of living into her own soul. And her skin showed evidence of this participation, this blurring of unique identity. It darkened, dashed the hope in Sonia's eyes, deepening the rosy hues of her Greek inheritance, moving away from the parenthood which her mother's Greek lover might have given her, travelling into the shades of Paramjit Singh Chahal's Indian skin, his fathering, and then moving beyond that, going deeper and deeper, travelling into the heart of India. Could she reach, finally, the heart of India, burrowing like a mole, making tunnels, changing direction if necessary?

Meanwhile she climbed the stairs, her feet leaden with injury. 'It's your fault,' she said to Anu. 'You sent me down to apologise. And you didn't have the guts to come with me. You don't mind that he talks to your wife as though she was a common prostitute.'

'I'm sure you exaggerate. What exactly did he say to you?'

'It wasn't his words only. I could tell you his words and still you would not know. It was his way of looking, the tone of his voice. Then you'd know about his assault.'

'Yes, but tell me.'

She could locate only Chaman Bajaj's words, which did not convey the burden of his attack. She could see Anu standing near the window, looking out at eucalyptus trees which she had gazed at hundreds of times when they had made love. He was weighing her words, weighing Chaman Bajaj's words, feeling them out judicially, putting them together. He was troubled, but the weight of the sentences did not bow him down.

'He didn't accept your apology. Both of you are wrong. He had no business to talk to you like this, but you should not have brought up the key. Oh, I know you felt strongly. So, I could have done something about that. I told my father I'm not taking sides in this. He asked me how could I bear to stand there and see Chaman Bajaj insulted.'

But he had already taken sides, as far as she was concerned, by moving from love to judgment. She was split wide open, watching him. Everything in her was floating now on the surface, open to view, unencumbered by her skin. There was no translation into the daily detail with which she had filled her life, attempting not to see the truth of her being. The sounds of dogs returning came through the open window and Bhim Lal Whig calling softly to them, his voice tender as it never was otherwise. She looked again at Anu, and knew that she did not love him.

'I'm going,' she said. 'I'm leaving this house.'

'But where will you go?'

'I don't know.'

She telephoned Madhuri, secretary of her College Board. 'May I spend the night with you?' she said.

Anu came in as she was putting the phone down. 'You don't have to call a taxi,' he said. 'You can take the car.'

'I am taking the car,' she said. She hated the fact that he nodded

his head, registering the information. 'You're letting me go?'
'You don't have to go.' But he didn't ask her to stay.

She was confused, her hands seemed to be wearing thick gloves, fumbling and clumsy as they tried to pack clothes and toilet articles into a plastic bag. And Sohail stood near by, getting in the way with questions and tears. She kissed him again and again. His face was full of fear.

She did not know what she was packing for. It was with slow wonder that she picked up her stick of mascara and added that to her plastic bag; she did not recognise it or its use. Layers of air were soft and dark about her head as she went into the night. She got out of the car to close the gate behind her.

Already she was on the flyover above Oberoi Hotel. On her left the huge claws of Jawaharlal Nehru Stadium pushed their warning lights in square abundance into the night sky. A high silver pole crowned with light broke the black air above her head. If she could go on driving like this forever, she would, but now she must go back.

With a start she realised that she was already past the decision, with no cognisance of how she had arrived at it. Sohail was in the house with Anu; as yet her life was there. She would leave, but in a different way. Why should Chaman Bajaj choose the time for her? She must go back now. To go back tomorrow would be much more difficult. She would have to wait for Anu to fetch her. Now she was not willing to pass the initiative to him any longer. It was enough. She had decided to go back.

When she drew up at the house the gate was open, as if waiting for her, and the dogs were silent. A man stood at the front door, just putting his hand up to ring the doorbell. He held her address in his hand, written down by her father. Ranjit Dhawan had arrived.

Ranjit had waited so many years to get here, to reach this point where he stood at the front door of her house and watched her long fingers and serious face breaking open like a flower towards him, coming to him through the darkness. He knew, looking at her, that everything in his life had wound itself like a spring to reach this point, every step away from Surjit Markand's camp in Jullundur after Partition, through his years in Kenya, where his family had migrated in 1950, and back, almost twenty years later, to Delhi, to join as senior surgeon on the staff of Daulat Ram Hospital. In 1970 the Red Cross had asked for medical volunteers to work in hospitals on the eastern border. He had been selected for a

Scandinavian-sponsored hospital in Kalidiggi, ten miles from Maldah, in West Bengal.

'Yes?' The Brigadier's daughter took the slip with her address on it. 'This is my father's writing. Has he sent you? I'm glad to see you. We haven't heard from him since he went to the border more than a month ago.'

He looked hastily at his watch. 'I'm sorry, it's very late, but I couldn't get here earlier. I came straight from the railway station, because your father said to contact you immediately.'

'That's all right,' she said, 'come in.'

*   *   *

9

Dear Images

The silence inside her head was broken by honking from a blue Fiat. A woman was driving it with considerable verve and energy. It turned, a shade too fast, from Lime Road on to Park West, clearly headed for the main road.

Now she became aware of the traffic on the main road, how the buses and trucks roared and came to a slow crawl when they reached the tractors working overtime to tarmac the road for the Asian Games, and then picked up speed again, hurrying to their destination. Office time, 9.45 am – half of Delhi was getting to work. She gathered up the splinters of her silence and turned her own car on the corner from M. Road.

'You are cold and unfeeling,' he had said, tears of hurt running down his face. He had come down the short, curling staircase which ran from their bedroom to the hall at the front door. Somehow she had struggled to get dressed. She stood waiting, her handbag over one shoulder, and in the other hand a plastic bag with some files she had to take back to the office, and clothes for two days. That was as much as she could plan for. It had taken great effort and much thought to lay one object after another into the bag propped up in front of her mirror, knowing he was lying on the bed behind her, full of pain, rejecting her, sending her hurling into unfriendly, strange regions she had never entered before. Being married meant that he had always been there. Now, suddenly, he had drawn apart. He was looking at her as a stranger, or at best an acquaintance. He was examining and assessing her, not looking out from the same skin which they had shared for so many years. It had made her curiously lonely, bereft of all human contact.

'I've watched you all these years,' he had said, 'and I know you well. You don't care about anybody. You just want to go out there into the world and get your own happiness. And, let me tell you, you're not unique. Though you think you are. I've seen many like you. I know your type.' His face was twisted with anger and bitterness and his voice was low, although the children had already left for school. 'Don't you come back here. I don't want to see you. All this is now over. It's finished. Why do you telephone? You don't need a taxi. You can take one of the cars.'

'Of course I will,' she had said. 'I'm not calling for a taxi, I'm calling Tara. I have to go somewhere tonight, after the office. I can't stay on there beyond seven o'clock.'

'Oh, yes,' he had acknowledged, then had turned and gone back up the stairs to finish dressing.

She was close behind the Fiat now. A shiver of familiarity ran over her, and all her fluid, numb senses concentrated on the woman who was driving the car. It was as if she knew her, and yet she had never met her before; she was close enough to see that.

Then, a sudden knowledge, the woman could be herself. Her hair was black and thick, and rolled in a heavy mass behind her head. Her arms were tight and neat, held in firmly by a half-sleeved blouse; her back was quick and square, moving sharply with the steering motions of her arms. The car shot out like a knife, adventurously, into the traffic on the main road, just in front of a three-wheeled scooter and a black Ambassador car.

She didn't trust her own reflexes too much this morning. On another day it was exactly what she would have done, but today she felt a slowness in herself, a need to calculate and direct each act. Already there were a number of vehicles between her and the blue Fiat when they reached the traffic lights near by.

Three lepers begged at that particular crossing each morning, spacing themselves out between each wave of cars that stopped. It was a different three each day, you could tell from their clothes, not so much from their faces – the same caved-in wrecks. The lepers were beginning their rounds, peering in, waving their stumps through the car windows. A little boy selling the *Morning News* came up, running cheerfully between the cars. This morning she couldn't turn her gaze from the road. The other woman had given a leper some money. Now she put away her handbag, settling down to wait for the green light, then reached down to the seat beside her for an apple.

The woman watching her knew instantly the sequence of events which had preceded that act. The driver of the blue Fiat was eating her breakfast. She had ordered food for the day, had noted the shopping to be done on the way back from work, had cleaned up the children's room, had switched off a light in the verandah which some careless inmate had left on all night and all morning, and, since by then there had been no time left to eat, had picked up an apple from the fridge in her hurried scramble down the stairs to somehow get to work on time.

The watcher's heart opened with relief. For a few moments she shared an ordinary life with the other woman. She thought about the daily collection of details which had made up her own life for so many years.

The traffic lights changed. A large ball of green came on, hanging over their heads, and a ragged stream of traffic turned right, carefully avoiding a collection of potholes. It was important to keep the woman in the blue Fiat in sight, who drove very fast, confidently, even a little recklessly, the car springing out of the regular line of assorted vehicles to move ahead, then cutting back in when the going got complicated.

It was exactly how she herself would have driven in earlier days; she recognised the style. Anu had complained about it often enough, but she had kept on with it because it had given her pleasure, a sense of risk and adventure sweeping over her life for a few moments, for at least the length of a journey.

But today she had no heart for it. She resented the speed at which the woman was moving. She wanted time to think about what had happened that morning, but just keeping the blue Fiat in sight took all her energy and concentration. They were crossing the bridge now. Then they were at the traffic circle in front of Rajdoot Hotel.

He was on the pavement as usual, standing under a *neem* tree with his black briefcase in his hand, waiting for her. He was making desultory movements within a small radius, scuffing his feet, feeling his beautiful thick black hair, embarrassed because he had been standing in the same place for so long. She was late this morning.

For one sharp moment she was surprised that the woman in the blue Fiat did not stop beside him, reach across to open the door and have him climb in beside her. She just went straight past, negotiating the traffic. Her head did not turn to search for him under the tree and her body did not strain with awareness of the waiting figure.

But then she herself did not stop either.

He had seen her coming. He had grasped his briefcase more firmly, his body collecting itself casually into lines of purpose, and walked to the edge of the pavement, his hand already reaching out for the car door. She saw his body spread out flatly beside the road, spreadeagled against the column of space behind him. Their eyes met as she passed. His face was amazed, then angry, and then understanding and awkward as he shuffled back under the tree, losing himself behind a *chabri-wallah*, anxiously searching the road behind her for her husband's car.

He would telephone her later to find out what was wrong. Or she would call him to say what had happened. There was nothing he could do to help her, however. She didn't even know what she wanted from him or from anyone else.

Except that she wanted to see the other woman's face, to look into her eyes. Maybe she would find an answer there. For that she would have to keep her in sight, try to pull up beside her at a traffic light, or even follow her to wherever she was going; it didn't matter any more where. It seemed merely coincidental and of no consequence, only confirming the magical nature of the circumstances this morning, that she was taking the same route Krishna followed each morning.

He would think later that her not stopping to pick him up was already a decision to abandon the affair. It hurt her to leave him under the *neem* tree, cut off from herself. But she had taken no decisions so far. She knew only that she must follow the blue Fiat. The knowledge released her from everything else for the time being; it absorbed her completely.

She felt like a Great Dane loping along the road behind the blue Fiat, the dog's great paws falling smooth and silent on the tarmac, its harlequin body compressed entirely into knobs of bone and

95

stretched skin, all its senses directed to the woman fleeing quickly along the road.

She had given herself up entirely to the other woman. Absorbed in the chase, she was released from the past and future. Her life was concentrated in these few moments as she negotiated traffic with determination.

Today the madman startled her. He stood on a narrow divider along the centre of the road, directly in front at the bus stop. Traffic flowed in noisy streams on either side, high tops of double-decker buses above him, rattle of *tongas* and three-wheeled scooters, bicycles, the twisting hum of the blue Fiat and then her own car.

He was oblivious to sight and sound. His face was radiant and a smile stretched the white stubble on his cheeks. One hand smoothed a grey, untidy mane of hair that fell to his shoulders, the other was cocked at his waist. His rags were bright and tied in swatches, his strong legs full and naked below them. He was an ancient warrior, a Rustom. His chest was wide with glory and his foot was on the chest of an enemy.

Empty as she felt herself to be and somewhat light-headed, she was all spirit as she passed him. He filled her with a strange joy, this figure of abandon, exposed and self-contained in his ecstasy.

They were on the new fly-over now, speeding, only the blue Fiat and her own car. Other traffic had fallen away. The road arched into the sky, dashing almost into the balconies of a white hotel. Shimmering street lights bent over their heads, one graceful arc on either side. The sun was no longer muted. It reflected in fierce splendour from a metal canopy which rose in a single spire at one edge. At the other, four huge arms climbed from the Stadium, clawing into the sky, armoured with plate-glass. Thousands of high-powered bulbs clustered behind the glass, switched off now but ready to come alive in a blaze of light.

A rush of traffic came between them at the foot of the fly-over. Perhaps at the next crossing she would be able to draw up beside her. She felt a slight thrill at the prospect of seeing her face; she would encounter the unknown.

The light was green. They went straight on to the empty pedestal that had once held King George's statue, round the Victory Arch of stone with a pale flame burning to the martyred dead, and then up Raj Path. The blue Fiat beat a light just as it was turning red. The waiting cars had been reined in, jogging back and forth, poised to move. They had already begun to cross but she herself could not

96

go through. She stopped and watched anxiously until she saw the blue Fiat also stop at the next crossing.

The blue Fiat turned right, headed towards the House of Parliament, graceful between trees. The car could take one of three roads. Soon it would disappear behind sandstone fountains. She would not know where it had turned and she would lose the other woman. The policeman put up his hand, palm flat out, but she did not dare to stop. The scooter driver in front of her was not expecting traffic; he turned hard and swift into the side of her car. It went on, impelled by the momentum of her foot on the accelerator. Events had not yet caught up with her hope.

Then the thud of impact, the hard sound of grinding metal. The car stopped. She got out. Metal pieces of the scooter were scattered over a wide tarmac space.

Everyone was in a hurry; it was office time; traffic went around the accident, the arena marked off by two phlegmatic policemen. She looked around. The woman in the blue Fiat had disappeared; the shadow she was chasing had gone.

An event had occurred, there was no doubting that it was before her; an accident, two men climbing out of the debris, staggering to the traffic island, sitting down, looking for their wounds under gouges in shorts and trousers – that was real. It pushed through something in her mind, like a circus lion hidden behind a paper hoop, bursting through suddenly, bright yellow and red.

The gates were open; now the huge dog padding along the road behind her was finally coming through, going past her, and then on. Her life, arrested for twenty minutes, was moving again. Into pain and desperate hurt. She had reached it now, what had happened this morning, what would happen. She sat down beside the two injured men on the rough, wooden barrel of the traffic island, and burst into tears.

She cried and cried, until finally the policeman moved over and touched her on the shoulder. 'It's not so bad,' he said, 'at least no one's dead.' No one dead, only the woman she had been until this moment, struggling to retrieve the past, the image in the blue Fiat, which she had lost.

These things happen again and again, images playing themselves over.

*   *   *

10
The Brigadier Gets to Work

Brigadier Paramjit Singh Chahal (Retd). A long enough name and designation, but still difficult to fit into, to be forever contained within an unchanging vessel of 'Retd' Inside he was still Paramjit, a growing, living creature, but now there was no further place to go. 'Brigadier Paramjit Singh Chahal (Retd)' was the last point of arrival.

But his name would not have included 'Retd', not on the sign board of his own front gate, if Surjit Markand had not joked about it.

The meddling man had managed to build just a tiny house, after all the important jobs he had had. They ranged from Superintendent of a refugee camp in Jullundur, where Paramjit had first met him, to Intelligence Officer doing special hush-hush work in Delhi. They said he was fairly senior when he finally left there, but Surjit did not talk about it. No doubt he was an intelligent man. Why quarrel unnecessarily with him, or with anyone else? But some things you could not help, when they made your blood boil. Like Surjit teasing and mocking until the Brigadier put (Retd) behind his name, which was like the kiss of death.

Surely he was jealous of the Brigadier's beautiful house, each time he and his wife, Sonia's friend Anjali, came to visit? He commented often enough on the *litchi* and mango trees swaying in the large piece of land around the house, and roses blooming in the garden. Everyone in the area was jealous of the Brigadier's house. Only Sonia did not appreciate her luck; she was too busy conspiring with his enemies. Technically, Surjit was right; retired army officers were required to put 'Retd' behind their names. This made the Brigadier all the more angry. It had been more than a year since he had retired, and he was not sure yet what that meant. He felt no change inside.

Then there were other changes. For example, here he was

getting off the train at Howrah Station in Calcutta and no one was there to receive him, to get his suitcase out of the first-class compartment. He had been in Calcutta before, a dirty, badly managed city, a hell-hole to drive in, an assault on the senses when you passed through it. Fortunately he had never had to live there, just had to pass through it every now and then. They should hand it over to the Army to manage for a while, he thought, they would clean it up immediately, put things in order. The Brigadier was convinced the most competent administrators in the world were in the Army; they really knew how to organise people. What did civilians know about discipline?

Getting a taxi was a nightmare, though there were long lines of them, yellow-topped and dirty, outside the station. He followed the *coolie* closely; they sometimes ran off with your luggage. They stepped over flower-sellers, emaciated children, beggars, vendors of coconuts and sweetmeats swarming with flies. He paled at the thought of the quantity of infection being passed on to unwary customers. He had to stop, taking a risk with his luggage, to speak to a woman buying the sweet stuff for her child. 'Please don't feed your child this poison,' he said.

She did not understand his words and was confused and frightened. Men standing around, including the disturbed vendor, assembled to attack the Brigadier, shouting.

Paramjit was ready to argue with them; he had not teased her, he was a doctor, going to help poor people, free, to give his services to a Red Cross Hospital on the border. He was a good man, even if his wife made him out to be otherwise. He wanted only to save the woman's child from certain cholera or typhoid which he would get from eating the poisonous, infected stuff. The vendor became more incensed and threatening. The *coolie* pulled him away towards the taxi; he had already loaded the luggage. He demanded an extra tip for saving the Brigadier's life. 'They would certainly have killed you. I got you away just in time. At least three rupees more, Sahib.'

'I'm not afraid of them. I'm an army officer. You think I'm afraid of some half-clad creatures in a railway station?'

But he gave the *coolie* the extra tip, anyway. One should always be generous with the poor, not argue with them as Sonia did.

The taxi was crossing Howrah Bridge. Calcutta people were very proud of this bridge – he could not imagine why. He looked from the window, down at the River Hooghly, not so far below. Hulks of abandoned river boats gathered and advanced towards him from its surface, like prehistoric creatures. A colony of black buffaloes wallowed at the edge of the slushy river.

The corpse of Dhiraj Kumari rose right up, straight from the steamy surface of the river, floating at him. He had left it in Dagra, running from it as fast as he could to this distant place. But there it was, floating through the air, dressed in a neat, starched *khadi* sari, gathered at one shoulder under the official epaulettes, and a long-sleeved white blouse. Not laid out neat and still like the dead body her brother had called him in to see two months previously in his house at the edge of Dagra. She had committed suicide, poisoned herself.

'She came here from Morenapur. She was posted in the Military Hospital there, did you know that?' Paramjit had nodded dumbly, looking at the body in a flowered *salwar-kameez*, laid out formally on the bed. He had not seen her for ten years. Difficult even to recognise her smoothened face, the full lips and bunched-up nose, cast in the artificial mould of death.

'She came to Dagra to kill herself under my roof. As if the fact of her death would not be painful enough for me otherwise. I can't understand why she did it, like this.' But even as her brother had expressed his grief, his shrewd, unpleasant eyes had watched the Brigadier over the top of his white handkerchief, assuring him that they both knew why she had come to Dagra to kill herself.

She had killed herself because the Brigadier had not kept his promise. Was it as simple as that? He had said he would marry her when he retired. The ignominy of divorce and remarriage to a junior lady doctor was impossible before that. 'Not the career, I don't have many friends in service. You know that Sonia made sure of that and that she conspired against me. I didn't rise very far, just to the rank of Brigadier. They played a trick on me, said I had a mysterious heart disease. You know I never had a heart attack. Good excuse for those sharks. On medical grounds they did not promote me, but really it was because I had embarrassed them with my honesty, and had refused to agree to their corruption.'

He had stood there, muttering to her for the last time, his eyes stiff with tears, not yet able to feel that she was dead or that he had retired.

'You know how miserable I am with Sonia. It's a kind of lethargy, an inertia. Like being tired and heavy at the edge of the jungle, though you know the excitement of the animals is waiting for you just beyond. Maybe I've got old, or just don't have the guts. Hate to think that, a man from my family. How my brother would mock at that! But you don't have guts either, to sit it out, to wait for me. You gave up, after all your brave talk of waiting forever. Waiting for what?'

That had been reasonable in the complete silence of death-side protocol, in the presence of a body which did not quite establish itself as related to a woman he had known in Sikkim. Not the body he had undressed again and again from its starched, uniform saris, unpeeling it, plucking it out like a pale brown kernel, unexpectedly soft, held in a firm case of fruit.

In Sikkim he and Dhiraj Kumari had gone up into the northern hills together to see the sun rise over the Kanchenjunga. You couldn't see the peak from Gangtok where they were posted. Parties went up in *jongas*, over narrow, dangerous roads to the *dak* bungalow at Binsing. If they were adventurous, they went higher; to Rangcha and Tim-Tim. This time there had been fifteen other men in the group and a couple of nursing officers. They crowded the photographs he took, their thick figures in uniform bunching around the tall body of Dhiraj Kumari topped with crinkly hair, faintly slanting eyes and full lips. Not beautiful – nobody could say if Dhiraj Kumari had ever been beautiful, especially as her skin had been disturbed by a bad case of acne carried far beyond adolescence.

Later, Sonia's broad white finger had stabbed at three photographs, picking out Dhiraj Kumari in furious accusation. Rumours had trickled to her as she stayed in Delhi year after year, guarding the education of Krishna and Gola, while he went from one non-family station to another. 'That's the woman,' she had said, 'and you dare to have her in your photo album, in your own home. Have you no shame! And she, bitch, trailing after you from place to place. Indian men, what creatures, my God!' And she had spat with a crude, heavy rasp that he had never expected to hear from a woman's throat.

Even so he had not thrown away the photos – just inked out Dhiraj Kumari's body, taking care to follow its outlines well so that he would always remember. He believed firmly in photographs; they captured life and held it unchanging while the paper and colour lasted. What other methods did one have for doing that?

The *dak* bungalow at Binsing belonged to the Border Patrol people. They were not especially friendly or courteous to the Army

Medical Corps officers who were visiting. Only the Colonel, in whose honour the trip had been organised, merited their heavy-breathing hospitality, their particular care and attention. On another occasion this would have angered Paramjit and raised fundamental doubts about his own worth. This time he had been glad to be left alone in the long tunnel of his desire for Dhiraj Kumari, a tunnel which wound with immense excitement to the closing ceremonies of dinner and departure to their respective rooms. It had been a prefabricated structure, walls of flimsy bamboo pasted on to thin planks. He had almost been able to hear her next door, sitting on her bed and waiting for him. When he went in, she had not been there at all. His throat had been gripped with a terrible despair until she had come from the bathroom, still in her uniform sari.

It had rained all through the night; there had been no question of seeing the Kanchenjunga the next morning, but he had never been less interested in natural beauty. The sound of the rain outside the window, wrapping him and Dhiraj Kumari together in a thick grey curtain, had been the most beautiful thing in the world.

She had followed him from Gangtok, getting herself posted wherever he went, a tender, faithful shadow, waiting for him to marry her. She had even come as far as Tezpur, where he had been posted during the 1962 Chinese Aggression. But it had been a mistake for her to have come to their home in Delhi and to have met Sonia and the children. She wanted very much to do that, to see the surroundings in which he spent so many hours of his life, and he could not deny her that. After all, she was truly in love with him, and her pale lozenge of a body still inspired him to violent excitement each time he was able to touch it.

Sonia had smelled the connection right off. Her nose was sharp as a panther's. 'So that's the woman you're riding, isn't it? I had heard but now I can see with my own eyes. You put your hands on her stomach, on those falling breasts, and God knows where else!'

'Don't be so crude,' he had said. 'You wretched, uneducated woman! You never learned to talk in decent society. Your daughter is here, at least have mercy on the child!'

Krishna had been listening. He had seen her throat and cheeks green with shock under her deep colour.

He had put his arm around her shoulders and had taken her out of the room, to a distant corner of the *barrack* in which they lived so that she would not hear her mother's voice. It still came to them through the walls, roaring and violent, but she could not make out the words. 'Don't listen to what she says; it's not true. I am a family man. You are my three gems, the most precious things in the world to me,' he said to Krishna.

'It's not true, what she says?'

'Of course not. How dare you ask such a question! Dhiraj Kumari is like a daughter to me. I've met her brother, who lives in Dagra. He says that suitors have worn away their shoes making trips to their house, asking for her hand in marriage.'

He had later overheard Sonia talking to Krishna. 'You don't know,' she had said. 'You're still a child. No woman comes to another woman's house and talks the way Dhiraj Kumari did, in a sort of belonging way, unless she is sleeping with the man, unless she has those intimate connections with his flesh.'

The Brigadier had stood looking at the body.

He had been aware of Dhiraj Kumari's brother standing behind him, thick and coarse, his moustache a rough, black animal crawling across his face. Then he had turned and walked out of the door. At that time he had known his duty very well, no matter how much pain it had caused him.

But now it was different. Now there was no walking away from her, she was coming up from the river in a decided arch, her eyes looking at him, not caring at all about his duty, completely oblivious to the protocols of space and time which he had put upon her through their long association. It had taken only death, and this short period of two months, for her to forget his long years of teaching. You could not teach women anything; they had no sense of history, no perspective! Just look at this ridiculous behaviour. Here she was, in Calcutta, pursuing him on Howrah Bridge, with a determination, tenacity and lack of consideration she had never shown before. He had thought to leave her firmly behind in Dagra, to start a new adventure, whereas she was slicing through the grey air, over the heads of ignorant Bengalis and the rusty railing of the bridge, through the window, into his arms.

He was deeply embarrassed; he would even admit to some fear. He tried to look, to focus on the loosely tied turban of the *Sardar* driving the taxi, to hear the downpour which he knew had begun, its harsh, heated thunder in his ears, but he could see nothing. His vision was entirely blocked off by the green uniformed body of his one-time beloved. It was all about his face, waiting to be embraced. His arms would not move; they were petrified with fear,

103

frozen absolutely. How would he survive this? Then he was not considering survival at all, his heart was suffocating in his chest, his hands grappling with clothes at his throat, his face was pressed up, unbreathing and agitated, against the soft contours of nothingness.

The *Sardar* was sloshing dirty water on his face; he could smell in it the scent of rancid fruit. The taxi was drawn up near a filthy verandah which ran along a line of ancient, blackened buildings. The place was crowded with half-drenched people sheltering casually from the rain, among baskets of fruits and vegetables. Someone was frying bread *pakoras* on a kerosene stove nearby, and the smell of hot oil and spices came strongly through the rain. Then he was hit by the smell of his own vomit. It was on his clothes. He raised himself from the back seat of the taxi; the driver was washing out the floor mats.

'Must be the heat, Sahib, and the journey. We people from the north find it very difficult to adjust to this city. Take myself, for example, I've been here twenty years and I still long for the villages of Punjab.'

'What happened?'

'You gave a loud cry, called on the name of the gurus, then you were sick and passed out. I must tell you, I was frightened. How did I know what it was? I was going to take you straight to the hospital, but the police would ask a lot of questions, so I came here instead.'

'Take me to the Great Eastern Hotel. Do you have some cloth? I'll clean up on the way.'

They had not heard of Brigadier P. S. Chahal at the Great Eastern Hotel. The Red Cross had not reserved a room. He wandered out onto the verandah to consider the situation. He seemed to be floating, carried by water, an unusual sensation, as if he were free, very anxious and fearful at the same time, he and Dhiraj Kumari, because now she belonged with him.

Shoeshine boys clamoured around him, fighting with each other to polish his shoes, taxi-drivers and *rickshaw-wallas* offered to take him wherever he wanted to go. Some broke away from time to time to follow tourists streaming out the front door of the enormous hotel. Its white, clean façade with green-slatted, wooden windows open to reveal thin net curtains tied in European style at the waist, rose in splendour above the shops. He returned to the importuning vendors who crowded around him. If he accepted, for that short period he would coalesce, become a person instead of a mass of retired, decaying flesh. But he nodded dumbly and fled back into the shelter of the hotel.

'Can you give me a room anyway? I'll pay for it myself.' Suddenly it was very important to crawl away somewhere and hide, to remove evidence of Dhiraj Kumari's entrance.

The sun rose very early the next morning, flashing into his eyes as he lay half asleep on a narrow bed. The room was tiny, a fancy green window took up almost its entire breadth. Already the sound of traffic and cries of street vendors rose from the road below.

The Governor's Residence was very close to the Great Eastern Hotel, on a large plot of land. He could just about see a large building through the trees, above a high wall which screened it off from the road. Three gates made up of high columns, with a huge seated plaster lion spanning the top. He could not make out which one to enter.

The Red Cross had been given some offices in the left wing of the Raj Bhavan. Mr Ajit did not bother to rise when the Brigadier entered. Must be a senior officer; you could not tell with these civilians. Not from the way he was dressed, in a crumpled bush shirt and greasy black trousers. Worse, his feet under the desk were bare and rubbed against each other, a worn pair of *chappals* standing close by. Slumped in his chair, one could not tell whether he was tall or short. The room was lit by fluorescent lights which glanced off the man's bald head and spectacles. But the eyes behind the glass were hard and shrewd, completely sure of themselves. 'Well, so you've arrived, Brigadier Chahal. We were expecting you yesterday.' His voice was faintly hostile.

'Today was the date in the letter, sir.' The Brigadier told himself there was no need to be apologetic; he remembered the date, but he could be wrong. 'They didn't know I was coming at all at the Great Eastern Hotel.'

'But we know. Don't worry about the hotel. We will take care of that. Just mention my name to the manager.'

'When do I leave for Kalidiggi, sir?'

'I want you to go right away with General Sitaraman who will survey the area by helicopter. You are to be Chief Medical Officer for the region right up to Darjeeling.'

The Brigadier need not have worried about talking to General Sitaraman, he was too busy. It was a large helicopter, the General was up in front with directors of the two refugee camps. They were flying over the camps and along the border, right up to Maldah District.

The Brigadier sat very still as the helicopter circled down towards the tarmac of Maldah airport.

11
Ranjit Dhawan Meets the Brigadier

'I'll start at the very beginning, then, Mrs Whig? Give you the whole story?'

'Please call me Krishna,' she said, drawing him inside. 'Come and sit down. From what my father writes here, you helped him a great deal. But the letter is confused and rambling, as usual.'

'I first met him at Maldah airport,' Ranjit said. 'I was waiting for a cargo plane due from Calcutta, which was very late. I had almost given up. It was the middle of May, and the air was stagnant and oppressive, the wind changing to the east. Then I heard the whirling of a large army helicopter, which landed near by. "How does one get to the Red Cross Hospital in Kalidiggi?" asked the man who had got off.

'"I'm from the Hospital and came to pick up supplies. I can take you there, if you like. I'm Dr Ranjit Dhawan." He put out his hand, and his face split in a smile of relief. I told him they were not expecting him until next week. I don't think he realised what that meant. He especially asked about game available in the area.'

'He's always been interested in *shikar*,' Krishna said. 'But he doesn't shoot any more.'

'Oh, he shoots all right,' Ranjit said, 'but not game. Anyway, to continue. At one time leopards were fairly common in the area, particularly near English Bazaar and Maldah, where undergrowth in the mango gardens and deep ditches of mulberry fields gave them sufficient shelter. They say there was a man-eating leopard near English Bazaar once which carried off seven boy cowherds before it was destroyed. The leopards are all gone now, together with the hogdeer. You do see some wild pigs now and again which damage the crops. I told him about the game birds, too.

'I have had to know all this. You see, those who are perpetual exiles are very observant. They cannot take a land for granted. So they create a safety net of details to hold them in case of sudden eviction.'

'Exiles?' Krishna asked.

Somehow, without knowing it, they had crossed a subtle line, beyond which such questions can be asked and answered. 'Yes, I was kicked out of Punjab with the Partition. Home was Sialkot which we left when it became Pakistan. Then I was pulled like a rotten tooth from the refugee camp in Jullundur. Flung to Bombay and across the sea to Kenya. I left Nairobi a couple of years ago, a guest who had overstayed his welcome. I then came to Delhi.'

Krishna resisted a strong desire to say: 'Come to me, I will be your home and your land.' Surely it was too early to say that, and in this case everything had to be said very carefully.

Ranjit continued his story, his long, thin body hunched up on the sofa, his shoulders bony and his hands full of shadows from old wounds. 'Having told him about Maldah, I thought I would tell him a little bit about the hospital. It has eight doctors, one of them a lady from the south, Miss Kuppuswamy. Of the others, three are Bengalis, three Biharis and one a German missionary who belonged to HART, a foreign missionary organisation with lots of funds. It is a complete field unit with 200 beds, 100 each for surgical and medical cases, and surgical equipment. It is housed partly in a school building which has a low wall around it, and partly in tents. These are field tents made of plastic, unsuitable for the tropical climate there, and have no ventilation. They should have been canvas tents.

'I continued my criticism to this man who was going to take charge, handing him the end of the thread which could unravel the whole web, expose us all, flies and spiders alike.

'"The hospital has been here for five months and it hasn't worked at all. It needs something to bring it together. Perhaps you can do that. Oh, there are patients all right, local people, not really the refugees. In fact, the hospital is full, but the patients just lie there. And an average of ten die every day."

'"They told me of the cholera," he said.

'I went on, told him about the corruption, about the equipment

107

and blankets and food that was carried off each day and sold in the market. Perhaps this added to the sense of evil which hung over the place, a vague, deadly miasma. You couldn't quite name it or pin it down. Then we passed through countryside full of holiness; here they make a man a saint in no time. Everywhere we saw evidence of the adoration of Pirs and signs of belief: small bamboo boats with sails, set afloat in the Kalindri in honour of Khwaja Khilji; five mounds of earth in honour of the Panch Pir, models of horses in honour of the Ghorapir, strips of cloth tied in honour of the Tena Pir, on trees, at halting places, tied by carters bringing rice from Dinajpur, or carrying mangoes to the ferry, the delicious juicy mangoes of Maldah, heavy and ripe, which even then were scenting the air.

'I told him about the most popular festival of the district, the *Gumbhira*, celebrated everywhere during the last three days of the Bengal year, the end of Chait, and carried over into *Baisakhi*. I saw it this year. It ended on *Baisakhi* Day, which your father told me is a very important festival among the Punjabis.

'The driver of my jeep sang a song from the festival. A welcome for the Brigadier. It went something like this: "O Siva, what song shall we sing to thee – there are no mangoes in the gardens – as we go from tree to tree nothing but new leaves are seen – our sole thought as we sit is what shall we do – oil, paddy and rice are very dear and also bran. Listen again, just at midday come hail and rain to harass the farmer and destroy the wheat."

'The Brigadier said that *Baisakhi melas* had figured a lot in the history of his family, right from 1849. He said, "In my family, everything important happens on *Baisakhi*. My daughter Krishna got married on that day."'

'Yes,' Krishna said, 'My marriage.'

She considered the song which Ranjit Dhawan had brought from Bengal. It crowded with other songs, one of them Swaranjit Kaur's, offered to her neice Kailash for her wedding.

Now her skin was usurped and Ranjit Dhawan took its place. He brought her father to her with slow, gentle strokes and somehow brought his flying pieces together. Shattered and destroyed, dismembered by a life time of marriage to Sonia, coated with a thick, slurry night-offering of a betrayed Dhiraj Kumari, the Brigadier was faced now with evil and corruption. A string of genius which wound from Chaman Bajaj to Father Sherifis, to a fat-breasted grey woman who was present at every betrayal, it was the string of

108

a lasso which tightened around the soul. The Brigadier stuck up stubbornly, like the back of a whale showing above the sea, a stupid white whale which drew attention and fire to itself. The Brigadier at the border, flailed by Dhiraj Kumari, was the true skinless one. In this skinlessness, never mind the doubtful sperm, Krishna felt his fatherhood. Ranjit Dhawan restored her to some of the pastures of her childhood, where her love for Paramjit Chahal was free, fresh and taken for granted. The Brigadier spoke to her again directly and introduced her to the terrors of being skinless. After all, that's what fathers are supposed to do, to bring their progeny to the business of living and show them how to survive, even if survival means death through exposure.

12
The Voice of Paramjit

I wanted to call all the staff together the very next morning. I told the young doctor who had brought me from Maldah to call them together and that I would speak to them right away. But somehow he was quiet. 'Maybe you should speak to Mr Sanyal first,' he said. 'Get the Deputy Commissioner back here with you and have him introduce you.'

I didn't think it necessary, but the young chap seemed to know a lot. 'All right,' I said. This Dhiraj Kumari, this uneasy feeling in my chest, it has me agreeing to all sorts of things. 'And you won't have to go far,' he said. 'Mr Sanyal is on tour: you won't have to go all the way back to Maldah. He spent the night in the *dak* bungalow at Kaliachak, just a few miles away. On the banks of the Bhagirithi. I'll take you in the morning.' This place gives me a peculiar feeling. How the people stare at me, as if I had descended on them like a working of the ways of God, mysterious and unwelcome. By now they must know who I am.

He drove me everywhere. He and the Swedish doctor waited in the jeep outside when I went to Mr Sanyal. The river was below, at the bottom of a steep slope. A light wind blew from the east. No sign of rain. I wished it would rain. But everything was so green, anyway. It must stay like that, lush, branches sending out vines and creepers all the time. They wrapped themselves around everything, curled over leaves and tree trunks. Mr Sanyal was much older than I expected. His hair was grey and sparse, standing stiffly on his head.

'Listen,' he said quietly. We were alone. 'You know there are troubles in this area. The situation across the border. Anything might happen. The Mukti Bahini keeps coming across the border to Mirzachak. It's near Gaur, the other side of the Mahananda, almost at the border.'

'The Mukti Bahini?' I asked.

'Guerrillas,' he said. 'Young Bengali guerrillas fighting the Pakistan Army in there. They have some doctors, but no medicines and no equipment. And they get very badly wounded. Besides there is the cholera. Maybe you can see what you can do?'

He was asking me. I knew what he meant. I've worked with the Red Cross before. You're not supposed to help any fighting men. The Red Cross is only for victims of fighting, the help I mean. But in this place everything was getting indistinct. Outlines were merging in the terrible lush green of mango and mulberry leaves. I didn't say anything to Mr Sanyal just then. You don't have to answer all the questions. That's what I was learning. Some things can just be left floating, looking for other things to complete them, you don't have to find an ending right away and impose it just for form's sake. In any case, form began to mean less and less, after the initial introduction which Mr Sanyal gave me, when he came back to the hospital with me. Standing out in the school courtyard, the hospital staff milled around in narrow spaces between red plastic tents.

I spoke to them after he had finished, mainly about treatment for cholera. An electrolyte balance, antibiotics, and a steady glucose drip seemed to me the most important things in the world at that time. Nothing else, I swear it. I had no bad intentions towards anybody. I also spoke of other things. About taking over stores, assigning duties and organisation. I trusted them with a blueprint I had worked out in the night. But it didn't seem to interest them. It angered me to see their bored, vacant faces. If Mr Sanyal had not been there, I would have shown them what discipline means. I spoke to them. I am like your father, we will live here like a family, helping each other, taking care of people. The German Missionary

110

objected. 'You are not my father,' he said. 'My father's in heaven.' I handed out money in salaries which hadn't been paid for months. Mr Sanyal had given me 6,000 rupees as he left. 'Shall I get it from you next time?' But he didn't answer, just shaking my hand as he got into his official jeep. I don't know when I will be able to pay them again.

There was hostility everywhere. The Matron, Miss Sushila, resented me, I had to correct her ways in the ward. She was lazy herself and the assistants could do what they wanted. An orderly would go to sleep, an intravenous drip would come out, and the patient would be dead in the morning. So many of them were children. So sad, those thin little corpses being carried out by the sweeper at dawn. I found it very difficult to eat breakfast afterwards.

I had to be strict about the deaths. Every single person entering the hospital was given a cholera vaccination and sometimes there were 800 of them in a day. They grumbled about it and went to Bimal Choudhry to complain. They also complained that I charged them twenty-five *paise* each. He came to see me one day, his round, fish-like mouth moving in anger, hoping probably to intimidate me with his huge fair body which towered above me in shining white clothes. His short very dark hair was like what my own used to be.

'You know who I am? My father was a magistrate in Maldah. We are one of the oldest families here.' I said, 'I am chief Medical Officer for the area. I've been here one month, and there are no deaths now, not a single patient dies. We need the small contribution of twenty-five paise for the hospital.' He seemed to imply that I was keeping the money, which made me furious. I was the one who introduced accounts into that mad chaos. Five thousand blankets were missing when I took over and stocks, injection needles and cottonwool were also missing – and injection needles and cottonwool were turning up in the Maldah bazaar every day. I locked everything up and stopped the huge remittances which the doctors and nurses and even the volunteers were sending home by money order.

It seemed out of proportion. Somewhere a link was missing, or maybe I didn't see it, though it was there. I once even thought of asking Ranjit if he knew, but I am not used to private talks. Dhiraj Kumari used to complain about that. She said that I never really talked to her. It's got much worse since then. No complaints from

111

her now. She's inside me; she can see all there is to see; she can be my voice.

The others were all my enemies, except Ranjit. They wrote to the Governor and to Mr Ajit to have me replaced, saying that I should be sent back. Of course I did not agree. But I was not foolish; I was making my arrangements. After the very first brush with B.L. Choudhry I spoke to Mr Sanyal. Choudhry is an important politician with a large following. I needed some protection. Mr Sanyal deputed a police *havildar* called Santosh, ostensibly to guard the hospital. He was huge, seven feet tall and very dark, bald except for a thin fringe of black hair around his head. He was accompanied by a faithful slave called Bhim Singh, whose thin black moustache stayed clamped on his upper lip.

But I didn't make anyone happy. Even patients whom I saved from death seemed to resent me. What was the heart of their hostility? Wave upon wave of evil like a poisonous gas spreading a blight upon the place, spoiling everything? Choudhry flourished in its shadow. I did not create him from my mind; he sprang like a mushroom in the lush, treacherous soil. Huge, *kurta*-clad monster. He was talking earnestly to the *havildar* at the party. A farewell party for Miss Sushila. She told me grandly about her future plans. A brother in Kerala who had come back from one of the Gulf countries with a lot of money, he was going to buy her shares in a Nursing Home in Trichur.

I wished her well. My relief at seeing her go made me feel kindly even towards her moustache, slightly subdued in the evening light. The next matron had arrived already.

Miss F.D.Pinto. Properly respectful and dignified, brisk and efficient, not flying away all the time like the thin body of Miss Sushila. In fact, Miss Pinto's broad, high-cheeked face and her small eyes looked uneasy without a white cap over them, out of place among the flimsy, torrid silks and rushing dresses of the lady volunteers at the party. B.L.Choudhry came early, rubbing the end of his *dhoti* between his thumb and forefinger, watching me all the time. He talked to the doctors, to Miss Sushila, even went from time to time to the wall around the school yard where many villagers had gathered to watch. Light from our makeshift hanging lanterns fell on their wondering faces.

I had invited Father Sherifis, too, and I was waiting throughout the whole party for him to arrive. He is Chief of the HART organisation in the area, and a VIP. An impressive personality, not like Choudhry, who wears a *dhoti-kurta*, with his legs half naked and dirty feet below. Each time a vehicle passed I came out to see if Father Sherifis had arrived; he has a fleet at his disposal but he favours a green Matador van. All the motor sounds passed on to the *kotwali* at the end of the road, to the ferry across the Mahananda some miles away, or in the opposite direction, to Maldah.

Ranjit took me to meet Father Sherifis the first time. He didn't come in with me that day, saying that Father Sherifis didn't like him. I can't understand why; both have a tremendous vitality. The priest is bursting with it. It pushes out against his skin and keeps him going at a tremendous, frenetic pace. Ranjit is like a tightly wound spring, ready to go.

I knew immediately that Father Sherifis belonged to the Mediterranean. His glowing brown skin, dark hair, shining black eyes and full lips proclaimed it immediately. Could even be Greek, from the mainland.

I tried a bit of Greek on him, but he pretended not to understand. He put aside my hesitant question about the country of his origin. 'We priests don't belong anywhere, Brigadier. Only with God.' I was always submissive and respectful in his presence, to the very end. There was something about him which demanded this. Perhaps it was the monocle which fitted into his left eye. Its utter elegance. There were also his beautiful white robes and then, combined with the force below them, his vibrant healthy skin, his square hands which were never still.

'So, you've seen Mr Sanyal,' he said.

I was surprised that he knew so fast. I had seen Mr Sanyal only an hour ago, and I had come to Father Sherifis straight from Kaliachak. I said, 'You have no problems staying in this area? They say foreigners are not allowed here.'

'Allowed?' He laughed as if the sound of earth was in his throat. 'I go and come as I please. Who will stop me? We are people of God. What does the colour of our passports matter? Your hospital? It helps the poor people, a lot of good work. I know that with you in charge, it will continue to do so.'

There was a faint question in his voice, and I hastened to reassure him, as if I were responsible to him. 'I'll do my best, Father. But I believe the hospital is not functioning yet?'

'It is functioning,' he said. Then he handed me five thousand rupee notes. I was looking at them in my hand; I had never seen a thousand rupee note before. He said, 'Many of my people are working in your hospital. Look after them well.' He was already moving towards the door.

'But how will I give you receipts? The Red Cross is paying me.'

Now he was laughing harder than before. I felt the doors shake with it. 'Who needs receipts?' he said. 'The money is for you.'

I didn't realise about the money until later. At that moment I knew only that I must give it back before he reached the door. 'Wait, wait, Father.' I had rushed across the room and held his arm. 'I can't take your money!' He shook my arm off. I felt thick and clumsy, like a child that sticks its finger in the tiny workings of a watch. He took the money back without a word. We've met several times since then – he's everywhere in the district – but neither of us mentioned money again.

Father Sherifis arrived at the end of the party. The music had died down, and small quantities of fish and rice, left over from the meal, had been carefully carried away. He brought the six nuns who worked with us in his green Matador. They unfolded like a flower, a bunch of white petals opened around him, smooth and impassive. He was the central force, the dancing, powerful spirit that twirled round and round, holding them together.

The guests had not left yet, I still had shreds of my identity as host. Then he pulled me in, inexorably, as if he had always planned this slow sucking in of my smiles and gestures of introduction, into the circle of his skill, until he dominated the scene. Father Sherifis had brought a farewell present for Miss Sushila. She was delighted even before he had opened it with its peacock blue wrapping. The stumbling pace of the party, dying towards conclusion, picked up speed. Faces were bright, arranging themselves for the drama of presentation. With a flourish, Father Sherifis unwrapped the present, and held it up. A foreign-made toaster, its yellow plastic sides gleaming in light from my paper lanterns. Miss Sushila gave one of her extravagant, bird-like cries and clasped it to her bosom. I was watching him, the vigorous neck moving in its white casing. B.L. Choudhry had left already, the only one to go, though he lived next door. He couldn't bear to be outclassed. Something was bothering me, too, festering below the surface, its strong vapours directed towards me. Father Sherifis had robbed me of my farewell speech. The nuns drew close to him and gathered into a song. Its words were unintelligible, but it was a song of farewell, soft and sad. Even the Bihari doctors who had fallen on the fish with such gusto were now hushed and listening.

114

13
Violent Events

Krishna could feel her body beginning to acknowledge fatigue. The nerves, drawn out and stretched in the evening's turmoil, were slowly shrinking back into place and she could feel knots smoothing out at the back of her neck. Her hands opened and closed, the fingers stretching out luxuriously, her feet flexed. She settled back in the chair. Listening to this man made her completely happy, his words were splitting up the ashen territory in her mind, as if she and her skin had been waiting for just those words, and yet they were utterly and terrifyingly new. Perhaps even Ranjit recognised that his words were unusual, not the ones he was accustomed to use, but it seemed to be the only way in which he could express himself to this woman. Her listening face had spread out before him directing him to where he must go.

'The period of maximum rain had passed by the time I made my first trip to the Mukti Bahini. Meanwhile, all through September and October, I drove your father through curtains of pouring rain, where mulberry trees appeared like shallow ghosts in their fields, or monster-black buffaloes reared at us from the roadside, as blind as we were.

'We were desperately short of money in the hospital, the staff hadn't been paid for months and doctors were threatening to leave. Your father had cut off their other means of income, through sale of blankets and other things on the black market.

'Mr Sanyal couldn't help. Mr Ajit had not authorised him to issue money. We began to barter tins of bully beef in the markets of English Bazaar, quietly, through arrangements made by a Muslim lawyer, Mr Rashid Saraf. The high, round tins had a picture of a smiling cow on the side, making the contents quite clear. We didn't want any Hindu to buy them by mistake. There was a room full of the tins just behind the operating theatre, part of the food stock donated by international agencies. We exchanged them for provisions: vegetables, mutton, wheat-flour, rice and milk.

'They must have heard of our desperate plight. Lieutenant Chatterjee, an emissary of Mr. Ajit, arrived from Calcutta with funds. I was pleased to see him. We laughed and joked a lot, even managed to persuade the Brigadier to accompany us to a Bengali film in English Bazaar. He told us about the time he had taken you to see the *Thief of Baghdad* when you were nine years old.'

Krishna was suddenly all ages together in the thin body looking out at Ranjit. He did not know why her eyes were wet.

'The rainy season ended and the cold began to creep in. The political situation in East Pakistan got steadily worse, but the continuous waves of refugees sweeping through the hospital stopped.

'The cold had settled in when I took him to Gaur. It was 14 December to be exact – the big attack began on 18 December. My first encounter with the Mukti Bahini was roughly at that time. They couldn't come to the hospital – donor countries had given strict instructions and of course the Red Cross does not help fighting troops. But many of the local luminaries were on the committee set up to help the Mukti Bahini. Iqbal and Mian Sarwar had contacted the Brigadier through Mitra and Saraf, who were the main people on the Committee. The only important person in the District resolutely not on the Committee was B. L. Choudhry. He would not be on any Committee to help Muslims. You see, his mother had been killed during the Noakhali communal riots just after Partition, by a gang of "dirty Mohammedans" as he calls them. The others were willing to follow Sanyal's lead. He always called them freedom fighters, not insurgents or terrorists, as Choudhry did.

'That was as far back as October, when it was still raining very hard. The freedom fighters were slipping across the border. I knew the Brigadier had been passing on small quantities of medicine and equipment. He made careful lists each time for Mr Sanyal. Iqbal and Mian Sarwar came for the stuff, slipping quietly into the dispensary at night. Iqbal was young, short and dark, with curly black hair, and huge liquid eyes. He had just got his degree from the Medical College in Dhaka University when Mujibur Rahman, their leader, sent him out to Rajshahi. Mian Sarwar was older, a large man with a rough voice. They sent an urgent message for your father to meet them in the ruins of Gaur, between Nachole and Mirzachak close to the border, where they had set up some

116

sort of makeshift camp. He asked me to drive him across in the *jonga*.

'We had planned to leave in the morning but B.L. Choudhry dropped in. He took an extraordinary interest in the hospital. That morning he had brought over a generator for the operating theatre. Electricity and power had been cut off for a week, because of a grave fault in Farakka. They suspected sabotage. Choudhry was snooping around in the dispensary when the Brigadier and I arrived.

'It was afternoon before we set off; the sun had not come out at all that day. We crossed a new bridge over the Bhagirathi, which still smelled of tar and building materials, and drove down past Bamangaon, Jambari, Khurd and Darbarpur to the ferry across to Gomastipur. Already the rush for the Hazrat Pandua *melas* had begun, and the ferry was crowded. We had difficulty getting a place for the jeep and sat in the jeep itself. Faces of pilgrims going to the *Baishazari mela* in Gomastipur crowded at the windows, breathing their piety down our necks.

'If your father had been killed there they would have worshipped him as a local pir. And if B.L. Choudhry had died instead he would have turned up in the Ban Puja at *Baisakhi* time. Fortunately, neither of them died, and the district was denied two holy men.

'After Gomastipur the *mela* was behind us and we were in the Barind area, relatively high land with red clay soil of the old alluvium, characteristic of the region east of the Mahananda. Large portions of it were once covered by the jungle locally known as *katal*, mainly thorny, scrub-bush land mixed with an abundance of *pipal*, *bar* or *bat*, *simul* and *pakur* trees and *nipal* bamboos.

'The shadow of a disappeared jungle was on the land; we were entering it like a hand going into a glove, each finger wriggling into its appointed place. Already the fear of being fully enclosed was upon me.

'We left the lights of Nachole behind us to the north. Mirzachak was a dim presence down to the south, coming to us through small sign-boards on the roadside. Then the turning was past, the road narrowed and there were no more signs to follow. We just kept going, the headlights of the *jonga* picking out the edges of the road like a thin, faint ribbon in the darkness.

'When we finally reached the Mukhti Bahini camp, erected among the ruins of Gaur, everything became confused in my mind – past, present and future, Hindu and Muslim, real things and

117

fantasy. History seemed to be an actual stream, a river in flood, running into that scene and pushing it out, launching it like a swollen corpse among floating huts, buffaloes and children perched on the tops of trees.

'Everywhere in the ruins, corrugated iron roofs, mud walls, and rough shelters of bamboo poles leaned against monuments and ancient public works, tombs and mosques lighted by kerosene lanterns and wood fires. The fires were the only pleasant part of the scene, warming the moonless night, cold and starry. Our friends crouched round the fires, or sat on old, crumbling steps.

'Weary guerrillas leaned against the stones and used them as they could. There was no discrimination between Hindu and Muslim stones. Who could tell the difference? They were jumbled together like dice shaken in the hand of history.

'I felt there were a lot more people among those ruins than were immediately visible. Behind the walls of the huts, the battered mosque, in alcoves provided by the gates, or wedged into angles and fissures in the thick surrounding wall. There was an uneasy, teeming multitude of sound, hinted at by an occasional groan, or a man crying out in a painful nightmare. The skin of the men, the whites of their eyes, glittered in the faint light. I realised later that I had been listening to the pure sound of pain. Also that Iqbal's move to bring the Brigadier here was very smart.

'He and Mian Sarwar, some other doctors, and a few men in soiled uniforms of the Bengal Rifles, were assembled on a dias, probably an old foundation with steps leading up to it. There was a woman with them, a sweet Bengali girl called Azma who was a doctor herself, married to Farooq. She seemed to be in a state of near hysteria, talking a great deal, pulling at a pair of trousers which she was obviously unused to wearing. This was the medical team, the ruins were their hospital, and they had no medicines or medical equipment. What's the matter, Krishna?'

Ranjit put his hand out. She shook her head, she couldn't tell him about it because she herself hardly understood. The strangest sensation. For the first time in her life she had actually wanted to be somewhere else, and couldn't be. Up to this point, she had arrived without choosing at places of pain and maximum passion, feeling them against her skin which deepened in colour, flushed with emotion. But she, the creature behind the skin, did not figure, did not intervene or participate directly, did not change anything. In fact, all her life she had not changed anything, she had folded

118

into it, like soil shaken over the surface. Moulding and shaping it herself and making choices was something else.

There had been nothing she had wanted, really wanted, nothing for which her being had rolled itself into a ball and moved towards, saying, 'This is what I want.' Amazing how difficult it had been, what a lot of resolution it had taken, how many years of growing, patting into shape, of depositing year after year of thought and feeling, before she had arrived at this point when she felt, with her whole being, 'I want to be there in the camp with Ranjit.'

Now here she was, listening to a man she had met an hour ago, whispering that she wanted to be with Azma, because Ranjit had noticed her. Could it be that she, Krishna, numb in her soul, was now actually jealous of another woman?

All in a flash, so of course it was the strangest sensation, to commit her new feelings, and all at once, to have them formulate suddenly and sweep in one huge cold wave. Stranger still, her skin, normally the recorder, did not register at all. Something kept it back, something would not let it enter. Something had decided that here was not territory for the skin. Here she must enter alone, unclothed, without her skin. She must start from scratch, begin at the beginning, take one step at a time, like a child. There was no easy entry into this area. She already knew the pain of arrival, the hot breath of another's despair which she could not change, the agony of observation, the free load of passion. But this was different. She could not sweep in, fly or move in like a wave, to find the scene already laid out. Now, nothing was known, everything was new and moved like hairs floating under water, with infinite delicacy and wonder, breathless.

She was uncomfortable, uneasy, shifting around in her chair. There was no more peace and calm. Ranjit smiled, his lips trembled faintly. Everything was different, as if an exile had been gripped by a dream of possession. Ranjit went on, but now his words included what had passed in the silence between them.

'As I said, Iqbal did a very smart thing. He received the Brigadier in a formal committee on the dais, and then took him on an inspection round of the 'wards', the poor huts with their dying patients. It brought back the Brigadier's memories of inspection tours in military hospitals during his years of army service. His heart was touched, and shadows of pity lay around his eyes when he got back to the dais. There was another thing. He felt after a long time that he actually had the power to do something, since he controlled medical supplies and equipment which the Mukti Bahini needed. Also, for the first time in the months since he had arrived, he encountered no hostility, only friendliness and pleading, in fact a complete dependence.

'"Well, you've seen everything we have, Brigadier." Iqbal's voice was soft. "We can use whatever you give us from the kindness of your heart."

'"I'll see what we can do." The Brigadier did not want to commit himself yet, though he would dearly have loved to make an immediate grand gesture. Shadows from the monuments pushed our voices down, as if burying them under their stones. We whispered to each other, voices in conspiracy.

'"There's something else, Brigadier. Something even more important for which we need your help."'

Ranjit said, 'This is the casual way in which the most important things happen, unfold themselves, a cat getting up and walking across the floor, just like that.' Krishna nodded.

He went on. 'Then Mian Sarwar spoke, and Farooq and Azma. A tent of whispering sound, a cloud of bees buzzing around the Brigadier's head. "We have to stay alive."

'"It affects the safety of the whole camp. And our people fighting across the border. There is a spying organisation, with a very clever man at its head. It affects your country too. There was sabotage, a small explosion at the Farakka barrage. You've been without power for one week now. People are saying there are guerrillas in the area and that they must have done it. But it was not us at all. It was this man. He managed it. He stops all help reaching us from the Indian side. Only you seem to have escaped his influence. That's why we're asking for your help."

'"He gives news of our exact whereabouts to the enemy soldiers. They attack and kill us, even follow us across the border. Now we're completely immobile in this camp, can't go anywhere with these sick men. If he finds out about us, and he will soon enough, we will be destroyed like sitting ducks."

'"The only way is to expose him."

'"Who is he?" the Brigadier asked.

'Iqbal stopped and looked around. The other voices fell into a hush. "The priest, Father Sherifis, you know him."

'The Brigadier's face was green with shock.

'"What do you mean, expose him?" I asked.

120

' "The Brigadier can tell the authorities; they'll listen to him; he is an important officer."

'The Brigadier was quiet and unhappy.

'Mian Sarwar took me aside as we were leaving, early the next morning. "Tomorrow we will send some men to Sahibganj. Two armed guards and couple of nursing personnel. With a truck and a trailer. They will bring whatever the Brigadier decides to give us. And remember the priest."

'The Brigadier wanted to see Mr Sanyal right away.

'We went straight to Mr Sanyal's official residence in Maldah. His wife told us that an urgent message had taken him to Siliguri. The whole area was agog with activity, the army was on the move, the war had begun. We met lines of trucks and marching soldiers in battle fatigues.'

'Tanks?' Krishna asked. 'Horses?' Her brain was alive with the scene.

'No tanks in that area,' Ranjit said. 'Here, more likely, they would have needed boats. From Farakka the Ganges swings across a bulge of Bangladeshi territory and becomes the Padma River. Water was a major feature. But we were going across land, in a direction contrary to the traffic moving on the road. Our concerns seemed so alien to those soldiers and trucks moving on the road. In fact, the whole scene in Gaur now seemed unreal: ruins lit by fires in the night, a story about a master-operator. How would he dare to conduct his machinations with so much Indian military on the road, the might of the Indian forces patently arrayed? Strangely enough, only doctors and patients dying in those primitive conditions were real.

' "If you take the true spirit of the Red Cross," the Brigadier said, "and never mind now who donated the hospital, how can we see injured men bleeding to death, especially when we know we can help them?"

'The uncertain, unusual conditions on the roads helped to dilute the sharp outlines of his instructions from Mr Ajit. He told me also that Mr Sanyal, as far back as May, had encouraged him to help the Mukti Bahini in small ways. He hadn't said so openly, but the Brigadier had drawn clear implications from his sentences.

'Then there was the spy story to deal with. The further we moved from Gaur, the more mythical it seemed. The Brigadier didn't say very much. It would have been easy enough to let go of the story, to sit back and do nothing and hand over responsibility to the

121

marching columns, so professional and capable of taking care.

'We were stopped and questioned several times on the road. We couldn't have got through if it hadn't been for the Red Cross jeep and your father's credentials as a retired Brigadier. So how would a foreign agent operate in such a close web? But we were dealing with the original spider himself, wily perpetrator, source of the evil I had felt all this time, who could leap unscathed from line to silken line of his widening environment.

'We had to go slowly; it was only after lunch that we managed to locate Mr Sanyal in the Martha Hotel, close to the airport. The *dak* bungalow where he usually stayed had been taken over by the Army.

'We went up the short drive to the Martha Hotel. Hill flowers crowded its edges in a riot of winter splendour with brilliant colours. I had never seen their like in Nairobi, which is full of flowers and flowering creepers, jacaranda and laburnum.'

'Nairobi?' Krishna said, wonderingly. 'Laburnum?' She knew nothing about this man. Nairobi. He was another stream coming into India, and she could not travel into him at all. With Ranjit she met a perfect wall; he put her firmly and entirely into the present moment.

'I have a lot to tell you,' Ranjit said, 'but I have a whole lifetime ahead of me.' First, he was bringing her this exposed father.

'The Brigadier went up to the Deputy Commissioner's room, I waited in the lobby.

'The walls were laced with calendars and tourist posters mounted on plyboard – dancing belles of Assam in tribal costume, teeth gleaming in the sun, *shikaras* on the Dal Lake in Srinagar, a snarling tiger set against the thick jungle of the Sunderbans. I stretched out on a dirty sofa near the window, my head pillowed on its arm, trying to sleep a bit. It was to be a long drive back to Kalidiggi that day. But the springs of the sofa had long since collapsed under the strain of travelling schoolchildren, officials, an occasional tourist and other traffic inhabiting the lobby of the only hotel in Siliguri, which was itself a passage, a corridor to the hill areas of Sikkim, Bhutan and Assam.

'In addition, I soon became aware of various species of insects, bugs and winged creatures, who bit red, scratchy welts into my skin. I got up and went to the window. Potato fields ran straight off from the side wall of the hotel, hidden completely from the front entrance. It was like coming into a secret place, looking at the

122

broad, green leaves of the plants, clean and bright in the sunshine, perched on their raised mounds of soil.

'Then I heard the Brigadier behind me, his feet dragging a bit. The sun was still in my eyes. He looked utterly confused and sat down where the sofa still retained a depression from my body.

'"What did he say?" I asked after a while.

'The Brigadier spoke slowly, as if searching among rocky columns of words for a meaning. "I don't know!"

'I waited. The sun was warm on my back and I felt curiously free and irresponsible. This man in front of me on the sofa had absorbed the whole burden of decision; he was heavy and struggling with it. Mr Sanyal had pushed him away; he was on his own now, a tree growing without support.

'He went on. "He said I should help the Mukti Bahini if I wanted to, but no more lists of equipment were to be transferred. I had to be responsible for this myself."

'"What did he say about the priest?"

'"I asked him."

'"Did Mr Sanyal confirm the story?"

'"He said he could do nothing. I said, it's your duty. You're President of the local Red Cross, representative of the government. Speak to Calcutta about it, or even to New Delhi. But he refused to talk to me. As if his body was drugged with afternoon sleep.

'"He kept saying, very kindly, Would you like to go back? Why don't you go back, since they are troubling you so much? I'll arrange for your tickets. I tried to be clever. At least give me the money to pay the doctors and volunteers in the hospital, I said. It is two months since they were paid their salary, and they're getting very restless. Then I can think of going back. Although, you understand, Ranjit, I have no intention of going back now. The war's begun. I can't leave. Mr Sanyal said that Mr Ajit had sent no money, but that it would be arranged as soon as possible."

'"But is the story true? About Father Sherifis?"

'"It is true that Farakka was sabotaged. He repeated that. We are to understand what we want from that."

'"What are you going to do?" I asked him.

'He was at the fluttery edge of the situation, risen up like a sharp line of earth, the wall of a furrow, and he was perched on it like a potato plant. He could, at this point, fall on either side – the situation still permitted it. He could, for example, get together

123

some minor pieces of equipment and medicines and despatch them to the camp at Gaur through Iqbal's emissaries. Thereafter he could leave the fortunes of war to take care of the Mukti Bahini and Father Sherifis. Alternatively, he could send them stuff in noticeable quantities which would make the difference between life and death for those patients trapped in the historic ruins. This would have consequences for the Brigadier. More than that, he could attempt to pierce the heart of the devious priest and attack his power. Morality was not clear on either side. He was not supposed to help the Mukti Bahini with Red Cross funds; instructions were precise on that. He would have to violate those on his own responsibility; there was no help from Mr Sanyal. Then, the story about Father Sherifis was by no means proved beyond doubt and the Brigadier had already done what he could. He had informed the authorities concerned; it was up to them to take action. What could he do, a single man whom everyone was trying to send back to Dagra, against a well-knit spy organisation? We were not even sure that such a thing existed. Perhaps morality lay only in the attempt. A shifting thing, which he himself had to pin down. Meanwhile, I had no idea what he was thinking, sitting there. He seemed to have grown into the dirty orange-coloured sofa. I thought of the potato fields gleaming pleasantly in the sun outside.

'I said, "I'll go for a walk, until you're ready to leave." But he wouldn't let me go; he didn't want to be alone.

'Soon it was time to leave. Somewhere along the way down, we both knew I was taking him to Father Sherifis' headquarters at the edge of Kalidiggi. If he saw Father Sherifis now, it would be a road already taken, with no turning back.

'It was late evening when we drew up before a neat, rambling bungalow with a gate which said, 'HART Organisation of India.'

'A nun told us that Father Sherifis was still at Sunday prayers. We were shown into the parlour to wait. I had never been there before, yet the place seemed familiar, with its dark drapes tied back from the window, thin, black chairs with flat cushions, coir matting on the floor, and framed photographs and pictures hung on the wall, behind thick glass plates. Then I realised why I found it familiar. It smelled exactly like my convent school in Nairobi, of stale biscuits, tea served in frail aluminium pots, and a lot of misplaced but sincere goodwill. When the Brigadier came back from seeing Father Sherifis and we were walking out to the jeep I

124

had a distinct, uncanny sense that Father Sherifis did not belong in these surroundings. He was an intruder here, in this innocence.

'The Brigadier was ashen. I have never seen his face so totally devoid of colour. "Others have told me to leave, have suggested it in various ways. But this man ordered me to go, as if he had assumed the power to do so. And he warned me, in fact threatened me, against helping the Mukti Bahini, making it obvious that the consequences would be dire."

' "What about the spy story?"

' "It's correct," he said, "I know it. This man is a foreign agent. I didn't quite believe it myself, before. The Farakka sabotage could have been anyone's doing. But I marched in and related the rumour to him, that he was being connected to it. Perhaps nobody has said it to him before. His face fell open with surprise, became red and thunderously angry. Then he laughed his strange laughter. At that moment, I knew when I had heard it once before, very loud, mocking and strong, a power which knew the futility of attempts to control it. I had returned the money he had offered me on our first interview. An anticipatory bribe. I had forgotten about the money. That day, when he arrived at Matron's party in his green Matador, I honoured him as if he were the chief guest. But now I understood his face and the laughter. Iqbal is correct about him."

' "What are you going to do?"

' "There's not much time. We have to pack all the equipment tonight. The man's been warned and, if he is as efficient as Iqbal seems to believe, he will act fast."

'In fact, he acted faster than we had expected.

'The Brigadier seemed to have decided to give whatever he could to the Mukti Bahini from the surgical equipment. He took it for granted that I would be sorting equipment and rolling tents with him all night. There was no way to detach myself from the enterprise now.

'He got *Havildar* Santosh and Bhim Singh to help. The four of us worked almost in silence, except for instructions from the Brigadier on what to select. We separated out a long list of stuff – plasma, antibiotics, tetanus shots, tents, and real surgical supplies for minor operations, including elementary anaesthesia facilities. I was exhausted; we had been travelling all day with very little food, and the previous night we had slept among the ruins of Gaur. But the Brigadier showed no signs of fatigue. After a while we fell into a pattern of automatic movement.

'We still had not finished when the sky began to lighten. I curled into the flat plastic of one of the tents, and closed my eyes for what I thought was five minutes. I awoke to the sound of voices. Matron Pinto, already starched and dressed for the day in the hefty triangle of her nurse's cap, white dress and sturdy white shoes, stood beside the Brigadier. "Why don't you have breakfast in your room, sir? I'll have it sent to you here. No need to walk across to the Mess as usual. You must be tired; you've been working all night."

'That was our first indication that everyone in the hospital knew what we had been doing through the night, but we were too tired for this to register properly. The Brigadier just stretched himself a bit, yawned, and said, "No, Matron. Thank you."

'When we sauntered out a few minutes later I saw B.L. Choudhry hanging around near the dispensary. Maybe he had come to check up on his generator. The *havildar* and his crony emerged. The Brigadier waited a split moment for a salute, which was not forthcoming. Then a crowd collected, drifting to us in twos and threes, until suddenly, as we made to pass Choudhry, there were at least thirty men around us.

'"Just a minute, Brigadier Sahib. Where are you going, in such a hurry this morning?" Choudhry's tone was deliberately insolent, and the Brigadier flared immediately.

'"How dare you talk to me like that?"

'"It's you who don't know how to talk to people. You shout and misbehave with us. Who do you think you are, bloody retired officer, pensioned off and come here to trouble us!"

'Choudhry flourished a gun. I was not aware until now that he had a gun, in fact he had once asked me how he could get one. Now here he was lifting it threateningly into the Brigadier's face.

'"You think we don't know what you've been up to all night? Packing all this good hospital stuff to hand over to those bloody Muslims? Betraying your own people?"

'The Brigadier raised his arm to hit Choudhry, who slung across it with the butt of his gun.

'"But the man himself is bad, a real *badmash*." Choudhry addressed himself now to the crowd, which was close and pressing up threateningly around us. "He eats beef, hundreds of tins, which he consumes in private. He drinks liquor. You should have seen

126

him at the Matron's party. Drinking, dancing, loud revelry, and this man, this Brigadier, was at the centre of it all. I tell you, I know for sure he drinks in his room and has no idea what happens in the hospital at night, who lives or who dies."

'I had been gradually pushed away from your father's side, and now I found myself at the fringes of the crowd. The *havildar* towered directly behind him, a patently hostile presence, and Bhim Singh was beside him. The crowd was getting more and more worked up. There was a sighing and fluttering in it, breathing became more hot and rapid, hands rubbed against sticks. The Brigadier was now cautious about what he said; he was aware of the crowd.

'"Here is the key to my room." He had a sense of the drama, too. I could see his hand, waving the key above the heads around him. "Why don't you check my room? I never drink; you will not find a single bottle in my cupboard."

'Choudhry spoke now as if he were on the dais of a public meeting.

'"Okay. So he is a *badmash*. But at least he should not take things which belong to all of you, for your health and treatment, and give them to those evil Muslim men who have been coming across our border for these many months, eating our food, making eyes at our women, interfering in our daily lives."

'The crowd was angry now and I was relieved to see the Sub-Inspector from the *kotwali* next door fully armed and pushing his way through the crowd. But when he spoke his tone was belligerent and hostile. "The *Kotwal* Sahib has called you for questioning," he said, catching at the Brigadier's arm roughly. They passed close by me and I hung on to the Sub-Inspector's tunic, determined to be dragged through to the *kotwali* with them. When we reached the wall of the school compound, I realised where the waves of sound were coming from. The whole place was surrounded by a sea of people, their faces flushed with anger and hostility, rustling with it, muttering and calling after us as we passed in a small knot to the *Kotwal*'s office. B.L. Choudhry waited outside, his hand steady on the nerve of the crowd.

'The *Kotwal* sat behind his desk. Two stars gleamed on his shoulder; his close-cropped moustache and wide, flaring nostrils were composed and steady. "Sit down," he said to the Brigadier curtly. I pressed up against the wall. "You see that the people of the area are very agitated and excited."

'The Brigadier pretended the *Kotwal* was his friend. "I don't understand this trouble, *Kotwal* Sahib. Why all this hostility? After all, what have I done? I've worked only for their good. I'm not getting paid for it."

'"Why don't you leave then?" There was an urgency, a bullying, harsh note. The *Kotwal* was repeating what Choudhry, the *havildar* and the crowd outside had been saying. As if they all wanted to squeeze the Brigadier out, like a pus-filled pimple in their flesh, to close over the space his body would leave. They wanted to return to their old comfortable state of corrupt torpor, once this alien element had been dealt with. "Why don't you leave?" he repeated. "There will be no problem then. No questions, no arrest. I will give you safe conduct to Maldah."

'"Arrest? For what?"

'The *Kotwal* went on, as if uninterrupted. "Otherwise, I'll just send you back into the crowd outside." The Brigadier was quiet. We knew that the crowd was the real issue. They would tear him apart. And Father Sherifis had given Choudhry a gun. I knew it.

'"What is the charge against me?" The Brigadier was playing for time.

'The *havildar* intervened. "You haven't paid the doctors and the other hospital staff for months. The civilian doctors are ready to leave."

'"Yes," said the *Kotwal*. "Already the people have taken two processions to the Deputy Commissioner's house this morning, demanding that you should be withdrawn. The doctors were at the head, yelling that you had eaten up their money. Mr Sanyal has been given police protection; he has barricaded himself in his house. The doctors have even telephoned the Governor in Calcutta and they have threatened to go there this afternoon. How will the hospital run without doctors in these war conditions?"

'I could not understand why the Brigadier didn't just agree to leave. Then I remembered the piles of neatly sorted equipment and the Brigadier's possessed, indefatigable air as he had gone about the task.

'"I will pay the doctors immediately," he said. "Just see me back to my room, disperse the crowd, and I will arrange the money."

'The money had only been an excuse. "No, now, in front of me," the *Kotwal* said. Everyone knew the Brigadier had no money.

'The Brigadier's face was ashen. I took him aside. I had six

128

thousand rupees with me, the remains of what I had brought from Nairobi. I offered it to him, but I had to get through the crowd to my room.

'Some inspiration took hold of the Brigadier. He leaned across the table and whispered; only the *Kotwal* and I heard him. "You know Mr Surjit Markand? Top Intelligence Officer in Delhi. He gives orders to your Deputy Inspector General here. He can get you a police medal if you help me now. He is so close to me, like a member of my family, I have known him for twenty-five years." The *Kotwal* moved back, his face changing. He knew Mr Surjit Markand.'

'My mother's lover,' Krishna murmured. Soon there would be time to tell Ranjit everything.

'The Brigadier didn't wait for further changes. He leapt up and grasped the *havildar* round the waist. "Please, I will see that you are rewarded. You are my friend, by brother. Take me back to my quarters now; we'll fetch the money. A remarkable sight, the Brigadier with his arms wrapped around the *havildar*'s giant frame, weaving through the crowd.

'"I am very tired. I'm going directly to sleep after this," the Brigadier remarked to the *havildar* who stood over him as he handed out my money to the ungrateful line of Bihari doctors, volunteers and the rest of the staff. The Brigadier was careful to take receipts.

'We knew that we now had to go to Calcutta. He whispered his plans. "Get the Mukti Bahini chaps here from Sahibganj to the area behind my quarters. But only after it gets really dark, with the engine running. We should be able to load the stuff in a couple of hours."

'It took much longer than that, though Iqbal had sent his best men – two nursing personnel to drive the jeep and trailer and the truck, and three armed guards who carried rifles. As soon as the truck was loaded, we sent it off with one of the guards riding in front with the driver. But it was dawn. Already there were signs of movement. The Brigadier had to leave as well.

'B. L. Choudhry was the one who heard us first. He rushed out of his house and straddled the road, waving his gun and roaring at the top of his voice. People came running out, materialising out of thin air. Even the Kotwali was active.

'"I will not let you go. That is our stuff which you are stealing. I

129

won't let you pass," Choudhry shouted, rallying the crowd which was assembling.

'The Brigadier stood in the jeep beside me. His shotgun, a .500, lay between us, but he did not touch that. "Who are you to stop me? I am still in command here. This is my equipment; it's for dying human beings. Move out of the way, or I will have you shot."

'Choudhry leapt like a ferocious beast at the Brigadier, intent on dragging him down. Abdul, standing in the jeep behind us, fired, hitting Choudhry in the leg. He rolled to the side of the road, shouting curses. Some men grabbed Abdul's rifle and dragged him out of the jeep. The Brigadier was yelling at the jeep driver to move. Another armed guard, Ghafoor, leapt off to rescue his companion. You can imagine what the crowd did to him. Meanwhile the jeep driver took off, the trailer jerking into motion. My jeep was already moving. I skirted Choudhry, who was trying to lift himself from the road. He mouthed a magnificent curse at the Brigadier as we left him behind. "You have a death inside you, you bastard. I can see it growing. It will grow and grow and finish you off. It will eat you up and destroy you."

'Then we saw a green Matador van. A face flashed at a side window, then the shades were drawn. We couldn't look in; we could barely see the driver's face, wrapped in some kind of cloth. It was moving rapidly, sliding like a fish from the side of the road to block our path. I pressed on the accelerator and we were through, but it seemed pretty clear that the Mukti Bahini jeep following us, drawing the trailer loaded with stuff, would not make it. The Brigadier pulled himself up in the front seat, grabbed his shotgun, and, like a seasoned *shikari*, shot open the two front tyres of the van. It caved in towards the road immediately, like a mouth deprived of teeth, and the jeep, with its trailer wriggling behind, slid past and speeded behind us. "Funny," the Brigadier said. "I've used this gun for years in the jungle, shot all kinds of animals. I shot my last panther with it, in the Cheela Hunting Block with my daughter Krishna. Now I'm shooting Matador vans."

'The road forked. The jeep with the trailer turned off towards Gaur, we went on to Farakka, four and a half miles from Kalidiggi, towards the NCC Camp in which Mr Sanyal had barricaded himself with his family.

'He came out to greet us, leaned across and casually lifted the shotgun from the seat, handing it to the Superintendent of Police who stood beside him. Then he led us into the building. His voice

130

was impatient, but a little regretful. "You know what you're charged with, Brigadier Chahal? Under Section 307, attempted murder. You have a gun with two fired bullets in it."

'The Brigadier shrugged. "I used it on a van, not a human being."

'"That's all very well, but who will believe you? There are hundreds of witnesses for the encounter with B. L. Choudhry. His leg has almost been shot off completely. The mob was just stopped from lynching those two Mukti Bahini people you left behind."

'"But Choudhry was waving a gun; he would have killed us, I could see it in his face," the Brigadier said, his own face white with shock.

'"The *Kotwal* says Choudhry's gun was not loaded." The Superintendent of Police left the room, with the shotgun, holding it carefully in a white handkerchief like a newly born babe. "Why did you get mixed up with Father Sherifis? I warned you not to."

'"But you know who he is. I told you the whole story."

'"I know nothing about that. I know only that you have to appear in the District Court in Maldah today. I've asked for bail, though this is a charge of attempted murder. Then I am sending you straight back to Calcutta."

'The Brigadier did not fight now against leaving; he had finished his task.

'Father Sherifis was inside the court when we got there, sitting alone in a single line of chairs reserved for the audience.

'When we got outside again Father Sherifis stepped into our path. For a moment I saw the green Matador barring our way, and I made an involuntary gesture to pull the Brigadier aside. I had taken charge of him. Father Sherifis' vigorous hands, flowing with white cloth, went out reassuringly and we stopped. He was exactly like he used to be, full of charm, his face brilliant and glowing with energy, his whole body ticking with laughter. But the Brigadier's face did not wear the slightly obsequious smile which he had previously worn in Sherifis' presence.

'"Oh, Brigadier," Father Sherifis said. "You know the Bahini camp among the ruins of Gaur? Well, a terrible thing happened there a short while ago. A jeep drew up with a loaded trailer, everybody crowded around it, and the whole thing just blew up, ruin returned to ruin. The explosion ripped through the stones, killing almost everybody. Your army reached there, drawn by the terrible sounds. I believe they found very few survivors."'

14

The Brigadier Celebrates Victoria Memorial

Mr Sanyal had a kind face. I'm wrong about people, always wrong. Kindness isn't enough. Maybe he was king. People: the priest brought them, man of God, bringing them to me, hundreds and hundreds of them, crowding, getting into my head. So many of them are dead. I gave them medicine. Did I hope to save their lives? I've been too proud, hoping to save people's lives. But still they died. The man in white, his golden-silver shining face. He held power; he could control everything. Not quite. With my beautiful shotgun, my weapon of the jungle, wrapped in green leaves, touched with love, I shot the green beast. I escaped.

You pushed me, dear Dhiraj Kumari. I was a house with mice scrabbling inside, going whoosh-whoosh through the paper.

They are here too. Up a staircase. I see garbage and flies outside the window, spreading death and disease. Coming in here to me, too. Death and disease. You gave me no protection. Pulled out layer after layer; threw me into the arms of the priest; you wanted him to destroy me. Who destroyed me? What is this thing reflected in the fan above my head? If I look carefully to the side I won't see the shape. A stretch of water on the other side of the wall, with trees around it. A huge boat, swaying from side to side in the sun. Crowded with people.

If I could get the people out for a while, maybe I could sleep. But how can I sleep, floating like this? Something must come together in a mass, a locked fist, and then that would sink in sleep. But there are so many pieces floating around. They can't sleep. Each separate piece can't close by itself. And they don't come together. Don't you see that? I'm talking to you. Some of them will gather round the centre of sound.

A young man collected all the pieces, a bagful of toys, brought them here, climbing the stairs, left them here on this bed, staring at garbage outside, and beyond that a stretch of water, palm trees waving. I could not put them together in a shape for Mr Ajit.

I must explain it all to you, I said. I wanted to tell Mr Ajit how it happened. If I could have told him ,how it happened, then this floating mass would have coalesced, a past established, event following event in a solid river of happening. But Mr Ajit did not want to see me, perhaps because there was nothing to see. Just this collection of words trying to gather round a voice. He said I should give him a formal, written explanation. Maybe he just does not want to know. I spent my whole life like that, not wanting to know. Until you floated in through a window. Not with grills and iron bars on it; this one might have kept you out. I would have welcomed anything which kept you out. You frightened me, floating up suddenly from the surface of water. But no palm trees then, no people, just myself. I knew your name, even though you settled in a furry mass around my heart, still separate enough for that. Then you went deeper, like a termite in a rotting house, eating me, creating empty space where I did strange things.

Now I have almost forgotten what they were. Certainly I could not write them down on paper, in sentences that Mr Ajit demands. At the most I could have lifted up a corner of the paper you stuck over your heart when you left, like some house-owner boarding up the windows of his house against prying eyes when he goes away. You will come back? If I had lifted up a corner, like now, the words would have told him something. Make out a case, he said, on the telephone. He thinks everybody can put their lives into written sentences. And then, to make out a case. The words must make the right sounds. I did that for so many years. Language got jangled because of the women. The others had roles, like wife and daughter. What did they call you? You wouldn't fit in a case at all. I've retired now, and don't have to make out a case. They can't court-martial me, suspend me, make cuts in my salary, or force me to resign. I am free. Who wrapped her love around me in the jungle? My daughter Krishna. My shotgun remembered.

This kind young man. Must return his money, I have all the receipts for Mr Ajit. Receipts are easy for holding truth; it is sentences that are hard, to make out a case, justify the truth, make it sound right. I must get the money. Can't be owing all the time. I've begun paying you back. Receipts exist, then go into a void. As messengers with wings they come back carrying twigs in their

133

beaks, there is land after the flood. Maybe the young man can tell Mr Ajit what happened. If he puts the details together carefully, end to end, maybe somebody will understand.

Did you leave because recompense was done? Never enough, so come back. I miss you. Clung to my heart like a burr, pushing me out into the world. I hated you. Now I am in little pieces, without the bag of your nothingness to hold me. You had a name when you first arrived, flooding up from water, rising from the backs of buffaloes. Then we mingled, became indistinct. Didn't you always want that to be a part of me? So, why did you leave? Was it the smell? An old man's smell, a common, slow decay? Or did the priest squeeze you out too?

Do you want to be the whole of me? Is that something to tempt you with? Take it gradually, though, there's not much time left, after all. Don't you see, I'm making a choice. Have I at least earned the right now to make a choice? In so far as fragments can choose, each sending out small lines of desire. Rays of the sun in a child's drawing. If they saw the rays of desire going from me, they would gather them in a thick rope and hang me with it. But with you it would be different, I don't know. Maybe even a different kind of death. These fragments are gills of fish opening in water. They don't have to surface to breathe. Only the whale's like that, its great hump rising above the line of water, exposing itself to suck in life.

I was a whale. Please agree with me. I am ready now to be a fish, sucking in life secretively under water. But without you I have no gills, I can't breathe. The weight of water, green water, will suffocate me. The murder of the green Matador released me into the jungle, took the great beast from me and hunted it down. Now it is another kind of death, my death. And new life. To give me gills. If only you would begin to take me over. You don't have to do it all at once. Give me the freedom of water, gradually.

Pictures hung around a room, ancient drawings. This woman sitting on a throne with a small crown on her head, her lips pursed in a business-like manner. Her nose is sharp; her eyes are young and firm; she makes proclamations. They are set out in letters of gold on long curtains of marble which circle round and round a central statue. Written in many languages. But the lady can't move. She sits at the top of splendid steps, her head open to a brilliant blue sky, and she can't move at all. She is made of brown stone, of block metal, of marble. She turns up all the time here, in

134

various shapes and sizes, gathering more and more people around her, adding elephants and fans, soldiers and canons, horses and brocade dresses. Yellow and frayed, she lies under glass with her empty dresses, much more dead than a dead body. When I look up she is shining in many colours, the sun flooding through her as she kneels or rises, accepts benediction, travels in open carriages, her horses waving their plumes, her train laid down through churches of magnificence. I look for her even under the wide, winding staircases, because she should be on the empty iron pedestals which stand there with scalloped edges and curling metal leaves, waiting for an occupant, in the exile of cleaning materials.

She is not up here, in this room. She has been left behind below, stern mother of fear, dear Victoria, whose love is power. She grasped me sucking to her milky bosom for two hundred years. I pushed her away with infant arms. I am released. I am free to read what is written under these pictures. The letters emerge from a grey, rippleless void, crawling out like a sudden line of black buffaloes, one after another, from the blank face of water. I climb on their backs and dangle my legs. I am at ease and the mud of Kohat is cool against my skin. I can hear the call of partridges and my father's gun going off in the early hours of the morning. The line of buffaloes takes me home.

Thin, black lines of mountains going up into a white sky. Boats with wide sails, horses, elephants and camels on the road. A feathery banyan tree with hanging roots reaching the ground, shading horses and camels, and soldiers at ease. The gleam of water in the distance. Ranjit is the young man's name, the kind young man, Maharaja Ranjit Singh. Taken over by the Big Mother downstairs. A young boy and girl fled from those wars, crossed the river Sutlej and went up to Kohat. I have ancestors. My line goes back, far back. Looking down from the central balcony, black and white tiles in the entrance porch leap into my eyes. A guard sits beside the dirty white rails picking at his toes. A cannon used at a famous battle stands beside him. Neither of them scares me now. I can see them; I know their names; I can look out to the city of Calcutta over the heads of cooing pigeons on the ledges beside me. The back of Queen Victoria's throne is towards me. Her prim little bun of hair appears over the top and, wonder of wonders, a midget lion, her utter baby, skulks at its base, reduced. He has come down from where he was rampant on the top of the gate to Raj Bhavan and Mr Ajit.

Beds of orange and yellow *cannas* go off from her on either side. The garden is neat, laid out with perfect symmetry, grassy lawns spaced with clumps of date-palms and the spreading fans of *mor pankh*. Two stretches of water, but a sign says 'No Bathing Permitted'. Beyond Chowranghee I can see a hideous apartment building with deep mustard walls, doors and windows painted green, and a red roof, the silvery dome of the GPO, multi-storeys of the Reserve Bank, and, like rising music strung across the horizon, the zinging, jaunty pylons of Howrah Bridge. Howrah Bridge. Where you entered. Above all, stretching forever in a cobalt blue sky with white clouds floating gently, painting in a most beautiful frame, the arch of entrance. I have arrived. This is the Victoria Memorial.

15
Ranjit Enters Krishna's Life

'I took him to the West Bengal Circuit House on Hungerford Street. It was all we could afford; the charges were only seven rupees a day. A dirty little room on the fourth floor, built around a well where everyone threw their garbage. Every now and again a bucketful of stuff came sloshing down and he jerked his head towards it.

'"Make out a case," Mr Ajit said. "Let the Brigadier give an explanation for what happened. Attach your receipts. Then we will see. Nothing works unless it appears right on paper. You know that. After all, you work in Daulat Ram Hospital. You have to be accountable to auditors."

'He refused to see the Brigadier. "What's the point of that?" he said. "I repeatedly sent him messages to come back. The local people were very agitated; doctors in the hospital kept writing letters, making representations to have him removed. They telephoned the Governor twice. The first .Matron, Miss Sushila, stopped here on her way south to report about a farewell party."

'"Let him write it out, then we will see. Meanwhile, he must not

136

leave Calcutta. There is a charge of attempted murder against him, and his bail confines him to this area."

' "But where will he stay? He is your responsibility, you sent him out there among those spies and thieves. You must pay for him."

' "Be careful what you say, Dr Dhawan. We are in a state of war. Any more loose talk like that could get you into serious trouble."

'Lieutenant Chatterjee met me in the corridor. He drew me aside, whispering in my ear that he sympathised with the Brigadier, who was basically a good man, but that he had been foolish.'

Krishna was listening. What was it about the quality of her listening, as if her life depended upon it, which made Ranjit talk so late into the night? 'I was sad about Lieutenant Chatterjee. There's many like him. Mr Sanyal, for example. You see the flash of a whale's back, just below the surface of water. They know what's happening; they want to stay clear of corruption. But that's not possible; it sticks to you. The alternative is to throw oneself out and away. That's when the back of a whale bobs up above the surface, exposed and breathing, a sure target of harpoons. But they are afraid and prefer to stay submerged and breathless underwater.'

She talked to him, going back and forth, as she had never done before, 'But isn't that the way all systems are, any system, the moment it coalesces? As it has to do to survive. You said bureaucracy. But I work in a college and it's there, too. And in my father-in-law's politics, our relations with his friend Chaman Bajaj.'

She had forgotten about the family, forgotten even about Anu's betrayal. Ranjit was waiting for her. She continued, 'Then all these systems gather up and run into the big one, the State, and that goes on, rung upon rung. You have the hierarchy of developing and developed countries, and so on, to Ecology. All systems begin and end with Ecology. They used to call it God.

'Some people got away from system, but at a cost. Sufis and mystics. For a while they had the freedom of God, the freedom of the beginning and the end. Then they were swallowed and stifled by the Shariat and the caste system, by the wars of Christian theology and the monasteries.'

He was not gentle with her, neither was he harsh. As if they stood side by side near a river, looking on to a valley spread under their feet. "I suppose one must have systems. But they all work by exclusion. Those who half-belong, like Lieutenant Chatterjee, are pulled or forced to conform with a kick or two. The only signs of temporary displacement area sympathetic expression, a kind look in the eyes, a carefully hidden understanding somewhere, a word or two which escapes when the soul gets extra heavy. Then there are those who can't belong. Those are the real dangers and threats. Everything is pitted against them, to destroy them. They die in boredom, ignominy or indifference. Or they start systems of their own.'

'And you? What about you? Seems to me you've been a whale already, for my father's sake,' Krishna said. It was coming close, very fast.

'I have the freedom of exile, of being a refugee. It has its own costs, but you should see the other risks. Your father was flat out for days on end, completely supine and exhausted. I could hardly bear to leave him, even to go out for food. There was no question of leaving him alone in Calcutta, although I was supposed to join back at the hospital two weeks ago. But he began pushing me to come here to meet you when he returned from the Victoria Memorial.'

'The Victoria Memorial?'

'It's that big British museum – a museum of the Raj – in Calcutta. Big marble statue of Queen Victoria out in front. One day I got back from breakfast and found him missing. For three weeks he had not stepped out of the door. I traced him to the temple at the end of the road. The priest said a short, plump, silent man, rather exhausted, had stood there for two hours listening to *bhajans*. He turned up at the end of the day, chatting like a tourist about the Victoria Memorial. "I had a lovely view of Calcutta from the balcony," he said to me. Then he was different, insisted I should return to Delhi and meet you.'

Just then Anu entered. 'Oh, you're back,' he said. He held the burden of her disgraced departure from the house, and now her return; she had forgotten both. She was full of kindness, she wanted to put her hands out and soothe him, to be gentle about the impossibility of return. 'Anu,' she said, 'This is Dr Ranjit Dhawan. He's just come from Calcutta; my father is in trouble and he wants me to see the Red Cross authorities here.'

Anu's face turned from anxiety to familiar patterns of knowledge. His father-in-law must have been quarrelling again; it had happened before. He was too polite to talk of it before a complete stranger. 'Give me the letter in the morning. I'll speak to my father and Chaman Bajaj - they know all the powerful people here.'

'No, no,' she said, 'I'll have to do this on my own.'

'Spend the night here, Dr Dhawan. It's too late to go out now.'

138

16
Assessments

It began as a dance, the slow advent of music into her life which she had never heard before. Her father-in-law's dogs were quiet, the ferocious Great Danes housed in a shed leaning against the house to protect it from the entry of disruptive creatures like herself. They fell silent the night she returned from her journey into the night to find Ranjit waiting at the door with her father's long, rambling letter in his hand. Their furious sounds, material of nightmare, faded into the rising passions of the dance. Its new, beautiful rhythms knotted her up and drew her out, strangely and irretrievably, from the grey, undifferentiated, silent mass of her pre-birth existence, forming features, adding fingers and toes, completing the creature.

But she was not rid of Chaman Bajaj. He had closed over her life like a hound; his teeth were firmly set upon her. She could not shake him off with her alibis.

Anu was checking out her alibis, too. He found her car with its dirty purple patch on one side, standing in front of the Red Cross offices, her college on the campus, all the places where she was supposed to be. Still he was frantic with anxiety, as if he sensed the strong, dangerous drum-beats which were drawing her life into a dance. He overwhelmed her with time and attentions, even love. But it was too late. She had begun to leave him from the moment he had sent her out alone into the night.

Chaman Bajaj was not so easy to fool. He knew most secret things, as if from evil instinct. He saw her possessed and happy, and he set out to discover what it was all about.

Anu was nothing like Chaman Bajaj; he did not want to destroy her. She felt affection for him, and a kind of gratitude, but no love. Not the kind of rage which possessed her whole being for Ranjit. She didn't even have to look at him, and she desired him. She stood under the trees of Lodhi Gardens with him, losing all sense

139

of time and reason, drawn into the thunder of bird-calls as they nested at dusk.

But there was a soft under-belly to her passion – Sohail, her five-year-old son. She was playing with his life.

Anu had not found her out yet, wrapped like a mouse in the love-nest of her uncle's house, within walking distance of Daulat Ram Hospital where Ranjit worked. He would be greviously hurt, but he would survive the knowledge. What would happen to Sohail, however? He was wide-open, utterly vulnerable.

Her skin with its darkening talents was worrying her, too. The way it steadily responded with bruising effect to whatever happened. She would become so black that one day she would just disappear into the night. No one would see her again. At one time that had been what she had wanted. But now she wanted to live, to change things, instead of just watching them happen from behind the dark cowl of her skin.

17
Working with Ranjit

After several phone calls, spaced over two weeks, Colonel Bhalla, Assistant Secretary at the Red Cross Office, had agreed to see her. She went to fetch Ranjit from outside his consulting room in Daulat Ram Hospital.

She sat on a bench with crowds of people who held slips of paper which numbered them for entry into various consulting rooms. A bunch of men crowded at Ranjit's door, comparing numbers on their slips. Now and again they parted ranks with enormous reluctance to permit a person without a slip to pass through, recognising priority on grounds of personal contact with the doctor. She felt guilty about taking him away from so many patients. 'How will you leave all these people waiting here for you?'

'I'll leave them,' he said.

'What's the matter? You look annoyed.'

'I've signed double slips for Ampicillin, Betnesol and malaria serum, several of them, this morning.'

She had been in hospitals before and had recognised the odour of pain, fear and disease. But walking with Ranjit through the corridors, details sprang alive for her. She was aware of them as never before. Ranjit was putting a different pressure upon her darkening skin.

They stood outside the main gate of the hospital to hail a three-wheeled scooter. A cold wind made her pull her shawl closely around her. Ranjit was under clad for the weather, and the thinness of his body offered him no protection against the coldest month of the year in Delhi. They waited beside a food kiosk. A stove stood on the counter, with an enormous *karhai* of sizzling oil. A man was frying *samosas* and *pakoras*, straining off the oil through a blackened spatula and piling up the hot stuff in large aluminium trays. A delicious, crisp smell came to her through the air, the smell of perfect happiness.

'I'm hungry,' she said. 'Will you eat a *samosa?*'

'You mean that stuff? You eat rubbish from the roadside?'

'Yes, and I also eat that stuff.' She was pointing to the *chabri-wallah*'s two baskets under the tree, displaying different kinds of *gram*, peanuts, puffed rice and *gur* toffee, arrayed around a central pile of unshelled peanuts, smoking and hot under small clay pots of burning coals. She bought a bag of nuts, shelling them as they walked.

Small, half-naked children, crying from cold and hunger, ran around them. The heel of her sandal caught on a stone and she almost fell. Ranjit's arm shot out to hold her.

'Do you think we will ever live together, Ranjit?'

'I don't know,' he said, looking at her. 'I certainly hope so. I feel as if I had come home to you.' His words slanted a bit, their accent slightly different, from years of living in Nairobi.

Colonel Bhalla turned towards them when they entered, presenting his double chins, slow eyes and short, dyed black hair. A file labelled 'Brigadier P.S. Chahal', already dog-eared, with a number on the top, lay before him on the table. He was waiting for her.

'Please sit down Mrs Whig,' he said. But he was looking at Ranjit. 'Is this your husband?'

'No,' she said. It annoyed her to have to explain. 'This is Dr Ranjit Dhawan, staff physician at Daulat Ram Hospital.' Years of training in protocol, in saying what was expected, what people wanted to hear, made her go on, clearing the way for social propriety. 'He was with my father in Kalidiggi and knows the whole case well. In case you have questions.'

'Well, what can I do for you?'

She was looking at his round belly and dimpled arms under rolled-up sleeves. 'Perhaps you know something of the facts already,' she said. 'It's about my father. He was commanding the Red Cross Hospital in Kalidiggi.'

'I know your father,' he said. 'I'm from the Army Medical Corps myself. Served with him for two years in Jabalpur.'

'Oh,' she said. This man had probably seen her as a child. 'My father was arrested on a charge of attempted murder, he's a victim of conspiracy. We don't know how many people are involved; a lot of money has changed hands, but it's worse than that. Perhaps espionage. The whole thing needs to be investigated.'

'It will be investigated. We have some papers already.'

'Who will do the investigation?' Ranjit asked. Colonel Bhalla turned to him, obviously wondering why Ranjit Dhawan had spoken.

'Mr Ajit,' he said.

'Mr Ajit!' Ranjit's voice shot out angrily. 'That's wrong. He might himself be involved!'

'Please be careful what you say. Mr Ajit is a very senior official. He will conduct this investigation.' Colonel Bhalla's voice was cold and inflexible.

'And what about my father? What will you do for him? He's been victimised because he interfered with conspiracy.'

'I don't know about conspiracy. Papers in the file don't mention it. I think your father's statement is here, too.'

'Can I see the statement?' Ranjit said.

Colonel Bhalla was annoyed. 'Don't you know these are official papers? I can't just hand them over to you.'

'Why not?' she asked. She was amazed; she had never ventured forth like that. 'My father has been charged with murder. We have to do something.'

'Yes. It was foolish, the way he did things. Forgive me saying so, you are the daughter of an old colleague, but why did he get into this mess? We kept telling him to leave, but he stuck on stubbornly. You see, it raises all kinds of suspicions. If there was a conspiracy, people might think that perhaps he was part of it.'

Ranjit rose like a wave from his chair, as if his body had been pushed out involuntarily. He was tense and stiff, stretched like a rope. 'What! The Brigadier a part of all that? It's a cruel joke. This murder charge will destroy him. The least you can do is to get him off.'

'I don't at all see how you come into this, Dr Dhawan.'

'I was with him the whole time. I know he is not guilty of any of those things. You can't just leave him to rot in Calcutta!' He was shouting now.

'Please leave this office.' Colonel Bhalla's plump, pear-like body, the soft pouches under his eyes, were quivering like a jelly.

She wanted to walk out with Ranjit, to put her arm around his shoulders. There was something very exposed and vulnerable about his emotion. Then she remembered the receipts and his own account of what had happened, neatly typed out and folded in her handbag. She whispered to him to wait outside for her.

She handed over the receipts to Colonel Bhalla. 'Dr Dhawan loaned 6000 rupees to my father, to pay the salaries of the hospital staff. The Red Cross must reimburse him for the amount. I'm sure my father has mentioned it in his statement of the case.'

'It sounds irregular. How will you explain to Audits that we are clearing Brigadier Chahal's debts?'

'I don't care how you do it. They're not his debts. Nobody sent him money to pay the staff.'

'Besides, how did Dr Dhawan have so much money at that time? How did he hand it over with no surety? People don't do things like that. I'm sure there's more to this than meets the eye.' He went on, 'And why should I take this note from him? We haven't asked him for his explanation.'

'Keep it, anyway. It gives a complete account.' She was surprised at her own unconciliatory attitude. She had abandoned politeness.

Outside, Chaman Bajaj stood on the grass, haranguing some construction workers, his back towards the Red Cross offices. She was startled; she had not seen him since the night of their quarrel.

'It's strange,' Ranjit said. 'Makes me think of Father Sherifis, turning up outside the District Court in Maldah.' The same band of evil ran from one to the other, like a fiery ribbon wrapping up the space underneath. She had trouble shaking off the effect of Chaman Bajaj's presence.

'I don't think Colonel Bhalla will help. He seems to have made up his mind already. Maybe I should write to the head of the Red Cross.'

'Do you know her?' Ranjit asked.

'No, but I've seen photographs. Miss Pratibha Anand. Tall, frail, with dark shadows under her eyes. She's still beautiful and wears a flower in her hair. Maybe you don't know about her, since you grew up in Nairobi. We learned about her in class, as children. Part of the Freedom Struggle – she worked in villages to organise people for the long *morchas*. She belongs to a different time, an earlier generation.'

'Where shall we go now?' Ranjit asked. Slowly she shook off the picture of Chaman Bajaj standing outside the Red Cross offices. There must be something to use against him and Father Sherifis, some protection against their insidious evil.

Delhi belonged to her. Ranjit was a visitor and was depending on her. She would draw him slowly into the city. Time stretched out, whole, fruitful, waiting for them.

The large, black dome of Rashtrapati Bhavan was before them. A beautiful, spreading building and wide gravelled paths laid out in splendour. They could see it through high, open gates, at the end of a straight avenue leading from the hospital. Trees were thick on either side. Here was a heart of democracy, North and South Avenues, where the MPs lived – Parliament House and the wings of the Secretariat buildings, turning out laws, plans, decisions and projects, the central bus stop, disgorging human beings, or sucking them in, carrying them in buses, in lines which radiated outwards from this centre. There was movement, going back and forth to far corners of the country, feeling out its edges, and then back here. Trussing up the country firmly, like her own body kept inside its skin, given a definite shape and identity, its wealth consolidated, its weakness, like slowly splitting cells, carefully concealed in a mass of flesh and blood.

'My uncle has a flat in Talkatora Road which he is waiting to rent out. Meanwhile I have the keys. My typewriter is there. It's where I work and study. There are too many guests at home. Also, some of us are trying to form an Anti-Dowry Organisation; we meet there from time to time. We're working on a Bill which we hope to have an MP present to Parliament.'

The flat had the damp smell of occasional occupation. Its untidiness did not worry her at all; she was content and peaceful to be with Ranjit, in the circle of his presence. He sat opposite her at

144

the rickety table which held her typewriter. 'I think I'll write Miss Pratibha Anand a formal letter, asking for an interview.'

'No,' he said. 'Maybe you should tell her why you want to see her.'

'But how to put it down? So difficult to formulate. I can't say "I want to see you to tell you why you should help my father who is booked for murder." The whole thing seems too far away, here in Delhi.'

'You have to think out the words,' he said. 'I am only a doctor, I've told you the story.' There was no indulgence to be had from him. She would have to do this herself.

'Delhi catches everything and rolls it together. There are so many streams flowing in here; it is the capital city.' He was looking out of the window, waiting for her to get on with her work. He had put responsibility firmly in her lap.

'You are a stream, too,' she said. 'You wandered out, stayed away, and now you have brought your riches back. Indians going out and coming in, so many streams going back and forth. So many talents, so much work, adding up all the time.'

Her words were only chipping away at the surface of things. 'Will you take me?' he said. It was growing between them like a sequined cloud, rubbing against them, pushing them together. Then he was making love to her where she was, and they saw nothing, neither the bed, the floor nor the table. She knew nothing except his hard desire against her. She was drawn at last into the yellow centre of the laburnum tree, into the silence of the jungle. Then he was coming inside her, his mouth opening in a scream which ran like a primal mass into her neck. His whole body shook and shuddered with it, she put her arms around him, holding him against the violence of it, comforting him for the loss and gain of everything. This was perfection; she would never go beyond this.

Then he was lying beside her, caressing her, whispering into her ear. 'I am making love to you; I am going back into your whole life, drawing it all here, to this point, and then forever, beyond time. Your whole life is lying here beside me; it is all real. I give you the freedom of that. From here you are released, you can go wherever you want, but I will never leave you. My love, my sweetheart, my child. Everything. All the love.'

Her life was springing out into his arms, spreading all over him, flowing up and down North and South Avenues, circling Rashtrapati Bhavan. This time it was different. She had gone to the past, the present and the future, yet had always come to a point where she had stood disconsolate and cut off from everything. Like the streams which flowed in and out of India, bringing in their wealth, depositing their sediment, going away but leaving traces behind, adding to the thickness of history.

A child stood at the Teen Murti traffic circle, three large bronze statues of soldiers at the centre of a grassy area guarding the exit from the Prime Minister's house. She lived near by, at the edge of South Avenue with her uncle who was an MP. At night she dreamed of the Prime Minister sleeping just beyond the hefty, expressionless figures of the soldiers. He was wrapped in the shelter of beautiful trees. The smell of flowers crept up from his garden, through the window, caressed his eyes and prepared him for work. Every morning she stood at the edge of the road, to watch his shiny black Ambassador car pass up South Avenue on its way to Parliament House. On exceptionally lucky days he turned towards her, looking through the window, his face spread out behind the glass, his kind lips closed and distant. The rest of the day would then drop from that high point, straight over the edge of a cliff to the sea of night.

Her uncle Satinder had said that he and the Prime Minister worked in the same building. 'Do you see him then, sometimes? Like, from close by, does he pass near you?'

Her uncle had laughed, as if that were the most natural thing in the world and not a miracle at all. 'Of course,' he had said. 'We often sit at the same table. He talks to me; we discuss things. Oh, there are other people, too.'

Was it in that moment of time that she had chosen Satinder as one of her fathers, her heart going out in a hot, breathless wave of natural selection? What a journey it had been, this collecting of fathers, incorporating them, until now, with Ranjit her lover. What a distance, from the moment of birth and confusion, the mixing up of fathers. Who was her father, white man or Indian? Her darkening skin, moving from pink to brown and black, had fooled them all, confusing them; there was no way of telling which one had shot his genes into her, had bestowed the original patrimony. Then she had lost both fathers. The white man withdrew across the ocean, on his own ship, and the brown man went from the presence of his love for her. Now Ranjit was all the loves. This was the final point, perfection, though she could not lay it out as landscape, with trees and flowerbeds, streams and little hills, picked out and

146

discernible to the eye. But there was no going beyond him, this was a cul-de-sac, the road's end. She drowned in this love. It was releasing her to live as herself, without fathers.

The first time she heard the Prime Minister criticised it was as if the three bronze soldiers, outsize and calm, had splintered with one stroke of a giant hammer. The occasion came tumbling out in a clear package, perfectly formed, no fuzzy edges, all details sharp and distinct. She was coming home from school, standing in the aisle of a DTC bus, balanced on the balls of her feet, barely holding on to the rails of a seat beside her, casual, in a style fashionable at that time, moving slightly, turning, to offset the lumbering motion and heavy turns of the bus, the criss-crossed pattern of aluminium sheeting spread out under the soles of her white sneakers. Then, through the crowd and jumble of hot afternoon traffic, she had heard his voice.

A man was talking to his neighbour a few seats ahead. His words were blotted out, she could not remember them exactly. But it was a criticism, something to do with the Chinese Aggression, and a failure. Had the shattering of fathers begun then, the peeling off of layer after layer of trust, moving out from the hot nests of love? And yet here she was, watching Miss Pratibha Anand with the same child's eyes of hope and belief, as if at the side of the road, in a shadow of statues, looking at a black Ambassador, and an honest, tired face at the window. Believing that she would take care of everything and that one could trust her.

Miss Pratibha Anand wore a flower as usual, white, spangled against her frail wisps of hair drawn into a bun with black scaling pins. She sat at a shining office desk. Krishna was opposite, telling her the whole story of Brigadier P. S. Chahal, omitting nothing, pretending nothing, not making out a case at all. This woman was natural and human; she had the strength to be real. There was no place for cant in the short space and opportunity for them. Miss Anand asked a few questions, doodled on the paper in front of her, a house with smoke coming out of the chimney, a curving path leading to the front door, and a dog behind a bus in the front garden. Then she became irritable, impatient and rough as more and more details unfolded before her. She buzzed her telephone, called in an aide. Her voice exploded in short white spurts, like cannon smoke seen behind a hill.

'What's all this nonsense going on in Calcutta?'

She pushed her chair back, and walked with Krishna to the door, her feet kicking out her sari in front of her. 'We'll see what we can do,' she said. Then, amazingly, she put her arm around Krishna's shoulders. It was the faintest touch, light, airy, as if dropping a mantle over her.

18
An Old Woman

Then came the time of waiting. There was nothing to tell Krishna which direction Miss Pratibha Anand's instructions would take, or whether there had been any instructions at all. Her shoulder retained the feeling of the light touch; something had passed on to her. Was it a mission, had Ranjit cleared the way for this to happen?

Meanwhile his presence began to burgeon into Delhi, to replace its tombs and monuments, its gardens where lovers met and, of course, her uncle's flat in Talkatora Road, patrimony of her elected father, sweet heaven. She wondered if the Mughal Emperors had ruled in Delhi, only to leave behind these tombs and gardens. Once, returning from Humayun's Tomb, she idly considered a proposition to induct the emperors into her growing company of fathers. But there were too many of them; they would swell the ranks immeasurably. So she kept to Ranjit, content and delighted to be drawn like a thread, round and round the bobbin of his heart.

All the *malis* and *chowkidars* of Delhi turned out to watch them, as well as all the old women who sat near monuments with huge clay pots of water balanced on wooden rings, waiting to dole it out to grateful visitors. At the gate of Humayun's Tomb, there was one who had heavy breasts, phenomenally large, spread over her chest in the huge advancing flotilla of her years. She wore dark, loose *churidar*-pyjamas, a thin muslin *kurta* and a dirty grey *dupatta* over her head. Her face was familiar, with a strong grey moustache and hairs sprouting from a mole on her chin. There was something about the way she sat, all spread out and dominating the scene

148

around her, or the way she moved her head slightly to follow Krishna and Ranjit's passage down the straight path, through the Elephant Gate, to the Tomb. Her gaze was glittering and inveterate, despite the ridiculously high tip Krishna had given her for a glass of water.

Krishna was close to Ranjit, sucked to his side like a new bride, glorious in her discovery of touch, wanting to press each square inch of her recalcitrant, desperate, darkening skin to his flesh, to rub her neck against his hard, encircling arm, feel his fingers in the roots of her hair, nuzzle the smells in the tender confines of his ear.

'Everyone can see that you are my lover,' he said, delighted at the thought, which sprang in a gratuitous wave from the surface of his ecstasy, the roofless delight of an exile. And she, skinless, without father or mother, in doubt about her country, Paros or India, she could belong anywhere, and she belonged nowhere; she belonged to Ranjit, an uprooted tuber he had drawn to his flesh, dragged from a still-life portrait, where she had been held with other vegetables on the kitchen table, seemingly fixed forever in a painted identity.

But the old woman's eyes went between her and Ranjit, prising them apart and sowing seeds in every small place they could find, which sprouted, bore fruit and leaves, a veritable beanstalk which grew and grew, threatening to strangle them. Krishna knew then why the old woman was familiar. She was the seed of corruption, present at every moment of betrayal. She would be there when Poonam was blown up by a grenade, when Ram Adhikari was shot dead, when Bhim Lal Whig was murdered in Sheetal Square in Jullundur. What had kept her from Kalidiggi, and from engineering the Brigadier's death? After all, she was a professional like Chaman Bajaj. War increased her excitement and opportunity. The prurient marshy land of the Hospital was her natural territory, the situation ripe for her consumption, like Maldah mangoes.

Yet the Brigadier survived. Ranjit received a reimbursement of 6000 rupees from the Red Cross, with a receipt 'to be signed and returned for our records.' They received good news from the Brigadier at the end of a long stream of telegrams. He always sent telegrams, their short, garbled language was almost his natural expression. The last telegram said that the murder case against him had been closed, thank you both. For your good efforts, wishes, love, Father. The first, perhaps the only one, to bracket her and

Ranjit together. He was released, his shotgun returned. He went back to Dagra.

What had kept the heavy-breasted woman out of her natural habitat, the threatre of war? Was it something in the Brigadier himself, naive, stubborn and full of nothing? Or was it the presence of Ranjit that had protected the Brigadier?

But Ranjit could not protect himself.

He and Krishna visited Humayun's Tomb in Delhi, walking up its perfect Mughal garden with dry channels between the paths, where, in better days, fountains rippled and poured, bringing water from the Jamuna river. They entered one of the little rooms which led off from the central portion of the main tombs. Ranjit was in the corner himself, kneeling on the stone floor. Shadows of the room collected round him, his face was grey, he was breathing deeply, as if the betrayed spirit of the last Indian Emperor struggled behind his eyes. She was spread-eagled and alone against the wall of the room, embarrassed and fearful, until he pulled her down beside him, and the open war of history went through her, thundering through the pitiful confines of her skin.

The heavy-breasted woman was upon them, yelling. 'What do you think you are doing in this dark room, in that corner? This is a tomb, a holy place, a place for meditation. This is India, not London or California. You have to behave like good Indians here.'

Krishna was struck dumb, her voice tied into acute knots. Ranjit's voice was gentle, still suffering from the stream of Bahadur Shah Zafar. 'Who are you?'

'I am the *chowkidar*. And I say you two have no business here.' But her voice was quieter.

'Why? What are we doing? We are just sitting here.'

She could see that now, her beady eyes had adjusted to the darkness. There was no hanky-panky here, no fondling of breasts, no exposed members, not even kissing or touching. She was foiled, her voice blustering. 'Get out,' she said. 'Go from here, at once.'

Krishna later discussed the old woman who had masqueraded as a *chowkidar*.

'I almost expected her to carry her heavy breasts into my staff meeting this morning,' she told Ranjit one day. She was snuggled beside him, rubbing her hand against his skin.

'It was an emergency meeting, called by the Principal to discuss the "Situation arising from the illegal and unseemly behaviour of Shri Dalip Mehta, Lecturer in Economics." I had to rush to college from the bus stop. All the time I was expecting to see the big-breasted woman, a kind of shadow. I looked for her among the chairs against the walls, at the table where the Principal sat. But she wasn't there. She didn't need to be – Chaman Bajaj was enough. He represented the Board.

'We knew the real situation, despite the Principal's summary. A *mali* dismissed because he had refused to work on the Principal's private farm, and Dalip on hunger strike to have him reinstated.

'So long as his hunger strike was at the Boat Club, the Principal had not worried. She had good administrative reasons for terminating the *mali*'s services. Now Dalip was shifting to the College premises. The Karamcharis' Union would gather around him. Maybe even some of the teachers. And he was popular with students.

'My eyes were on Chaman Bajaj, wondering what he would do. People spoke for a while. Nobody dared suggest that the Principal should do what Dalip wanted. Chaman Bajaj terminated the meeting abruptly. "When Mehta comes here, have him thrown out physically. Don't let him enter the premises. We cannot have him dying in splendour in the courtyard, spitting into the lily-pond."

'The Principal seized upon this. "I take it the staff meeting supports this line of action." And she brought the gavel down. Subsequently the Principal's *goondas* threw Dalip out, beat him up, and broke his leg in three places. He is in the All India Institute now, his leg stretched out in traction. Not only that, but they have issued a dismissal notice against him and have lodged a report at the police station for illegal trespass on college premises and causing disturbance on the campus.'

'You opposed the decision?' Ranjit asked.

'I! What could I do? Against Chaman Bajaj? Besides, guess who is the Principal's lawyer? Anu! He is known to be one of the best young lawyers in the city.'

'Anu! Can't you speak to him? Tell him not to take this case?'

'It won't work. His principles are clear; the case should be strong on legal points. The morality of his client is for the judge to decide.'

'But what did you do?' Ranjit asked again.

She stopped and stared at him. It had never occurred to her that she could do something. 'Nothing,' she said. Reverberations from her answer went back and forth. Hitting against her skin with the dull thud of a drum, raising echoes.

A message from Mr Surjit Singh Markand, Deputy Conservator of Intelligence, was waiting for her when she got home. Anu was out when he came. She was glad not to have to explain Mr Surjit Singh to him. Her mother's lover. She could not pass on the pain in her skin. Would she one day pass on her skin itself to Sohail her son, as his inheritance? Let him take from her the burden of its darkening. Could her skin one day let her go, release her from its bruising pressure, let her return to rosy innocence, to the white curtains of ignorance which had hung about her? She would hide with Ranjit behind them, draw him in with her. After all, how much longer could she go on darkening like this? One day she would disappear altogether. She was afraid of that. Even Ranjit wouldn't be able to see her then.

Meanwhile Mr Surjit had been her mother's lover. Ex-lover? Why go into all that? Everything did not have to be clear, Anu was not asking questions any more, not chasing her or tracing her movements. His anxiety about her love was at rest, secure again, his attentions had fallen off. She did not have to sum up and formulate to provide him with answers. But she could not be sheltered in her skin again, like before, not since she answered Ranjit. 'Nothing,' she had said, 'I did nothing about Dalip Mehta.'

She met Mr Surjit in her uncle's flat on Talkatora Road, the scene of rendezvous and of farewell. Her own father had taken the shelter of this house from her, had willed it to her brother. 'Who leaves an inheritance to daughters?' he had said. So she used the borrowed patrimony of her uncle's flat. Women, they said, were born opportunists, making something from nothing, stitching together a patchwork quilt to cover their nakedness, making things for their unfathered loneliness.

She had not seen Mr Surjit since the time the Brigadier had been in Sikkim, when he had visited the Brigadier's family in their barrack quarters often, taking the children out for ice-cream. What else? What did he do? He had still been handsome then, his hair silver-grey and thick, falling in a smooth, unparted wave to his neck, his skin slightly soft and wrinkled, his lower lip protruding and heavy, his eyes bright with information. Deputy Conservator in the Intelligence Service.

'Ranjit Dhawan is a friend of your father's?' he asked.

'What do you know about Ranjit?'

'It is my business to know. What is Ranjit to you?'

Was he talking to Sonia's daughter? Wheat fields were in his mind, crushed stalks, and the tops of eucalyptus trees puncturing the blue sky above their heads. 'Chaman Bajaj has been talking to us, Krishna,' he said slowly.

'Chaman Bajaj?' An anxious fear was in her heart. 'Uncle Surjit. What do you want to say?'

'I know you have a relationship with Ranjit. And that he saved your father. I have no business to be telling you this. It's a professional secret. But one has other obligations.'

She said, 'I must fetch Ranjit. He's very close by, in Daulat Ram Hospital. It won't take any time at all. Please.' She could not bear the heaviness alone.

Uncle Surjit was waiting when they returned. Ranjit made a sign of recognition. 'This is Mr Surjit,' she said, wonderingly.

'I had forgotten your face,' Ranjit said to him.

'Do we know each other?'

'I was part of a refugee camp in Jullundur, straight after Partition – you were in charge of the camp. On Republic Day, 26 January 1950, you made a speech and someone distributed sweets. That was my best function in camp. Soon afterwards, my family went to Nairobi.'

They waited a while. Mr Surjit was remembering a foreign woman, blonde and fair as a goddess, with blue eyes and a blue satin suit, a beautiful child with curly, black hair and a rosy skin nestled beside her. It was the day he had first met Sonia and her daughter, Krishna.

'What do you want to tell us?' Krishna asked him.

'The Brigadier is off, all charges dropped. Miss Pratibha Anand's instructions. But her power has faded, she cannot protect completely, so they've got another scapegoat – our friend Ranjit. The investigation's been done in double-quick time. The evidence is complete; he is to be arrested. This means sure indictment, and twenty years in prison for treason in war time.'

'But what is the evidence?'

'That he had large sums of money with him, some of which he gave the Brigadier to pay the doctors. That he was seen with Father Sherifis, who, incidentally, has been expelled from the country. That he was seen in the Mukti Bahini Camp a day before it was blown up by a mysterious bomb. And that he was using a Red Cross jeep to cross army lines.'

'But he was with my father!'

'Nobody's mentioning the Brigadier any more, thanks to Miss

Pratibha Anand. It's as if he didn't exist. Now they're out for Ranjit.'

'What shall we do, Uncle Surjit?'

'I had thought only to warn you, but now I'll make some arrangements. Bombay. It's a big city, easy to disappear in. He will have to go underground, perhaps for many years. You must prepare for that.'

'How?' she asked Ranjit later. 'I don't know how it will be tomorrow or any single day after you have left. Your absence will just arrive, new and fresh. Nothing in my life, no knowledge, not even the strength of your love, can prepare me to cope with that.'

'What does coping mean?' Ranjit asked, 'or survival?'

'But you have opened a passage into me, an air-vent through which the world flows, back and forth. I don't think that will close now.'

'It should not,' he said.

'And you? What will happen to you. How will you take it?'

'I'll stay like a child in your belly,' he said. 'I'm at home there, with no more exile. You've grown up. It's your responsibility. No more searching for fathers.'

Krishna said, 'Miss Pratibha Anand's power does not work any more. The new generation's here, to balance her out, neutralise and overturn her. Her strength came from her own life, in her own time. But that's over now. She's outstripped. She's the old moon with the new moon in its arms.'

'There must be others to take over. People like you, Krishna. There's you.'

'Yes, I suppose we're all grown up now.'

'There's a lot more growing to be done, Krishna. You can be a leader. There's work for you to do.'

'What do you know?' she asked.

'Only what you know already,' he said. Then he took her in his arms. She could feel a cold clinging in them, a fear of absence, a knowledge of intermittent spaces in love. But through it all was a curious, lovely hope. It was the empty drop into freedom.

19

A Journalist's Account of Krishna Chahal's *Padyatra*

This report is from notes kept by four of us who accompanied Krishanaji from the very beginning, right through the padyatra – *Suryakanthi Tripathi, Dhoomi Rattan Prasad, Gaurav Mishra and myself. In fact, many of the passages are intact. We considered that this way the report would be more comprehensive, and that nothing would be left out. So the 'I' of the Report is really four different people. R. L. Negi merely made a compendium, which is why my name is put as author. I am a Gandhian social worker. I don't want to make false claims to any fame which might come from publishing this Report. I have been asked if Krishnaji is a Gandhian. She, too, has been asked this question. I do not really know her views. I can only tell you what I saw and heard as we went along. She says she does not know enough to belong to any organisation or school of thought. Her* padyatra *was to reach the country and people among whom she lives, to convey her feeling for the trees and hills and a few simple facts which everybody could see around them, anyway. Nothing new. The* Chipko *women had begun the new thing already.*

This long foot-march gave all of us an opportunity for self-education, and strengthened our faith in the wisdom of the common people. We gained more self-confidence, as independent social activists who performed the whole padyatra *without help from any organisation or establishment. Of course, we had the guiding force of Krishnaji to lead us and keep us going.*

We started from Poonch. Krishnaji chose that place, her only personal decision. Her father had been stationed there during the Kashmir action in 1948, and in the history of women in her family someone called Kailash Kaur was connected with Poonch. The decision to start from there was a personal tribute 'to women

155

pressing out against envelopes which hold them,' she said. And it's quite right that this should be a tribute to women. After all, at its heart, the Chipko *movement is very feminist. It consists essentially of a string of spontaneous confrontations, triggered and managed by women of the region, in which none of the so-called leaders were present. In some cases they were struggling against their own men, who saw their immediate economic interest tied up with the decisions of the district administration. In Dungari-Paitoli, for example, the battle was so bitter that it set wife against husband and mother against son. Their men sold off the forest, its destruction would have meant the women walking at least another five kilometres every day to fetch fuel and fodder. The women won, and saved the forest, but only after a long non-violent struggle. They were even threatened with arrest.*

Miss Pratibha Anand was arrested several times, but that was during the Independence Movement. After Independence she lived for many years in the western Himalayas, working among the hill people, before she moved to Delhi to head the Red Cross organisation. We received news of her death just as we were starting off from Poonch. A really saintly woman.

This report would have been much improved and enriched if I had had access to Krishnaji's own notes. Perhaps one day public pressure will persuade her to release her own account of the journey. Meanwhile, this Report is available to all those who might wish to take follow-up action right away, to come forward and begin such programmes to awaken the masses to protect and heal the wounds of Mother Earth.

The *padyatra* began in Poonch, in the State of Jammu and Kashmir. We had given some publicity to Krishnaji's walk through the hill regions, so a small group of journalists, local politicians and forest officials had gathered to see us off. Someone read a message from the Chief Minister. Krishnaji was asked for her own message. We had just heard of Miss Pratibha Anand's death and Krishnaji was quiet. She gestured for me to speak instead.

I was ready. I said, 'We are distressed by the conditions of the Himalayas. The situation is critical. Wounds have been inflicted on the body of Mother Earth through landslides and soil erosion, caused by the cutting down of forests. It has also led to floods and a scarcity of water for drinking, irrigation and power. The problem is not a local but a global one. If we can solve it here we will be able

156

to solve it all over the country and the world. We have nothing but our legs to walk on, and our backs to carry our luggage, so we will walk from Poonch to Srinagar, through Himachal Pradesh and Uttarkhand to Dagra, carrying the message that forests are for soil, water and pure air, and not for timber, resin and foreign exchange.

'We have just heard of the passing away of a great soul, Miss Pratibha Anand, who belonged to the old generation of devoted leaders. She walked in the Himalayas and I am sure in her long walks she must have seen the pathetic sight of the bleeding mountains and overburdened hill women. Fortunately, in spite of their hard life, the hill women in Uttarakhand region revolted against the exploitation of Nature and showed us a new light through the *Chipko* Movement. This light is in our hearts, and we carry it with us as a religious devotion and love of Nature.'

Krishnaji was restless and uncomfortable. Perhaps I said too much. We set off for Srinagar immediately afterwards, where we attended a small function organised by the Ecological Society. We assembled in Rajbagh Extension, quite close to the Canal. The Society is poor and has no office of its own. A lawyer had loaned us his house for the occasion. He himself stood at the edge of the small group, listening intently to Krishnaji, as if he believed everything she said. He was Shri M. B. Hussain, now Member of Parliament from Jammu and Kashmir, and one of the chief exponents of the new Forest Policy which the Government is trying to develop. He is leading a crusade against forest contractors in Kashmir.

It was drizzling so we stood in the verandah with our rucksacks at our feet. A message was read out from the Governor. We were to begin our journey from Srinagar with the good wishes of government leaders, scientists, journalists and others, all of whom were convinced that forests were not for felling.

'There is not much to tell you,' Krishnaji said, 'since my journey has just begun. Just a few simple facts to bring to your notice. A forest is a society of living things, of which the tree is the greatest. Big and small trees of different species in a forest, and grasses, bushes, herbs, insects and animals, form a vast, complex entity that offers human beings a range of natural resources for their use. For their economic and social growth, and to meet their material and spiritual aspirations. One leading forestry expert told me: "Forestry is not, in essence, about trees, it is about people. It is only about trees in so far as they serve the needs of the people."

157

'There are divergent philosophies with respect to the use of forests. Some leaders are fiercely ecological in their approach and regard the regreening of forests as the top priority. They say the self-sufficiency of hill people in food, clothing and shelter is important, but secondary to the major ecological objectives. They are suspicious of all types of forest-based industries, including those set up by local people, and want commercial green felling stopped altogether and no new contracts entered into with industrialists to supply raw materials.

'For others the search is for a new eco-development process, so that while the environment is preserved, the benefits of controlled exploitation accrue to the local people. They say that saving the trees is only the first step; saving the hill people is the real goal.

'I don't know which is the right belief. Perhaps you have already worked this out for yourselves. I know only that there is probably no other area of India's environment that has been more viciously attacked and destroyed in the last century than its forests.

'I will end with a small story. In the year 1730, a *saka* was offered by a band of Vishnois of Khejadli village in Jodhpur, Rajasthan, when their forest was invaded. They were led by Amrita Devi. She tied the first sacred thread round a tree and offered her head, saying that it was too cheap for the price of a tree. Three hundred and sixty-three men and women hugged the trees to save them, and they were hacked to death.'

In the first phase we walked through the beautiful Kashmir Valley up to Daksum. We saw its enchanting beauty, with the slowly flowing Jhelum, and saffron and paddy fields, and willow, poplar and mulberry trees by the road, as well as ornamental trees in the old Mughal gardens – which we had no time to visit because a speaking engagement had been arranged for Krishnaji at Palampur University. She described what we had seen on the way, as if bearing witness. 'When the trees go, the mountains crumble,' she said, and described the effects of a killer landslide which had buried the hamlet of Kranla. We passed it on the Jammu–Srinagar road.

We saw thick forests in the catchments of the Jhelum and Chenab, but as we reached the southern slopes of Chenab Valley the treeline was fast receding and streams had turned paddy fields on either side into spreads of sand and pebble. Suddenly the Chenab Valley was a graveyard of fir, spruce and other conifers. At the confluence of rivulets and on the roadside, logs were piled up and trucks plied day and night transporting timber to Jammu. We heard saw mills buzzing in the virgin forests and cut logs crashing down the hillsides.

We crossed the 12,450 foot high Symthan Pass and walking became difficult over the snow. In the past, the damage of heavy snow falls was minimal, because older trees protected the growing, younger ones. Now there are monoculture timber fields, which allow trees of only one age group to survive. These become victims of any calamity which strikes the mountain slopes. The trees become dried out, and they snap in the wind and snow. Most of the pine trees littering the hillside had not lived even half their expected life span of one hundred years.

We entered into Himachal Pradesh through the 4,000 foot high Padhri Pass, which makes the parting ridge between the catchment areas of the Chenab and the Ravi. We walked there for sixty days, covering a number of villages in Chamba, Kangra, Kulu, Mandi and Simla districts and passing through remote villages far from motor roads, especially fascinating for Krishnaji.

Those who have never walked in the Himalayas picture them as they are shown in geography books, as a single mountain range represented by a fat, elongated caterpillar. In reality they are a vast mountainous district some 1,600 miles long, by at least 200 in depth. The most curious feature is its sharp definition along the southern edge. It terminates abruptly, almost the whole way along the belt, in a ridge varying from 6,000 to 7,000 feet which drops sheer down into the plains of India.

Krishnaji stood on the summit of this outer ridge, looking south over the flat country 5,000 feet below, which stretched far away into the hazy distance. Turning to the north, an endless series of ridges met her eye, line upon line, none seeming higher than the ground on which we were standing, though a spur here and there rose to 10,000 or 12,000 feet. In the far-off distance was a long array of snowy peaks, averaging mostly about 21,000 feet. From that distance, the snows standing up against the skyline were like one long backbone to the Himalayas.

There was always sharply defined contrast. On hill sides facing north, which are shaded from the sun and so retain more moisture, pine forests covered the slopes; on the southern sides, a treeless red soil was covered with short, brown grass, and little lines of terraced fields. Midday light made these slopes hard and ugly, but morning and evening transformed them miraculously. As the sun

159

began to fall, all the brown, water-worn, tree-denuded, herring-boned ridges on the bare mountain sides cast deep blue shadows, as if to veil their nakedness. Flat slopes seemed to start into life as the lengthening shadows revealed each little roughness. Then a sudden softness came over the hard lines; distance became opal in colour, then indigo blue, which passed suddenly into black, and the stars came out in clear, cold points of fire.

At several points Krishnaji stopped to look at the view with intense stillness, as if she were impressing the scene on her memory or taking possession of the mountains. We went down to the Sutlej river, crossing it at a point where it is forced between high banks, and forms a deep, dark green pool above a foaming rapid. The river had already come a long way from its glacier and had lost the grey of snow water; it was a beautiful solid green, rather curious in a mountain river.

We had difficulty climbing up on the other side, because of heat from the sun, combined with the extreme dryness and stillness of the air. But Krishnaji did not seem to feel the effect of the rarefied air. She darted like a deer among the deodar cedars at Jibbi and burst like a small, dark piece of thunder from the deep shades of the pine-woods into the open valleys.

Once we were caught in a mountain storm. Magnificent echoes, repeatedly fed by new clashes, rolled down the mountain side, and were flung to the steep hills opposite, until the whole valley was shaking with billows of sound. By the time we reached the bottom, rain, driving mists and this strange, tumultuous sound, as if we had entered the beating heart of nature, had reduced us to trembling, dwarfed creatures. But Krishnaji was magnificent as ever and delighted.

Then she was enchanted by rhododendrons. She moved in a slow daze among bushes which grew higher than her head, in great masses on the mountain-side above the level of the forests. The flowers were bell-shaped, white and red, with the consistency of wax, their leaves broad and backed with red-brown velvet. We went much higher. Taking our last look at the Kulu valley, we got into the rhododendron forest at Kandi, the top of the Dolchi Pass which leads into Mandi. The rhododendrons here were some of the best of the few now left in the Himalayas. Most of them have disappeared, together with the broad-leaved oak forests. These, however, were a glorious blaze of crimson, with an occasional white flower showing up between them. Some of the trees were twenty-five to thirty feet in height. Seen from above they were one mass of large crimson flower-balls which made the mountain-side a huge flower bed skirted with dark green foliage. Krishnaji was quite lost among them.

Some of the villages we visited were most curious. Manikarn, for example, which lay on the right bank of the Parbati, across a rough wooden bridge, its small cluster of brown houses and temples wedged in on both sides by enormous precipitous hills. A dark shadow was cast all day long over the village by the immense heights opposite, a shadow which disappeared for a short hour at sunset when light streamed straight up the narrow valley. As we approached the village a strange smell of sulphur filled the air, while steam rose in clouds from numerous boiling springs that bubbled up out of the ground. It made me think of hell and destruction reaching out to touch the mountains, though we were told that many travellers come here to wash away their sins in its steaming pools.

We visited Pulga, too, the highest village in the Kulu Valley. After an hour's walk through a thickly-wooded ravine, by the banks of a rushing torrent, we came to an open space. Pulga lay a few hundred feet up, surrounded by magnificent deodar forests. We hurried up the mountain and, rounding a bend, saw the snowy mass of the 11,000 foot mountain above us, towering almost in our faces. It was 3.30 pm, but already the sun had dropped behind a high ridge and had a cast a shadow over the village.

Pulga, with its great white mountain and beautiful deodar trees, was one of the things that Krishnaji spoke of when we finally persuaded her to speak to the women at the Nagar Fair. An ideal opportunity to convey our message. It was a Kulu holiday, and villagers from the hills above and the valley below had gathered for the *mela*. We heard the sound of distant drumming and ear-piercing blasts on their curved trumpets as, gradually, one by one, the village gods were carried in on chairs and stationed towards the edge of the gathering. It was a *Baisakhi mela*, to welcome Spring. The scene was gay, brilliant and noisy. Everyone wore their best and brightest clothes. The women were dressed in soft woollen dresses of white and red, grey and brown, with checks in all colours, bright-coloured handkerchiefs tied over their heads, and their ears, necks and arms heavy with silver jewellery. For a while they wandered around with their children among the booths of sweetmeats, toys and jewellery, then they settled down in rows on the terraced hillside to watch the men dance. An incredibly monotonous dance. I could not understand how Krishnaji could sit amongst the Kulu women for hours that day, just watching the long lines of men with linked arms shuffling back and forth, fuelled with *lurgi*, their special rice liquor, and continuous, unchanging music emanating from drums and trumpets. The women looked at her curiously and then gradually gathered around her, smiling, dividing their attention between her and the dance.

She looked different from them. Her nose was as clear cut as theirs, but an unusual shape, perhaps from her Greek mother, and her eyes were huge and shining. There was a peace in them, which deepened as she sat among the women, watching the dance. As if the stillness and power of the jungle had entered into them. Her skin was much, much darker than theirs, which was fair, or pale olive. They had not seen such a dark-skinned person in those remote areas before.

We urged her to speak to them, but she was extremely reluctant. 'What will I tell them? They know much more about these hills and mountains. It is their life. I don't live here. By being with them for one day, or even some months, I can only enter a little bit of their lives, that's all. I'll speak in Shimla, to people like myself, who are destroying the jungles.'

But we insisted, seeing from the women's faces how much ready response she would get, so she told them about Pulga and Manikaran and how much beauty she had seen in the rhododendron and deodar forests. They prayed together to the village gods sitting in a line there before them, to keep the forest intact, to keep the harmony between humanity and nature. The forests gave them fuel, fodder, wild nuts and roots for their families. Already they had to walk long distances to fetch these things, keeping their children from school to help them carry them back. What would they do, if the forests went even further away from them? She told them of the women of Gopeshwar, in Uttarkhand, and others who had embraced their trees to prevent them from being cut down, and she sang the *Chipko* women's song for them.

The forest is my mother's home,
it gives me food and succour,
do not cut my trees, my friend, my brother,
do not cut away my life.

162

The women giggled at the word *Chipko*, the picture of sticking to trees, so she used another word instead: *angwaltha*. They understood the embracing of a loved one, and they were quiet as they thought of warm summer nights under the trees, of the touch of love, of wrapping themselves in it.

By the time we were walking through the Shimla bazaar and up to the Mall, the town had heard of Krishnaji and her *padyatra*. Journalists had covered it fairly thoroughly. Voluntary organisations had put out questionnaires asking 'housewives/other women' how they felt they could contribute to protection of the environment. Also, news came trickling in from the hill people who spoke of a woman with strange, glowing skin who was walking in their villages, stopping often to talk with them. The woman of the trees, they called her.

Krishnaji was somewhat changed. She no longer hesitated to speak, as if in the months we had spent walking in the forest she had crossed over and now touched something she was ready to offer. She was confident and could assert herself, like a woman of property. For now the mountains and the trees belonged to her, as they do to anyone who will love them. If you love a god enough he will belong to you, she said, and this is the god of Ecology, higher than all the others. Of course she didn't say this in public; she would have been accused of being irreligious, and a leader has to know what to say and how to say it when she speaks to an audience. But to us she often spoke of her innermost feelings. Travelling together for many days in difficult terrain opens each heart to the others, and many things, many obstacles drop away as irrelevant.

Admittedly, the saving of trees and mountains is not the most interesting subject for a town audience. We walked along the ridge above the Mall, to Scandal Point and above, to the flat area where so many 'seditious' speeches had been made against the British when Shimla was still their summer capital. The air was clear and dry. I hoped there would be at least a few people to listen to her.

My lack of faith was belied. There was already a crowd, and it grew larger and larger as she talked. Even her presence, at the very place where so many speeches had been made and *morchas* begun, was strong and somehow alight and it attracted them like a torch.

She spoke of glaciers receding, hill slopes becoming barren, rivers and lakes turning muddy, valleys becoming deserts, water sources drying up and drinking water getting scarce. The Himalaya was geologically young and unstable, subject to periodic seismic shocks that bring down crumbling slopes. In addition, human beings had interfered with the land-water-animal-plant-climate cycle. Forests acted as a sponge, softening the impact of rain and retarding run-off. Now floods and soil erosion were a regular thing.

Then she came to Shimla's immediate surroundings. The hornbeam tree, used all over the state for fodder, was being devoted exclusively to the bobbin-shuttle industry. Two and a half million tonnes of apples were produced per annum. Packing cases for the apple crops came from forest timber. The Kulu Valley, once a picturesque sea of deodars 150 feet in height and 10 feet in girth, was now almost bare. The Chamba Valley, once famous for its honey, was losing its glory. Bees live in a single Semal tree for hundreds of years. Now the bees were leaving.

I looked around me at the people listening to Krishnaji, who stood firmly on a bench, and realised that many of the audience were tourists. This perhaps, was not of much use; they would go back to the plains when the heat became bearable. To act further on the basis of facts we have gathered in the mountain forests, we would have to reach those who pulled the levers of power up here, or in the government at Delhi.

After Shimla we camped at a place called Mira, near a suspension bridge across the Son Ganga, which is the main tributary of the Mandikini. We had seen where they joined, at Sonprayaga. The waters of the Mandikini were extraordinarily clear, almost blue, in sharp contrast to the muddy, greenish aspect of the Alakananda, which meets it at Nandprayaga. Both the Alakananda and Bhagirathi have their source in Uttarkhand, the *Deva Bhumi* or sacred land of the eight northern mountain districts, dotted with *ashrams* and *rishis* and other seekers of peace and worship. For us Uttarkhand is memorable also because it was here that the three chief incidents of the *Chipko* Movement took place – Chamoli-Gopeshwar, Rampur-Phata, and Reni.

As we came down from Rambara, we noticed a distinct change in the surrounding hills. It was the dividing line between mountainous and alpine regions. Above were thickets of bushes and dwarf trees, below a thickening forest up to Gaurikund. Beyond Gaurikund the illegal felling of trees and faulty *lisa* or resin tapping had mutilated the jungle. Even where we saw new plantations, these were of conifers, not the broad-leaved oak forests.

We stared questioningly at the tired, bearded young stranger

164

walking into our camp. He clearly did not belong to these parts. But Krishnaji recognised him right away as M. B. Hussain and greeted him joyfully. He had come down a small road on the right which branched off towards Tungnath, Mandal and Gopeshwar, ultimately joining the Rudraprayag–Badrinath highway. The path climbed steeply above the right bank of the Mandakini, and entered a thick forest of oak and rhododendron with its big red flowers. Though the sun was up, it made absolutely no impact on this heavily shaded forest.

M. B. Hussain and Krishnaji talked in the shadows, long, long into the night.

'I have a friend called Ranjit,' she said. 'He opened up the world for me, let me go out to it, freed me, instead of always being closed up inside my own skin.'

'I don't think I understand,' said Hussain.

'Well, how do I explain. Take these mountains and beautiful trees, all the Himalayan countryside we have been walking over these many days. I feel at last as if they belong to me. Oh, not exclusively, but they do belong. All of India belongs to me. Once I was a woman with no country, no property, no possessions, no relations. Nothing came in to me. Objects and experience, passions and pains, passed over me and left their shadow on my skin, but it was always as if a fur of some kind existed around me and muffled me. Ranjit stripped it off. Left me exposed and vulnerable, but free. And now the mountains and streams and trees and people come into me as if they are really there, not something passed on to me second-hand through the medium of my skin-experience. I'm seeing all these for the first time; they come in to me so fully and wholly. It is the only way things can belong to you without tying you down. They belong to everybody. You can never lose them.'

We were more interested in what M. B. Hussain told Krishnaji: that the biggest auction ever in that area was to be held shortly in Dagra to award a contract for the felling of 20,000 trees in the Tons Division. It was vital to stop it, and only she could do it. The *padyatra* had given her the necessary power, those in authority would be forced to listen to her. The kind of reception she had got in villages along the way, the huge numbers of villagers who had turned out to hear her and who would follow her if she called, were clear indications, even to them, of her popular support. She called us all to attend to this.

She said, 'Let us see how we can do this. First, our demands must seem reasonable. We will ask for a total and immediate ban on tree felling in an area of 1,500 square kilometres for a period of ten years. This will cover the whole Tons Division and beyond. Meanwhile, a committee of experts should study the ecology of the region.'

'This committee idea will really catch on. But how to stop the immediate auction? Once they award the contract it will be difficult to postpone the felling.'

'Only the villagers themselves can do that,' Krishnaji said. 'They've done it before, the ground's been prepared by the *Chipko* Movement. We w··· have to persuade them to travel further than they've done before – to Dagra.'

She was drawing designs on the damp ground where we sat talking, her stick going deeper and deeper into the soft earth below the huge rhododendron bushes.

Hussain went to Dagra to make arrangements.

Krishnaji spoke of the forthcoming auction when we reached Karchi-Regdi, in the Reni area, on the slope of the Kunari Mountain. *Regdi* means landslide in the local language. Krishnaji looked over our heads at a bald, mutilated hilltop which faced us, mute reminder of past landslides. She did not mention the forest auction immediately; instead she talked of the great flood of 1970. A torrential downpour into the catchments of the Alaknanda and its tributaries had swelled the rivers. Seething and swift, they had pulled over their banks and flooded the entire region, taking with them bridges, roads and *bagads*, the small winter fields on the river banks. Fifty-five people had been killed, 142 head of cattle had been swept away, and crops had been devastated. The villagers had good reason to remember the monsoon of 1970.

'Floods are not a natural calamity,' Krishnaji said. 'They are made by human beings. When the forests are cut down the rivers are bound to swell their banks and overflow.'

Then she told them of the proposed auction of trees. 'In the name of those swept away in the Balacuchi flood, I implore you to come to Dagra and tell the authorities that you don't want your trees cut down.'

She repeated her appeal in village after village. Some of the villagers left with us; others caught up on the way; and some went directly to Dagra. By the time we reached there about 3000 hill people had gathered at the outskirts, where Shri Hussain, with the help of students from local colleges, had put up tents and had made

166

arrangements for food and drinking water.

Krishnaji refused to attend a function organised for her by the District Magistrate. She had already had separate meetings with him and other officials responsible for the auction, who had pleaded helpless to even postpone it. Their orders had come from above. 'Then what is the use of speaking to you in a formal function, with garlands round my neck, if you can't do anything?'

The college students whom Shri Hussain had contacted had by now got very involved in the campaign. They were enthusiastic and eager for action. 'We must interrupt the auction forcibly, there is no other way,' they said.

Krishnaji refused to permit this. She got them to paint posters, all of which began: 'For the welfare of mankind . . .' and went on to tell the town about the auction. She spoke at various places, wherever she found about a dozen people standing together, which was not difficult.

'This Himalayan crisis is not an isolated event,' she said. 'It has its roots in our materialistic civilisation of today. The ecological imbalance is the result of the spiral of demands, ever increasing and never satisfied. It is this which has destroyed the harmony between humanity and nature.'

Dagra was in the centre of the holy land. It was familiar with *rishis*, and heir to centuries of worship and renunciation. Its citizens understood very well what Krishnaji was saying. If things had gone a bit further Krishnaji might well have been accepted as a saint at one of the local *ashrams*.

Krishnaji seemed to know the town well: where to speak, where to find printers and stationery and whom to contact. 'My parents live here,' she said quietly, when I mentioned this. 'My son is at school about twelve miles away.' She was so busy she could not even visit them. She fell asleep standing up among the villagers at the camp at night. Her feet still bled from the blisters of the long walk, there were black pouches under her eyes and her voice shook with fatigue.

On the morning of the auction our camp was agog with excitement and anxiety. Day after day we had explained to our hill friends what was being done. Now they were ready, assembled behind us at the Conservation Office where the auction was to be held. Then the townspeople began to arrive, shepherded no doubt by our enthusiastic friends from among the students. Meanwhile the contractors and their men who were to bid at the auction also

167

drifted in. Krishnaji stopped each one at the door and explained our case, handing them a copy of the pamphlet Diwan Singh Chawla had printed for us. It set out the whole case, relating all the facts and figures Krishnaji had conveyed in her talks during the *padyatra*, and repeated our two-fold demand: a ten year ban on the felling of trees in an area of 1,500 square kilometres, to be applied immediately, and a select committee of geologists to go into the effects of deforestation. The contractors took the pamphlets, smirked, shrugged their shoulders and looked away. None of them turned back from their objective.

News came through a *chaprasi* that the auction had begun. It seemed to electrify the gathering, now more than four thousand strong. Spontaneously, without a word, they stood up and began to shift around. Slowly the sound of feet and voices seemed to grow. 'Save the trees, Save the Trees, SAVE THE TREES,' they were chanting together, villagers, students and townspeople. They had now surrounded the office on all sides; the building seemed to have shrunk in size, floating in a sea of faces. I was standing next to Krishnaji. I could feel her body trembling. I knew the thought of possible violence disturbed her intensely. Otherwise her face showed no change; she was quiet and watchful. It was no use trying to control the crowd, her voice would not have been heard above the din.

Just then a shiny black Ambassador car and a line of official jeeps drew up at the edge of the crowd. Shri M. B. Hussain and a minister emerged from the car. The latter was very impressed by the size and determination of the crowd and its devoted chanting. The crowd parted ranks to let the minister through. He negotiated his way to the door of the office and stood beside Krishnaji, who was waving her green-coloured pamphlet. Someone put forward a chair for him and he climbed above the heads. The chanting stopped for him to speak.

'The auction has been halted,' he announced. A wave of clapping greeted him. 'I have read what Krishnaji has said in this book, and I am amazed. The forest is sinking. At this rate, we will soon destroy the mountains, and ourselves. I agree to the demands; no more trees will be cut for ten years.'

20
Transition for Krishna

Krishna had now received the secret of *angwaltha* from the *Chipko* women, their spirit of love reaching her as she walked through the *Deva Bhumi* of Uttarkhand on her *padyatra*. And from Ranjit, who had connected her to a passion for living.

Going out to wrap herself around people, objects and events past and present was nothing new for Krishnaji – the colour of her skin bore witness. Its colour showed the pain and passion it had observed, deepening from a tender, rosy pink of Greek fathers, to the dark perpetual bruise of India, which had put its loves, griefs and beauty to her, and had hung her in dark curtains of its corruption. India's streams and rivers flowed in and out of her, people moving back and forth, taking its wealth to foreign lands, coming back with the spoils and talents of living, from Asia, Africa, Europe and North America.

The other like that had been Lord Krishna, stung blue by a serpent in a brave exploit upon a river, shortly after his birth. He had been dark ever since. He travelled from Mathura in Uttar Pradesh to the plains of Punjab, and affected the fortunes of a great war. A short *yatra*, which took him everywhere, to the whole world.

She drew closer to the passionate, colouring god. His music and enchantments were in her soul, her endless hours of dalliance and love-play, the stillness of Vrindavan, its beautiful trees, the entire wonder of life opening out petal by petal. She still went out in her watchfulness, wrapping herself, squeezing over awkward contours, spreading over the earth like a dark lake, closing over particles like a long, darting lizard tongue. But now it was an *angwaltha*, a warm embrace of the loved one, holding so tenderly and with such infinite contact, as if her life depended on that, in the utter stillness which is at the heart of passion.

Shortly after birth came the octopus tentacles of special rules for her. But with Houdini-powers she could escape from anywhere, even chained in an iron box let down into the sea. She could travel out to others, bound and gagged and fired with life, as naturally as an arm going back in a yawn. Connected thus, touching the world, wrapped with love, she would pirouette in the streets, defiant, like a string of blind men behind dark glasses, each part giving faulty warning to the next, but out in the open air, willing to be assaulted by light. They say Houdini died by drowning, but she was not about to die. Not yet.

One after another her fathers had left her. One travelled across the sea in a ship before she was born; another withdrew his love, as he withdrew his rights, his name and his property when she went to another man in marriage. No matter. She was rich with fathers, gathering ancestors from the air and from history, free to choose, taking what came along. Belonging now to no family she had made her own family of the hill people, a large family, rich, all with different names, each bringing its own wealth.

Denied patrimony, deprived of inheritance, land grabbed from under her feet, she was earning the right to a whole country. Slowly, inch by inch, she was drawing India into her with love. Mother India for the orphaned girl. Her rights would continue to grow. No point stopping with being Lady of the Manor. One day she might be Woman of the World, distinctions blurring between country and country, her skin encasing the whole twirling earth in a faint dark film, visible from space-ships and the dulcet eyes of extra terrestrial beings. Who is this Krishna Chahal, self-created being, separated from chaos by her own skin?

Bombay excited her. Going through the steamy suburbs, past seedy railway sidings, coconut palms, thatched huts, pigeon holes of government housing, the sky cut up and criss-crossed by electricity lines, past the splendour of skyscrapers split into offices and the crawling frontages of tenement buildings, chugging into Bombay Central. There was a particular tenement building where, in a *chawl* in the central section, four flights up, looking over the teeming courtyard with its single water-tap, lived a shrivelled old lady, Ranjit's aunt, cousin of his father, ignored by a family departing to Nairobi in the haste of Partition, fleeing the wrath of refugee camps. She was dug up like a termite, a small, gray Dadar insect, by her exiled, itinerant, hiding, underground nephew, who had found his home with Krishna for a while and then was separated from it like a child slowly distanced from its vision of paradise. A nephew who moved in with the silent button-creature waiting for death because a termite-hole was his own natural habitation, while he darted out to revolutionary trade union activities with Gola Chahal and others. Passing into the great metropolis of Bombay, scene of her Greek mother's arrival in great Mother India, of the biological battle of Krishna's two fathers, scrambling their semen in the relevant female channel, of the departure of the young Ranjit Dhawan and his family for a new life in a distant continent. And scene of his return ten years ago, fleeing from a false case of murder and treason, which had since been dropped, but the knowledge of that cremated in Dagra with the corpse of Mr Surjit Markand formerly of Jullundur and Delhi. It was as if the great city of Bombay released a sack of dreams inside Krishna's skin, swelling it, making it soft and rubbery with expectation, pushing her out with excessive excitement and trembling love to greet Gola who stood at Bombay Central to receive his sister and mother, two women arriving alone for his wedding, sole representatives of his family.

The legal part of the ceremony was simple, a signing of the marriage register in Shalini's home. The heart of the marriage was elsewhere, in a dingy meeting hall in Dadar, where the two associated political organisations, Shalini's Student Body and Gola's Workers' Manch, were to celebrate the wedding of their two leaders.

In the mornings the meeting hall was a school classroom. In the evenings it was rented out to political parties, cultural organisations and feminist groups; it became transformed, taking on the spirit of its occupation. It was directly below an ancient and popular theatre. Frequently, the shuffling feet of the audience and the thump of histrionics from the stage above provided background noise, masking the quiet but well-known activities of spies and informers who hovered at the door of the meeting hall. They were turned away firmly by vigilant office-bearers from both organisations stationed strategically to check out entrants to the hall. Those turned away went skulking down dark corridors between empty classrooms, haunted by the ghosts of reluctant children and scarred furniture, or down the main unlit staircase, the once-polished wood of its broad stairs broken or caving in at various places, waiting to catch the unwary foot, or down one of the several unknown side staircases where a murder could be committed and no one would know for days.

171

Whom did they meet, dodging and darting down one of those side staircases, trampling down those dangerous steps with unseemly haste? Surely if it had indeed been Ranjit Dhawan he would not have been refused entry? Was he turned away? Whom did Krishna see, in a glimpse, turning between dark shadows, that sent her heart beating like a mountain thunderstorm through her breast? Why could she not pursue him down the corridor, draw him back, pull him into her heart, where she had longed for him since the day she was born? Like a fisherman's net going deep down to the floor of the sea, raking up magic treasures, she had brought in fathers, a country complete with streams and mountains, chosen families, even trees, yellow laburnum, gleaming in the heart of light. But before this most important creation, soul of her life, she could do nothing. Her powers to see and connect fell away charmless, her intense magic exposed as a cheap bag of tricks, a sleight of hand merely, a secret hidden in a sleeve. She could not follow him, or even tell whether it was indeed Ranjit she had seen, or only a misty concoction of her dreaming heart, infected by the warmth of her brother's marriage and the pure, patent joy of the occasion.

Happiness had transformed the meeting hall into a long, joyous tunnel, leading to the smiling couple at the end. Their friends had hung the walls of projecting pillars with red flags, bright, varicoloured buntings, photographs of Bhagat Singh, Baba Sampuran Singh, his sister Poonam, other Indian revolutionaries whom she did not recognise, and a bearded Marx, an open-eyed Lenin.

Even Sonia recognised Karl Marx, the picture of a bearded man with full lips and small, intelligent eyes. The communists who had infested her island of Paros during the war carried small pictures of the same man, had handed them out to the children, corrupting their minds, just as if they had been long-robed priests distributing holy pictures of saints and martyrs. Her brother had pointed out the communists to her, nudging her when they passed a wildly gesticulating group of handsome young men. She had thought them harmless and enthusiastic and liked to look at them, until the killings and bombings began, the kidnapping of little children and the blowing up of churches. Then everybody on Paros had hated the communists, a menace to respectable people.

Sonia realised, looking at the buntings, red flags and at the pictures, that her son Gola was a communist. Gola, elixir of her heart, whom she loved more than she had loved Paros, Michael

172

and Paramjit put together, certainly more than her other child, the dark changeling Krishna who had grown reluctantly from her own flesh, half-tying her to this painful country. She had known that Gola was in politics; he did not have a respectable, paying job like Surjit, or a lucrative profession like Anu. But now she knew he would never be able to support her, and that she would never be able to leave Paramjit to live with her son. He was a communist and therefore cut off from her, drawn into a world to which she had no access, in fact its centre. The smiling, buxom woman at his side, his bride, could not separate them as firmly as this fact. Decorations in the hall, the friendly, unknown faces of his friends, adding up like a pyramid towards the couple at the end, made it clear that she was alone, self-enclosed, and now there was no further hope of getting out. No other lover, husband, child or country was permitted to her.

Krishna was alone in her waiting for Ranjit, with the terrifying beating of her heart. Before he left ten years ago, she had had no idea what missing him would mean; his absence meant nothing, she had no information of how it would be. That some days she would wake up with the wonder of life unfolding petal by petal, and she alone at its heart, the single canker. That she would grow heavy with desire. That her limbs, tortured and unmoving, would want to tear it from her like a hair-shirt that grappled and shrank with her. Longing for him, wanting him, was simple only in the purity of knowledge that this was desire, not in the heavy force of its despair. With Ranjit she knew perfection, and she could not go beyond it. There were no alternatives.

There were other men. Hussain, who had helped so much in the *padyatra* and the action at Dagra. She was glad he lived in Delhi now. And Shanta Prasad, who wrote articles and learned reviews for newspapers. He never heard a word she said to him, but she was delighted by his innocent self-absorption. They were drawn by the warm, glowing sensuality which greeted their approach, by the clear, evocative strangeness of the woman behind it and her dark beauty. She knew all that. It was not easy to come back alone from plays, receptions, parties and even from political meetings. Often she wanted the physical comfort of touching another body during her nightmares. It could even have been Anu's. Or to sink simply into a circle of warmth, going deeper and deeper, faster, flailing towards orgasm and release, desire as a rough edge in her flesh fading until the very next time she thought of Ranjit. Just to sink, instead of creating herself, having to stand upright in each moment.

Now she was occupied with taking care of Sonia. Her own resentment, her orphaning, was forgotten in this new *angwaltha* of her skin, its embrace of Sonia. Paramjit Singh Chahal had not come for his son's wedding, pleading a heart ailment. His absence freed Sonia's personality from disturbance and distortion, from the tragedy of terrible interaction with her husband. Krishna was now mother of mothers, gathering up Sonia's wasted life, patting a stardust of nostalgia on her eyelids. Krishna felt more warm and loving towards her mother than ever before in her life.

'Have you been to Bombay before?' Manik, Shalini's mother, made a neat, quiet unit with her husband. Not threatening fumes of hellfire which always hung over Brigadier and Mrs Chahal when they were together. Manik did not really belong in the meeting hall, just as Krishna, smiling, and Sonia, angry, hostile and resentful with betrayal, did not belong there. But she greeted many of Gola and Shalini's friends, recognised through years of attrition and familiarity, as her daughter stayed involved in political work.

'Oh, I know Bombay very well,' Sonia said. 'I had a very grand wedding reception here, shortly after arrival from Greece. At Wilson House, one of the poshest hotels at that time. With a lot of jewellery, a beautiful tissue sari, nice, well-dressed people, a very fine occasion.'

For a moment she was transformed. The ageing, grey woman bent over with spondilitis, eyes dim, face drooping with misery, stood proud and high. She gleamed and glittered, her head tossed, she was blonde and glorious, the beauty of Paros. And her rich lover Michael Stavros stood over her like an archangel, his spear looming, his arms full of gifts and good tidings. Here in Bombay, the stage had been set for the activities of two fathers and one mother. From here a darkening, orphan child called Krishna had gone into the world.

Who had taken her two fathers from her? Was it Mother India, wishing to leave the field wide open for Krishna's choice? But who was responsible for the misery and agony of being without a father? Who had taken his father from Sohail, the son of Krishna? Did fatherless women generally swallow and expel the fathers of their sons, send them shelterless and without love into the world? Was that Sohail's sole maternal inheritance, or could she roll up her darkening skin and slip that in as well, as part of his baggage?

174

Having taken the roof from over his head, the wall from behind his shoulders, the arms which held him up over the crowds, the voice which broke into his dreams to fill them with warm, flowing laughter, could she also give him her way of seeing and surviving? Give him both her curses, her two burdens, her two gifts?

Sonia was almost crying though only Krishna could see that, since they were seated now in a straight line, on folding aluminium chairs against the wall. 'My wedding was not like this shabby, stupid little wedding which my son has chosen.'

'Hush, Mummy, don't talk like that!'

'You wait and see how you will feel, if Sohail grows up and abandons you in your old age.'

The two women held each other's hands. Through the sweat and disturbance there was a feeling of love. Gola had got up to speak. He looked handsome and earnest, standing there, waiting for the loud, affectionate clapping to die down. The women's eyes were soft, they looked at each other happily. Something in this strange wedding celebration had caught them. It was pared down, all the dross removed, reduced to the bare essentials of happy union. Despite Manik's efforts at occasional translation, they had not understood much of the other speeches, since even Shalini's had been in strict Marathi. But Gola could not speak Marathi.

'I have been thinking a lot about marriages,' said Gola.

There was loud, raucous clapping and sounds of, 'Yes, yes, why not?'

He smiled at the teasing. 'It's really a problem to which we will have to give increasing attention. Marriage is important for so many reasons. But how do we, all of us in these two organisations, find suitable wives, or husbands, as the case may be? Given the nature of our work. And not just what we are actually doing, but the whole state of mind, the attitudes which go with it, a whole new way of living. Men amongst us whose mothers insist they marry nice girls from their villages, or girls whose parents put pressure on them for arranged marriages, they all have difficulties when they agree to such marriages.

'Shalini and I have been very lucky to find each other, both of us doing the same kind of work. The streams of our two organisations flow into each other. Even so, we will have problems. For example, both of us are anxious that Shalini's contribution to political work should not fall off because of babies, or housework etc. These are things we will have to solve...'

Her mother's hand, rough and moist, had fallen away and a faint smell of sweat came from her body. Krishna could not hear Gola's voice any more, though she concentrated on the movement of his lips. She went to the end of another marriage, her own, years ago, just before Ranjit left. The door opened again and again. Her uncle's flat on Talkotora Road, his unknowing contribution to her happiness, had been split wide open, snatched from her, and a silent wind of destruction had blown straight through walls which had seemed impregnable. The wind was Chaman Bajaj, his nameless, general vengeance, the intense passion of evil which was his face, staring at her from the door he had opened. Again and again she had looked up from Ranjit's arms into his face. And beyond that, looking over his shoulder, his cheeks, his laughing brown eyes dropping for ever into the horror of knowledge, the face of her husband Anu, brought in to view her with her lover. She had wanted to hold her happiness in Ranjit, but Chaman Bajaj had been a knife, prising the pearl from her soft, oyster-flesh, condemning her to a wound, an empty space, over which she could never close.

21

Ancestors

Manmohan Singh and his sister Swaranjit Kaur were fifteen and ten years old respectively. They were all that was left of the family in Kotli Loharan, a village near Sialkot, famous for damascened work on iron. The family made beautiful caskets for jewellery, ornamental handles for swords and daggers, bases for *chillums* and *hookahs* and occasionally, on commission, a decorated trunk to hold a bride's dowry. Sales had gone down since the death of Maharajah Ranjit Singh, ten years ago, in 1839. The great, one-eyed ruler had been born near by, in Gujranwala. Then he had moved on to Lahore, a city more capable of expressing his power, which had perished nevertheless, with the poison which caused the Maharajah's death. Unrest broke out on his land – the

176

warring princes of Punjab could not hold it together. Bands of aimless soldiers roamed its length and breadth shadowed by the creeping British, cleverly pulling the red threads of annexation behind them, to tie this last morsel to their Indian empire.

It was not the best time to hold a fair in Gujarat. Trouble was brewing in the area, Swaranjit's father was aware of that. He said as much to his family of five children and two younger brothers who had assembled to eat, while his wife handed out lentils, butter milk and *chappatis*. But a *Baisakhi mela* is difficult to resist, even at the worst of times. They had relatives with whom to stay in Gujarat. A lot of the family products, piled up in the workshop, could be sold.

The reasons for going were many and expedient. The old man made one concession to his fears. The two youngest children were to be left behind. They deeply resented their exclusion from the happily departing party, even as they helped their mother pack away the carved objects, touching goodbye to their highly polished surfaces as they disappeared into cloth and straw that would cushion them against jolts on Sher Shah's Grand Trunk Road to Gujarat.

By the time *Baisakhi* actually arrived, everything had changed. The Sikh soldiery was massed under the Attarwalas' horseshoe formation, between the town of Gujarat and the river. They were few in number, and they had 59 guns compared to the British, who had 66. The British attack began at 7.30 am. The Punjabis opened fire too soon, exhausted their ammunition and betrayed the position of their guns, which the British then silenced. Their cavalry and infantry charged the Punjabi positions. Afghan cavalry, which had joined forces with the Punjabis, could do nothing to help them. The British occupied Gujarat and destroyed all the Punjabis it could find.

Soldiers fled from capture by the British, in small, disorganised bands going in all directions. A distant cousin, formerly in the army of Gulab Singh, was in the group that rode and limped through Kotli Loharan, on its way to Shahpur. He sat before the fire talking to the two children, relieved to be alive and full of food, willing to impart details of the murder of their family. They had been mown down by British guns, which had seen only the dark faces, making no difference between soldiers and vendors of iron caskets. No quarter had been given; it was a war of extermination.

The children's terror infected the soldier and he took them along when the group moved on, as if to erase the burning pain from his own mind. At Shahpur the group ran into trouble with a small detachment which had accompanied Nassir Khan, one of Sultan Mohammad Khan's several sons, down from the villages of Upper Miranzai, the fiercely independent reaches beyond Kohat and Peshawar. The children were the most easily dispensable of their group, they were left behind by the fleeing Sikh soldiers. Nassir Khan welcomed them. He had come a long way to see the sights of the Second Sikh War, the end of Sikh power. Now it was time to retreat with his father to Kabul. He was on his way to tell him that they must go, since they could not accept the yoke of plumed British residents. He would take these two young morsels with him. Swaranjit Kaur was seated in front of him on his horse, and her brother protected Nassir Khan from the winds that came up from behind.

Horses and ponies were not common in the area, people were more familiar with sheep and goats, donkeys and sometimes camels. Villagers came to the doors of their houses to see the big brown horse passing through. How handsome was the tall, fair man astride it, in his large, loosely tied turban, quite different from the style of the plains, his black, *zari*-embroidered waistcoat, and the white *salwar*! And his two children with him, for of course this was a family travelling through, a family of some note because of the soldiers accompanying it, also on horses, though not such fine specimens as Nassir Khan's horse. The boy behind him sat with easy confidence, as if he had been born to fly with the wind, seated on a fine horse. Only a few of the staring villagers noticed and asked each other why Nassir Khan's hand was between the little girl's legs and why she had doubled up and pressed her back to his chest, full of unfamiliar sensations which made her want to laugh and cry at the same time.

The children had crossed one river already with Nassir Khan, after leaving Shahpur, but the Indus was quite different from the Jhelum. The river was low and slower, but most extensive. The point at which they were to cross on the ferry was three miles in breadth; Swaranjit could not see the other side. The horses were lined up, constantly restless and hungry as they stood waiting for places on the boats. Many more boats had been brought in to cater to the crowds wanting to cross over. A famous *Baisakhi mela* was being set up on the opposite bank. Nassir Khan fed the children lumps of crystallised sugar-candy while they waited. He knew that

178

he and his horse would have to leave them soon.

Swaranjit Kaur knew it too; she could sense approaching abandonment. The opposite shore drew near, with its wide expanse of sand, and scanty reeds and shrubs which fringed it. The scene was so lonely and desolate that she held her brother's hand and hid her face in his shoulder. It had begun to be hard and lumpy with muscles. He was intent on the tracks of tigers, which were numerous in the sand where the boat drew in.

Nassir Khan's horses quickly lost themselves in the rush of traffic. In addition to the slow, constant stream of people crossing the Indus on the ferry, there were those who had come in from Isa Khel, from Lakki and even from as far off as Bannu. They came on foot, on horses, in bullock-carts and *tongas*. The women wore *salwar-kameez*, *burqas*, *dupattas*; the men's turbans were bright blobs of colour moving through the afternoon air. Manmohan Singh was looking at a little boy in a pill-box red velvet cap with gold embroidery, brightly striped shirt, and new white pyjamas cut away at the back and front, who rode on his father's shoulders just in front of them. It could easily have been himself on what was now a thousand *Baisakhis* ago.

The sandy bank of the river was the fairground. Shops were bamboo poles with gunny sacking stretched over them. Some sold brightly-coloured sweets and soft drinks, others birds, animals and wooden toys. Right in the centre was a large general merchandise shop whose goods had clearly come from the plains: glass bangles, beads, mirrors, combs, *kohl* and highly perfumed oil. There were showmen all around, wherever the children turned to look – acrobats, conjurors, animal tamers with bears, monkeys, snakes, a mongoose, men with medicines for teeth, stomach-aches and women's diseases, handing out pills and powders. The boy and girl stood haggard and hungry, near a wooden giant wheel which, slow and full of children, was creaking round and round. Bells were suspended from its edges and rang sharply with the sound of tin. The children were seized with terror and longing.

They heard a strange voice behind them, clucking at them to have courage, not to cry. It spoke a familiar mixture of Punjabi and Dogri, exactly what their mother's parents had spoken in Bhimbar. They turned in joy and found themselves face to face with a *feringhee*. They could tell that straight off from the cap he wore, and from the white face and blue eyes smiling at them from below it.

179

'Charles Masson, that's my name,' he told them. He fed them at one of the magical shops they had been looking at and bought a wooden horse on four wheels for the girl who was now almost too old for toys.

'Where are you going? No parents? You come with me, we can keep each other company, travelling. The usual route from this part of the country to Peshawar leads along the banks of the Indus to Kala Bagh, famous for its salt mountains, and thence by Shakr Darra to Kohat, in Bangash. I have been recommended to follow this route because it is considered the safer and because it is likely I should receive every assistance from Ahmed Khan, the chief of Isa Khel, who has so great a predilection for *feringhee* that it is known throughout the country. As Mr Elphinstone's mission in 1809 has traversed this route, I have decided to follow the unfrequented one of Marwat and Bannu. First we will go to Lakki.'

He had not spoken to anyone for a long time, and he enjoyed his speech, though he saw that the children were asleep, leaning against each other. The names would have meant nothing to them, anyway.

It rained heavily the next morning, and he drew the children under a *karita* bush for shelter. They lay there, crouched like three shells, one within the other, until the rain stopped, and then went on to the frontier post of Kundi.

The road from there was tolerably good, and brought them to the mouth of a pass through the small encircling hills. The last hill in the range was an extensive burial place. They reached its top, and stood like three trees silhouetted against the unclouded sky. The plains of Marwat and Bannu burst upon their sight. They could see its villages, marked by their several groups of trees, the yellow tints of ripe cornfields, and the fantastic forms of the surrounding mountains. In front and to the west the distant ranges were glorious, being pure white and diversified by streaks of azure, red and pearly grey. The variously coloured hills, stretching westward from Kala Bagh, held the salt mines, some pink, some blue, infinitely more beautiful than the grey stretch of salt at Bahadur Khel, but much less pure in quality.

The plain gradually descended. They could see the river Khuram flowing in the hollow beyond the town of Lakki. But first they had to cross an enormous ravine of great depth. Before they descended they drank water which had collected in a cavity in the rock. It was clear and wholesome, but tasted strongly of animal skin. 'You see why?' Charles Masson said, instructing the children. He pointed to some *Vaziri* women, giggling at the strange *feringhee*. They had come to fill their *massaks* in the pool. 'These are the skins of goats. They can carry water for miles in that.'

They had done well to drink. It was intensely hot in the ravine, and they sweated profusely. Then the clash and jingle of weapons and shields, the sound of mule hoofs trotting on the rock, came up behind them. Charles Masson was in a panic. He knew these were the armed *dacoits* of Sirwar Khan, an outlawed *Vaziri* who hated the British because two years ago a contingent of soldiers had murdered his children. Masson knew what would happen. They would take his gold, then tear open his trousers and cut off his testicles. He could hide in the pile of straw which lay drying against the rock face, but what would explain his horse? The bandits would search and find him.

The children decided to help him. Swaranjit lay on the pile of straw which covered the motionless *feringhee*, her brother leaned against it, playing casually with the reins of his horse. The bandit party was en route to waylay Mohammad Khan, Sultan of Kohat, Haagu and Teri, who was returning to Kabul with his son Nassir Khan, his followers and all his wealth. The bandits stopped when they saw the children and, of course, took their horse. Charles Masson was sweating so hard under the pile of straw that his perspiration made a small stream which flowed out and lapped gently at Sirwar Khan's feet.

'We have to go quickly.' He rallied his men, who were beginning to have thoughts about the children, especially the girl. 'Nassir Khan leaves today for Kabul, and he is carrying his father's wealth. It would be very useful to us, especially now that there are so many cursed British in the area.' If Swaranjit had understood Pashto, and had known that Sirwar Khan was to attack Nassir, she would have gone with him. She still remembered the hands of Nassir Khan and what they had done to her. But the bandits went on without her. Charles Masson emerged from under the pile of straw and thanked the children for his life. They had played the game very well, he said. He was cool, in command of the situation again. But the children had grown in that space of time; they were strong now, released from his patronage.

Charles Masson was ready to receive hospitality when they reached Lakki. A small group of British soldiers was camped there on their way to Bannu to help with the road. They gave him all the news a British traveller needed. When Sikh troops took up arms at Peshawar at the outbreak of the Second Sikh War, George Lawrence, the British Officer there, had taken refuge in Kohat. Sultan Mohammad Khan had played him false, and had delivered him over as prisoner to the Sikhs. Now Sultan Mohammad Khan and his son Nassir Khan had fled to Kabul. Swaranjit Kaur, listening carefully to the gossip of the Indian sepoys in the contingent, at last secretly said goodbye to Nassir Khan's hands. Khwaja Mohammad Khan, chief of Teri, had taken the British side in the conflict. He was permitted to continue managing the *tahsil* of which he was made a per; 'tual *jagir*. Meanwhile the whole district, with the rest of the Punjab, was annexed to the British dominions.

The road the British had begun to construct immediately on annexation, from Bannu by Bahadur Khel to Kohat, was giving them a lot of trouble. The area was swarming with insurgents, resisting the takeover of their lands by foreign soldiery. The rebels were now in control of all the salt quarries, at Jatta, Malgin, Bahadur Khel and Kharak.

Charles Masson was fired with enthusiasm. His aimless journey suddenly took on a purpose. He would help his fellow countrymen recapture Bahadur Khel. He cared about the smaller quarries too, the possible revenue from those for His Majesty was certainly not to be sniffed at, but salt was found in greatest quantity at Bahadur Khel. The rock salt could be seen from a distance of about eight miles and the thickness exposed exceeded 1,000 feet. Moreover, the salt was very pure and grey. He could see it in his weary mind's eye, all stretched out, gleaming in the pale mountain sunlight.

He decided to bypass Bannu, taking the children with him. They ascended the hills and crossed three successive ranges. Their route led west, until they crossed a small but rapid stream, after which they turned to the north. The hills since leaving Bannu had been tolerably well wooded, but in the smaller ranges the quantity of wood increased and pomegranate, with other wild fruit trees, were abundant. Then they came to a long valley, where trees laden with small, green aloes grew densely beside the water course. They halted at a spot where two or three vines hung over a spring of water, sheltering it from the heat of the day. The group was joined by a riotous company of British soldiers who had just finished constructing a designated stretch of road, and were now intent on celebrating the occasion with a potent witch's brew which His Majesty's ships had brought for them all the way from Scotland.

182

With them were a batch of mountain tribesmen. They had done the actual breaking of stones and laying out of the road, and were equally relieved that their work was done. They had spent a part of their wages in the village of Asmat Kozah, which they had passed on their way to the valley, well known for its strong liquor. The Hindu contractor, who had recruited and accompanied them, was cold and dry, he drank nothing and was anxious to move on to the next job. He tried to dissuade them from stopping with the British soldiers, but to no avail. Now he sat, a small man with a thin moustache and heavy rings on his fingers, and watched them drink.

Evening shadows began to fall, and the moon came out in the clear night air, a large silver ball that jiggled and shook from one edge of the valley to the other. The whole party, except the two children and the sour Hindu contractor, had passed out. Their fires burned down, embers glowing like the last eyes of day, their feet got colder and colder and were drawn up under rough covers.

Swaranjit Kaur stirred away from where she lay against her brother's back, unwrapped their mother's thick shawl from around their bodies. 'Let's go,' she said.

He was sleepy and startled. 'Where? At this time of night?'

The contractor was awake now. 'Listen, look here,' he said. 'You can't do that.'

'You stay here, if you like,' they said.

'But the British will wake up tomorrow and kill me when they find their guns and horses gone.'

The children shrugged their shoulders. 'Come with us then.' They had grown strong and wiry in their months of journey; they knew they could easily overpower the contractor if he attempted to stop them. He knew that too, and agreed to go along with them.

Travelling was no problem in the bright light from the moon. By morning they had left the soldiers far behind. Nevertheless, they left the beaten track, following a narrow path shown to them by a passing Sayyid. He glanced with curiosity at the young girl and boy with long, grey guns slung over their shoulders, followed by a thin man on a horse he could barely ride. Two more horses followed them at the end of the line.

The scenery became extremely diverse. There were many trees heavy with flowers they had never seen in the plains, and small copses of fruit trees laden with plums and peaches, which they ate with cool delight. They had almost reached the insurgents' camp at Bahadur Khel when they had to deal with the contractor again.

183

They were back now on the regular track. The sound of rough *feringhee* voices came over a low hill. They took the horses carefully behind a large outcrop of rock and kept them very quiet. Todar Mal, the contractor, saw a chance to reestablish his credibility with the British. Just as the group of jingling red uniforms was passing, he opened his mouth to shout. Swaranjit shoved her fist, wrapped in her *dupatta*, straight into his mouth. Her long fingers clung desperately to the back of his head, shoving it firmly against her stifling hand. Her arms bore for the rest of her life the marks which his flailing rings inflicted on them.

Once the soldiers had safely passed they tied Todar Mal firmly to the rock. He yelled and cried and pleaded with them not to leave him there. His eyes were white with terror, his voice followed them for long stretches of the road, calling out, 'There are wolves and leopards here, they will eat me!'

The rebels' camp opened its arms to greet the children. They had bought their welcome with guns and horses, but it was the first welcome since their parents had died, and their hearts flowered with happiness. The core of the group belonged to the *Vaziri* tribe, but rebellious elements from several of the annexed villages had drifted up to join it. This particular splinter of the insurgent party was led by a tall, lanky young man who was not a *Vaziri* at all. He stared resolutely at Swaranjit Kaur as she sat beside the fire with her brother, devouring the food they put before them. Her lively voice was telling their story between mouthfuls, as if she could not bear to wait.

'You're a brave girl,' he said, finally, when she had finished. 'I want to give you something. We captured the salt quarry at Kharak, near Kohat, but the section of us which is guarding it has to move on, beyond Peshawar, so we cannot keep it on any longer. We will give it to you for the guns you have given us. Both of you can manage it, but it will belong to the girl. Be sure to tell the British that she is the owner when they come to register it and collect the revenue.'

He went with them to Kharak, and settled them into the business of salt quarrying. Then he left. Swaranjit saw him again five years later when she looked out of her window in Kohat. A handsome man crossing the wheat fields. His calves rippled with muscles; his shoulders were broad and the most beautiful she had ever seen. She ran down to him, again and again. But he could not stay with her; the British would hang him. Nor could he take her with him.

184

She did not even ask his name, so when her husband threw her out on their wedding night because she was not a virgin she could not even say who it was that had deflowered her, and retreated into long-lasting silence.

Manmohan Singh's only son, Sucha Singh, was contemptuous of his father's continued interest in making rifle barrels. 'Let us concentrate on the salt quarry, Father,' he said, as respectfully as he could manage. 'That is where the money is. Why do you waste your time making these elaborate designs on metal?'

But Manmohan Singh's fingers had recovered their childhood memories from Kotli Loharan, where he had done beautiful damascened work on iron caskets, following his father's strange, elaborate designs. He had an attachment for rifles after his long odyssey over the mountains. He continued to work on rifle barrels long after the industry, discouraged by the British after the Mutiny of 1857, had departed from Kohat city to the villages of the Khyber Pass, where it flourished.

Meanwhile Sucha Singh concentrated on the salt quarry in Kharak. He bore the periodic inspection visits of his silent aunt, Swaranjit Kaur, with a patience imposed by his father's authority. He did not understand his father at all, and he did not trust him. There was a peculiar freedom about his personality brought perhaps by the difficult journey from Sialkot to Kohat. The journey seemed to have changed more than his father's locale. The old man actually believed that the salt quarry at Kharak belonged to Sucha's licentious aunt Swaranjit Kaur, at a time when nobody believed women should own property.

People still told stories about the occasion of his aunt's marriage. On her wedding night her husband discovered that she was not a virgin, and threw her out of his house. She arrived crying, a trembling, red bundle, back at her brother's house, where the marriage decorations were still being taken down from the *deorhi*. She had not been seen to cry before or since; nor did anybody know exactly what passed between brother and sister, who had for a long time been each other's whole family. But no one heard her speak after that discussion with her brother.

One week later, Manmohan Singh was standing, alone and steadfast, at the erstwhile bridegroom's door. He was greeted by waves of abuse, but he stood unmoving, repeating that his sister's jewellery should be returned to her. It belonged to her, not to her brother, and not to the injured husband. A peculiar, self-contained dignity about him kept them from touching him. Besides, he stood tall, towering above all the other Sikhs in the town, and his arms were strong and bulging from working with iron. They could not meddle with him; they returned the jewellery, which was handed over to Swaranjit Kaur.

When Sucha Singh wanted the jewellery he spoke to his aunt with all the charm his intense, mean heart could muster. He needed to buy large quantities of salt immediately. The profits to be collected were enormous, and they moved him to a flurry of emotional activity. He need not have tried so hard; his aunt gave him the jewellery as soon as he asked.

At the time of annexation the British had imposed light duties on salt obtained from the Kohat salt quarries. Allowances were made to the Khan of Teri and other chiefs, to secure their co-operation in the new arrangements. Of course, no allowance was made for the salt coming from Swaranjit Kaur's quarry in Kharak. They did not need her political co-operation, and were still a bit puzzled by the story which Manmohan Singh, her brother, had spun to explain her ownership.

In 1883 the duty on salt was raised to eight *annas* per local *maund*. Then in December 1895 Sucha Singh received a piece of very interesting information from his wife's uncle – who worked as a confidential clerk in the office of the Deputy Commissioner of Salt Revenues. He did not generally divulge such information, but he could not resist telling his niece. Within six months, the duty on salt would be increased to two rupees per local *maund*; although prohibition against export of Kohat salt to the Cis Indus territory was to be maintained, the preventive line that had been established on the Indus to stop export was to be withdrawn. What did a prohibition count for, if it was not enforced by British arms? Salt sold in those hitherto prohibited areas for twice the price.

Sucha Singh gathered all his resources – profits from the salt quarries, his wife's dowry, his aunt's jewellery, the gold his father had collected from the sale of rifle barrels to the rebellious tribesmen in the border areas. Everything the family owned was sold to buy more salt, huge quantities of it, which was stocked in a long shed just outside the city wall. Then Sucha Singh waited breathlessly, poised on the edge of truth, everything gambled on the veracity of the clandestine information he had received. The gamble paid off. Duty on salt was raised, just as the uncle had

186

projected, and the salt he had bought so cheap brought him an enormous price when carried and sold across the river. Suddenly, the family, descended from two waifs who had wandered from Sialkot to Kohat, was flowering and had become rich.

There was enough money for Sucha Singh to satisfy the burning ambition of his son, Gopal Singh. He paid for him to travel to England and become a barrister. It made good business sense for a branch of the family to go into the professions, and law was being especially encouraged by the British. Besides, his other son, Makhan Singh was there to help with management of the salt, and to arrange for the marriage of their sister, Kailash Kaur. The marriage was fixed with a handsome *sardar*, Sobha Singh Palji, who had drifted into their neighbourhood one day, all the way from Bhimbar.

Gopal Singh returned from England for the wedding, qualified and suave, with 'Bar-at-Law' behind his name. The new barrister soon tired of Kohat's small-town pressures, and the penny-pinching ways of his father and brother. They all lived in the house that the grandfather, Manmohan Singh, had built many years ago, just inside the city wall. To curb his restlessness, Gopal Singh was married to a small, sturdy girl from Bannu with a large nose and a skin pink and beautiful from the mountain air. She fell in love with her husband the first moment she saw him.

Although Sucha Singh aged, his grip on the salt quarry and on his fortune stayed as tenacious as ever, but he was full of fears and suspicions. He wandered in quite often in the early morning, to sit with his son Gopal Singh in the law office he had set up on the first floor.

Despite the barrister's preference for Western style, the office was exactly as law offices had been for at least a century in Lahore. Sucha Singh would not permit expensive, new-look furniture into the house. Thick white sheets covered the cotton *durries* on the floor. They were changed every morning, sometimes under Sucha Singh's personal supervision. He would be settled on a bolster pillow against the wall, a brass spittoon on the floor, drinking from a pitcher on a small, inlaid table beside him. He watched Gopal Singh lay out his files, select books from wooden revolving shelves, and seat himself with some difficulty at a low desk with sloping sides on which his writing paper lay.

Then Sucha Singh filled his ears with stories about various members of the family. At first he had complained about his aunt,

Swaranjit Kaur, that she was eating them out of house and home. News of these complaints reached her, and she strode into the office one morning while Sucha Singh was there. Silently she thrust under his nose the original registration papers for the Kharak Salt Quarry. Each yellowing sheet of paper bore her name and signature. Then she handed him a wad of notes, gathered from the sale of her beautiful *phulkaris*. There was no need for her to make even a mute reference to the jewellery which he had not returned to her. Her nephew Sucha Singh did not complain about her thereafter.

When Sucha Singh's suspicions and fears extended themselves to Makhan Singh, his other son, Gopal Singh began to hope that the property would be left to him. His father asked for advice about legally securing the salt quarries. Gopal Singh became soft and tender towards him, carefully hid his contempt for his father's mean ways and instructed Prabhjot Kaur, his wife, to send the best samplings of food to the old man, the expensive delicacies which she concocted in her kitchen under his direction.

It was a well-meaning but mistaken gesture. His father noted that his habit of extravagance extended to food. He had seen the clothes already: three-piece suits ornamented with a gold watch chain draped across his chest. Expensive food finally undid Gopal Singh in his father's eyes. The real immorality lay in carelessness with money. He was convinced that, within months of his death, Gopal Singh would fritter away his share of the salt quarry. He decided not to leave him a share at all. In fact, he left him nothing except two rooms and the office in the family house within the city.

The will was read right through to the assembled relatives. At the end there was a small mention of Gopal Singh. The utterly absorbed, watchful faces which surrounded the clerk as he read out the will stayed forever in Prabhjot Kaur's mind. She often wished later that her husband, Gopal Singh, had lived to see the sole inheritor, his brother, Makhan Singh, leap from rooftop to rooftop with a pistol in his hand when the rioters came to get him. It was during the first riots in Kohat, years before the long, bloody night of Partition. The rioters surrounding his house were workers from his own salt quarry, inflamed by his slave-driving ways.

Gopal Singh constructed the new house outside the city walls soon after the will was read, which excluded him from his father's fortune. He died, shortly afterwards, of an unidentified illness. Their youngest child, Paramjit, was only three years old then.

Prabhjot Kaur, after the initial period of indulgence in grief, concentrated on bringing him up and the other two older children, Satinder and Lajwanti.

Taking care of Satinder was not easy, even while her husband had been alive. One summer she was in Amritsar, visiting her brother, a sub-divisional engineer in the Indian Service of Engineers. Satinder came in agog with news picked up in the bazaar: great trouble was brewing in Guru-ka-Bagh, fourteen miles out of the city. His eyes were alive with excitement. 'Volunteers are lined up at the *Akal Takht*, to take vows. Tomorrow the *jathas* begin to go to Guru-ka-Bagh. Their vow is to be silent and peaceful, no matter what happens.'

Prabhjot Kaur's brother was angry. 'Your boy should not get mixed up in anti-Government stuff. I have my job to think of. The British are supporting the Mahant, the priest at Guru-ka-Bagh. They don't like these Akali *jathas* at all. The new Akali party is gaining a lot of power among the Sikhs, and they fear they might join up with the Congress fellows.'

His friend, Sharma, a local doctor who accompanied him on morning walks, agreed. 'The Udasi Mahant at the Guru-ka-Bagh shrine has asked for police protection. You Sikhs are too emotional. If he doesn't want to have people pick firewood from his plot of land, that's up to him.'

'But people have been doing that for years. It's like God's gift, which they take for granted. What will those poor people do?' Prabhjot Kaur was fired by her son's enthusiasm.

'It's not his land, he has no right to stop anybody. It is God's land.' The boy was passionate and serious. Prabhjot Kaur should have been warned. She should have confined Satinder to her brother's European-style brick bungalow, retreated with him into her brother's fears of the new politicians who dared to oppose the British rulers. But passion was springing in her heart, which drew both mother and son to Guru-ka-Bagh.

Five Akalis were arrested on 9 August 1922 for felling a dry *kikar* tree on the plot of land which Mahant Sunder Das had said belonged exclusively to him. The men were convicted of theft and sentenced to six months' imprisonment and a fifty rupee fine. To protest against official highhandedness, to assert their right to chop wood for the free community kitchen, *jathas* of five volunteers each began to march to the shrine.

'A good opportunity for the Akali leaders,' her brother said wryly, 'they're smarter fellows than I thought they were. They're using this to rouse passions all over the State.' Akalis from surrounding areas were pouring into Amritsar. Official arrangements to prevent them from coming in by rail and road were to no avail. By 28 August 4,000 Akalis had courted arrest. Police pickets were placed all along the road to Guru-ka-Bagh. Beatings began long before the volunteers reached the garden. Even so, *jathas* of 55 or 100, and sometimes even 200, Akalis went each day to the garden after taking their vows at the *Akal Takht* of the Golden Temple.

Behind this barrage of news Prabhjot Kaur sensed excitement growing in her son Satinder. She saw his face in a film made by the American cinematographer Captain A.L. Yorgos, who had filmed the Akali Diwan at Amritsar. Swami Shardhanand, Hakim Ajmal Khan, Maulana Kifayat Ullah, Kumari Lajawanti and Sayed Atta Ullah Shah, all great leaders in the Independence Movement, sat on the dais beside Akali leaders. Behind them were the calm, shimmering waters of the holy tank, a narrow pathway crossing it to the temple, and the magnificent dome of the temple itself catching the rays of the afternoon sun and reflecting them into the black and white film. Satinder's face appeared suddenly in a corner. Something in the hard, intense look of the boy's eyes must have caught the camera's attention, because it concentrated on his eyes for a moment. Prabjhot Kaur recognised them from the small welt above the left eye, where it had been stitched when Satinder fell on barbed wire as a young child. The image mingled in her head with what the film showed later: *jathas* of Sikhs in black turbans going over mile after mile of muddy, water-logged roads. A *jatha* was stopped at Ranewala Bridge, kept there a whole day, then allowed to cross the next day with a newly arrived *jatha* under a heavy shower of *lathi* blows. A picture flashed on the screen, of a booklet prepared for the use of police officers. It described the sophisticated use of the *lathi*, which parts of the victim's body should be attacked and how to get in blows with maximum effect.

The face of her son stayed with her when he pleaded to be allowed to join spectators at Guru-ka-Bagh. Then her husband Sardar Gopal Singh sent her a message from Lahore, where he had come for an important case. A friend, the Reverend C. F. Andrews, who had helped him in London, was arriving in Amritsar on the morning of 12 September 1922. Indian leaders designated him eyewitness for the violence and beatings at Guru-ka-Bagh.

190

Prabhjot Kaur must accompany him to the site of the shrine. She remembered the slanting eagerness in Satinder's face and decided to take him with her.

The party went in three *tongas* and Satinder sat beside her. She noticed him glancing often at the open, acutely gentle face of the Reverend Andrews who sat in the front seat. They left at 1 pm, and from the main road pr(ceeded along the bank of a canal. When they had gone some distance, they saw two Sikhs in black turbans on the opposite bank, waving their hands at them and pointing to the sky. A great bird was circling there, a golden hawk, the bright blue of the sky rising from its wings like columns of glory. Satinder clutched at the white man's arm, laid along the back of the seat, and whispered to him urgently. Every day, as soon as the beating began at the Guru's garden, the hawk circled its way through the sky to Amritsar, to the Golden Temple, the gold of its body fusing with the gold of the dome, telling the breathless congregation that cruel violence was being perpetrated at the shrine.

The Reverend Andrews acknowledged that he had seen a great bird in the distance, but he could not say whether it was a golden hawk or not. The three *tongas* stopped and made a circle; their occupants stood in the centre, looking up. Despite his precise caution the white man had entered into the sanctity of the moment. Like the other faces, his showed faith and reverence, a solemn awe mixed with joy. But Satinder was outside this circle, he was hard with excitement, intent only on joining one known truth to another, grabbing at phenomena, as if reality could be experienced through an accumulation of detail. The colour of the canal, muddy and thick, flowing fast between its carefully constructed banks. The small clusters of people near the waterstands, pouring water from bulging earthenware pots for passers-by on the road.

Soon their *tongas* were passing a *jatha* of about a hundred Sikhs in black turbans, their ranks orderly and quiet. Very young boys and old men were in the centre of the group, protected by the big, healthy bodies of other volunteers, mostly ex-servicemen, who walked in the stiff-legged way of soldiers and fell naturally into straight lines. This time it was not the Great War, fought for the British in Africa and Europe; their turbans were arrayed with small, stiff wreaths of white flowers. This was a non-violent war of faith, and much more difficult. The *jatha* arrived at the shrine long after the *tongas* had reached it. The men were muddy, dripping with perspiration, but quiet, as if a stillness of prayer and religion had entered their bodies.

Meanwhile, the Reverend Andrews and his party waited sitting crosslegged on the grass with a large group of spectators at the shrine. Their faces showed signs of pain, many of them praying as they waited in absolute silence. Prabhjot Kaur registered a singular stillness, a complete lack of excitement. She thought they were waiting for the beatings to begin, but Satinder came back with news, the beating had begun already.

'It's back there, on an empty plot of land, near the dried-up trees.' He picked up the Reverend Andrews' *solar topee* from the ground and helped him up.

'It must still be yesterday's lot they're dealing with,' said one of the men who had come in from Delhi, lifting his stiff body from the ground.

Then Prabhjot Kaur passed from suffering reflected on faces around her to the suffering itself.

A dozen policemen and two English officers stood waiting for the slow, orderly rows of Akalis to reach them. Four at a time, they went up and stopped at a yard's distance. They stood perfectly still, their lips moving in silent prayer, their hands joined, their eyes looking through spaces between the men. It was a moment of offering. Then a British officer lunged forward, a heavy wooden staff bound in brass gleaming in his hand. A reflected ray bounced off into Satinder's eyes. He did not blink but watched the staff go forward and hit the man with all its clenched force, straight on the collar bone.

Satinder waited. He thought the pain would explode; a flower of fire danced inside his chest. He waited for something to happen. But there was nothing, no sound or movement, no change in the air. Perhaps it was silence that disturbed him. That a body should be offered and pain inflicted so casually. It made a gap in his heart, established an emptiness of space, a hyphen between him and events, a gap which continued to exist long after its origin was buried deep inside him.

Krishna's kinsman brought a hot breath of familiarity, a young boy violated by Non-Violence, muffled and distanced from life in that one instant when the blow descended and was received in silence. The space, the padding was well known, it was across just such a medium that her skin shadowed its colour-signals. Satinder had no darkening skin to protect and service him, he had to trust

192

instead to the Babbar Khalsas, apostles of violence, to reach through these layers of wool which covered him, for pistol shots and the sharp points of destruction to puncture this nervating fabric.

The Brigadier, Paramjit Singh Chahal, had no darkening skin either. The corpse of Dhiraj Kumari clung to his soul, made him vulnerable and released his stream of spontaneous actions into the Bengal countryside. What a family triumvirate of mighty Caesars, set to conquer the world – Krishna of the darkening skin, Satinder victim of non-violence, and the crumbling Brigadier gazing from Victoria Memorial, clad in the fires of betrayal!

The man who had been hit rolled over, felled by the mighty blow. He did not flinch or scream with pain. For a short moment, the muscles in his face and neck twisted involuntarily. He lay there gathering strength. Then he rose to receive the next blow.

One companion lay unmoving after three blows. His waiting friends moved forward to lift him up into a transport lorry which served as an ambulance. Just then a policeman leapt on the prostrate man with his full weight, landing with both feet on the man's stomach. Satinder was filled with fury. It gurgled in his throat, and his body shot forward to defend the injured man. The Reverend Andrews' hand was on his elbow and his mother held his mouth, stifling his cry of rage.

'We can't do less than the others; they have been watching for days,' she said. He saw, as if from a great distance, the pain on her face. She was murmuring into his ear. 'Those poor, injured men will travel in lorries over a road which has broken my healthy bones getting here. What an agony it will be for them, each time the rough truck goes over a pit in the road! There is a perfectly good, smooth road on the other side of the canal, going all the way to Amritsar. But it's closed, reserved for officials, and they won't open for the *jathedars*.'

He envied her immediate reaction, the way she spread naturally into the details of taking care. He saw her eyes streaming with tears, her words diffusing the hard fury in his heart, he saw an Akali standing beside his prostrate, injured companion, waiting to hand him up into the lorry, he saw a policeman walk across and kick him, so that he fell like a tree across the body of the injured man, and he, Satinder, did nothing. The details reached him slowly, across the hot, enclosing layer which had established itself around him.

193

22
Satinder in Lahore and Kohat, 1930-36

The first thing Satinder noticed about the people of Lahore was their strange pallor, as if their skins had been shut up inside the city walls for too long, shaded by tombs, the sun's rays filtered off by trees, buildings and bazaars. In spring the men practised the sports of flying pigeons and kites, their pleasure was in Heera Mandi, visiting prostitutes who wore large nose-rings and bells on their feet. He felt a foreigner in the city, breathing the air of Kohat on it, his lungs still stiff from the memory of cold walks to his father's new house outside the city walls, or shooting partridges near his uncle's salt quarries ten miles away near Kharian.

Krishna's skin would have offered a contrast to the Lahorians' sticky pallor. It was already brown and rich, suffused with the blood of her ancestors and rubbed red and raw by the craving pressures of their lives.

Satinder felt spiritless and alone in Lahore, though there was no obvious reason. His mother's uncle, a railway ticket-inspector, had taken care of the fatherless brood that had arrived as part of a streaming convoy of Hindus fleeing riots in Kohat. He had somehow managed, through contacts in the government, to obtain admission for Satinder in Dayal Singh College. The trek to and from college kept Satinder busy. His mother had sold her jewellery to rent a set of rooms above the old Lahore Gate. They were tiny and airless and the noise from the Dabhi Bazaar nearby was intolerable. From morning till night, shopkeepers, vendors with pushcarts and hawkers, with baskets on their heads or slung over their shoulders, sold cloth: velvet, cotton, silk from Kashmir, woollen cloth from Bhimbar, *khes* from Kohat – everything except *khadi*.

Gandhiji's bonfire of imported cloth had reddened the broken

194

walls of the Old Fort in Delhi; primitive wooden spinning wheels were beginning to go click click click all over India, but as yet there was no *khadi* in Dabhi Bazaar. Meanwhile, Satinder woke up every morning to the noise and rattle of buying and selling. But these sounds did not touch the silent, empty space around him. His mother had made a home; he went from the springboard of her love, from Paramjit's young, avid admiration and from his sister Lajwanti's casual disdain, completely absorbed in the doings of her girls' school, but he always carried his invisible monk's cowl held closely around him, padding him off.

He sat for hours in the snack shops outside Shalimar Gate, a cup of tea cooling before him on the plastic sheet which covered the table, and thought of the death of his father. Like uprooting a huge, ancient, healthy tree, its roots pulled with enormous difficulty from acres of land bringing out the hearts of subterranean insects like himself and his mother, frightened, turned over, exposed to sunlight for the first time.

His sense of fear and freedom had deepened with the riots in Kohat. His hard, oppressive uncle, Makhan Singh, had leaped from rooftop to rooftop with a pistol in his hand, a white poplin *salwar* billowing out between his legs. Satinder had been in the crowd looking up, watching, protected by anonymity and thin detachment. But there had been something in the thick, black shoes leaping through the air in panic which had brought back to him the confused, curdled silence of Guru-ka-Bagh.

It was the mention of Guru-ka-Bagh in Sampuran's speech which caught his ear as he passed a group of students listening to a young man with flashing, round spectacles and a slight American drawl outside the college gates. Satinder, on his way to the bicycle-stand, joined the fringe of the crowd. A bystander whispered information. This was Sampuran Singh, Lecturer in Political Science at Government College, with a Master's degree from Berkely University in California, USA. His parents still lived in the United States. He had come back to India because of Nankana Sahib.

Sampuran was even then talking of the outrage at Nankana Sahib. 'You all know what happened there. Mahant Narain Das sat every day with his mistress in his lap, and watched prostitutes dancing within the sacred precincts of the *gurudwara*, in the Janam Asthan where Guru Nanak Devji was born. When the Sikhs could not bear this desecration any more, Bhai Lachman Singh Dharovalia and his *jatha* went to the *gurudwara*. Mahant Narain Das was waiting for them with 400 thugs. As soon as the *jatha* entered the main gate, Pathans posted outside shut it behind them and the firing started. Not a single warning was given to the Akalis. Every one of them was either killed or wounded severely by swords, hatchets and firearms. Mahant Narain Das supervised the butchery himself, urging his men to spare no long-haired Sikh in the vicinity. Then he and his men collected and burned the dead and wounded. According to an eyewitness account, "in these burnt heaps there were traces of arms, heads, legs and other parts of bodies chopped into small bits...and practically the whole compound was full of blood."

'I don't want to give you any more details. I want to impress upon your minds who was really responsible. It was the local British authorities, who knew all about the Mahant's preparations, and rather than stop him they urged him on by offering him police protection. The Commissioner of Lahore, Mr C. M. King, visited the *gurudwara* to reassure the Mahant. He is surely responsible. And the Superintendent of Police, Mr J. W. Bowrine. It is against them that we must now seek revenge; they are responsible for the massacre. Only then will we be able to turn to what happened at Guru-ka-Bagh.'

Sampuran was handing round copies of a cyclostyled newspaper, the *Babbar Akali Doaba Akhbar*. Satinder listened carefully as Sampuran read out excerpts from a passionate appeal. '"As the Indian movement has subsided, the Tenth Guru has, therefore, in his infinite mercy, sent the Babbar to help the nation out of its critical situation. The Babbar will make his appearance in the Doaba where the Sikh army stands drawn up in battle array. He will expose the secret of the *feringhees* who will shriek with pain.'"
It called upon them to bring about anarchy by means of the *khanda*, cut down the foreigner and purge the land of sinful deeds, to burn police stations, plunder the treasuries, place gunpowder under the railway lines, raid the magazines, steal arms and sing the song of liberty.

Later Satinder sat on a bench facing a *casuarina* tree heavy with blossoms. Behind him was the stony presence of a huge Gandharva Buddha which seemed to hold up the museum roof. He thought of Sampuran coming down Government College Hill. Then he looked up and saw him.

Sampuran had long since abandoned his turban. His hair was black, curly, and thinning at the top. An early bout of smallpox in

196

his village near Jullundur had put some distended, indelible pits in his dark skin. That, and his serious eyes, made him look much older than his age.

His eyes had been sad and heavy with tears when he told Satinder about the death of his dear friend Karam Singh, editor of the *Babbar Akali Doaba Akhbar*. He had been travelling to Doneli village with three other Babbar Akali friends: Udai Singh, Bishan Singh and Anup Singh. The latter turned out to be a police informer who had quietly destroyed the party's guns and ammunition, with the exception of one gun which Karam Singh carried on his person. The Babbars had seen the police party and had rushed to a *gurudwara* across a small stream. Mr Smith, the Superintendent of Police, wanted to arrest them alive but they had refused to surrender. He therefore set fire to the *gurudwara*. The men had emerged wielding their *kirpans* and were killed in a hail of bullets.

Satinder, however, had been more interested in Sampuran himself. 'What brought you back to India?'

'I read about what happened at the Nankana Sahib *gurudwara* and I was outraged.'

Satinder thought about a clear feeling like outrage emanating from Sampuran. He remembered rage, gurgling in his throat at Guru-ka-Bagh, then returning like an incestuous stream into his own stomach. Would rage and destruction, going out of him the moment it arose, resolve the fact of violence? Sampuran seemed to have the answers. He was a stream that had flowed back to India, strongly and by choice. There were many streams going back and forth. Satinder was a pebble thrusting its rounded lump into the water of the stream.

'I took the next ship back to India,' Sampuran went on. 'But it was not until October 1922 that I reached here, just missing the *jathas* that went to Guru-ka-Bagh in which 5,605 Akalis were arrested and 936 were hospitalized. Everyone followed the trial with close interest. When the convicted leaders were being removed to gaols, mammoth crowds greeted them en route. I was among the thousands who laid themselves on the rail track at Panja Sahib *gurudwara* to stop the train, so that prisoners being taken to Naoshera gaol could be fed.

'I was at the edge of the group facing the engine. Before my eyes its great black wheel came slowly to rest, crushing two men whose bodies were almost touching mine. I felt as if my whole life were wound up and stretched tightly across that wheel in those moments, watching its approach. I flopped down with relief at being alive; the stones on the rail track hurt my cheek and my face streamed with sweat. I knew only a deep disdain for the human beings around me. The feeling came in wave after wave; it rendered my stomach wretched and hard and I burst into loud tears.

'Slowly I became aware of a tender hand held quietly on my shoulder. I looked up; it was a very old man from my father's village, Baba Santa Singh. His face had so many wrinkles, you could climb them like a ladder. And his eyes were pale with love. He took me in his arms and I finished my crying on his shoulder; it smelled of raw onions and wood smoke.

'When I moved away it seemed to me that I left twenty-five years of my life in his arms. I sought out Master Mota Singh, Kishan Singh, and the others, and joined the Babbars whom Baba Santa Singh told me about. I knew I did not belong with the pale, dedicated eyes of the non-violent *jathas*.'

Satinder paced the streets of Lahore, wondering where he belonged. Sometimes he went out to the villages near by, wherever he could reach regularly. A general meeting of different *jathas* of the Babbar Akalis was convened at Gojowal. It decided on a programme which was principally Kishan Singh's idea. The appeal to come forward for passive suffering, which the other Akalis had put forward, was getting too strong in the area. People must be systematically told about the alternative cause and its method of execution. The plan was that small groups would distribute their paper, the *Babbar Akali Doaba Akhbar*, which Sampuran now edited. The boys would arrive at colleges and split off among the students, going back again and again to the same college, picking up students who had talked to them on previous occasions. Or they would go to markets and talk to vendors in the streets. Sometimes they would go to private houses in Sikh areas.

Satinder travelled willingly with these small groups. It was comfortable and filled up the empty pockets of time, the raw, anxious moments which Lahore opened to him. Kohat had become a dream of paradise, filled with love of his dead father. But he could not really feel the presence of his young companions. A space yawned between Satinder and the happy, excited, arguing boys with whom he walked. They could not reach him beyond a certain point.

Guru-ka-Bagh had established the empty space. He saw again

198

and again the white fist and the gleam of brass and wood coming through the fingers, going towards an exposed collarbone, a praying Akali, his black turban crowned with a stiff chaplet of flowers. Satinder's whole body, its muscles, flesh and blood, his entire soul had strained to the point of impact, waiting for an explosion. It had not come. The man had fallen in silence, had lain still, and his disarranged flesh had adjusted itself around the intrusion. The rage inside Satinder had been pushed back, delayed, and there was now this emptiness, this woolly distance which sat between him and those he met and dealt with. He longed for their presence to reach across and touch him through the padding.

The young men spoke of Satinder's aloofness. Some even said he was a snob, since they knew that his late father had been among the first Indian barristers to train in England. But Satinder rested nowhere. His connection with Sampuran, meticulously pursued, renewed every day, attended to with care and love, was more in the nature of a hope that Sampuran's force would reach him.

Once Sampuran sent him as far as Rawalpindi with a pile of pamphlets. He went down the first line of shops which sold dried fruit. On the ground were high piles of almonds from Kashmir and long, thin and seedless raisins from Afghanistan and Iran. Thick, brown snakes of dried figs hung from the low raftered ceilings. He descended a few steps to another market near by, much larger, criss-crossed with brightly lit lanes of shops which sold goods imported from Japan, Germany and England. Satinder had never seen such shiny, varied merchandise before. It made him uneasy.

The shopkeepers refused to talk with Satinder, fearing trouble with British authorities, but some accepted copies of the *Akhbar*, tucking away the rough, cyclostyled sheets under thin mattresses on which they sat.

Satinder tried to tell Sampuran about his sense of desolation. He had offered a complacent shopkeeper the full force of his intensity and been received with blank indifference. Sampuran listened.

'You're right. It's no use trying to convert shopkeepers in the big cities. They don't listen and they don't do anything. We should try to reach the peasants instead and go to the villages. They understand their own exploitation. We will have to change our strategy a little. In any case, the police are too close to us here. But meanwhile I want you to do something else.'

Three hard-core activists had arrived in Lahore from Jullundur, on their way to the North West Frontier Province, to collect arms

199

and ammunition for the Movement. They were seated with elbows pressed on the aluminium top of the table, drinking tea and talking. Bhaskar was clearly the leader of the group, a small, fair-skinned young man with a narrow frame, curly hair and thin, intense eyes, their pupils almost luminous. Satinder remembered their abstract excitement as Bhaskar looked up from making plans. He reached across the table to shake Satinder's hand.

The three were to fan out and cover the areas around Bannu, Dera Ismail Khan, and even as far north as Hazara. Bhaskar was to go to Kohat, which might be the most fertile source of arms. The others would join him there later.

'Will you take Bhaskar to Kohat?' Sampuran asked. 'You're from there, aren't you? Just introduce him to a few people. He'll do the rest; he's very good at talking.'

'Yes, but ...'

'Please go with him. You are one of us now.' His tone was casual; it took Satinder's allegiance for granted. Satinder longed to feel the excitement he had seen in Bhaskar's eyes, but he felt nothing. Maybe Sampuran's answers would become his, if he tried them.

'The people I knew are not in Kohat right now,' he said. 'Everyone left after the last communal riots. That's why my family is in Lahore. But they have called on us to return. The Hindus are beginning to trickle back. My mother has been saying she wants to go back, too. We can do that.'

Bhaskar travelled to Kohat with them on the train and they made a family unit in the compartment. Bhaskar was keen to talk to Paramjit, Satinder's young brother, but the boy was sulky and withdrawn, looking out of the window.

'You must be wondering whether your house is safe,' Bhaskar asked Prabhjot Kaur.

'Yes.' She was grateful for his attention, turning to him.

'My husband built the house. He died just before we left, four years ago.'

Soon after she reached her old home in Kohat, Prabhjot Kaur learned of Bhaskar's mission to collect guns for use against the British. She called Satinder into the courtyard, among the jasmine bushes, dry and dusty, their leaves yellow. There were signs that someone had been living in the courtyard: three blackened bricks where they had done their cooking, a damp, shallow depression near the water tap where cooking pots had been washed, which had kept the jasmine roots going. Now the bushes had put out some flowers, Prabhjot Kaur drew their fragrance round her like a veil. She stood there with a large pail of water at her feet and a mug, about to water plants.

Satinder was irritated. 'There's so much chaos in the house, and you're out here.' He gestured to the bushes.

She put her hand out appeasingly to touch his shoulder, stroking it through the worn sweater. He felt exhaustion and emotion in the fragile bones of her wrist and the thick, raised veins on her hand. Returning was not easy.

'I want to give Bhaskar your father's revolver. And some old guns hidden in the house. They belonged to an ancestor, your father's grandfather, Manmohan Singh. He is supposed to have made them himself. Your father showed me where he stored them when we first moved to this house.'

Bhaskar and Satinder went with her to what used to be the old law office. She lifted the covers she had draped over the sofas when they had left Kohat. Clouds of dust filled the room, smudging their cheeks and settling in a grey film on their hair. Satinder thought of Lajwanti, his sister, and young Paramjit, playing and quarrelling in a corner of the same house, in a different world. He could not connect them with the bemused woman leading them to a board in a corner of the room.

Her hands trembled with silent excitement. She reached down to the bottom of the bookcase, a neat panel below several shelves of law books. She squatted on her haunches, her *dupatta* falling away from her head to expose a thin plait of greying hair. Her fingers, like a blind person's, felt the edge of the panel. Suddenly it shot out as a drawer, opening a band of darkness in the wood. She moved away a little and directed Satinder to reach in. The smell of dust was strong as he knelt beside her, reaching into a dark nest of scorpions. His fingers encountered a clutter of hard objects of varying sizes, wrapped in thin, woolly cloth.

He and Bhaskar unrolled a crusted string that ran around and up the length of two guns and an assortment of pistols. His father's revolver was easily accessible, dismantled in a cardboard box. Bhaskar's supple, familiar fingers put it together in a few minutes, and a highly efficient-looking black weapon lay beside him. They cut the string that held the other weapons. The metal of gun-barrels and the beautifully worked silver of their butts came to view as the cloth fell away. 'These should be in a museum; they're real vintage stock, we surely can't fire them. But we'll take them, anyway. We can always melt the silver down and use the parts in the guns Ajit is learning to make.' Bhaskar was murmuring almost to himself. He had forgotten the middle-aged woman beside him. Her face was blank with disappointment that her gift might be useless after all.

'What about the revolver?' she said at last.

'Oh, certainly, we can use that,' Bhaskar was vibrant once more, the waves of his emotion gathering her back from the corner to which she had retreated.

It drew Satinder back too. His father's sister, Kailash Kaur, had told him how two children had arrived in Kohat many years ago. The boy, Manmohan Singh, had continued to work on these beautiful guns. Now his mother had offered them to Bhaskar as a precious gift, which Bhaskar had not really appreciated. Then he thought of Kotla Loharian, a small village near Sialkot, where a man and a batch of small boys had sat outside in the sun working elaborate designs on iron, until they were overtaken and drowned in waves of British soldiers. It was right, after all, that Manmohan Singh's guns and his father's revolver should go to Bhaskar. Satinder turned over the pistols lying on the ground, holding them up, one by one, to the sunlight that came in through the window, until he came to an exceptionally beautiful one, with a long barrel curving away from a silver stock, the hammer black and smooth above it. 'I'm keeping this one,' he said. He rubbed at it with one of the moth-eaten bits of cloth lying on the ground and put it inside his coat.

Bhaskar smiled at them, taking his attention from calculating the price of silver on the guns, to the mother and son who stood before him. They were drawn back into the vortex of his charm and enthusiasm.

Gathering arms from Kohat proved much more difficult than they had anticipated. Many of the people Satinder and his mother had known were not back yet from Rawalpindi or Lahore where they had fled from the communal riots, though the returning trickle was rapidly increasing in volume. Bhaskar decided they would spend some extra days there.

Prabhjot Kaur said one evening, while she sat shelling peas into a wide, shallow basket, that Sardar Sobha Singh Palji, husband of her sister-in-law, Kailash Kaur, had come from Bhimbar to Kohat on business. He was staying with relatives in the house next to

202

Makhan Singh's in the walled city. He was a restless man who travelled a lot and had many contacts. Perhaps he might help with the guns.

Bhaskar and Satinder went to see him. He was in the room next to the kitchen, a tall, bony man in a *salwar*, with a long shirt and black waistcoat. He stood near the window, looking out into the narrow street below. He smiled at Satinder. 'I was just thinking,' he said, 'that I was standing at this window when I first saw your aunt.'

Satinder remembered him only as a child knows an adult. They had not met since Satinder's father died. Now he looked at him carefully, wondering how to tell him about Bhaskar's mission. In the intervening years, wrinkles round his eyes had deepened and swung in arching circles to the edges of his face. They sat talking on a hard bed covered with a white sheet.

'Yes, I know some people in the hills who could help. Provided you are prepared to meet them,' Palji said.

Satinder wondered why his uncle was looking at him in such a steadfast manner, as if he were at the edge of meaning. His manner was short and swift, the speed of a lonely man, not used to talking.

'I know a band of roaming tribals, you could even call them *dacoits*. They live in the hills. Their leader is connected to you.' He stopped to acknowledge Satinder's surprise. Then he went on more slowly. 'The grandfather of this man was Swaranjit Kaur's lover. Swaranjit Kaur was my wife's aunt, who lived alone for many years in a back room of the house next door. You never knew her; she died long before you were born. The story goes that her husband threw her out on her wedding night because she was not a virgin. In fact, she had conceived a child out of wedlock. The father of the child was a tribal chief who had given her a salt quarry in Kharian which your uncle, Makhan Singh, now owns. She first met this fellow as a very young girl, coming with her brother, Manmohan Singh, through the hills from Sialkot. Then she slipped out to meet him, again and again. When the child was born, he took him back into the hills with him. Garkal the *dacoit* is the son of that child of Swaranjit Kaur, so he is your distant cousin. He can get you guns. Do you want to meet him?'

'Yes,' Satinder said.

'It will have to be near the salt quarries. I know how to contact him; he helped me once before.'

Meanwhile, Makhan Singh's family had returned to his house in the city after the riots. Bhaskar and Satinder went with Prabhjot Kaur to visit them. Makhan Singh himself had not returned. Even when the others came back he refused to return to Kohat and had stayed out at the salt quarries at Kharian.

Palji said that Satinder should come alone to a rendezvous near the salt quarry with Garkal the *dacoit*. 'His name comes from *gar khel*, which means "one who plays in caves".'

Satinder could not take Bhaskar. Now in sole charge, he felt a shifting of responsibility. Something had been handed over, almost without his choosing, and its weight gave him more substance. But the centre of his being was still lonely and untouched, like virgin territory. Empty moments, when he turned, saw and felt nothing, were strung around him like points of cold fire.

He and Palji left their horses tied at the salt quarry in Kharian and walked up into the hills.

Garkal was waiting for them under a tree, his arms hugging his knees, an army cap on his head. In a reflex motion his hand lifted the rifle which lay beside him on the grass, and he rose to greet them. He embraced his cousin. The cartridges in a band across his chest cut into Satinder's flesh. He could smell rough sweat through the man's clothes, the hairy smell of horses and dull comfort of rifle grease. Garkal pushed him back and examined his face, as if searching for a resemblance. Then he smiled, his white teeth suddenly breaching the blackness of his beard and moustache.

'You want guns?' he said. 'I have them for you.' He handed him a leather sack which lay behind the tree. It held five guns and several rounds of ammunition. There was not much further talk. Satinder felt he had left something behind unfinished. He realised he had wanted to talk about Swaranjit Kaur, Garkal's grand-mother, but now it was too late. He and Palji went back via Makhan Singh's salt quarry. His mother had sent a gift for the old man. Palji waited with the guns near a long windowless shed used to store salt, while Satinder went in search of his uncle.

It was already late afternoon. The sun slanted down on an untidy, furrowed network which ran through grey beds of salt. After years of working it there was not much salt left on the surface, but enough to shine with a grey, dull gleam. Thin threads of tunnels led into the earth, to mine the richer veins that lay buried inside. There was some activity near the black mouths of these tunnels. There was not much talking; it was still a long way to the end of the day. Occasionally a child cried or a woman emerged from a distant line of huts where the men lived. One of the men near a vat directed him to a small shack covered with tin and asbestos. 'The office,' he said.

The door of the shack stood open, its only source of air. In the dim light he could barely make out a thin figure lying very still on a string bed in the corner. Close by were a desk and chair and open boxes stuffed with papers, which were probably accounts. Makhan Singh sat up. Satinder was shocked to see how flesh had dropped away from the man's large frame. Skin hung loose over his muscles, bones and tendons. It stretched tight only over the face, defining its bony structure. Darkness had collected in the sockets of his eyes. 'Are you sick, Uncle?' he asked, as he rose from touching his feet.

'No. I can still walk as fast as ever. Perhaps I walk too much. I go into the hills every day.'

Satinder gave him a small sack of green almonds which his mother had plucked from their garden that morning. Then he told him about Bhaskar and the Babbar Akalis. His uncle looked at him for a while, then he stopped him. 'I don't care about all that. But I have something for you,' he said. 'Before my father died, he gave me a small packet of jewellery. It belonged to his aunt, Swaranjit Kaur. He sold the rest to buy salt at the time the taxes rose and he made his fortune in the deal. He should have given it back to her, but he never did. It bothered him, when he was dying, and asked me to give it back. You see he had forgotten that she had died long before him.

'I was carrying this pouch, on my way to sell it, the day those bloody rioters came for me. I've carried it against my skin ever since, like an evil talisman. I must get rid of it.' He reached under his shirt and pulled out a leather pouch, worn smooth and thin through constant rubbing against his skin.

'Why are you giving it to me?' Satinder asked.

'I don't want any more ghosts. Your father has haunted me ever since I inherited his share of the property.'

Satinder emptied the pouch on the bed. Gold sprang into a small rosette of light; the darkness of the room deepened and swung around it in a slow wheel. Satinder looked at the pieces one by one: thick bangles made from gold wires twisted together, strings of carved gold beads, ornaments for the hair in the shape of broad clips with chains going up, pins, and two heavy, decorated combs. His uncle had distanced himself already from the jewellery. He gave out his last piece of information like one speaking from the fringes of space. 'My father said that Swaranjit Kaur once had long, beautiful hair. That is why there are so many hair ornaments.'

He chewed on almonds. A crackle of shells followed Satinder all the way to the horses.

Prabhjot Kaur was not expecting Satinder to go back to Lahore with the three young men who finally collected in her house. 'What will I do? How will it be here, with these two children and no one to help me?'

'I'll keep coming back, but I must get my law degree. I have only a year left.'

The pouch of Swaranjit Kaur's jewellery lay heavy and cold in his pocket. Once, as he swung himself on to his horse at the quarry, he had thought of giving his mother the jewellery. But when Palji asked, 'Did you get anything from the old...?'

'No,' he said.

He kept the leather pouch and Manmohan Singh's beautiful silver pistol for himself. He was carrying them on his person when he got off at Lahore station. He felt as if the brother and sister who had travelled from Sialkot to Kohat now had him by the hand and were pulling him away from the heap of luggage, guns and a basket of almonds with gunny sacking sewn over its mouth which stood near Bhaskar and the other two on the platform.

Satinder went to locate his mother's cousin, the senior ticket collector. He had recently been promoted to station master of Lahore railway station.

'He can take us to the railway canteen to eat,' Satinder said. He located him at the end of a maze of corridors and small offices, standing near a desk talking to two British police officers.

Satinder began to back out of the room, but his uncle had caught sight of him.

'I thought you were in Kohat with your mother,' he said.

The British officers were examining a railway schedule, making notes. 'I've just arrived with some friends. We were looking for a place to eat.'

They would have to get the long, unmistakable shapes of the guns off the railway platform before these two red-faced, brawny men wandered out and saw them. Soon he was back in the verandah which ran along the length of the station building. A fan overhead creaked noisily, not disturbing the heavy layers of air.

206

Satinder's hands were sweating, he wiped them on the seat of his trousers. He looked down the length of the platform, to where he had left his friends.

A tight group had gathered. Policemen were pushing at Bhaskar and the other two. Their hands were bound behind their backs, their luggage and guns shouldered by two constables.

Satinder ducked into the shadows of the verandah and hurried back to his uncle. A small choking sound came from his throat, like an animal caught in a trap. Then he fainted.

His uncle lifted him to a dirty orange sofa that ran along the wall and splashed his face with water until he regained consciousness. His hands were like two separate animals on his thigh; he did not have the energy to raise them. Desolation and panic wrapped around him like a mist, cutting him off from the three men who had been carried away like dead leaves. Had he deserted them?

Could something in his face have betrayed them to the British officers in the station master's office? The police would come for him as well. Perhaps even now his companions were being tortured in Lahore gaol, hung from the ceiling by bound wrists, stripped and beaten with *lathis* on their naked legs and back.

He must get away from the railway station. Nobody would look for him in the station master's house. His uncle sent the office *chaprasi* to show him the way to the railway colony. He walked behind the turbaned man in a white and red uniform like a bridegroom following a loud band to his wedding. Everything else faded and became indistinct. He concentrated utterly on the narrow back in front of him and the brown, hairy neck which rose from it. They went past platforms for goods trains, through railway workshops where silent engines waited to be repaired, with piles of tools and equipment abandoned by mechanics.

As soon as they reached the house Satinder collapsed on a string bed in a courtyard which had recently held red chillies spread out to dry in the sun. He slept immediately, without dreams, like a dead man.

It was dark when he awoke. The lights were on, his uncle was back and sounds of activity and voices came from the house. A smell of frying food floated out into the dark air and grabbed his empty stomach almost before he was fully awake. Then the dead heaviness of his hours of sleep dropped from him and he left the courtyard rapidly, heading towards Sampuran's house. He would find it easily enough: 23 Shahi Lane. It led off the Lower Mall,

Sampuran had said. Even so he felt he was heading into darkness.

A circuitous route skirted the area of the railway station. Soon he was at the foundries and hardware shops, at the markets that sold wool, metals and fruit. Shops and *godowns* were shut, their goods pulled back firmly behind wooden cross-barred doors or iron gratings. A couple of the foundries were open. A red glow from their fires, the huge black shadowy shapes of men working at them, the sound of hammers striking on iron and the grating crunch of metal sprang out to Satinder. Everything after his recent sleep seemed to be abnormally vivid and distinct.

There was much more life in Anarkali Bazaar. Eating places buzzed with customers and most of the shops were still open. Sample goods hung out on to the street, swinging from protruding shelters of tin and asbestos sheets, or from canvas awnings looped on wooden poles. He walked under brightly coloured hair-pieces, rows of glittering glass bangles, floating banners of Dacca muslin and newly arrived nylon saris from Japan.

A big board saying 'Razak's Tailoring Dept' rose above his head, on the second storey directly under the eaves. The outline of a folded shirt with a pointed collar was picked out on the board by a thin tube of light; it came on and off as he waited outside Hashim's 'Tasty Snacks' for a place to sit. Then the light went off and the board became a dull, white blur: Razak had finished for the day.

Satinder was eating with the urgency of one who had not eaten for several days. He gobbled two *samosas*, a pile of *naans* gleaming with butter, a glass of tea and finally a huge piece of *tandoori* fish, the crisp layer of spices and batter crackling in his mouth, crumbling under his fingers to reveal the pure, white flesh inside.

Sometime later in the night he would have to go back through Bhati Gate to their old quarters in Dabhi Bazaar. A large rusty key for the padlock shifted in his upper pocket as he rose to pay his bill, clanked dully against the silver pistol inside his coat. The leather pouch containing the jewellery was on the other side of his chest, soaked with sweat.

He left the Anarkali behind and walked fast. The shape of the museum rose on his right, shadowy and dull in the light from a small moon. His head was crowded with buzzing sounds from his past hours of talking with Sampuran. Shahi Lane turned off the Lower Mall, just beyond the law courts. Number 23 was a small, two-storeyed house which Sampuran shared with a lawyer.

He knocked at the door. A face peeped through glass panes at the top, then ducked down. A woman opened the door. She stood there, still holding it, framed in light, looking at him enquiringly. Her head was uncovered, her hair cut short, falling in black, curling waves over her shoulders. Blue flowers sprang to him from her *salwar-kameez*. He had an impression of a large, rounded frame, firm breasts, and a froth of blue chiffon around her neck. Then light caught the balding fringe of Sampuran's head as he entered the room, and made shallow pools in the pockmarks on his face. He hurried forward, his plump arms stretched out to embrace Satinder.

'This is my sister, Poonam,' he said. 'She arrived some days ago from San Francisco. She will live here, now.'

Sampuran's enthusiasm battered against the glass pane of Satinder's silence, a terrible, cold heaviness, which shut him in even more than before.

Sampuran looked at him questioningly. He drew Satinder towards cane chairs in a corner, settled an embroidered cushion behind his back as if he were sick. Satinder saw his waiting face, and Poonam standing behind him. He found his voice with enormous difficulty. Hot, sour juices were rising in his throat; he felt he was choking on the food he had eaten.

'What happened?' Sampuran asked, 'Did something go wrong? Where are Bhaskar and the other two?'

'They were picked up by the police at the railway station. The guns, too. Our friends went from the station with handcuffs on their wrists. I don't know where they are now.'

'How come they didn't pick you up as well?' he said. 'Weren't you travelling together?' His question made Satinder feel resentful and helpless. He said nothing.

They went carefully over the event, detail by detail. 'What made you wait so long before you started to come here?' Sampuran said. But his voice was kind. Satinder clung to it like a hurt animal and was ashamed. 'It's going to be so difficult, in this darkness, to find a friendly lawyer, then go crawling from one police station to another to locate them. Meanwhile, God knows what the police will have done to the poor boys. They have their ways of getting information out of prisoners.'

Waves of shame washed over Satinder. 'I went to sleep in my uncle's-house. I just could not keep my eyes open.' But at that point Sampuran was intent on what to do next. He refused to take Satinder with him on the search.

'There might be a witness from the train or station who would recognise you. Just put off the lights and stay upstairs. Don't open the door to anyone.'

Sampuran's presence and his questions had kept Satinder alert and responsive. After he left he sank into inertia. Poonam struggled with the chain which secured the door. From a great distance he heard her scratching efforts at the door. To have been picked up with the others would have taken care of so many questions in his life. But also he was aware of being glad to be free.

Poonam was shaking his elbow. 'You should go upstairs now. It's very late.'

He followed her to Sampuran's bedroom. His books were all around, in piles on the floor, in chairs, on tables, at the narrow desk where Poonam made him sit. Then she settled herself cross-legged on the bed. The curtains were drawn to keep in the dim light from the lamp. He was uncomfortable to have her sitting there. 'Why don't you go to sleep?' he suggested.

She shook her head. 'I'd rather wait for Sampuran to return, I can see that you are not going to sleep, either.'

Her voice was soft. He wondered vaguely what she meant. Then he dropped into deep lethargy, and it was difficult to focus when she put her next question to him. Then he was wrapped in a beauty and warmth which seemed to be reaching out to him.

'You haven't asked about me at all,' Poonam said. 'About how I happen to be here or anything like that.'

'Sampuran said you came from San Francisco.'

'Yes, I arrived in Karachi a week ago, by an P & O steamer that came via Tokyo. Then I took a train. I'm still adjusting to being on firm ground again. A long journey. Have you ever been across the Pacific Ocean?'

'I've never been outside India,' Satinder said.

She continued to offer him her life piece by piece, to hold in his hand.

Her first journey had been nine years ago, straight after she had finished her BA from Berkely University in California, when she had come with her parents and two aunts to Jullundur, and had gone immediately to their village. 'Gyani Basantpur,' she said, 'Post Office Barparvaha, Block Hainsar Bazaar, District Jullundur. It was my address for three years after that. They married me to Seth Chaman Lal's youngest son, Jagdish. A solid land-owning family, very active in politics, Arya Samajis, staunch

210

followers of Gandhiji and Swami Dayanand. Sethji went often to Delhi, to Amritsar, even to Lahore. He was one of the important Hindu leaders to address a mammoth gathering at the Golden Temple after the atrocities at Guru-ka-Bagh. Often he took his elder sons with him. Between them they covered the various groups and factions in politics. My husband was left to look after the land and it bothered him that he was cut out of the excitement.

'Gandhiji began to encourage women to join the Independence Movement. Even my mother-in-law went to a *khadi*-spinning session organised by Sethji's group near Jullundur. I begged to be allowed to go, to join *morchas*, but my husband resolutely refused. Perhaps he resented my education. Then he began to beat me. The more he sensed my restlessness of spirit, my desire to get out, the more he beat me. And he began to talk about the insufficient dowry my father had given me.

' "I'm educated," I said. "I can help with the accounts, I can type out your letters, do many things."

' "I don't need you for all that," he said, leering at me, making it quite clear what he needed me for.

'I pulled out my heavy *zari* saris, laid out what remained of my wedding jewellery, since most of it had been taken for his sister's wedding, pointed to the Honda motorcycle which had come across the sea as a wedding present, to the Willy's jeep which stood at his door. "All that was my dowry," I said to him. It made no difference.

'Then, one day, in a state of excitement, he almost killed me, pressing his fingers deep into my neck and shutting off the air. You can see the marks even today.' Her hand rubbed reflectively at a faint, bluish tinge at the base of her neck. Satinder was listening now, drawn completely into her story.

'My father took me back to the United States, and a divorce was arranged easily enough. Jagdish, my husband, was frightened.

'Sethji let me go; he was worried that if my story became public it would affect his political standing.'

She told him of how she had continued with her studies and had got a Master's Degree. Sampuran had written to her to come to Lahore to help him in the Babbar Akali Movement. He was going out into the villages and needed women to talk to the village ladies. He had got her a job, to teach English Literature at the Government College for Women.

Poonam made Satinder a gift of facts, the story of her life,

211

throwing him a line to pull him out of a trough of silence. His face turned away from the glare of the reading lamp. He saw her on the bed, sitting, shifting, talking; the tones of her skin were suddenly immensely alive, warm and attractive. He saw his hands laid flat on the top of the table, each finger separate and distinct.

He put his hand under his shirt. 'There is something I want to give you,' he said to Poonam. The room had closed in around them. Its darkness was a cocoon. Light lay in soft swathes. Slowly he took Swaranjit Kaur's jewellery from the leather pouch and put it in a neat circle, edge touching edge, in the light. Her fingers ran caressingly over it.

'Whose is it?' she whispered.

He told her about a young girl who had come through the hills with her brother, had captured British guns and rifles for tribal insurgents, about bright eyes over a camp-fire that had locked into hers with passion. He had hardly known of these things until he began talking to Poonam.

He told Poonam about the gift of a salt quarry, of how Swaranjit Kaur had gone to her lover in the wheatfields under *babul* trees beside the Kohat river which flowed underground at a distant point north of the city. Then he told her about the wedding night, when Swaranjit Kaur's new husband had turned her out of the house for not being a virgin.

'She should not have married,' Poonam said, and shivered.

'She never betrayed her passion again. She died in silence.'

'Why are you giving me this jewellery? It must be very precious.'

'Please, take it. She would have liked that. Makhan Singh, my uncle, wanted to return the jewellery taken by his father, but Swaranjit Kaur had been dead twenty years by then. It hung heavy on his soul, so he gave it to me instead. But it doesn't really belong to me, either. If you like, you can sell the jewellery and give the money to Sampuran for the Movement.'

'I don't want to sell it; I want to wear it. Will you help me put it on?'

At first he was clumsy with clasps and pointed hooks. Then ease came into his fingers, into his whole body; they became one co-ordinated urge of grace, picking up speed under the skin, moving to her with a pulsing, unknown energy. He fixed the last comb in her hair and her neck was still arching below his face, soft and sleepy, her head given to the movement of his hands. Then his lips were on her skin; he was kissing her with a desperate, happy

212

knowledge that he could not leave her now; she was cleaving to him, melting into his flesh.

His hands were in her clothes, his eyes closed. All his past, his hurt, his guilt, his fear, his silence, he was burying in her body. It was running through him, flowing out into the band of the dull, soundless vacuum that had padded him from the world, filling it and stripping it, cleansing him, making him whole, as if now he would always hear her smallest whisper, feel the faintest movement of her skin. Guru-ka-Bagh was finally left behind and he did not need Sampuran's guns any more.

At first her body was flashing and bewildered, fastened immobile by the terror of his passion. Then she was moving under him, taking him in, grinding her own violence and pain into his bones.

As if their flesh had always known that here, finally, there would be release and freedom in joy and delight, in the birth of passionate mystery. That when they rose at dawn their bodies would be full of the thunder of bird-calls.

23

Marriage and Death

The interrogation centre was ringed by towers, each equipped with a powerful, rotating searchlight. Soldiers with guns stood at close points around the electric fence. Perhaps he could manage to escape the coils of electric current by jumping across to a tree twenty yards outside the fence, but the snipers would certainly get him. There was no possibility of freedom. Better to find a more accessible form of death.

Sampuran managed to get to him the first two volumes of Gibbons' *Decline and Fall of the Roman Empire*. What would happen to the British Empire? His cheeks were too stiff to smile at the hopeful choice of title. For twenty-four hours they had kept his face pointed to a powerful light, forcibly open to the glare, until blood had welled from his eyes. But still he had told them lies.

Nothing about the murder of Captain Rawlings, who had conducted the shameful beatings at Guru-ka-Bagh, nothing about their plan to kill Bowrine, for which the guns had come from Bannu and Kohat, nothing about Satinder, his mother, or the *dacoit* from the Kohat hills, who had supplied them the guns. So far, all this information had been safe with him. He wondered what Gurmukh and Ajit, his two companions arrested at the railway station with him, had told the police.

The police *havildar* smirked as he handed over the books. 'Some woman brought these. Her head was covered with a blue *dupatta*. Good-looking woman. You sleep with her? What do you do with her? Tell me about it, eh?' He dug him hard in the ribs.

Bhaskar winced. They had hung him from the ceiling and had beaten him severely, swinging him round and round to get at any portion of his bare skin the thin, wet stick had left untouched. His skin was sore and throbbing; he could hardly bear the touch of his clothes. The *havildar*'s rough hand hurt him. 'I don't know who she is. Why didn't you ask her?' he said. He really had no idea who the woman was. It must have been someone sent by Sampuran or Satinder. Meanwhile he was concentrating on keeping the *havildar* in good humour. He would have to persuade him to let him keep the bathroom door shut when he went in there next time.

'Quite a spirited woman! She was tossing her head like a horse. Even the Sahib could hardly keep his hands off her; I could see he wanted to squeeze her breasts. Otherwise you think he would have let her give in two books for you? You're only permitted one, under the Defence of India Act. But he couldn't permit the other thing she wanted.'

'What was that? What did she want?' he asked, although his heart had sunk like a stone to know that they were putting the Defence of India Act on to him.

'She kept insisting on a lawyer and a trial and such like. So the Sahib got very close to her and showed her the Act, going through it line by line with his finger.'

Bhaskar longed for the *havildar* to leave, but the man was obviously in a garrulous mood. 'I stood there for an hour watching her,' he said, 'though the Sahib wanted me to leave; he kept gesturing towards the door. We have women like that in Kohat, brave women. You don't see them here.'

'Oh, you're from Kohat!'

214

'Why, do you know Kohat? Have you been there?' The *havildar* was beginning to loosen up.

'Do I know Kohat! Of course. I love it. If ever I get the chance, I'll live there,' Bhaskar said.

'I agree with you one hundred per cent. These pale people of Lahore are no comparison. Their skins never see the sun. And their hearts are mean as hell; they wouldn't do a thing for anyone.'

'Everyone is so warm and friendly in Kohat. I felt as if I were in my mother's house.'

'Were you there recently? It is three years since they gave me leave to go back there.' The *havildar*'s voice was eager.

'Not recently,' Bhaskar said carefully. 'It was some time ago. The North West Frontier Province Government employed me to examine salt quarries, for fixing the amount of tax.'

But the *havildar* had already embarked on his dreams. 'What excellent partridge shooting near the quarries! What a pleasure to go out at dawn with a gun and hear your dog going through the bushes, flushing out the birds. And then to eat partridge pickle! Nothing in the world like it, except the women. They are really great. This woman of yours, in the blue *dupatta*, reminds me of them. My grandfather's first wife was a woman called Swaranjit Kaur. Also a woman of spirit. He turned her out of the house on her wedding night. They say she was in love with someone in the hills. Can you imagine that?'

There was no time now. The afternoon bell had rung, his new-found friend would leave soon, 'Listen, *Havildar* Sahib,' Bhaskar said. 'You know I am suffering from this terrible dysentery. It troubles me greatly to keep the bathroom door open when I go in, and have the smells and everything coming out to you.'

The *havildar* was still dreaming about Kohat; there was a bulge in his trousers. 'Okay,' he said. 'It's against regulations, but you can keep the door closed.'

Bhaskar scraped with a piece of broken glass at the rubber insulation on wires leading to the electric light overhead. Soon he had exposed enough of the wire to kill himself if he put his wrist against it. The scene was prepared.

Then he got back to his cell and opened the books, forcing himself to turn the pages casually. There could be a half-open eye at the official peep-hole in the door. Even so, his body jerked when he came to the first encircled letter. There was another one in the second book. 'G' and 'A'. So, both Gurmukh and Ajit had broken

215

in the interrogations. There must have been widespread arrests already – Master Mota Singh, *Havildar* Major Kishan Singh, Sreedhar, and others whom the two boys knew.

But there could have been no hangings yet, since the two boys had joined after Captain Rawlings' murder and knew nothing of who had committed it. And they did not know of Satinder's political contacts in Kohat. He had to protect them; he had the knowledge. He couldn't afford to let them break him down.

Bhaskar killed himself on the day Satinder got married.

Satinder and Poonam had reached Maharajah Ranjit Singh's *samadhi* early in the morning. Seven o'clock, the Bhaiji had said, agreeing rather reluctantly to marry them in the *gurudwara* attached to the *samadhi*.

A big *pipal* tree in the courtyard, sprouting tender brown-green leaves at the beginning of summer, was still hung with the mist of early morning when they arrived. The priest's regular business had not yet begun.

'No relatives?' he asked curiously.

Poonam shook her head. Sampuran, her brother, was in Jullundur. Satinder smiled. It seemed to him that he wanted to smile and smile infinitely. 'My family is in Kohat,' he said.

With one wave of his hand, Bhaiji called in people who were camping under the *pipal* tree, two families of Sikh traders from Afghanistan on a long pilgrimage. They had come from the Punja Sahib *gurudwara* near Taxila. Bhaiji spread a cotton carpet on the flat stones of the courtyard and the group seated itself as audience and witnesses of the wedding.

Poonam's *dupatta* was tied to Satinder's *kurta* and the priest performed a few minimum ceremonies, chanting prayers in a loud, smooth, sweet voice, which filled Satinder with pleasure as he walked in slow circles round the Holy Book.

Satinder's mouth carried the taste of soft semolina *pershad*, running with *ghee* and swollen with raisins, which the priest had distributed at the end of the wedding. He walked with Poonam towards the Badshahi Mosque. Her body fluttered very close to his. He could feel her delight; that she wanted to touch and hold him. He longed to put his arm around her waist, to pull her close and feel the length of her body against his. But the time was not yet, he could not hold her as they walked between the rising stones of the Fort and the low wall of Maharajah Ranjit Singh's *samadhi*.

She smiled at him; her face was open to him. 'I want to hold you,' he said, 'but if I did, someone would tell us that this is India and not California, that the place is holy, and that men and women should not walk here, holding each other.'

The ache of his desire went out to her. 'I've seen the Badshahi Mosque before,' she said, 'but now it is like seeing everything for the first time.'

They climbed the steps which led up to the three foot high base platform. She put her slippers neatly beside his brown, shabby pair of shoes and wandered off to read a plaque which gave a history of the mosque.

'I love the feel of these old stones under my feet,' she said. 'They are already warm from the sun.'

A low, marble-screened raised rectangle for the Imam was at the opposite edge of a central square. The square was so large that the beautiful dome and minarets rising above seemed to belong elsewhere. It was punctuated by a flat-edged pool whose water, disturbed by hands being washed in it, quivered above blue and silver paint in the bottom.

'This square could hold *lakhs* of people,' Satinder said.

'Can you imagine!' Poonam was excited. 'Millions and millions of prayers must go up from these stones!'

He looked into her eyes as she spoke, and the air around his head was thick with twittering sounds, as if millions of birds were preparing to sleep at dusk. He closed his eyes under the weight of sound. Then he put his hand out and pulled Poonam gently down beside him on the stones she had made alive with her spirit.

There were not many people in the mosque that morning. Women in grey *burqas*, veils thrown back over their heads, had settled on the stone floor near by. Their children played in sunlight and shade, going between high columns that held up the fluted corridor which skirted three sides of the square and ran at either end into the main structure.

A few men cleaned and polished the marble, reaching up with long sticks to wipe dust from the walls and ceiling. Others stood near an office behind a green door, which held a heavy donation box and an official chair and table. Yet another bastion of bureaucracy stood near a side gate which opened to the Old City, not as big as the main one, but high and studded with a heavy, iron pattern. A chair and table, with two men to give out eight *anna* tickets, guarded the entrance to the one minaret that visitors were

217

permitted to climb. Satinder felt for coins in his pocket, looking at a group of women who sat near by.

'They're obviously from Kashmir,' he told Poonam. 'You see their long, loose *phirins* and *salwars*, and the way the headcloth is tied, over the forehead and knotted at the back of the head? And the silver jewellery? I recognise it from my aunt, Kailash Kaur, who lives in Bhimbar, which is part of Kashmir State. Her husband travels all over the place, especially to Poonch and Srinagar. He got us the guns which were confiscated from Bhaskar on Lahore railway station, that night when we first met.' Slowly he was letting her into his life.

She had her back to the ticket desk, looking up at another minaret, much closer to the central dome. A wide, shallow grey cone jutted from one of the thin supports, a loudspeaker tied to the stone with thick wire. 'Is that where they address the congregation from?' she asked, pointing. 'Whoever speaks from there would have the ear of *lakhs* of people on Friday, at the time of weekly prayers. I would love to see you do that, though you wouldn't notice my face in the middle of a huge congregation.'

'A Sikh addressing Muslims from up there?' His voice was sharp and excited.

'A man speaking to people.'

'But first I must have something to say,' he said, lightly, laughing, moving her towards the entrance to the minaret. He translated a board in Urdu which hung on the wall. 'It gives the times of the daily prayers. You see the pictures of five clock-faces, showing the times? That's in case you can't read. And the board tells you how to behave in the minaret. Not to jostle or push, which could be dangerous.'

'Make sure you don't push me off,' she said, giggling. Her palm was flat against the cool, beaded exterior of an earthenware pot balanced on a wooden stool at the entrance. The man beside it tapped a long-handled scoop lightly against his teeth as he waited to pour water on demand. A long line of glasses stood ready and waiting.

Access to the minaret was in stages. A broad staircase led up to the parapet. A narrower path led along the edge to the next staircase, which wound up to the minaret itself. They could see clustered domes beyond it. The stones were much hotter under their feet than they had been in the courtyard. They passed six huge iron rings set at intervals into heavy blocks of sandstone.

218

'They must have tied prisoners or horses to these.'

At the edge of the parapet, they leaned over curved, punctured arches which both decorated and guarded the edge. A strip of the Old City lay between the mosque and Hathi Gate, one of the thirteen which opened in the encircling wall of Lahore. A low shack of rough, cemented bricks, nestling against the wall of the mosque, proclaimed itself as a 'reporting room'. Policemen in brown berets, with fringed yellow cords across their chests, stood at the door, leaned against the wall, or lay in string beds in the shade, their cracked heels in black sandals turned up to the sun. Satinder moved Poonam on; he did not like policemen.

They were now standing over a large tree, barren and leafless until he saw its small green shoots. The entrapping arms of its twisted, spreading branches had destroyed several paper kites, their clinging remains fluttered a warning, like wedding decorations. Undeterred, young boys stood at its base, flying more kites. Maybe the wind was good in this section. Across the road, barred windows were set into high buildings, a few freshly painted, with special attention given to wooden frames, and narrow balconies crowded with potted plants. The bright green and blue of their paint exposed the shame of neighbouring grey façades. All the ostentatiousness of paint gathered into the splendour of Hotel Vakil, its frontage covered in green, white and orange stripes, punctuated with elaborate grilles at the windows. Satinder turned to look down at the road.

A cow with narrow horns, her back stained with large patches of colour from a recent celebration, strolled across and stopped to rub her swollen udders against parked cars, cyclists, *tongas*, itinerant buffaloes and rickshaws. Pedestrians avoided her carefully. Some looked up to read a banner strung above their heads, which announced a *Mushaira* inside Bhati Gate.

'Can you smell tea boiling over?' he asked Poonam, suddenly a little anxious, turning towards her. A huge kettle bubbled by the roadside, beside an open box arrayed with *paan* and cigarettes. Their owner tried hopelessly to cope with two trades. A *rickshaw-wallah* sat idly in the back of his parked vehicle, waiting for tea or a customer, whichever came first.

Poonam had gone on. She stood staring at a cluster of domes and thin, fluted minarets which tumbled out from the central dome. They were too close to her eyes, too close to each other, for any pretensions of symmetry, order or grace. Curved brass spikes glowed at the top of each dome, casting radiance on layers of untidy bird droppings which festooned the sandstone, and lay along white lines of inlaid marble which traced the lines of the minarets. The air was pregnant with the sound of cooing pigeons.

'How awkwardly the domes cut off the sky,' Poonam said. 'These sections of blue sky are all jumbled up, as if nothing was born from them, no grace or beauty. Though we saw it as beautiful a little while ago, standing below in the courtyard.'

'Their beauty is artificial and is meant to be looked at only from the courtyard, from where the artist planned it. But I can look at you from anywhere and always find you beautiful.'

'We'll see,' she said, delighted.

They were at the base of the minaret now. A long, narrowing spiral led up to the slim eyelids at the top. They were drawn into it, to climb three wooden steps and then be in the stomach of the world where chaos would be resolved. He had given himself to homogenous darkness; air fell away from him in layers; he belonged with the woman climbing before him, as with nothing else. He took off his socks at her command, his feet spreading very white and clean on the well-worn, smooth stones. Then he couldn't see them any more, in the soft velvet spiral, which was utterly dark.

Poonam went ahead, they had to feel each step. There was no getting used to this darkness, no possibility of light through the thick stones. Their hands encountered narrow air- and light-holes, but they were blocked with twigs and leaves from old nests. Their breath brought in the smell of age and of stone rubbed smooth from bodies that had brushed past the walls.

He lost shape and identity, belonging entirely now to a vacuum, to the aura which had surrounded him for so long. His soul spread and spread, until it joined with the queer band of silence and he was rising, floating up behind Poonam, as if through water, weightless, with no name, generous and unknown as a species, a nothing.

Then Poonam's hand reached down towards him. It arrived and touched his skin with an electric silence, as if sensation were born in that moment, with a strange newness and wonder. His flesh coalesced around her hand, pieces coming together almost out of the air, like a jigsaw puzzle whose edges had never previously known or recognised each other or fitted any picture until they belonged around Poonam's hand. His body surged, resolved, locked into the strongest erection he had ever known, his whole life went into it. His head threw back, his mouth opened in a scream which would burst the stones. His arm and jacket were in his mouth. He could feel blood bursting through his bitten skin and a wetness running down his leg. A series of deep shudders went through his body, running up and down it, taking it over. He leaned against the wall, still holding her hand, though she was pulling at it faintly, urging him on, wondering why he had stopped in the silent darkness. Would he break up into little pieces now if her hand left him?

'Wait,' he said.

She felt him then, the twitching of his body in the last throes of orgasm and came down to his step, holding him even as her own desire rose and bubbled inside her, trembling like a stormy pool against her lips and her skin, straining and rubbing against him, as if every inch had to fuse with him.

The long sound of a cough came travelling down the stair, hollow and picking up speed as it hit off and ricocheted from impervious walls. An old man cleared his throat loudly and spat over the edge of the minaret. They stood still, as if listening for the spit to land on the ground a hundred feet below. Then they laughed and continued up the stairs. The old man was at the top, squatting on his haunches against one of the pillars, a small, rolled-up fragment of humanity. He did not even look around as they brushed past to reach for a place on a narrow, curving platform at the head of the stairs.

'It's quite different from here,' Poonam said. 'You can't see the City at all. It is as if it didn't exist.'

Satinder was looking around. 'I don't see the river,' he said. 'Those are the wholesale markets. It should be just beyond.' He stepped back, and then cried out, rocking his body forward. He had regained his balance by the time he reached her arm, but his voice was still astonished. 'I didn't realise the opening of the stair was right behind me. I could have dropped straight down that black hole.'

The fear of it shadowed her face, as she watched donkeys with saddle-sacks of bricks and grain leaving the markets. A camel train loaded with firewood went along the canal. A timelessness of stone and centuries hung about the animals and sweetened his own sudden fear.

A large group of boys of varying ages had crowded up behind them. He tried without success to put his body between her and the sweaty, aggressive creatures who wanted to press up against a pretty woman. The loud clatter of their footsteps coming down the stairs was behind them all the way down, past the five clock-faces and the *mutka* of cold water and out into the central square. Then the group melted away, diminished and silenced by the stature of the dome and the arching beauty of the embellished ceilings. Satinder and Poonam were left alone with the stones.

They were strolling towards the entrance gate. 'Wait a moment,' she said, moving him to the edge of the central pool. Its waters were shallow and clear above bright blue paint. She knelt on the splashed cement of its edge, scooping water between her cupped hands and slowly washed his feet. He looked down, his body held like a statue. Her bent shoulders were embarrassed but absorbed, as if the whole weight of the mosque and its meaning had gathered in them. When she had finished and was still, he sat beside her, and in turn washed her feet. Now the men hanging around the courtyard were really staring, amazed; they had never seen a man washing a woman's feet before. Satinder felt his love like a warm, beautiful stream, dripping from his hands to her feet.

'Shall we go through the Old City?' he said, when they were out of the mosque. 'I want to show you the place in Dabhi Bazaar where we will live.'

'Not yet,' she said, 'we must go to the Fort.'

'Today? But it's late afternoon already, and you must be tired. Can't we go another day?'

'I had a dream last night. There's something I must see,' she said. 'I dreamed I had built a beautiful house, an enormous palace, a fort, actually. The most beautiful thing. Its walls were red and green with light; they shimmered and glowed, radiant and exquisite. It was on a huge, steep rock that dropped in a precipice to the sea below, and on the other side was a lake with a forest behind it, covered in yellow flowers. But the fort, the house, was not complete. I could not complete it and the sadness of that hung heavy and sweet on me. I gave the sadness to you, and to the third person – I don't know who he was, who travelled with us as we went from room to empty room, where windows and doors hung vacant and gaping.

'I told you that maybe I should have built a smaller house and that then I would have been able to complete it, but you did not answer, only conveyed to me that you too were sad, and struck by the utter beauty, the marvellous light, which came from the stones

222

that I had built. You could not answer, because really I was asking the question of myself.'

He saw the light of her dream behind her skin like the beauty of creation.

'I can still feel the sorrow of wanting to complete my fort. It was so beautiful, Satinder! I can't describe the colour adequately — sort of red, with an intense green coming from behind it, full of light.'

He felt tired, his limbs laden with a strange, heavy fatigue, as if they were full of sleep. They followed a line of people walking across the Fort to a small cupola that nestled on a central platform. He sensed that she was absorbed, anxious to get on, looking for something. At last they were on the parapet, gazing out at the river Ravi where evening shadows first gathered.

Already the quietness of his body was beginning to affect her and she stood very close to him. The river was a harsh, wide-eyed, fickle creature, meandering towards the southwest, washing and cutting into the north-west corner of the Old City which belonged to him today.

She was almost supporting him now, holding him as they walked. He stumbled so often, like a sleepwalker. They had left the Masti Gate far behind and were in the heart of the Waksawali quarter. Streets were familiar and evening life was beginning to gather in them. They unfolded sinuously, dark and comforting. He resented the wider roads, few and far between, unnaturally lit up, full of honking cars and trucks, barbarians in the delicate flavour of the old streets. Heat increased as they got further and further into the Old City. Four-storey buildings with flat roofs tilted closer and closer to each other across the streets and lanes. Latrines at the top, and flowing, open drains released vile gases into the air. Poonam had covered her face with the end of her *dupatta*. Finally they were at the last street before his house over Dabhi Bazaar. Here the shops were small and open fronted. On one side they sold copybooks, stationery, skipping ropes, and plastic toys for children; on the opposite side piles of spices: turmeric, red chillies and fragrant cardamom.

He was relieved to reach Dabhi Bazaar. Here, the cloth merchants, even the vendors with carts, knew him. They called out as he passed, asking after his mother and the rest of the family, gazing curiously at Poonam, waiting to put their questions. Then he and Poonam were climbing the narrow, dark flight of steps to the door.

He gathered her in his arms and took her straight to the bed near the kitchen. Like two creatures going into soil they burrowed in the dank sheets, feeling their age and softness and how the cloth had been untouched during months of absence.

Their lovemaking went out against the walls, the door, the unswept floor. It ballooned out of the window and spread as a dream of glory over the Fort, the Old City, the Badshah Mosque, full of prayers and consecrations. Then they were asleep, their arms around each other, and their bodies sweaty with summer heat.

The letter, in a brown envelope, was waiting for them on the doorstep when they reached Sampuran's house in Shahi Lane, later in the day. A typed sheet informed them that Mr Bhaskar, arrested under the Defence of India Act, had committed suicide in prison. His personal effects could be picked up from Room Number 8 in the prison annexe. Poonam had given her own name and address when she had delivered the books; it was the only connection the prison authorities knew, since Bhaskar had told them nothing.

'They've already cremated him; I have been asked only to collect his "effects".' She was crying, crumpling the coarse brown sheet between her hands. 'Don't wait. Go to Jullundur; Sampuran's called you. I'll do the rest here. I know you don't want to go. I never want you to go, but you must. There's work to be done.'

Satinder travelled on the same cement truck which had brought Sampuran's message and met him as arranged, in a tea-shop near the railway crossing coming in to Jullundur on the Ludhiana road. Lines of buses had stopped there; he and Sampuran would be taken for bus passengers, waiting for the trains to pass. Sampuran's body was relaxed and he was tilting back his straight-backed chair against the wall. Urgency showed only in the speed of his words, which gave Satinder no time to think or question. Sampuran's eyes bulged from their crinkly lashes; one hand went up to rub at his throat. It was his only gesture of nervousness. He had lost a great deal of weight since they had last met in Lahore, the skin at his neck hung above a brown-checked bush-shirt.

'There's something you have to do, Satinder. But first to fill you in on what's been happening in the Movement. A great deal in the last month; arrests, a couple of hangings, large-scale investigations. I won't give you details, there's no need – and the less you know the better. But there hasn't been a single trial yet. They're trying to keep the matter quiet, to destroy the Babbar Movement in silence.'

Satinder was listening, his legs crossed and one hand slowly rubbing the other, exactly like the rickshaw-man waiting under the parapets of the Badshahi Mosque. He knew, certainly and definitely, that Sampuran's answers were not for him; he didn't need them any more.

A young boy came to take their order. 'What's that new building coming up?' Satinder asked. A large structure had begun to be built on the other side of the railway crossing, visible above its crossed white bars and the large, glowing red eye of the closed gate.

'A college,' the boy said.

Then the owner of the teashop came up behind him, and added, 'Khalsa College. The Akalis are building it. The Sarkar gave them the land. Trying to keep them away from the Congress and the Babbars. But the British have finished off the Babbars now.'

The two men moved to another teashop, almost against the wall of the prospective Khalsa College. 'We have to do something right away,' Sampuran said. 'You heard what he said? We need new recruits, and something to boost the courage of our present cadres. You can do it, Satinder. No one knows you are here.'

'What do you mean?' he said.

'Tomorrow morning, Colonel Fisher of the Sikh Regiment is to cross a suspension bridge across a deep canal which runs close by my village of Gyani Basantpur, forty miles from here. He will be accompanied by officers on horseback and foot soldiers. Today he is in the town of Sarsawan, where he has sentenced Master Motia Singh to death. We can do nothing about that; the poor man will be hanged this evening. But tomorrow morning, when the whole party is on the bridge, you must blow it up and kill them all. It will be seen as fitting revenge and that the Babbars are still alive and active.'

Satinder was stunned. 'Tomorrow morning? What are you talking about, Sampuran?'

'It's possible to do it. We will never get more notice than this. Bhai Dhian Singh will lay the dynamite charges under the bridge, I've already informed him. He is a reliable but ancient man in my village and manages the *gurudwara* which my father has funded for years. He will do what I say. He'll hide you until the heat has passed. Then you can return to Lahore and no one will be the wiser. The village people will not give you away.'

Satinder interrupted him. 'I've just married your sister,' he said.

Sampuran stared at him incredulously. 'You've married

Poonam?' His body was stiff with excitement. 'And you've waited all this time to tell me?'

'Did you let me speak before?'

Sampuran pushed his chair back, came around the table, embraced Satinder. 'And I'm sending you off to possible death! She'll never forgive me. But you must go all the same,' he added hurriedly.

They began to walk down the road to the bus stop. A bus came at once and Satinder got in. He was talking to Sampuran through the window. 'When I was at the Guru-ka-Bagh beatings, some years ago, something broke in me. The *jathedars* did not hit back or cry out. For years I've needed something to bridge the space those *jathedars* emptied out with their silence. Your sister's done that for me; she is my life. Some months ago I would have offered myself willingly to do this killing. But now it's different. I'm at peace now. I don't need to do this. I understand a little bit now what non-violence means – taking life entirely and wholly, not violating anything. Sampuran, I can't do what you're suggesting.'

Sampuran was looking at him with barely concealed disdain. 'I don't understand. I'm not asking you to do this for yourself. It's for us. I've explained why.'

'I'm not sure that I agree this is the best method of publicity,' Satinder said, his voice clear and confident, pompous in his own ears.

'There's no time; it has to be done tomorrow, and you have to do it. Everything that's happened in the past few months – your journey to Kohat, the arrests since then – whether you like it or not, has carried you past the threshold of choice.'

'But there is a spark that must connect past events to an act like this. I don't feel it.'

'Are you telling me that you are afraid?'

'No, it's not fear. But I don't have the need to kill, anymore.'

'Nevertheless you must do it. As part of your life. I won't ask you for anything else again. Please, this you must do. For the sake of everything in the past year. Then we'll let you drop out and become a Gandhian, if you want.'

'But, I already am a Gandhian.' Satinder was surprised to discover this truth inside himself; it was like touching something soft and perfect and healthy in his body.

'No. Please, Satinder. You must get off at the bus stop near Gyani Basantpur. I'll see you later in Lahore. I'll tell Poonam where you have gone. She'll be proud of you.'

'No. I'll tell her myself.'

The bus was moving off. Satinder nodded to Sampuran through the window. Then he reached inside his coat to feel his ancestor's silver pistol. Perhaps he should have given that to Poonam as well.

Bhai Dhian Singh was much older than Satinder expected. His body was thin inside a flapping shirt, the collar limp and well washed around his leathery neck. His hair was grey and wispy under a loosely tied turban and he wore round glasses with ancient black frames. Looking at him Satinder wondered how the old man had made the fifteen-mile journey from Gyani Basantpur to the bus stop to receive him, let alone fix three heavy packs of dynamite under a suspension bridge.

'Don't worry,' Bhai Dhian Singh assured him. He folded his legs into the open cart behind a small pony as they set off from the bus stop. 'Everything is being looked after. Fixing dynamite is simple stuff. I was a soldier in the First World War and fought for two years in Africa.'

He explained the arrangements. The apparatus was under some bushes near the other end of the bridge from where the British party would enter. The last steps of connecting a wire from the packs of dynamite to the detonator would have to be done just before dawn, to avoid discovery, as the wire would cover open ground. Satinder must flee from the scene of action as soon as the bridge began to blow up, going across the fields, through a newly planted eucalyptus copse, across a mango orchard and to the village. Bhaiji would wait for him near the *harijan* well at the edge of the village.

Satinder was startled by the old man's use of the word '*harijan*', it was still so new, a word confined, he had thought, to the newspapers. 'Bhaiji, you are a disciple of Gandhi then?'

The old man smiled. 'Does it look that way to you? An old man who goes through the darkness of a storm to tie slabs of dynamite under a bridge? He's a great man, but I have different things to do.'

It was quite dark when Satinder reached the bushes. They were easy enough to locate and close to the bridge. He could not move much under them or walk across the bridge, to check out the other two packs of dynamite, for fear of being spotted. He would have to take Bhai Dhian Singh's work on trust. He settled down under the bushes, near the cold, metallic corners of the detonating equipment.

227

He did not recognise the bush. Its leaves were slightly hairy, rough on the surface and strong-smelling. He rubbed one between his fingers. It prickled his skin and released a smell like a mixture of spices into the cooling air. He tried to avoid having the leaves touch his body, at least his face. But the bush grew very close to the ground, and a bunch of berries rubbed against his cheek. Most of them were unripe, so they felt hard and smooth. The ripe ones were purple, pulpy, with large seeds. Then he decided that his investigatory activities were making the bush shake too much. He pillowed his face on his arms and lay still.

Gradually everything grew silent around him. Insects playing in the grass near his ear ceased to move. Krishna stretched herself out beside her ancestor, touching him, spreading over him, covering him like a shawl, fitting snugly over his private parts, smoothing over his buttocks, stretching over the long ache of his legs and the huge, rounded knobs of his shoulder bones.

Krishna was a woman who belonged everywhere and belonged nowhere, neither with father nor husband. She did not have the male power to impart belongingness or to draw the attribute of belongingness into herself. In this she was like her mother, shorn of glory, deprived and dramatic, or like Kailash Kaur, lover of her nephew, or Swaranjit Kaur, creature of silence. But Poonam was an exception and Satinder was full of the power of Poonam. The wholeness, the sure-footed confidence of being alive with which she had filled him.

That night he paddled back and forth in the half-region between sleep and wakefulness, his mind unable to formulate where his efforts should go, beyond the fact that he must be fully conscious one hour before dawn. Something hard around him was cracking, chipping and breaking loose; the silence of night was flooding him. He breathed the darkness in terrible gulps, dizzy and uncomfortable. A dream possessed him with the grip of pythons.

It was probably the hold of a ship, a small, dim rectangle of space deep in its belly with a narrow corridor running round it, to which it opened through ancient panes of glass, cracked and shattered, crusted with deposit and strung with a filigree of cobwebs. He saw indistinct figures, thin and cadaverous, without clothes, almost without flesh. He could not even tell, from the skinny outlines of their bodies, whether they were men or women. They were seated in the corridor, leaning into the central space through broken openings in the glass, poking with useless oars at the dirty bilge

228

water which sloshed around in the base. Their arms were bone, covered with skin like poor pieces of cloth, through which he saw the hump of veins and arteries. With movement, their skin stretched taut or hung in folds, and it was the most miserable thing he had ever seen. But it was their sound which terrified him, a low, rough accusing moan, in different pitches and volumes, as of fluttering spirits tortured with pain. Every now and again they turned into the recognised drama of his mother's voice, heavy with reproach.

She was vaguely beside him, seated sideways, on a raised platform at one end of the central rectangle, with some other people whom he did not recognise. He was aware that the others' flesh was solid and substantial, firmly enclosed within a definite shape of skin, their lips closed in reasonable lines, their eyes clear and slanted, focusing on present problems.

Then he was a little boy with his mother, in Patiala, mysteriously despatched by his father to visit relatives, leaving behind the beloved streets of Kohat. Adrift in an alien environment, he left his mother's side only to fix, in fear and fascination, on the lips of an old woman they had met at a friend's house. The mouth moved incessantly, shaping words, joining them into long sentences, stopping for pauses between paragraphs, her face travelling into a variety of expressions, its wrinkles and small, bright, laden eyes with straggly brows, stretching and turning with her thoughts. His wet, urgent fist dug into his mother's side, demanding that she notice his terror. It lay in channels through the agitated silence. He could not understand why his mother was amused, explaining within earshot of their subject that the old woman's son and daughter-in-law, with whom she lived, talked so much that for years the old woman had not been able to get a word in edgeways. So, long ago, she had begun a parallel, running conversation, soundless because she never hoped to be heard, but nevertheless shaping the words in her mind.

Even European women in the State of Patiala laughed at the old, mouthing woman. They sat with the other women in a high, screened balcony of Patiala's only cinema hall, the women's section. Patterns on the screen, empty leaves and flower petals, were big enough to permit them to look out at the movie, but none of the men seated below could see them or desire them. He was conscious of being the single male permitted into the protected bastion of women's virtue, carefully preserved for his exclusive enjoyment. Nobody but he knew that he was not a little boy any more. He looked at the sharp, clear line of an Englishwoman's jaw. She was frail and wispy, her scanty, brown hair drawn up into a small knot at the top of her head, her hazel eyes crinkled with laughter. The other foreign woman was of Teutonic origin, her arms in a sleeveless frock were heavy, red and shaking as she laughed, her huge breasts swelled and spilled over his hands as he hung on to them, his feet slipping and sliding on the smooth marble columns of her thighs. He struggled to be steady; he got closer to the screen than any of the women dared; he looked to the area below where the men sat. Their turbans, pink, white, yellow, crimson, green and purple, were spread like flowers on the white floor.

A deep pain went through his whole body, disturbed the bushes, startled the birds so that they cried out in the eucalyptus copse. His pores were springing with sweat. He realised that the women behind him could never, never see that beautiful garden of turbans swirling like flowers below. The women had been pushed and jostled by the backside of the world, which had crowded them into a tiny screened-off portion on a high ledge.

He felt Poonam against his buttocks; her flesh was warm and luscious. Then his mother was pulling her away. His body was thin with agony. He was out near the the salt quarries of Kohat, with a gun and his father's dogs, to shoot partridges. A carved silver pistol glinted in his hand. The early morning air was cool and fresh. Soon it would be time to get up. But first he looked through the stone pattern again. His eyes fell on the cinema screen which the whole hall was watching; men, women and thirty children of the Maharajah, with their English nicknames and European nannies. He saw that the screen was blank. There was nothing on its grey-white surface except light, plain, dancing and empty. He understood then the nature of silence, Swaranjit Kaur's silence, the ambivalence of her being; he was looking into the heart of her silence.

The diaphanous film of dawn slid between leaves and tender shoots, touching his eyes with early morning dew, misting his cheeks, falling in cold fingers on his knees, stiff and burning from the long, hard climb through the night. He awoke with the training of a *shikari* who has to be out in dusty places, among bushes or beside water holes, while it was still dark, before birds awoke, to spot their first movements in the early light. His father had taken

230

him out day after day among the broken rocks near the salt quarries into barren empty spaces beside a disappearing river, and had given him nothing with which to live his life except this training. Satinder rose into the thinning darkness. Something about the quality of sound told him it was time to start.

The light metal frame of the bridge was visible, piercing the faint mist in a criss-cross pattern of tense wires, dark rods and flat planks. The river, a tributary of the Beas, was very deep but also at this point at its narrowest. A ravine dropped in straight, black walls with a bottom he could not see. He wondered if the timing of the fuse-wire would permit the whole party to get on the bridge before it blew up. He did not know the length of the fuse; he did not know how many people or horses Colonel Fisher's party comprised. This business was like the bosom of a river, flowing without his control, spinning him round and round, but holding him in its arms and not letting him go.

He secured one end of the wire firmly to the first pack of dynamite, lying flat on the damp wood to reach it. He carried the other end back and parted the bushes to make sure it was properly attached to the heavy handle of the detonating equipment.

It was still misty when they appeared. The wait had been long and tense. He was surprised by the first figure taking shape at the opposite end of the bridge, a soldier leading Colonel Fisher's balking horse on to the planks. Once one horse was on, the others would follow, unafraid of the bridge looming through the white air or the sound of the river below. For one split moment Satinder felt a deep longing. To lie down under the bushes and close his eyes to the peaceful procession of events taking shape at the other end of the bridge, to let it unroll itself without his intrusion, a fist bursting through its paper hoop, scattering the scene.

Then a soldier coughed and he was galvanised into action, forgetting everything except the coiled sequence of steps which he had to take. The first horse was already on the bridge. Soon the others would settle into a steady rhythm. The fuse had to be lit, but he found it difficult to raise his body sufficiently under the bushes to push the metal handle down. He cursed for not having practised this before. It had seemed easy enough in theory, but now the bushes shook and rustled dangerously with his slightest movement. Very carefully he slid his body alongside the equipment. He supported himself on one elbow, his forearm flat and knotted against the ground. The muscles of his right arm strained to bring the lever up at this awkward angle and with a minimum of movement. As he brought it down, with a grinding of metal, the entire equipment tipped over and fell on his arm, pinioning it to the ground. The curling snake of burning wire ran along his arm; there was no possibility of moving it without major disturbance. The flame got stronger and brighter as he watched. Soon it was at his flesh, searing the skin, burning the red blood underneath. He smelled the burning even before he felt the great, ugly slicing of pain. The flame was moving fast; it would not reach the bone. He bit his tongue to keep from screaming. The whole strength of his body concentrated on the red, smoking gash travelling across his arm, cutting off at the wrist as the fuse went along.

He could barely watch its progress, through a dim, red haze of pain. It was a tiny, dancing speck pulsating like a firefly, hidden now and then by the scrubby grass. Mechanically, without urgency or curiosity, he noted the movement of figures, on foot and on horseback. They were all on the bridge. Colonel Fisher, in the lead, was a few steps from the end, his face under a plumed riding hat clearly visible as he peered into the mist. The first pack of dynamite exploded almost under his feet. The shape of the man and his horse suddenly broke up, tearing the outline with a terrible roar. The searing, throbbing pain in Satinder's arm joined him with a rope of fire to the terrible, flying pieces of flesh, bone and cloth going into the air.

The others behind Colonel Fisher had turned to run back across the bridge when the second pack of dynamite went off and then the third. The air was full of pirouetting, shattered puppets, men and horses. Satinder was sick, vomiting as if his insides would wring blood upon the ground. Then he blundered from the bushes, running without sense or direction.

When Satinder regained consciousness Bhai Dhian Singh was beside him, his shoulders hunched patiently under his white shirt. 'All the men on the bridge are dead. You fainted near the well, at the edge of the village,' he said. 'I dragged you in here. This is my cattle shed.'

The old man had tried clumsily to tie up his arm. Bits of straw stuck out from the rough, grey cloth of the bandage. His arm was completely numb. He felt nothing except the trembling of his body with a raging fever. Bhai Dhian Singh's grey head seemed to wobble on a thin chicken neck. 'Everyone's killed. There are no survivors. The job was done well.'

232

Satinder turned and burrowed into the straw like a wild animal, covering himself with the spiky, slithering mass, going into its dark silence. Even the dim light from slits high up in the wall, the faint, quivering tones of the old man's voice, made his skin ache with pain, as if its tolerance had been permanently destroyed. Fatigue and an odd anxiety lay on his limbs like a pile of small stones. Movement was difficult. The smallest gesture would send stones rolling and clattering. He did not dare open his eyes, but that did not protect him. Every now and again, behind his closed lids, straight shoots of fragmenting flesh went off in all directions, a monster plant, or bizarre fireworks from a tragic fantasy beyond his control.

He was aware that this condition lasted quite a long time. A rough surface of worry came to Bhai Dhian Singh's voice. Then one morning Satinder managed to pull himself from the straw, exposing the wound on his arm. A thin scab had formed on the crimson welt, but inside it was still raw and throbbing, as if a heated rod of metal had been buried deep in his flesh. He dragged himself across the floor until he reached the door. It was securely shut and bolted from outside, but its wood was so old and warped he could see through irregular gaps between its edge and the frame. Just outside, at the end of a stretch of hard, packed mud where children played, stood a low *peepul* tree. It was in a rage of tender shoots, masses of pale green leaves growing so close together he could not see the wood except when a wind blew through gently, parting them like hair, so soft that each was a cushion for sunlight. Slowly the tree picked up the movement of the wind, dancing and glorious as the sick man's eyes watched from his frame of wood.

He knew that now was the time to return to Poonam. He gave his silver pistol to Bhai Dhian Singh when he left. 'You looked after me like a father,' he said.

The old man was delighted with the gift, polishing it on his shirt-sleeve, smiling, waving goodbye.

Lahore was an impersonal mother when he reached her, uncomprehending, self-contained and beloved. He was still too weak to walk much. He felt his legs wobble as he went carefully from the train platform to the exit; past the ticket collector. Only when he was getting on a *tonga*, did he realise that the last time he had been in the railway station was the night of Bhaskar's arrest. Another life; a period of time when he had not known Poonam.

The city was still gentle and silent, in early morning. Vendors, shopkeepers and office-workers had not begun yet to pour in from farflung homes on buses or cycles. He recognised advertisements, banners, shopfronts, workshops and houses, and forgave them all for their obliviousness to what had happened in his life during the past few weeks.

It was enough that he saw them clearly. They dawned on his consciousness like messengers of peace. The large buildings on the Upper Mall were his friends, their solid presence greeted him, pushing down the jungle in his heart. Lahore meant to him simply that Poonam was here.

He did not know where to find Poonam. The message had been to go first to the shop attached to the museum. It was still two hours before the museum opened. A grassy *chowk* before the Anarkali Bazaar had trees and benches. Men in striped underpants or loose pyjamas, with a following of small, serious boys, were performing the last stages of their morning exercises.

The *tonga* lurched away with the driver clucking to his horse. Satinder lay down on a bench, his arms wedged beside him, his feet pointing away from the statue of a British general which stood under a mantle of pigeon droppings, at the centre of the *chowk*. Its fine, granite head with empty eyes reminded him of Colonel Fisher.

He saw blue sky through a circle of leafy *ashoka* trees. Wisps of cloud and dark smoke from trains and industrial chimneys wandered across it. Everything in him strained towards meeting with Poonam. Excitement ticked with rolling wheels of blood through his veins. He could not close his eyes to sleep, though he had not slept at all since he handed his silver pistol to Bhai Dhian Singh. He had added his own violence to the memory of Poonam's village and had left his pistol in her family house. Now, only to reach her would be happiness. He could hardly bear to wait; he kept his back against the bench with definite effort.

The museum shop had just opened. A smiling young man with masses of black hair and a moustache which drooped past the corners of his mouth was setting out books and reproductions on the shelves. Satinder approached, and the man turned towards him, impersonal as the buildings on the Upper Mall, his body in readiness to fetch an object.

Satinder mentioned Sampuran and then his own name. A change came over the young man's eager shoulders; his hands upon the counter were suddenly serious and self-contained, his eyes

234

friendly. Very quickly, he gave an address in Shahadara and explained how to get there. 'A new suburb, north of the Fort,' he said. 'Across the river. Houses are still being built there, private ones; there is no government housing in the area.'

A plump woman in late middle age opened the door. Even in his exhausted state Satinder noticed her huge, loose breasts. They lay spread out under her shirt like round, pulpy shields of a Roman emperor. She smiled from under a white muslin *dupatta* when she heard Sampuran's name and led him to a narrow open staircase at the back. 'These two rooms at the top are for paying guests. Sampuran is there.'

He was ushered into the room. It was so small, only a thin strip of space ran between the single bed and the walls, and it smelled faintly of bird droppings. But the view from its huge, high window was magnificent. The plots between the house and the river Ravi had not yet been built upon; he could see clearly to the Fort far away on its other side, the river glinting like a jewel in the late morning sun. Satinder was intensely conscious of the Fort as he and Sampuran stood wedged against the window, so close that he could see the riddled, light-coloured bases of the pox scars on Sampuran's skin.

Sampuran put his arm around him. 'An excellent job,' he said, 'but you got hurt?'

Satinder held out his arm to show the red welt hardening already into scar tissue. 'Where's Poonam?' he said.

'I didn't know when you would be back. And we're very short of people, as you know.' Sampuran was apologetic.

'Are you saying that Poonam's not in Lahore?' Satinder's body was stiff and angry; he felt a strong desire to grip Sampuran's throat and shake him very hard. 'Where have you sent her?'

'To Kot Lakhanpur. She's gone with Dhanno Singh and Saroja, to distribute leaflets. I wanted her to talk to the women there. It's time we brought in the women. They could be very useful to the cause.'

A deadness and lethargy entered Satinder. He could feel his shoulders droop, his whole body collapse as a result of Poonam's absence. He hardly had the energy to say another word to Sampuran or to go down the stairs. He could not bear to look from the window at the Fort; its light would burn him.

'Let me know, I'll be in Dabhi Bazaar,' he said.

Like a dark, transparent veil, a diaphanous funnel of misty

excitement, the dismal, disappointed, silent heart of Satinder moved like the slick tail of a cat up and down the streets of Lahore until it found the necessary opening to Kot Lakhanpur. A fruit-seller's shop and a *halwai* at the corner of the road which specialized in *ras-malais*. Then down a narrow, busy lane which wound past open stalls, a street thronged with men carrying loads, the nightmare of vehicles blocked at various points by stationary trucks waiting to be unloaded: the bazaar of Kot Lakhanpur. The name was from a collection of villages that fed themselves from this warren of shops. Barla was the last village in the group, an arterial wedge of mud houses where Poonam, Saroja and Dhanno Singh were resting their weary, proselytising bones that night.

Everyone was asleep. Giggling, curious women who had listened with rapt attention to Poonam, and landless, bonded labourers, to whom Dhanno Singh had spoken earnestly about why their cotton sold so cheap to the mills of England. Also sleeping was the mistress of the house where the three Babbar Akalis rested, one man and two women, terrorists, distributors of leaflets, subverters of His Majesty's government. She had invited them in, fed them with her own hands, earned their praise as one who helped those who could make her no return. She bore a remarkable resemblance to the woman who had opened the door to Satinder in Shahadara, pointing up the stair case which held Sampuran at its head, aloft as a dancer perched on the twirling head of Shiva's snake and to the woman in Humayun's Tomb, who had expelled Krishna and Ranjit from its sand cave. Her breasts were huge and bulbous. They spread out as she slept, and she settled them comfortably, sighing softly in sleep, the strong, sparse hairs of her moustache ruffled by her outgoing breath.

In another room Poonam and Saroja lay in one bed, twisted in sleep and, near by, Dhanno Singh, his bleeding travel-worn feet tucked under a sheet and an odd, uncomfortable object cradled under his arm.

They came in the middle of the night to arrest Dhanno Singh for the murder of Colonel Fisher and his company. The large-breasted one, the mistress of the house, had betrayed them. She hastened to push her guests out into the arms of the police. Her eyes were sharp and as pointed knives as the three people were led out with handcuffs on their wrists.

Dhanno Singh did not see Poonam and Saroja who were directly behind him. He was intent on dislodging the pin from a grenade

236

under his arm, which was seriously hampered by his manacled hands. The grenade exploded just as the whole group bunched around him, outside the door, preparing to depart. Shards, travelling out of the filthy mess of blood which was his body, killed the two women behind him, nine intervening policemen, and a buffalo tied patiently to the doorpost. There was no one left alive on the scene except the old women, her greed melting in profuse tears over the dead, black bulk of her beloved animal, and a police *havildar* who had loitered at the end of the street to drink tea while his men went on ahead to make the arrest.

The police *havildar* left the big-breasted woman crying over her dead buffalo and went into Lahore to tell her brother Sampuran. He described the accident, his mouth so full of words that he had to restrain himself from relating to the woman's grief-stricken brother his own memories of Kohat. 'I saw her in prison, with a blue *dupatta*; she came to give some books to a convict called Bhaskar who had visited Kohat. That's how I remembered her, and I delivered the note about the convict's death to this door.' He felt very honest as he handed him a worn leather pouch full of valuable jewellery, found on the woman's body.

Satinder had just woken when he saw Sampuran's familiar dark, balding head through the wire-screened door. His heart leaped with joy. A wave of Poonam's smell still came from the pillow. Sampuran had come to tell him she was back. His eyes were fresh from a dream. He was trying to climb the side of a high building which was steep and sheer. Without getting higher he moved from one window ledge to another, each wide and old fashioned, with a strong, gleaming frame of wood. There was no danger so long as he went from one to the other, just a slight jump and a safe landing. He wanted very much to get to the top, but he could not jump down the steep drop to the ground and try a different route. The ground was swimming far below. He thought desperately of going higher. He was filled with terror and began to fall. Each time what saved him was a plain, yellow-painted, vertical rod, set into the side of the building as if on the outside of a passenger train. As he clutched it, in dizzy, sweating moments of horror, he knew that the rod would never give way.

Gradually the whitewashed sides of the building deepened in colour, became red-green and luminescent, glowing, glorious with colour and light. The ledges he balanced on became narrower and sharp, mere slits to let in air and sunlight into the thick walls. It was not a house he was climbing any more; it was a fort. This alarmed him, made him more fearful then ever before. Then he found a rod; it would save him, so he grasped it strongly. Immediately it gave way, wrenching out of the wall; stone could not hold it. But instead of dropping down to his death, Satinder was floating to the top. It was unutterably beautiful, lonely and sad. He now no longer wanted to get to the top, but he could not get down; he could never go down.

He was now in another part of his dream. The atmosphere was different, no longer severe and solitary. There were people around, garrulous, homely and ordinary. The top now was not a wind-strewn, terrifying, ecstatic parapet, glowing with light and dropping to the sea below. It was a partly covered terrace, lined with grey paving stones and looked after by an old man, a caretaker, completely helpless in getting him the bird.

It was a rust-red bird, almost maroon, with black, curling antennae. Its beak and the tips of its wings were thin, black and elegant. The bird was like a Chinese painting on silk and it flew round and round on the terrace. He could not reach it and he wanted to, very much. Soon it would fly away. His father had been watching him climb. Now he was on the terrace, too, walking slowly into the space between him and the caretaker. He opened his hand and a bird was there as well, exactly like the other only smaller, a fledgeling.

He wanted to cry out to his father: 'Don't lose it now. Close your hand, or it will fly away!' but he could not say a word. The baby bird, just as beautiful and desirable as the large bird, did not fly away. It was now in his hand and clung to his fingers with pointed, scratchy claws. He tried to dislodge it, rubbing at it with his other fingers and the back of his hand, but it clung more firmly. He knew then that the only way to get rid of it was to sit very still and wait until it grew up and flew away.

Opening the door to Sampuran, Satinder waited in a short breathless space before he greeted the news of Poonam's arrival. His life was already bubbling with happiness. But Sampuran waited, too, until Satinder looked at his face. Then he handed him the leather pouch of jewellery, and put his arms out to hold him, so that he would not fall down the stairs.

The women were already there at Shahi Lane when Satinder reached it, keening, helping to bathe Poonam's body and to lay her out on the bed. Poonam's death had been taken over; she did not belong to Satinder any more. Her face was beautiful on the bed, the marks of the grenade on her body covered by silk.

He smoothed her clothes as if the group of women watching from the wall did not exist. He was floating now, and he carried her in his arms. Slowly he took the jewellery from its leather pouch, piece by piece, and fixed it in her hair, on her arms and around her neck. It glittered and shone on the silk, collected light from Swaranjit Kaur's body which it had first adorned.

24
Satinder Becomes a Politician

Kailash Kaur and her sister-in-law, Prabhjot Kaur, stood in a patch of sunlight on the Mall, watching Satinder lead the demonstration. Just being on the Mall filled them with apprehension, since Indians were not permitted there. No board or sign announced the prohibition, but everyone knew. Only the British were permitted to walk under the shady plane trees of the Mall, on its red gravel whose edges had been finely maintained, sharp and clean as a knife. The students' careless, marching feet had just sent it slithering in fine sprays across the tarmac. The procession had been organised as protest; the police would arrive any time now to arrest them.

The two women were infected by the gay warmth of the students, and the awkward seriousness of the young lawyers whom Satinder had persuaded to join. He had recently been elected President of the National Party of Kohat, and its members marched behind him in careful array.

Kailash Kaur was smooth and peaceful in the knowledge of her love, heavy with her lover's child, wondering casually, a little fearfully, if it would have his green eyes. Persuading her to join the march had been easy enough. She was at her brother's house outside the walls of Kohat.

The two women moved to the roadside to see Satinder better and stood talking softly to each other.

'You must be proud of your son,' Kailash said, admiringly. 'He looks so handsome, standing there, so grown up. I still remember him as a little fellow toddling around trying to get my brother's attention. But Gopal Singh Bhapaji didn't have much time for his children. Not like Palji, my husband. You should see him with our little Gulshan. She's only three years old, and she rules him completely.'

'Now she'll have to share him with the new one.' Prabhjot patted her sister-in-law's full stomach approvingly. 'Satinder came back very different from Lahore this time.' She was looking at her son. 'Sort of empty.' As if he were on the top of a mountain, with nothing under his feet. Suddenly his childhood had left him.

'Lahore does strange things to people.'

'Most certainly it was his friends, particularly one of them called Sampuran. I shouldn't talk about him like that because the poor man is in prison, and for a good cause.'

'In prison? You mean he's a *satyagrahi*?'

'No, nothing like that. You know the Bhagat Singh case?'

'In Bhimbar we don't hear much, being in Kashmir. The State authorities try to keep Congress news out, for fear it will stir people up.'

'This isn't Congress news. Bhagat Singh shot Colonel Saunders about five months ago. Satinder says that they will probably hang him for this. Well, now they've traced the gun he used to Satinder's friend, Sampuran. Somebody came up from Lahore just yesterday and told Satinder about it.'

The police were in a hurry. Prabhjot Kaur watched in horror as their *lathis* came down with full force on Satinder's shoulders, and he laughed into their faces. She threw herself in front of her sister-in-law's swollen stomach, screaming as the *lathis* came down on her own shoulders, a strange, endless stream of abuses running from her mouth, as if all the years of grief, restraint and suffering with her husband had suddenly been opened and let out.

It was an apt beginning to Satinder's life in active politics. May 1942 saw him as a member of the Muslim League Ministry in the North West Frontier Province. He drew up a careful agreement with Dr Amir Khan, leader of the coalition Ministry, which contained twelve terms that explicitly protected and safeguarded the rights of Hindu and Sikh minorities. Even so, historians of the Freedom Movement wrote that Satinder Singh Chahal had sold out the Sikhs for power in the Peshawar Ministry.

240

In 1940 he returned to Lahore, for the first time since Poonam's death. A central board had been set up, with nine members, to draw up a plan of action for Sikhs in the coming months. Satinder was the member from Kohat.

He was afraid of Lahore. His feet moved like soft, woolly creatures through the streets of the city. His did not dare go near the Fort; it still held the strong memory of Poonam.

One of the princely rulers, the Rajah of Marmot, had offered his state house on the Upper Mall for the meeting. It has been called to consider the steps the Sikhs should take when the Viceroy invited Jawaharlal Nehru to form the Interim Government, just before Independence. Satinder emphasised that Sikh representatives should join the Interim Government only after an understanding was reached with the Congress as to what safeguards were contemplated to be written in for them.

The other members concluded that Satinder opposed the entry of Sikhs into the Interim Government. He was asked to go to Peshawar, to consult with Dr Amir Khan, leader of his Ministry. When he returned to Lahore, the Board had resolved unanimously in favour of Sikh entry in the Interim Government, without conditions or assurances about the future of the Sikhs.

The Rajah of Marmot himself escorted Satinder to the front door. 'Sardar Chahal, I want to appoint you my legal adviser. I am involved in complicated discussions with the Government of India, and I need your help.'

It was less than a year before the country was partitioned, and India and Pakistan emerged as two independent countries, in August 1947. Sardarji visited Delhi on the Rajah of Marmot's work just before Partition, and took his two daughters with him, left them at his sister Lajwanti's house. There was talk that Hindus and Sikhs were no longer safe in Kohat, and many of them were moving out.

Lajwanti's house was full of commotion and activity. Satinder's younger brother, Paramjit, was marrying Sonia, a beautiful, golden-haired lady from Greece. Numerous relatives came for the reception in Lajwanti's house, and just stayed on. There was fear in the Punjab, wherever Hindus and Muslims lived together. Nobody knew what would happen, but Delhi was the capital city; it was expected to be safe.

When Partition came, the number of *tongas* stopping in front of the house increased, and people with vanquished faces and small bundles got off, to swell the numbers of the family inside. When the house could no longer hold them. Lajwanti's husband, the worthy Dr Talwarji, set up a tent on the lawn. But Sardarji's two daughters, the children of his second marriage, still played on the lawn, and nobody took any notice of them. They could see clear across to Circular Road, which ran in front of the house, and watched as Muslims were pulled off *tongas* like peas from a pod, killed and left on the road in soft heaps of blood, in reprisal for the brutal deaths in the new state of Pakistan.

Then the girls were taken off hastily to the suburb of Basti Nao, in Jullundur, where Sardarji's family, fleeing Kohat, had moved into the huge house of a Nawab who had taken his family to Lahore.

All kinds of exchanges were taking place.

Sardar Satinder Chahal was an important official in the city. There were 720,000 refugees in Indian camps. The Resettlement Department set up in Jullundur had a staff of 8,000 and Sardarji was in charge of transfers from one camp to another. One day a man called Dhawan and his young son, Ranjit, came to see him.

Ranjit stared at Sardarji's eyes. They were like pieces of rock, firm, as if everything inside was solid, and had come together. Sardarji looked at him, then turned to the application form put before him by the boy's father, who was explaining, 'I've come from the camp of Mr Surjit Markand, just outside Jullundur.'

'You're an engineer, and you want to go to Bombay?'

'Yes, sir. To catch a ship to Mombasa, in Africa. I want to take my family to settle there. India has become very difficult for us now. We are like animals, in the refugee camp.'

'But you will put yourself back under British rule.'

'I'll earn enough to feed my family. That's all I want, just now. If you put my case forward. I'll get some money for the train fare to Bombay and then for the ship to Mombasa.'

'Another stream moving out,' Sardarji murmured, looking again at the young boy as he signed the paper.

25

Gola Goes to Chandigarh

Gola had visited his uncle in Chandigarh several times over twenty-five years since he had first settled there in the late fifties. Sardarji made it clear that he disapproved of his nephew's kind of politics. His own non-violent, religious preferences were now inflexible, a composite image. Nevertheless, Paramjit's son was the only other person in the family active in politics and he felt a special warmth for Gola.

In recent times, travelling to Punjab to renew contacts with the groups there, Gola had always travelled the same way: a train from Bombay to Delhi, a few days there with his beloved sister Krishna, and then on to Chandigarh by bus. She was divorced and lived alone; there was no trouble, staying with her. But this time Krishna was away in London. He had not been able to contact her, even though their father had had a heart attack two weeks previously.

The scooter from the bus stop in Chandigarh lurched over potholes and through puddles, sending rain water up in huge grey sprays. It splashed his knees.

He was familiar with the road, past the cinema houses in Sector 17, around the glass expanse of the printing press, past the new *gurudwara* now finally complete, through side lanes, as far as the dead end where his uncle's house stood. His mind was seething with plots and schemes and beyond that was a rippling, sick sheet of pain.

Shalini, his wife, was in gaol on a charge of murder. They had picked her up immediately after her long train journey from Punjab to Bombay. The Bombay group of the Progressive Students' Forum had decided that its General Secretary, Shalini Chahal, should establish contact with a similar group in Punjab, through a Dr Sripal Singh who had worked in the labour unions in Bombay until three years ago. Now he ran a small clinic in Dinga Village. He had the trust of villagers in that area, and of students in the nearby Agricultural University. Shalini had met him in his village and had talked a long time with him. Then she had made the tedious journey back to Bombay. The police had picked her up the moment she had stepped into her house.

Prabhurao Ghatke, *goonda* leader of an extreme right wing group in the university, had been murdered. His brain had been smashed in with blows from a stone. It was well known that his group had been formed out of pure hatred for Shalini's PSF. Time and again they broke up its meetings, clashed with its supporters.

All the PSF leaders were picked up for the murder: Shankar, Nilima, Sujatha, Vanshidhar. But in the eyes of the sub-inspector, the chief trouble-maker was General Secretary Shalini Chahal.

Gola, who had just got back himself from Dagra and his father's heart attack, had rushed to her parents' house in Trombay Lane, hoping to intercept her before she got in, but he was too late. The sub-inspector was crowding her and her family into the main room. Her mother screamed at the handcuffs.

'But she wasn't even in Bombay,' Gola said. 'She was in Punjab at the time of Ghatke's murder. She's just got back.' But the sub-inspector was not interested.

'Tell it to the Magistrate,' he had said. They had let Gola see Shalini once in the police lock-up. She had looked out at him through the bars, her face tearful and dirty, a viral fever raging in her eyes. There had been no trace of her bubbling vitality, the tremendous energy which constantly amazed him and filled him with joy. Now, with her shut away like that, he just could not function normally. But he no longer expected his life to cohere and come together in developing patterns as before. He just lived from one chunk of time to another. A single thread ran right through, informing every moment, tying together his erratic existences. The thought of Shalini in prison and how to release her.

He thought of one of the signed affidavits that she had brought back from a civil rights fact-finding mission in a backward hill region. It was signed by Kum Sauler, 22 years old, Shalini's age. First she had referred to the capture of her father by insurgents. Then she had told of her own interrogation, in the bald manner of affidavits for judges who have very little time.

'I had no information. A large group of men surrounded me. We were in a room behind a cycle shed. They insisted I confess and admit that I had given food to the hostiles. Finally the commanding officer got very angry. He made me take off my skirt and

244

personally felt my thighs, my buttocks and all the way up to my abdomen, with his hand not sparing my private parts.' The pathetic phrase, 'not sparing my private parts', came whipping back at Gola like a heavy ball on a chain, again and again, breaking his heart.

Or he thought of Shalini sleeping on a lice-infested blanket beside mad and vicious women put away for years. He did not dare to think about the other details of her daily life, of what she ate and drank or where she relieved herself.

Better to concentrate on getting her out. His own freedom chafed sourly against him, but he had used it. Her trial began in a week's time. He had to persuade Dr Sripal Singh to leave Dinga and go to Bombay, to testify that Shalini had been with him when Ghatke was killed. It was absolutely vital that he should do so – no one else could save Shalini now. But it was not likely that Dr Sripal would agree to do this. He would know that police would keep tabs on him as soon as he stepped out of court; they would know the kind of political work he did, and he would be a marked man. Gola could not even contact him directly for fear of giving him away.

His mind went cold and greedy for a while, turning over schemes. He had worked out so many other cases during the last five years, when comrades got themselves picked up, that it should be easy now, sliding along on well-oiled channels, a plan unfolding with clear precision in his mind.

Would Ram Adhikari, his uncle's servants, help on this occasion? He was an intelligent, efficient young man on whom Sardarji's entire household rested. Meera Aunty, Sardarji's second wife, depended upon him completely. But he was not militant or radical; he did not understand class war, though Gola had tried to talk about it in the past, and he had never responded to talk of revolution. The other problem was that his aunt would try to prevent Ram Adhikari from leaving on any mission whatsoever. She was deeply attached to him and clung to him with all the strength of her clouded mind. He had really looked after her and had given her a son's love, though he was a servant in her house. And she imagined people were kinder than they actually were. There was no other reason why she should worship her husband, whom she loved more and more as the years passed, offering to cling to him when the only thing he wanted was to be left alone.

Gola found himself in the porch of his uncle's house. Meera Aunty was coming down the front steps towards him, framed by coloured glass in the front door, her arms out to greet him. Then he fainted.

He woke to find his uncle rubbing good whisky into a wound on his forehead. The room was full of the smooth smell of alcohol. Sardarji's hands were strong and deliberate, fingers square-tipped against his skin. He watched him, eyes open in small slits, not acknowledging yet that he was awake, his body limp and relaxed as it had not been for a long time now.

His uncle never seemed to change. His clothes always hung loose and shapeless, as if somewhat irrelevant to the hard body which moved in short, bullish fashion below the cloth. Only his beard, which had been thick and lush, padding his cheeks, was thinning rapidly and his saffron turban had got looser and more unsteady on his head.

His own body could not now any longer keep from the relentless march of event and circumstance. Something about the way his muscles lay told his uncle that he was awake.

'Tell Ram Adhikari to bring the telephone in from the verandah, the wire's long enough. I'm expecting a call about the *morcha* to the Beas-Sutlej Project.' His wife was not usually given these details; orders were issued without explanation. He was watching his nephew's face. 'Our people were to oppose the opening of the project today by blocking all roads leading to the site. Sant Singh estimated 20,000, but I think abut 10,000 must have turned up.'

There seemed to be no point in lying there with his eyes closed and a small trickle of whisky dribbling into his ear. He sat up in the middle of a long description.

'The whole project is eyewash, just to collect credit for the coming elections. If they were serious about water for the State, they would have begun the Khera Dam. Voters are smart now; they can't fool them and this *Rasta Roko* campaign will make sure that they understand.'

A feeling of great exhaustion sat on Gola's shoulders and about his arms. He was slumped in the sofa, unable to move. Even so, like a well-trained warhorse, his political antennae began to wiggle with interest at the thought of a large-scale campaign.

'Ram Adhikari is not here,' Meera Aunty said. She had been sitting beside Gola, putting out a hand to touch him vaguely now and again, obviously delighted that he was there.

She went out of the room. Her whole being was now intent on

fetching the heavy, clumsy wooden box with a handle, which held the telephone.

Both men sat on dusty sofas facing each other, their bodies turned towards the door, waiting for the instrument to arrive. Gola could think of nothing to say and his recent fainting spell released him from the awkwardness of silence. His uncle was distinctly older this time. His mind filled with evening shadows, coming in determinedly through windows around the room and from the dining room beyond the green curtains.

Meera Aunty and the telephone box were banging against the screen door. It worked on a hard spring whose vengeance had not diminished during the last fifteen years, though many of the other fittings in the house had fallen to pieces, one by one. She was breathing a little hard as she put the box down near his uncle's feet. Gola's heart ached to see her thin shoulders bending over. She straightened up and smiled at him, her false teeth too large and shining in her mouth. A few grey hairs escaped from an untidy knot, and her bedroom slippers slapped against her heels as she made her way to the kitchen. She always wore the same kind of slippers, rubber, covered with cloth in different patterns, but always brightly coloured, her feet sweating in them through the summer. She insisted they were comfortable on her callouses. For many years his uncle had hated those ugly slippers, but it was the one thing he could neither persuade nor bully her to do something about.

He seemed very restless now. Every now and again he pushed at the telephone with his foot, as if working out a mass of energy.

'We're the last of the older generation. There are just a few of us left, relics of an older, strongly nationalist, past. I fought in the Independence Movement and went to gaol many times.' He felt the white scar which snaked along the inside of his left arm.

'Younger people, those your age for example, are different. They take freedom from foreign rule for granted. Now they're looking for the enemy right here, amongst themselves, and that's more difficult. They're hot-blooded, strong, confident, they want everything.'

Gola listened, absorbed, although this right-wing manipulation was different from grass-roots work among the peasantry which his groups were effecting in different parts of the state. But at some point the radical elements of the left and right must be meeting in a way which his uncle could not begin to understand. The old man's hands were destroying the fried peanuts in a bowl before him, smashing them into small pieces which dribbled on the carpet.

'Rita!' he yelled, 'Rita!' A moth-eaten, scruffy Alsatian bitch nosed her way through the screen. She crouched, keeping a safe distance from her master's feet, and licked every last peanut crumb from the carpet. All his uncle's dogs had been called Rita, regardless of sex.

'Well, you should rest now.' After a while, Sardarji could not stand company.

They walked down a wide verandah on one side of the house. Gola knew the family guest room well, its bright blue walls, a mirror wedged between two halves of a cupboard, in an alcove where no light could possibly reach, and the photographs on the wall.

His favourite was a family photograph which showed his father, Paramjit, at three years old, very grumpy, leaning a fat baby face with oiled, curling hair against his own father's knee. Sardarji was then a young boy with smooth cheeks, already sporting a turban, standing behind the child. Their sister, Lajwanti, stood on the other side from her father in a frilly cap embroidered with *zari*, lace pyjamas and a long satin shirt, holding her mother's hand. In the photograph Gola's grandmother was a beautiful woman, tall and thin, elegant after a fashion, not a woman in white *salwar-kameez* with a string of gold beads, a caved-in face and eyes blue with cataracts, as he last remembered her alive.

But his uncle was steering him towards a narrow dressing-room where his grandmother had lived for many years.

'The other bedroom is a prayer room now,' his uncle said.

'But you already have a prayer room!'

He remembered it well, separated from the guest room by a thin door, through which he had heard his aunt reading the scriptures. Her voice grew increasingly thin after a clot of blood had travelled to her brain and the words ran into each other, but they were loud enough to waken him at 5 am whenever he had visited and stayed with them.

'We needed a prayer room to accommodate more people. Your grandmother would have liked it.'

As they moved towards the prayer room, he said, 'Gola. You know Sudershan, my son-in-law, married to my younger daughter, Anita? A good Sikh boy from an excellent Ludhiana family, now settled in Nairobi. He and Anita have lived there since their marriage. He is a successful chartered accountant. He comes here often on business. I think he wants to move back to India. He and Anita will be here tomorrow, on their way back from Sinawar. They put their son at boarding school there. Sudershan hasn't seen the new prayer room. It contains a very beautiful painting of Guru Nanak, which he gave me when he sold his father's house in Ludhiana. It was too big for the earlier room. Besides, since the agitation started, I've been having many more prayers in the house; we needed more space.'

'You have been getting more and more religious, haven't you, Uncle?' Gola felt the harshness in his voice. He resented having to sleep in the dressing room. 'How does it mix with your politics?'

'From the very beginning, religion and politics have gone together. The sixth guru, Arjun Singh, wore the *miripiri*, the two swords, one for temporal and the other for spiritual power. For me, religion has always been important but what I feel now really began with Partition. The killings and terrors. Then sitting day after day in the Resettlement Board. When I came out of there, and set up my law practice in Shimla, something had happened inside me.'

A moment in the Resettlement Board office, Shetal Chowk, Jullundur, when a strange exchange had taken place between Sardarji and a young boy called Ranjit Dhawan. Perhaps Sardarji had passed on his heart and his courage to the boy and had turned back to his mother's religion.

Gola's uneasiness increased. He had read about troubles in Punjab, *morchas*, talks and demonstrations. But actually being here was different. Walking towards the new prayer room, feeling his uncle's attention straining towards the black telephone for news of the *Rasta Roko* campaign, Gola groaned at the knowledge this brought him.

The police would be out and watchful all over the State. Sripal would definitely be under close scrutiny; perhaps he had gone underground already. He would be difficult to contact. If Gola tried to do it himself it might mean his own arrest. And then there was the workers' movement in Bombay to think of.

The police would be watching all the buses and trains. Perhaps even Ram Adhikari would not be able to get to Dinga unnoticed. A brown-haired, fair-skinned stranger like himself would be spotted immediately. Hardly anybody would be getting off at the tiny bus stop in the village.

As General Secretary, he was accustomed to moving pieces

around in his mind, planning strategy, reacting to sudden situations. But this time it was a question of Shalini's life. Somehow that made all his schemes waver and turn false and crooked at some point, like a stick pushed half into water.

A couple of days before Shalini had set off for Punjab they had read about a suicide in the newspaper. A thirty-two-year-old engineer in Delhi had wrapped himself and his four-year-old son in live electric wires and had turned on the switch. Both had died instantaneously. His wife had died of accidental electric shock earlier that year, and the man had been in a state of depression ever since.

He had read out the news item to Shalini who had been getting dressed for the university. 'What an immensely stupid thing to do,' he had said. Something about the death, and the manner of dying, stuck in his mind.

Shalini had giggled and cooed in good imitation of Bombay film love scenes. 'And what would you do if I died? Would you kill yourself instantly? Surely life wouldn't be worth living without me?'

But he could not let go of the picture of a young man and little child wrapping themselves in lethal wires. Had the man hoped to rejoin his wife by dying exactly the way she had died? The remains of a small family winging its way through the shock of electricity to a dead unity.

It was not the time to be thinking about love, trailing down the verandah behind his uncle. The smell of dogs and dust was very strong. Gola turned to his aunt. After her one sentence she had not said a word. His uncle managed the situation, as usual, but she had been hovering at his elbow, one hand outstretched, the other making hurried little movements from time to time to cover her mouth.

Now she smiled at him. 'So nice,' she said, stroking his arm. 'You must stay long this time. You see my teeth. My dentures fell and broke two days ago. New ones. The dentist takes so long. These are my old ones.' Her nervous hand was trying to hide them.

'Don't worry,' Gola said, wanting somehow to comfort her for her whole life. 'They don't look so bad.'

His uncle's voice meant to tease, but it was mocking. 'She's been talking about her teeth to all our visitors for the last two days. I don't know what's happened to her; she's begun to talk a lot. Come in here; I'll show you the new prayer room.'

The floor was laid with mattresses, covered in sheets now grey

250

from the passage of devoted feet. Suspended by strings leading down from the four corners of the room was a large, white, embroidered satin frill. It hung over an open-sided cabinet swathed in purple velvet, where the Holy Book lay open. A white plume-brush in an engraved silver cornet was wedged in beside it. It was the family Book, carried over by his grandmother from Kohat. 'Your parents were married around it,' Satinder said.

The old photographs had disappeared from the walls. Gola had especially liked one in sepia tones, taken on a beach in England, of his grandfather Gopal Singh as a young man in Western clothes, an elaborate watch chain draped over his waistcoat. He had not discarded his loose, starched turban with its long tail. It set a dreamy shadow over his spend thrift eyes, distinguished him in a group of thirty-two men, the first batch of Indians to go to England to qualify in the Bar-at-law examination.

Now the walls were lined with framed calendar prints depicting scenes from the long history of Sikh martyrdom, men being run over by a train, sawn in half, dipped in cauldrons of boiling oil, roasted slowly over an open fire. The colours were vivid, the figures slightly misshapen, as in a child's art, trying to record all the angles of the body.

A huge painting on the wall, of Guru Nanakji with his legs crossed, seated under a shell-blue sky, was in quite another class. The face was gentle and peaceful, a kind of powdery haze hung over its pastel colours, and faint gold spokes of his halo shaded naturally into the dull gilt of the heavy frame.

His uncle was right, the new painting was much too big for the old prayer-room. Still, Gola thought longingly of the bed, its musty cover smelling of damp and age, which had once been in the room. He did not like the idea of sleeping in his grandmother's room, which had not been used since she died five years ago. He was sure to find a few limp suits of *salwar-kameez*, neatly folded in the cupboard. That is, if he ever had enough energy again in his life to open the door to any cupboard. Or walk into any room.

His uncle said 'You see, it is all this that is real.' He gestured vaguely towards the artifacts of the blue prayer room. 'It is God that is real, not human beings.'

Gola was filled with regret; fatigue made him more vulnerable to sentiment. His uncle was letting go. He and Krishna often used to laugh at their uncle's fierce pride in their rather bizarre ancestral past. But this new attitude of dependence on religious experience

251

was a definite loss, like the withering of a strong nerve. It made him feel even more depressed about sleeping in his grandmother's room.

He has last been there five years ago. His grandmother's dead body had been lying inside it. Krishna had sent him to bring Sohail out. The boy had been pushed up near the bathroom door by a line of people jostling for a last ceremonial look at the shrivelled lady who lay on a slab of ice, which leaked into puddles and small rivulets in the summer heat.

Sohail had refused to leave, standing like a rock against the bright blue door. He had been only six years old at the time, but very large and tall for his age, his head resting squarely on his body. When he made up his mind about something it was difficult to change it. It was quite clear that Gola could not get the boy out except by carrying him, kicking and screaming, through the door. That would anger his father and his uncle, both men of violent tempers. Gola had let Sohail be.

The child had been deeply upset by the time a black van had arrived for the body. His eyes were red, the muscles in his body woven into tense ropes. Gola had kept him out of sight in the very last car, with two political workers who raised their eyebrows at a young boy going to the cremation ground. Gola had not cared about them. He had been by then already used to separating people into categories on the basis of their power to affect a given course of action.

It was Prabhjot Kaur's last journey. She had been inextricably tied up with Gola's birth and had insisted Paramjit must have a son. It had been a defeat for his mother, Sonia, who had not herself chosen to have this child, though she had loved him excessively.

Sonia had refused to acknowledge Prabhjot Kaur's authority. The old lady had said she was not taking proper care of her son, Paramjit, and received abusive language from Sonia. She had broken into copious tears, then had taken to arriving at the breakfast table, where Paramjit sat consuming eggs and toast, and slipping a muslin-wrapped bundle of blanched almonds into his pocket. 'To keep your health up, my son. You have so many trials in life.' She had sighed in the direction of Sonia, busy in the kitchen.

Because of the violent quarrels Prabhjot Kaur seldom visited her younger son. Krishna tried to explain to her mother Sonia. 'She's a foolish old woman. She's treating you with Indian custom.'

Sonia had said, her face flushed and ugly with anger, 'If my sister-in-law Meera wants to be a door-mat to her husband and mother-in-law, she's welcome. They say Satinder was married before and that he is still in love with his first wife, Poonam. That's why he treats Meera so badly. But I'm different. I won't stand all this nonsense.'

Their father had arrived, as always, at the wrong moment. 'Of course your mother hates everything Indian. It's that white skin of hers; she thinks she's so superior. But she really knows nothing.'

'Your mother says I don't look after you.' Sonia's beautiful, chiselled lips had been stretched tightly over her teeth. 'Who takes care of me here? Who bothers about me? I have no one here at all, no parents, no family.'

'You have me,' his father had said, in a rush of sentiment. 'But you don't want me; you reject me; I don't know what you want.'

That had been a slight dip in the storm for a short moment, a fine, quiet widow's peak coming down the forehead of their disastrous marriage.

Nevertheless, when Sonia had left to visit Paros to see her own dying mother, the old lady, Prabhjot Kaur, had come to take care of her son's household.

Gola had stood very close to Krishna, watching his grand-mother's arrival. 'Mummy's coming back, isn't she?' he had asked.

Now Meera Aunty was settling Gola into his dead grandmother's bed. She had said that they would get dinner when Ram Adhikari returned. He had to talk to Ram Adhikari. Then she slip-slapped out of the room, leaving him with the ghosts.

There was silence from the verandah outside, except for the distant sound of Rita chasing her fleas, the rustle of mammoth cockroaches in a stack of newspapers on the dressing table and raucous tones of starlings quarrelling in the mango tree outside his window. It did not add up to a shield against blue-painted doors, and the slow trickle of water in his mind, dropping from a slab of ice and finding its way to the door. He decided to go out in search of his aunt.

She was in front of the mirror in her bedroom, examining her dentures. There was very little light; her face was held close to the mirror surface, almost as if she were seeking to enter it. Nervous fingers, pushing up her cheeks, threw enormous shadows against the opposite wall. A cupboard was open beside her. It held some rusty suits, a few ancient, discoloured ties straggled warily across the inside of the door. Meera Aunty had preserved them from the

253

short period just before Partition, when Satinder had worked as Legal Adviser to the Maharajah of Marmot.

Gola had never seen him in anything but *khadder churidars* and *kurta* and a saffron turban. In winter he added a beige Nehru jacket with slightly shrunken armholes from which his upper arms bulged out strongly.

Gola's figure loomed in the mirror behind his aunt. She turned towards him hurriedly, patting her cheeks into place.

'You're feeling better now?'

'Yes. I came in to talk.' It was not a room for talking, too dark, unventilated, nothing in place. But it did not seem to matter to her.

'So, you have a new prayer room!'

'Yes,' she said. 'Ram Adhikari painted the room. He does everything in this house. Ever since he came; I've forgotten how many years ago he came.' Her voice kept trailing off at the end of a sentence; he had to force himself to pay attention.

'What has happened to the old photographs which used to be on the walls of the bedroom?'

'Those old photographs? I threw them all away.'

'All the old photographs of my mother's wedding as well?' They had been taken on his aunt Lajwanti's front lawn, only a couple of months before the first Independence Day celebration. Everyone stood in straight lines, carefully arranged according to height. Right in the centre were three figures on chairs: his aunt Lajwanti, her mother Prabhjot Kaur and the hot, uncomfortable bride, Sonia. His father Paramjit and Sardarji had stood behind them.

26
Preparing for the
Punjab Journey

Gola had almost given up hope of Ram Adhikari's arrival. He returned to Mataji's room and collapsed on the bed. Fatigue and the throbbing lump on his temple put him in a haze.

His head felt hot and full of a desolate, sick fear for Shalini. His breath came in short jerks and he felt completely helpless. There was so little he could do for her, apart from the enormous caring in his heart. He could not reach her or make her feel less alone. He left the light on in the room.

Ram Adhikari pushed open the netted swing door, and a swarm of mosquitoes preceded him into the room. He edged a tray through, smiling at Gola.

'Oh, you've grown a moustache,' Gola said. The boy's face had always been long and young-looking. Ram Adhikari touched a line of hair on his upper lip.

Gola saw rice, a piece of meat and some watery curds and realised he was hungry. But there was no time; Ram Adhikari was already turning towards the door.

'Wait, I want to talk to you.'

The young man turned back, but Gola knew he could not talk of Shalini in this room; it was closing in on him, full of the past, like a buried time-capsule.

He led Ram Adhikari down the verandah steps into the garden, a narrow strip of lawn with scraggy grass which went around the house on two sides, shaded by fruit trees.

Gola did not go as far as the trees. A wooden frame held up some flourishing grape vines, which Ram Adhikari guarded zealously against the urchins for Meera Aunty, who made a wine from them. Mohinder Singh, her architect cousin, had sent her a gift from the United States: home equipment to make wine, with instructions which she could not follow. She set it up successfully anyway, with its test tubes, beakers and long glass pipes, under a back staircase that led to the terrace.

Year after year she used her white grapes for a light, fairy wine which became famous in Chandigarh. Many had asked her for the recipe, and she had told them what she could remember, hiding nothing, but each string of instructions was different, and nobody could duplicate the wine's perfection. As if losing touch with things around her, she put her being instead into the clear liquid poured into lemon-squashbottles and set out in quiet lines beside the illicit still.

The grape season was past; the vine had shed all its leaves, parched by summer. Gola could see a thin moon and many stars through the crooked lines of its deceptively dead stem and twisted branches. He was glad for light from the moon; he wanted to see

Ram Adhikari's face. Nothing could be written down for Sripal; the boy had to be told the whole story. But first he must be persuaded to undertake the journey.

For years now Gola had explained to Ram Adhikari the intricacies of revolution and the straight line of history, but to no avail. He had expected the boy to fall like a ripe fruit into the basket of his thoughts. He had offered to put him in touch with the Jullundur people. But Ram Adhikari had clung to Sardarji's house like a migratory bird come out of winter. Perhaps he would cling even more firmly now, since he had a two-year old daughter and his wife was pregnant again.

Gola told him the story of Shalini and why Sripal must be contacted, and asked that he meet him in Dinga as soon as possible. From there Gola would take him on the train to Bombay in time for the beginning of Shalini's trial.

He studied Ram Adhikari's face. Its handsome lines were a sculpture of dark shadows and moon-lit surfaces showing no response. 'Shalini is my wife,' he said suddenly. 'Please help me to save her.'

'It's a bad time to go. Punjab is troubled these days. People come to the house all the time, especially since the new prayer room was opened. Your uncle is a very important man, everyone says. I don't want to go to Dinga; there's police all around.'

Gola did not dare to look at him, waiting for what he would say next. He looked instead towards a hibiscus bush, thick and untrimmed, near the edge of the verandah. A pair of red velvet bedroom slippers stood under it. Meera Aunty was never far from her pair of slippers; she must be listening.

'Besides, I don't think this man will go just because I carry him a message. He has no reason to trust me.'

'He will trust you when you tell him about Shalini. There's no other way you would know about her.' Even as Gola began to hope about Ram Adhikari's going, he realised that he was right; Sripal would hesitate about beginning a long, hazardous journey asked for by a stranger. Gola himself would somehow have to get to Dinga, once Ram Adhikari had make the initial contact. Sripal might not go even if Gola asked him to; it was many years since he had known him· in Bombay.

'I want to go myself,' Gola said. 'I'm trying to find some way. But the police probably know me; I've come too often to Punjab. They could nab me under Preventive Detention if I went to Dinga without a reasonable explanation.'

Ram Adhikari considered Gola's face. The only feature he had not inherited from his Greek mother was her bright blue eyes. He had the rest: nose like a Greek god, fair delicate skin, mounds of pale brown hair. Certainly distinctive.

'Whereas I could pass easily as a labourer from Uttar Pradesh, come in for the harvesting season,' Ram Adhikari said. 'And I know the area quite well, already.'

'How?'

'Because of Baba Sampuran. He's your uncle's friend. They were together before Partition. He's old, maybe more than 80. He used to come here a lot; he and Sardarji used to talk of the old days in Lahore. Then the police told Sardarji that the old man had connections with terrorists. So Sardarji told him not to come here. It would affect his political image. He's been known for the last forty years as a leader of the Non-Violence Movement.'

Ram Adhikari went on, 'But I continued to meet him, I worked with him sometimes. I'll contact him now. Maybe Baba will know your friend Sripal.'

'Then you will go?'

Gola kept an eye on the red bedroom slippers near the hibiscus bush while he gave Ram Adhikari details of how to contact Sripal in Dinga and what to say. He never found out if his aunt had actually been there, listening, but a heavy sadness hung about her early next morning and he knew that Ram Adhikari had left.

She came in from the garden as he sat in the verandah, carrying a basket over one arm which held pale green tomatoes still wet from their stalks and a large, curling marrow. She tripped over Rita's sleeping, scaly body and kicked out at her with surprising vehemence.

Angry shouts came from the front of the house. His uncle's walking stick was hanging at the gate held together by a large padlock and a long metal chain.

'I'm already late for my morning walk. Who locked the gate?' Meera Aunty produced a large, iron key and handed it to Gola. Her effort to stop Ram Adhikari had been unsuccessful.

A dusty taxi with two eager faces in the back seat drove in, and Sardarji gave up his morning walk. For his son-in-law, Sudershan, he would relax even the principle of regular exercise. And Gola had forgotten how attractive his cousin Anita was. She threw her head back and combed out long, rippling hair which fell below her waist. It framed her fair, freckled skin and hazel eyes which were just like Gola's. It was said in the family that their ancestor, Swaranjit Kaur, had had the same unusually beautiful hazel eyes.

Anita's husband, Sudershan, was immediately absorbed in an enthusiastic conversation with Sardarji, who led him to the verandah. He was asking insistent questions about the *Rasta Roko* movement. Sardarji's replies were vague, hiding the fact that his contact Malik had not telephoned him the previous evening.

The son-in-law did not notice. 'What is this?' he said. 'Each time I come from Nairobi, things are worse for Sikh farmers. I had so much trouble selling the house near Ludhiana, nobody in the village had money to buy it. They exist on credit from the banks, for their tube-wells and their tractors, for everything. In fact I got much less for the house than I expected. It hurts me to see the problems of my friends and relatives in the village. I have been seeing them all my life. I was brought up in Nairobi, but my father insisted we return regularly to the village. To keep in touch,' he explained to Gola.

'That's why he came back to marry me. To keep in touch.' Only Gola, walking beside her, heard Anita's wry words. Her husband's energy continued to concentrate on her father.

'They work from morning till night, with all the strength at their command. Sikhs are the best farmers in India – in fact, they are among the best farmers in the world. Yet they are refused water, which is their life-blood.'

'That's exactly what I told Gola yesterday.' Sardarji looked over his shoulder almost appealingly towards Gola. Sudershan's barrage of words was exhausting him.

But it went on, as if the enthusiastic young man had said all this before. 'It's been thirty-five years now, striving to establish our own identity. Now we have finally run out of patience. I'm glad. Their tactics are to lure Sikh leaders into endless rounds of talks that only leave them empty-handed. It won't work any more. Sikhs demand action. You know the words of Sahib Guru Gobind Singh. Blessed are those who keep God in their hearts and swords in their hands to fight for a noble cause. When there is no course open to man, it is but righteous to unsheath the sword.'

Sardarji looked clearly uncomfortable and disturbed now. This was infringing on his cardinal principle, as dear to him as religion. 'You know, Sudershan, my son, there is a power in Non-Violence...'

But Sudershan was not listening to him at all. It was as if the old

258

man had not spoken. 'The only thing is, what effect will an outbreak of violence in this area have on the entire country? For one thing, it would decrease the food supply. And then, look at the geographical location of Punjab. It's very difficult, all this.'

'You are concerned, then, that violence would spread to the rest of India and destroy it.' Gola did not want to take part in the conversation, his mind was fuzzy with fear and indecision, but his uncle needed help.

Sudershan was cautious but still vehement. 'Whether I care or not doesn't matter; it will happen if things continue like this. Everyone knows that Sikhs fought in the forefront for India's independence. They fought in wars to maintain the country's territorial integrity. They are loyal by nature, historically patriotic. They have proved it without doubt, nobody should question it. But when they ask intensely for autonomy, the Hindu communal majority screams labels at them: "Partition", "Separatism", and so on.'

They had reached the verandah now. 'Ram Adhikari!' Sardarji called out. There was no response and Meera Aunty was silent, offering no word of explanation. Sardarji controlled his annoyance with difficulty and pulled out the chairs himself.

He took up the conversation. 'Whatever we do, we mustn't pull away from the country. In 1946-47, the British asked us if we wanted a separate Independence. I was with Master Tara Singh, the great Sikh leader, when they asked. But we refused. We staked everything in India. My own brother, Gola's father, fought in Hyderabad and Kashmir, to keep the patchwork of this country from flying apart. This is my own family, my flesh and blood. We have been like needle and thread, sewing the country together, attaching piece after piece firmly to the map. We didn't go through the horrors of Partition in order to leave India again. I will never leave India now.'

Gola had heard of his father's army postings, in Poonch when the raiders came across the Kashmir border, and in Hyderabad during the Police Action. It had been long before he was born, but the family albums were full of photographs. Sardarji had seen his brother, the young army captain, as a Sikh soldier battling in the cause of national integration.

Sudershan settled on a chair and bent to take his shoes off, preparing to go into the prayer room. But he had not finished talking yet. 'If we advocate autonomy, it doesn't mean we are anti-

259

Indian. India is a diverse country, too diverse to ever become a homogenised state where everyone thinks and talks and acts alike. This country has so much potential, but to fulfil it we must move away from the idea that it is no more than a large village commune.'

The old man already looked tired and the visit had just begun. 'Wait,' he said. 'Have some tea before we go into the new prayer room. Unfortunately the servant is not here.' He winced with suppressed irritation. 'But my wife will make some arrangements. Meera!' he yelled out.

Meera Aunty came out of the bedroom with Anita, who returned to the front door for the luggage. Her mother went to the kitchen. Suddenly there was a crackling sound and flames showed through the open kitchen door.

'Meera has set herself on fire again. She can't do anything right.' The old man and his daughter rushed to the kitchen, with Gola trailing after them. The end of her sari-*pallav* had caught fire on the gas stove. 'I banished kerosene from the kitchen, but it didn't help,' the old man was muttering. Anita doused the flames under a tap and emerged later carrying eggs, tea and neat piles of bread and butter. But there was no time to eat it.

There were voices and commotion on the front lawn. When Gola and his uncle got there they found Sudershan talking animatedly to Malik. An empty green Matador van and some jeeps were drawn up under the blazing *gul-mohor* trees which came over the wall from a neighbour's garden, and behind them was an empty green Matador van.

People from the jeeps were already drifting towards the front steps where Sardarji stood with Gola. The men wore short *kurtas* and *churidars*, some with a leather strap holding *kirpans* slung across their chests. There were blobs of colour between them from the few women in the group, whose bright *salwar-kameez* and *chunnis* covering their heads stood out against the grey-white of the men's clothes.

His uncle's face was suddenly calm and absorbed, thrust a little accusingly towards the man in the blue turban coming towards him from Sudershan's side.

Gola had not met Malik, but he knew about him from his uncle's references to him over the years. Meera Aunty broke into a fit of severe coughing when she saw him and had to be led away. Malik's presence always brought this on; she was allergic to him. In her own emotional, scattered way she distrusted him.

260

Malik was a powerful man, Secretary of the Party's Executive Committee for many years now. He was generally known to be a moderate, but he had no really defined views. He and Trikha, his alter-ego, were interested only in power; that their Party should form the government in the State. They would bend in whatever direction, right or radical, and make whatever electoral alliances were necessary, to achieve that goal. Standing there, watching him move slowly and dramatically towards Sardarji, Gola felt for the first time a strange connection with Malik. He recognised that he was just as determined as Malik. His own purpose was to get Sripal to Bombay and save Shalini. He would use any means to achieve that objective.

Two years ago, during the general elections, Malik had persuaded Sardarji to stand for Parliament for Jullundur, his old constituency. Long ago, he had been elected MP there, for the first Parliament after Independence, but he had been out of active politics for ten years. Nevertheless, Trikha, with his sweet tongue and large, sincere brown eyes, had flattered and cajoled Sardarji into accepting the nomination and spending all his money on the election campaign.

Meera Aunty had barely recovered from a stroke which had destroyed part of her brain, but she went from house to house, knocking at doors, greeting people and recommending her husband's name. Then Malik had come to an overall understanding with the two opposition parties, and the Jullundur seat had been set aside for the Doaba Congress. Meanwhile they had assured Sardarji that party workers were going from village to village, chanting his name. He had expended his rhetoric, his wife's precious energy, and his money on the campaign. When the results had been declared, his votes were so few that he had even lost his deposit. His old friend Baba Sampuran had told him of the electoral alliance and the hurt of betrayal had almost killed him.

Now Malik was coming towards the steps. The sun caught the large gold bangle he wore on his right arm and he glanced into Gola's eyes.

'How did the *Rasta Roko* campaign go yesterday?' Sardarji asked, and then in a more querulous tone, 'You were supposed to call me yesterday.'

'We couldn't telephone; we were running from hospital to hospital to find out what had happened.' The smiling was left for Trikha to do. Malik never smiled. His words were clear and even,

261

with proper space between them, 'But I came in person to tell you, as soon as I could get away.'

The people from the jeep were restless and angry. They were milling around Sardarji, waiting. 'What happened?' he said.

'The road blockade was a complete success. Our people used anything they could find: trees, trucks, burning buses, bullock-carts. When the police tried to move them they fought back with whatever they had: swords, stones, knives.'

'And bullets!' Sudershan added. He had been talking to the others, and now joined the small group on the front steps.

Malik continued, not looking away from Sardarji's face, 'Police responded with gunfire of their own. As far as we can see, thirty persons have been killed in the police firing and not fifteen as the government is saying.'

'They're also saying there was unprovoked violence from our people, and that 175 policemen were injured. How was it then that not a single policeman died, and only a few were admitted to hospital?' Sudershan was excited.

'Where did the fighting take place? How many of ours were injured? Which hospital are they in?'

'We are still collecting figures. Mr Gurmukh Singh Sharifa was not allowed by the police to go inside the hospital at Malerkotla. He is saying the post-mortem reports are false.'

'But more than 200 have been injured! My son is in hospital in Malerkotla. He has a bullet in his arm.' One of the women in the crowd burst into tears.

Malik looked at two men in the crowd. One of them said, 'Sardarji, we have come to take you with us.'

His uncle was startled. His face was still grave, digesting the news which Malik had brought. 'Me? What can I do?'

'We have to carry information of the *Rasta Roko* campaign to the people and tell them what happened. This is a good time to continue the *morcha*.'

'We can't let the iron get cold. This is the time to strike.' Trikha's voice came to them from the middle of the crowd.

Malik turned to let him through. Trikha had warm eyes and cheeks full of sincere good feeling. 'We must mobilise our supporters, collect them from all over the state and send them to Amritsar to take the Pledge.'

'What pledge?' Sardarji asked.

Trikha said, 'To dedicate our lives and our blood to the service

262

of God and the community, to make whatever sacrifices that are necessary for the betterment of our people. Master Montek Singh Nirala is to administer the Pledge at Amritsar.'

The old man was suddenly a fourteen-year-old boy watching orderly and silent *jathas* of Sikhs, their hands folded and small, white flowers drying in their black turbans, take another pledge at the Golden Temple and then march through the mud to the Guru-ka-Bagh. The boy still watched, silent screams ripping through his stomach, as a British officer's thick stick bound in brass descended on their unprotesting flesh and struck them to the ground, one after the other. Then Poonam's love had come like new thunder, ripping off the padding which had settled around him at Guru-ka-Bagh. He had finally abandoned his search for answers in the terrorist methods of the Babbar Akalis, and his dear friend Sampuran. Poonam had died in violence, and he had wanted nothing more to do with violent acts. Now Malik's mention of Gurmukh Singh Sharifa disturbed him. He disapproved thoroughly of Sharifa's political ideology, which used violence as a tool, and had said so several times, openly, though many had warned him that it was not wise to earn the enmity of a man like Sharifa.

'Our people are in deep crisis,' Sardarji said, speaking as if from a great distance. 'I trust that the struggle will remain peaceful.'

Gola had heard of Sharifa. He was leader of a band of highly communal religious extremists who had fanned out all over the State and had organised themselves well, dividing the area into three zones and concentrating on small towns within these zones.

Though their ideologies were totally different, Sharifa had tried consistently for the past few months to establish contact with Dr Sripal's *Mazdoor Sabha*, which was a large leftist group, and its ancillary student groups, in order to set up a network of people at grass-roots level. But Dr Sripal's determined opposition had prevented any expedient linkages, and Sharifa had turned instead to Malik's party.

Malik had been pleased enough to receive Sharifa's trained cadres. More than that, he and Trikha had seen which way the wind was blowing. The young men were angry and frustrated; they felt they were not getting enough returns for their talent and hard work and were not satisfied with the patient methods of Nirala, Sardarji and his kind. It was time to turn to new ways, the kind that Sharifa offered. But the break could not be sharp or sudden; that might be disastrous for their political fortunes. The Party still had to fight elections. So Malik and Trikha had persuaded Nirala and the others to accept Sharifa for a trial period. Nirala as Chairman of the Party was especially important.

'The Party is like a *peepul* tree,' Trikha had said. 'Wide and spreading. We must cover all points of view, all methods of working, in order to truly serve the people.' It was not a style which the Executive Committee could easily counter. But Sardarji, as member of the Executive, had retained his deep uneasiness and had opposed all connections with Sharifa's group. His voice was now sharp.

'What do you want with me?' he asked Trikha.

Malik came in at this point. 'We want you to go with us, address many public meetings between here and Jullundur, and gather the people together.' He gestured towards the waiting crowd which murmured and moved its feet in anticipation of departure.

Sardarji was tired. He showed no interest in accompanying them. 'You have plenty of leaders who can speak. Let them go instead. I am a tired old man. It is many years since I addressed a public meeting.'

'But everyone knows what an excellent speaker you are.'

'Oh yes. You have worked all your life in this cause.' There was a palpable edge of anxiety in Sudershan's enthusiasm. 'Everyone knows you as a man of Non-Violence. We need you. You must go.'

'Yes. Your image as a disciple of Non-Violence is very important, especially at this time. That's what we need.' Gola was standing next to Malik. He sensed that the man had said more than he intended and was regretting it. 'You see,' Malik went on, unexpectedly loquacious, 'people are accusing us of carrying unlicensed arms, of provoking violence. It spoils our image in the press and with the opposition parties. Your active presence would restore the balance. They will understand, through you, that our methods are democratic and constitutional, that we do not believe in destruction and violence.'

'What you really want is to win the next elections so that Malik can be the next Chief Minister,' Sardarji said acidly. 'How would I help you appear Non-Violent when you have men like Sharifa with you? Won't he address meetings too?'

'Sardarji, you are being unfair.' Trikha's voice was warm and reassuring. 'Even if Sharifa addresses meetings he will take a different route. You won't see him until Jullundur. It won't be too tiring. We have planned only four meetings for you and we have this comfortable Matador van for your family. You can leave in the van straight after the last meeting, in Jullundur.'

They did not say that they wanted Sardarji to participate in the pledging ceremony at Amritsar.

'What is the route you have planned?' Sardarji asked.

'From here you would take the national highway through Kharar, Cham Kaur, to Ropar. Then through Balachor to Naoshera Doaba and Koriha. Then, beyond Banga and Kultham Bahram, but before Phagwara, is the village of Dinga which is becoming increasingly important. Lastly, of course, is Jullundur.'

After Dinga was mentioned Gola did not listen to the man's litany any more. He was concentrating entirely on the scene before him, like a man watching a snake enter the room. He saw himself travelling to Dinga and talking to Dr Sripal under the perfect cover of Sardarji's cavalcade. He moved to his uncle's side.

'I think it's an excellent idea. This is the time to catch the flood of their hearts. It will be a trail of glory for you,' he whispered.

'But there is not a single major *gurudwara* on the way. None of the meetings you mentioned...'

Gola interrupted his uncle with new-found enthusiasm. 'The areas near the *gurudwara* don't need you. The *bhaijis* can get their *jathas* together in no time.'

'Gola is right. Everyone in the family is keen that you should go,' Sudershan said.

'And we will go with you,' said Gola.

'Of course.' Sudershan was proud and eager, already swelling with reflected importance. 'We'll see that you have no problems.'

Malik made his final move. 'This would be good experience for Sudershan. He wants to leave Nairobi, come back here and join politics. We will give him his first chance to speak in public.'

27

A *Yatra* through Punjab

Gola did not sit in the green Matador van with the rest of the family; it would be easier to slip away from the jeeps when they reached Dinga. He established himself in the last one in line. Then his mind relaxed its hold. He did not notice the others in the jeep. A strange, feverish spirit took possession of him. The journey and the countryside came to him in vivid, intense detail, as if there was an intermediary observer.

Straw stacks were like inverted beehives in the fields. String cots and aluminium chairs stood beside *dhabas* selling tea and boiled eggs and men looked up at the line of jeeps festooned with flags, led by a green Matador van. Water was heated in tins which once held *ghee*, now blackened from use on outdoor fires kindled between bricks. Logs were piled near the road. Tractors pulled small trailers full of children.

Now they were going through Kharar. Slowly the jeep came to a standstill, almost touching the one just before it. The van had stopped before a long, low building which said 'Martin Girls' High School'. Shed-like structures clustered nearby. The headmistress emerged and stood at the door, a thin, dark, South Indian woman with a sari wrapped tightly around her. Her teeth, very white and even, spread across her face in a wide smile. 'A lot of patience is needed to deal with people like you, who know how to fight long battles,' she said. 'But meanwhile people should be assured of complete safety, and efforts should be made to solve Punjab's problems.'

Meera Aunty looked at her, a little bewildered, waiting with difficulty. 'I want to use your bathroom,' she said.

The meeting in Ropar was fixed for late evening on the day after they reached the place. Meanwhile, people from the jeeps fanned out through the town and outlying villages to collect an audience. They hired rickshaws, three-wheeler scooters, bicycles and taxis.

266

All five jeeps were put into operation.

'Come and hear Sardar Satinder Singh Chahal, renowned Sikh leader, jailed several times by the British, famous disciple of Non-Violence. Great sacrifices for the Sikh People!' they shouted through huge megaphones.

There was competition from more enthusiastic voices, also using megaphones, advertising a *Baisakhi mela* which was to hit the town ten days later. Instead of drab yellow pamphlets they handed out brightly coloured photos of a handsome motorcyclist dressed in a red shirt and blue satin trousers, whose machine would travel at breathtaking speed round and round and up the walls of a circular steel structure. There was no time to lose, no time to permit confusion.

People from the jeeps were camping quite close to the guest house where Sardarji and his family had been housed. The *shamiana* for the meeting was put up there.

Crowds on the carpets under the *shamiana* collected slowly, coming from offices, from shops which had been shuttered early, from the roadside where they had been selling toys and mangoes or cobbling shoes, making tea and *samosas*, vending lottery tickets, or preaching the virtues of *bambola churan* to the migratory population of the bus stop. Gradually they flowed over the edges of the carpet, settled on the grass, stood deeper and deeper at the edges, and climbed the few scrawny trees to get a grandstand view of the low dais. It was covered with a clean, white sheet, arrayed with hard bolster pillows and that essential piece of political equipment, a microphone, was put out well in front, its complicated wires trailing to a large box set up on the side under the watchful eyes of a technician.

The intense, feverish attention which had gripped Gola was now a fog. He felt through it the familiar excitement which political meetings always generated in his blood, the discharge of adrenalin which had pushed him into heavy organising and speaking. He could not remember ever being such a passive participant. Even when he and Shalini had been on hunger strike in front of the Vice-Chancellor's office, completely still, conserving energy, they had still been the centre of the show, with banners, flags and an audience weaving around them. The thought of Shalini returned with joy into his body. He had been so intent on schemes designed to persuade Sripal to go to Bombay that the pain of her absence had been pushed aside. Now it washed over him in a wave, pushing

267

up against his sudden, strong desire for her.

Trikha was sent across the bridge to fetch Sardarji, who came out alone. His large, untidy figure, put together as if by accident, detached itself slowly from the shadow of the house and walked across to the *shamiana*, his movements grave and dark. The straggling line of his family followed, with Trikha bringing up the rear, one hand stroking his *kirpan*. When flashbulbs from the photographers' commissioned cameras had died down, Malik rose to introduce Sardarji.

'You know him well. Sardar Satinder Singh Chahal. An established and brilliant lawyer of Chandigarh, and our renowned leader, active in the people's cause since a very early age. *Lathi* blows were delivered to him by the British and he went to jail several times during the Independence Movement, fighting for our freedom. Nobody can question that Sardarji has followed faithfully the teachings of our gurus, who have preached Non-Violence through the ages. He was Minister in the North West Frontier Province Government before Partition and was elected Member of Parliament for Jullundur in the first elections held in free India. You have not seen him recently at public meetings because he has stayed in his house, thinking and praying, away from trappings of power, deep in the worship of God, in which glorious task he is helped by the devout lady who is his wife, sitting right here.'

Meera Aunty's legs, already stiff from the hard board of the dais, moved uncomfortably, her feet shuffling in the red bedroom slippers.

Malik went on. 'In fact, even now Sardarji and his family were on their way to pilgrimage at Hemkund Sahib. We pleaded with folded hands for him to come and address you here. Fortunately his habit of serving the people is strong. He has agreed to postpone his pilgrimage for a few days so that he can address you here in Ropar and at a few other places, including Jullundur. I will ask him now to tell you about the Pledge which the community is asking from you.'

Sardarji pulled himself up and moved towards the microphone. He was staring at the black wires that led away from it. Already something in him had begun to open up. The Pledge had recently admitted a remembrance of Guru-ka-Bagh. Now black wires wriggled into the wedge fanning out in his heart. Slowly they attached themselves to a big, heavy box of detonating equipment. A faint, searing smell of burning flesh was in the air, and a flash of

268

pain went across his arm. His fingers ran along the dramatic white scar on the inside of his arm. When he began to speak it was as if the words were remembered from somewhere else, coming back to him, repeated. The audience recognised the familiar arguments. They were waiting for a spark which would fuse all arguments, transform them to a glittering diamond.

'You must have heard what happened in the *Rasta Roko* campaign,' he said. 'Our people blocked all the highways leading to the Beas-Sutlej project, which will take more water out of this State. Thirty people were killed and more than 200 were injured and are in hospital all over the State. I am sorry to say that some policemen were also injured, although fortunately none were killed. There has been too much killing already. We have known how to die like soldiers, whether at the hand of the enemy or the police, but we must not kill. Firing was resorted to without warning. Nine trucks were burned as they stood in the fields. These atrocities must be opposed; morally, legally and constitutionally.

'But that is not why I have come here. I know the *morcha* will continue and that talks and negotiations and demonstrations will continue. I did not need to come here to tell you that our cause is a good one, and that you must continue the struggle. You will do that anyway. I have come here to tell you that you must all proceed to Amritsar and take the Pledge on *Baisakhi* Day. It is a pledge to serve the community with your heart and soul and body. Martyrs are people like you and me; they are formed from ordinary clay. When the spirit goes out and fires them, they become men of significance. This Pledge will give you the spirit, so you must go to Amritsar to take it.

'We need to restore to ourselves a sense of wholeness, a sense of identity, of knowing who we are and what our shape is. And others must know it, too; they must see us before them, clean and whole.

'That is why the issues we have taken up are so important and vital to our existence. They are just demands and must be satisfied.

'After Independence, the States were reorganised on the basis of language, but the Punjabi language was ignored. It was only after fifteen long years of struggle that a linguistic State was set up, but large Punjabi-speaking areas and the city of Chandigarh were kept out. Punjab lost its capital three times – first Lahore, then Shimla and later Chandigarh. We want Chandigarh back.'

There was clapping at this point. He was beginning to catch at them like a cog at a wheel.

269

'Partition reduced the Land of Five Rivers to a Land of Three Rivers. Two-thirds of the total water from the rivers has been diverted to Rajasthan and Haryana. Many of you here today are farmers yourselves. Others have lands to which they return at harvest time. You know what it means if river waters are diverted. Your land will go dry. Water is the life-blood of the Punjabi farmer. Without that his fields will be converted to parched land. It would mean death for Punjab.

'The people who are here today live in Ropar, and nearby areas. For years we have been talking of the Khera Dam which was to have come up on the Ravi just behind Ropar, and brought prosperity to the whole area. Why has work on it not started? Because those who control the purse-strings of the State do not allow the construction. They say Haryana must first be promised fifty per cent of the water and electricity. We refuse to accept such a demand. When such talk is going on, no one remembers that Punjab is the granary of the nation. It is we who produced the wheat surplus which reduced our dependence on the United States. We have made our contribution to the Indian nation.

'And yet, when I wanted to go to Delhi from Chandigarh during the Asian Games, I was forced to go by air. Sikhs were not allowed to enter the Capital by bus, train or car. I am a poor man. I could not afford to go by plane, but I went because my daughter and son-in-law were arriving from Nairobi. They are sitting here with me, keen to return to India, to take part in the destiny of their own people. For years I have been telling them: come back here, return like a stream that will make this land rich and bring the wealth of your hands and heart back to the land of your forefathers.

'We have our memory of independent identity. It goes back to the great Sikh Empire, established by Maharajah Ranjit Singh when Punjab stretched from Peshawar in the north-west to Ladakh in the north-east to Montgomery in the south and Delhi in the east. Punjab continued to exist on that scale until 1947.

'Then we were asked by the British as to what we wanted for the Sikhs. I was actually there when all this took place. Everything I say is from my own experience.

'The British asked us if we wanted an independent Sikh State. They had just agreed to give Pakistan to Jinnah. What difference did it make to them if more bits and pieces were carved out of this beautiful country? In fact the more we were broken up into small fragments, the more it suited them. But it made a difference to us:

270

we did not want a place which would further splinter our beloved land which we were fighting to keep together. Sikh soldiers were in Hyderabad and Kashmir at the time of Partition. My own brother was there with the Indian Army. We refused to take a patch of land, when the whole of Mother India belonged to us. We said no.

'We have always fought against invaders who threatened the integrity of this country. We fought against the Mughals. Then we fought against the British during the Freedom Movement; shoulder to shoulder with the rest of the country. When Partition came, we did not question for a moment that our fortunes were with our brothers here. Thousands of us made the terrible journey from East Punjab to Amritsar and Jullundur.

'We have produced grain and cotton for the rest of the country. We have been called the sword-arm of India. We have fought in three wars against Pakistan, in which many, many Sikh officers and *jawans* have laid down their lives. We have given the army great Generals, like Kulwant Singh, Harbaksh Singh and Jagjit Singh Arora.

'I have seen what sacrifices the Sikhs are capable of making. I was 14 years old when my mother took me to Guru-ka-Bagh, just outside Amritsar. *Jathas* of Sikhs took a pledge of Non-Violence and piety at the Holy of Holies in the Golden Temple. Then they marched through the mud and the heat to Guru-ka-Bagh. I was a young boy then, and I watched while the British and their lackeys beat them down brutally. I have never forgotten the silent strength of their faith, the power, energy and wholeness which their moral vow gave to them. Before my very eyes, purity seemed to enter their souls.

'This purity is what I want for all of you, who are like my children, just as much as these two, my children, sitting here behind me. That is why I am asking you to go to Amritsar on the holy day of *Baisakhi* and take the pledge of sacrifice. No matter what anybody might tell you, there are no short cuts through the gun or through methods of destruction. Only the purity of your heart and your inner strength will take you to the truth.'

Shortly after the meeting dispersed a fever took possession of Gola. It had been coming on for some time, but now there was no resisting it. His body trembled and shivered; he could not stand on his legs, and there were bright patches behind his eyes. Meera Aunty took him into their room in the dilapidated guest-house. All night he could smell the strong odour of bad plumbing in the

271

bathroom as his aunt went back and forth to fetch water to cool his raging forehead.

The next morning he was examined by a doctor from Ropar. He pronounced it to be the strange viral fever which, during the last few months, had been spreading out from Delhi into Punjab. Whatever else, it was a self-limiting fever. It would rage for five days, and then shut off like a water torrent shored up suddenly behind a dam, leaving the body drained and weak.

His uncle refused to listen to Gola's protests. He went out to arrange for the green Matador van to take him back to Chandigarh.

For some reason Malik was reluctant to loan the Matador. He came in with Sardarji to Gola's bedside; discussing the matter gave Gola the necessary opening. He was determined to get to Dinga and meet Sripal. 'I will go with you,' he said firmly. 'I'll be much safer that way. Who will take care of me in Chandigarh?'

'Your aunt could go with you,' Sardarji's voice was doubtful; he was not convinced of his wife's efficacy.

'It will be a journey, either way. We will be comfortable in Naoshera Doaba. We are to stop a couple of days there; the fever will work itself out.' Malik was helping Gola, who by now eroded by fever, was clinging only to the thought of Naoshera Doaba, one more stage on the way to Dinga, and Dr Sripal. His mind coalesced around the golden circle of Shalini. The wandering, fever-ridden images, the painful absence of shape and lucidity, when he just hung, suspended, in a red miasma of distress, came together in some reasonable entity only in the thought of Shalini. She was the central Pledge which told him that he still existed.

His cousin Anita made up a bed for him on the floor of the green Matador van. The doctor said the fever would pass, but, lying there, it was difficult to have faith in survival. The lower half of the Matador under him seemed hollow, like an empty coffin. Jerks and sounds from the road below, fully two feet away, came to him directly, as if right under his ear. The ceiling above his face seemed a picture of his life, a chart, with the graph of a thin wire, slightly crooked, held down with shining aluminium clips, clawing between two overhead lights like a black snake on cream-coloured paper.

Sardarji was talking to him. The words came to him slowly, in straight, black typewritten lines laid out behind his eyes. The Crocin tablets were working; his fever was rolling off in huge, sticky drops of sweat.

272

His uncle was saying, 'There's still time to go back to Chandigarh. There is another reason for you not to go to Naoshera Doaba. I don't know if you remember, but Bhim Lal Whig lives there. He is the Chief Executive Councillor. They say he could be the next Chief Minister of State, if the present Movement of our Party fails. Both he and his friend Chaman Bajaj are very powerful. He controls the politics and the finances of this whole city and of the area between here and Jullundur. His timber mills and trucking business cover the State in a network. And he owns the *Punjabi Tej*.

'The *Punjabi Tej*?' Sudershan's voice shot out, hard with anger and hatred.

'What is the *Punjabi Tej* which you're getting so excited about?' Anita asked him.

Her father answered instead. 'It is a newspaper with a huge circulation in Punjab, published in Jullundur. I worked in an office next door, in the Resettlement Board, when we first came over from Pakistan. But you were very young then.'

'The *Punjabi Tej*! A newspaper which says, "*Kacha, Kara*, and *Kirpan*! Send the Sikhs to Pakistan!" Day after day it is full of insults and hatred. It mocks us and condemns us as separatists and anti-nationals.'

'That man is afraid you will snatch his wealth from him,' Meera Aunty said, in her bemused way, her first contribution to the conversation. 'I'm glad Krishna is out of all that.'

'What do a few slogans here or there matter,' Anita said. 'I remember one of yours from the *Punjabi Suba* days. How did it go? Oh yes. "*Hindi, Hindu, Hindustan! Dhoti, topi, Jumna-par!*"'

'You just keep quiet, Anita! It's not the time to talk like that, even amongst us. I've had enough patience with your so-called sense of balance. You're my wife, you have to take sides! And your side is with us,' said Sudershan.

'Gola! Are you asleep?' said Sardarji. 'Bhim Lal Whig! Do you remember who he is? Krishna's father-in-law.'

'Not any more,' Anita said, unrepressed. 'Or have you forgotten that she and Anu have been divorced for ten years now?' Anita's voice proclaimed that Sudershan had not hurt her. She could not be pushed into the patient submission of her mother. Anita had built up an armoury which her mother had never possessed.

'Bhim Lal Whig,' Meera Aunty said. 'I remember him. A very young lawyer from Bhimbar who worked in Papaji's office in

273

Kohat. When Papaji died, he returned to Bhimbar. It was before I got married. I used to learn embroidery from Mataji, and he came in often to sit and chat with her.'

'You learned embroidery, mother?!' For a moment Anita was a little girl again, amazed at her mother's unexpected talents.

'I can't do it any more. My mother was preparing me for marriage into your father's family,' Meera Aunty went on vaguely, like a rumbling stream. 'Then Bhim Lal Whig told Mataji some rotten gossip about Kailash Kaur and her husband's nephew, Prakash. Your aunt Kailash Kaur's husband, Palji, and Whig's father were sworn enemies in Bhimbar, throughout their lives. Some dispute over land. Mataji loved Kailash, who was her husband's sister and the only one who understood how lonely she was. From that day she refused to see Bhim Lal Whig again, saying that her husband had harboured a snake in the bosom of the family.'

'Oh, yes. He is indeed a snake; there's no doubt about that.' Sudershan was chafing under the fact of betrayal, which came in from all quarters. 'Your niece was married to a Hindu boy?' he asked Sardarji belligerently.

'Yes.' Sardarji was not apologising. There was a new strength in his voice; he was on a journey. So long as he travelled, Sudershan's disapproval was irrelevant. 'In fact, my brother Paramjit arranged the match. He remembered Whig from Kohat, as a child. There was a great difference in their ages, but Whig was very warm with him. Paramjit said that he was like an elder brother to him. I was so busy in politics that I had no time for him.'

'I thought you had forgotten Kohat,' Meera Aunty said.

'Well,' said Sudershan, unable to control himself any longer. 'From what Malik and Trikha tell me, this one-time relation of yours has made some interesting arrangements for us in Naoshera Doaba.'

'What arrangements?'

'Your meeting has now become a public discussion to be held in the grounds next to Bhim Lal's timber mills. He has put up a big *shamiana*, and has arranged for cold drinks and *jalebis*, so there is bound to be a big audience.'

'Does Malik approve? And who is going to speak?'

'Malik has no choice regarding the arrangements, and he said that you would speak on our behalf. The other two speakers will be a well-known Sikh academic who opposes us and Bhim Lal's old

274

friend, Chaman Bajaj. It seems they have already arrived in Naoshera Doaba.'

'I won't speak,' Sardarji said. There was a moment's silence, the family was startled. Something in his voice brooked no persuasion. 'This time it is you who will speak, Sudershan.'

The dust storm started soon after, while they were still on the road to Naoshera Doaba. Yellow, black and red swirls drove around them in thick curtains. There were no vehicles on the road apart from Sardarji's cavalcade, which crawled like a string of circus animals towards the town.

The number of people travelling with them had increased many-fold. As Gola was carried from the van to a hot, stifling room, he had the impression of crowds milling around. More jeeps, a couple of trucks and some buses had been added. These were parked around the cluster of buildings which Malik and Trikha had commandeered at the far edge of the town from the canal. The area between them almost had the air of an enclosure or a fortified camp. Bhim Lal Whig strode right into the heart of this Sikh camp to fetch Gola.

He stood at the door, a bull of a man, much shorter than Sardarji who walked towards him. His stomach pressed out against his bush-shirt and trousers. His eyes were large and full of energy, despite the fat which welled up around them, and there was a sense of vibrant power behind his dark skin. He returned in full measure the obvious animosity which Sudershan thrust upon him with all the movements of his body and ignored the hard stares of the other men in the room. He addressed himself to Sardarji.

'I've come to take Paramjit's son, I'm told he is sick.'

'Don't worry, we'll look after him.' Sudershan was unbearably aggressive, but the older man was not provoked.

'That poor sick boy must be Gola. Your father is my good friend. I loved him when he was a sweet child in Kohat. This is the first time you have come to my home town, and in what circumstances! I suppose this old man thinks that because your sister divorced my son I have no more feelings left. Bhim Lal Whig is not that sort of man. I am a man of very warm feelings. I love or hate forever.'

Sardarji went towards him in protest. Bhim Lal Whig gestured to him to stop. 'I have an ambulance waiting outside. Since you object, I will not take him to my home, though my wife is waiting for him. I will put him in an air-conditioned office in my timber mill, right beside the canal. The air is cooler there. Otherwise he will collapse in this duststorm. You can see him on your way there. He'll be safe with a doctor and a nurse.'

While his words built a temporary screen, he was gathering Gola together. He was an old man but there was an extraordinary strength and vigour in the arms which scooped him up and handed him to the two orderlies who waited with a stretcher.

The dust-storm was still raging next morning. Gola could see its yellow wall when his uncle opened the door of the cool, air-conditioned room. His beard and turban were thick with it and his clothes gave off a cloud when he shook them and stamped his feet as he entered.

'It's dying down at last,' his uncle said. 'It should be all right by the time of the meeting, after all. How do you feel?' Gola felt he was coming back from a long distance.

'Much better. You're going to Dinga tomorrow? I'll be able to travel with you. Please open the windows, I'm tired of just lying here.'

'Are you sure you're well enough?' When Gola nodded, his uncle switched off the fluorescent light and the air-conditioner which had worked valiantly through the dust-storm and was now creaking like a tired animal. He opened the windows. The dust came in immediately. They sat in the dim half-light, listening to sounds of the *shamiana* being put up, voices and a microphone being tested. Everything grew less and less ghostly as the dust settled. His uncle seemed to have absorbed it. His voice was dry and crackly.

'Something strange is happening to me,' he said. 'As if this journey is opening up my life behind me. Like a black fog stretching to the time when I was a young man in Lahore, when I fell in love and got married the first time. Sometimes I think she was not a woman, but a spirit; I knew her for such a short time. But my life came together around her; it had unity and cohesion. Suddenly I was connecting with things and events, with the world and people around me. I felt an inner integration which gave me tremendous energy and courage. Then she died. After that it was an act of will to keep the hope going, to survive. I heard Gandhiji, I listened to the teachings of the Sikh gurus, and I believed that the programme of Non-Violence which I adopted would give my life some structure, some point of cohesion. The *satyagrahas* and marches, going to jail and hunger-strikes, all seemed to work. It

276

released an enormous amount of energy and faith in me, I was comforted to work with other people in a shared cause. But listening for the past few days to Sudershan and Malik, and now Bhim Lal Whig, I feel again a deadness and irrelevance which waits inside me. The heart has been absent behind my long series of actions, there was no love, it had died. Only the scaffolding remained. Now that will not do. There is no more time.

'I'm an old man. I'll die soon. I want some spark which will set all this on fire – fuse it somehow, my past, my future. Maybe not like what happened then, in Lahore. But something. I cannot die in this chaos and confusion. Just a couple of days ago I was asking the others to take a Pledge and now I feel nothing in myself, no commitment. Not even to God. Just an emptiness.'

Gola realised why the old man who shuffled out of the door would not be speaking at the meeting that afternoon. He had nothing to say.

Gola lay as near the wall as possible, on a work table used to slice logs. Its planks were hot from the sun beating down all day. His head was in the shadow of a tent of logs balanced against the wall. The dais for speakers was directly against the other side. He could hear every word.

A huge, magnificent *shamiana* went up, with maroon and purple stripes, stars of green with yellow centres, and a heavy blue frill at its edges, quite close to the fast-flowing canal which carried logs downstream to the Ravi river. Beyond the canal, on the other side, was the Home Guards' Armoury, guarded by three armed constables and a squad of highly-trained police dogs. Bhim Lal Whig, too, had a special fondness for large, salivating dogs: his Great Danes.

By afternoon, the dust storm was over. Under the command of Bhim Lal Whig himself, who was Chief Executive Councillor, sweepers turned out in full force. Their long, scratchy brooms swept up and piled the dust which had covered roads, houses, buildings, people and dogs. Trucks came and carried it off. The town criers had been out day and night. Every man, woman and child knew about the meeting, and who was paying for the *shamiana*, carpets, cold drinks, tea and *jalebis*. They murmured, 'What a kind and generous man! Harbouring his enemies in the nest of his bosom.' Everyone turned up to hear the discussion, since all offices, shops and especially the timber mills, the largest organisation, were closed that day directly after lunch.

277

Naturally the District Commissioner had made necessary arrangements. The entire police force in the city had been spread out at various points under the *shamiana*, at its edges, on the roads leading to it. A faint, incipient tension stretched between the small units of constabulary, like a network of veins and arteries with blood beating out from the heart, which was the high, beautiful dais set up against the timber mill, at one end of the *shamiana*. But the network neatly skirted one group, setting it aside, isolating it like a pool of casual splendour.

This was the pack of police dogs, held on leash by three Home Guard constables. The audience thought it was part of the police arrangements. The dogs lolled at the edge of a vast sea of faces turned towards the dais. Their tongues were spread to cool themselves; they did not share the alert, expectant air of the rest of the spectators. The men holding the ends of their leashes paid no attention at all to the proceedings, diverted by the progress of cold drinks among the assembled company.

The Superintendent of Police, going by to check on the arrangements, raised a quizzical eyebrow in the direction of this ring of smooth-skinned, spotted dogs that had spread itself in the outskirts of the crowd. He did not remember them as part of the list made available to him: constables, jeeps, rifles, batons, *lathis*, shields, pith helmets and other equipment.

The Deputy Superintendent caught the direction and curl of his boss' eye-brow.

'I've already checked them out, Sir,' he said. 'Those dogs are from the armoury across the canal. Their guards must have come across to watch the fun.'

Gola, waiting on the other side of the wall, felt the afternoon settle upon him like a blanket. The fever had exhausted his body but his brain was unnaturally alive, following the disembodied words coming across the wall.

Bhim Lal Whig opened the Convention. One of his speakers had come from Delhi, Mr Khetrapal Singh, a well-known, versatile man, from a family highly respected in Punjab. Impeccable intellectual qualifications. Another speaker was Bhim Lal Whig's old friend, Chaman Bajaj, the only other non-Sikh on the dais. He was a well-known politician who seemed to turn up everywhere. The national papers carried photographs of his tall, portly figure always in an *achkan* which sloped gently outwards over a large stomach and crisp, white *churidars*. Even local papers in a small town like

278

Dagra carried his pictures. It was not known where he resided permanently and no one was quite sure which political party he espoused – certainly none claimed him. Nevertheless, the tentacles of his power reached into odd crevices and distant corners. You turned around and it was there, unexpectedly, and sometimes with force.

As Bhim Lal Whig described his friend and their long association, it struck Gola that the two men made a perfect pair. Whig had a rough hardness which was muffled in the indistinct, dangerous, evil of Chaman Bajaj.

'As for my own views,' Whig was saying, 'this whole town, in fact the whole state of Punjab, knows them through my newspaper, the *Punjabi Tej*. The paper has been criticised for the strength and fire of its views. I do not care about such criticism. I am interested only to see how many people read it. People know what I think of the issues, and I will not repeat my opinions here. I would rather ask Sardar Satinder Singh Chahal to speak. His father, Sardar Gopal Singh, was my benefactor, in Kohat, in North West Frontier Province, when I first started my legal profession. I abandoned that profession soon after, I have done many things since then, but I have not forgotten his kindness.'

Gola wondered how Malik had agreed to be so publicly beholden to the organisation and arrangements of the editor of the *Punjabi Tej*. He waited to hear whether Sardarji would speak after all, but it was Sudershan who took the microphone, his rage thinly suppressed. He owed his first opportunity for public speaking to a sworn enemy, to Whig, editor of the *Punjabi Tej*.

'Indeed we are all familiar with Mr Bhim Lal Whig's views. Who does not know what poison and hatred is released each day by his dirty newspaper published in Jullundur. The views of my father-in-law, Sardar Satinder Singh, who is sitting with us here, are equally well known, and so he has declined to speak. But there are others of us who will speak. I will speak, and Mr Whig's kindness in creating this occasion here will not deter me from being frank in expressing what I feel.

'It appears to me that the moment of our trial has arrived. We must rise and attract the attention of the world to our noble principles, or die as traitors to our gurus. This is the most critical moment for the Sikh people, and we must make a sincere effort to save ourselves from the threatening disease of domination. It is a disease which needs immediate and desperate remedy.

279

'The Sikhs are a prosperous, proud and outgoing people. They have made themselves at home in places all over the world and in diverse company. They are not quarrelsome by nature and they are not interested in fighting battles with their Hindu brothers. But when we cry for Hindu-Sikh unity, some Punjabi Hindu spokesman like Whig Sahib here will reply that unity can be obtained only if we submit. They committed the original sin of repudiating their mother-tongue and of introducing religion into the politics of independent India. When we cry for brotherhood, unity and equality they offer slavery and death.

'You know how many people have been killed and injured in the recent *Rasta Roko* agitation? In the name of the great gurus, Tegh Bahadur and Gobind Singh, and in the name of the minor sons of Guru Gobind Singh and the innumerable martyred ones who were done to death in their effort to protect Hinduism and Hindu culture, I ask: how long will this continue? How long will our young men be killed under one pretext or another for protecting this sacred cause?

'The Sikh has everything; he has strength and hard work and faith in God. But he can never hope to gain the levers of power in the State. Dignity is missing from the life of the faith, that dignity which comes from participation in the country's administrative and political affairs.

'The basic cause of the trouble in Punjab is the Hindu-Sikh hostility which is like a virus infecting us. There are very fundamental distinctions between the two faiths which cannot be bridged by occasional intermarriages among neighbouring Hindus and Sikhs. Whig Sahib's son was married to a good Sikh girl, the niece of Sardar Satinder Singh Chahal. Does that mean that he feels kindly towards the Sikhs? Not at all; you have read his paper. This virus will continue to flare up until the identity of Sikhs is completely accepted by the Hindus and their allies. It is then that the instinct of survival and self-preservation will subside among the Sikhs.

'We have definite remedies. Malikji will be able to tell you more about them when he speaks. What we want is dignity and the chance to participate. We must manage our own public affairs. We must have power in the State.

'People ask us why there are so many armed men inside the precincts of the Golden Temple at Amritsar, why so many of us carry arms. We tell them about Guru Tegh Bahadur who wore the *miripiri*, the temporal and spiritual swords. We love weapons. For us they symbolise self-respect and self-defence. They form part of our religion. When the country needs us during external conflicts, nobody criticises us then for carrying arms. Now we carry them to describe our dignity.'

No one saw the green Matador van drive out of the Sikh camp and through the streets emptied of police and people, rattle across the rough bridge whose white stomach soared across the canal, reaching to the Armoury on the other side. Only a thousand particles of sunlight watched it go. Beautiful, spangled segments wrapped around the driver's face in a mask as they neared the Armoury, covering everything except the slanting shadows of his eyes. They covered the beards and determined faces of the men at the back of the van, covered in startled caress the guns on which the men's hands lay, hidden under a checked bedcover. They twanged a sharp, unheeded warning to the Head Constable. He lay sleeping on a *charpoy* in the shade of a *peepul* tree, not knowing until they woke him up, that masked men armed to the teeth had arrived to rob the Home Guards' Armoury.

Three constables, holding a pack of dogs on a leash, waited at the edge of the crowd under the *shamiana*. One of them felt a big iron key in his pocket, the key to the heavy steel door which closed the Armoury.

The afternoon was a huge, yellow ball behind Gola's eyes as he lay in the timber yard. His fever had returned, pushing everything else out of him, all love and judgment, even the smell of freshly-cut timber close to his head. Malik's dry voice, the sound of cracking wood after the thunder of Sudershan's speech, came through the wall and possessed him. He was virgin territory, open to all assault.

While his three constables enjoyed Malik's speech, their mouths full of hot *jalebi* juice, the Head Constable, sole guardian of the Armoury that afternoon, lay bound hand and foot on his *charpoy* under a *peepul* tree. Six masked men had bandaged his eyes. Then they blew a gaping hole in the back wall of the Armoury. This time destruction was wrought with modern equipment which would not touch the explosives and ammunition stocked inside. The terrorists were freshly trained in new-fangled technologies. They had no use for equipment like the heavy metal box and long, searing wire, attached to sticks of dynamite which had been used by Satinder, a previous incarnation of the revered Sardarji on the dais, to blow up a bridge, to throw the jumping, twisted bodies of Colonel Fisher and his men up into the air.

The explosion was loud and quick. It shattered brick and mortar, and red shards flew to a great distance. The dust was blown away quickly by the breeze from the canal which had already vanquished a dust storm. Nevertheless, dynamite fumes lingered in the Armoury and six men spluttered and coughed behind their masks as they pushed their legs gingerly over the rough edges of the newly created opening and swung their bodies into a small room stacked with guns and ammunition. They were men in a hurry; they had to slide the cold steel objects of their desire from the Armoury to their green Matador van, which waited with its floor lifted up to expose a secret, hollow space below.

The men proceeded to hand out 14 sten guns, 28 rifles and 859 rounds of sten gun ammunition. All this was carefully layered into its new coffin in the van, padded with a thick bedcover, and bolted down. Gagged and bound, the Head Constable was dumped on the floor of the van. He heard not the slightest rattle from the stolen artifacts under his head.

Meanwhile across the river the speeches went on. Gola, on the other side of the wall, turned away from the discussions. He had heard all arguments; his head was stuffed and he felt it would burst with the huge quantity of words. But he could not get away from the next speaker, and the next, and the next; he could not descend the table on his own and reach the comfort of Bhim Lal's room. He clung tenaciously to the sound of a single voice to save his consciousness. The welter of words threatened to sweep him off the table and away from Naoshera and Sardarji, far from Dinga and Sripal and away from Shalini forever.

The Head Constable in the green Matador van had time enough only to see the ceiling before they bandaged his eyes again. The van was put on a ferry across the canal and the dog squad was unable to trace its Head Constable for four days. By that time the rats had bitten through his legs, and he was babbling about the inside of a green Matador van and a black snake which wriggled slowly between the two eyes of the electric lights.

The voice coming through the wall now to Gola had grown vague and indistinct, blurring in outline, merging like a patina into the vast, red area of pain spreading through his head and body. It was the voice of Chaman Bajaj, who was the perfect man for an imperfect situation. Gola would hold on, at least until this master-artist finished.

'If we are speaking of figures,' Chaman Bajaj said, 'everybody can quote figures. I am not very good at it. I am a simple man, not an intellectual, I know only a few truths. When I quote figures, I have to look at this piece of paper to do so.' He was jovial, seductive, lilting.

Just before Gola fainted, he saw with the complete clarity of one passing out that a thread of evil connected Bajaj and Malik, who were currently adversaries. Krishna's skin registered other connections; its darkness was the greatest connector of them all. Like glue, sticking the patches together. Joining Father Sherifis, to Chaman Bajaj, to Malik, linking a fat woman with bulbous breasts, who showed Krishna and Ranjit out of the secret, emperor-ridden confines of Humayun's Tomb, to Sampuran's landlady in Lahore who opened the door to a searching, passionate Satinder, to an enormous betrayer who was present at Poonam's death. Linked sounds, too – of Colonel Fisher's bridge blowing up, the Mukti Bahini camp disappearing in Father Serifis' smoke and a hole opening in the Armoury. And now what next? What sounds of rifle-fire, what death, what destruction to close the links?

'And what does this paper say?' the voice of Chaman Bajaj went on. 'That according to the Public Enterprises Survey, investment in Central Public Sector Enterprises in the Punjab has gone up significantly over the last decade.

'Several letters of intent and licences have been cleared for the State. Not just heavy industry. It is the hub of the small-scale industrial sector of the country – Ludhiana is known as the Manchester of India.

'People say the Punjab farmer is forever in debt, but I say that credit is a way of modern life. All modern business and modern farming survive on credit. It is a common practice to take advances from a bank for business purposes...

'Sikhs, one of the most advanced communities in India ... contribution in all fields, brilliant, industry, trade, army, science, art, administration education.'

The voice, repeating itself, repeating others, faded into the dim regions of Gola's consciousness, which now let go. The speakers were winding up. Evening shadows lapped at the crowd and lights began to come on one by one under the *shamiana*, including a large spotlight over the dais where a lonely old man called Satinder Singh Chahal nodded with fatigue at the table.

An amorous *rickshaw-wallah* was returning from a secret rendezvous with a married woman of Korilia. Cycling back to

Naoshera Doaba by the usual circuitous routes he took to avoid being seen, he passed by the Home Guards' Armoury. Veils of dust had settled down. A gaping hole in the back wall, and its abandoned look, were clearly visible. He was gripped with fear.

The pack of dogs under the *shamiana* was getting restless. Fear and anxiety travelled down the leash from the wrists of the constables. They had heard the whispered word and did not know whether to go or stay. Slowly, fear stretched over the assembled public like a fragile web of light blue net which farmers fling over fruit trees on a hillside to keep the birds away. The oppressed fruit, kept from the sun, shifted and shuffled underneath, waiting. Then, in quick succession, the District Commissioner, Superintendent of Police, DSP and the whole police force heard the *rickshaw-wallah*'s news. The Armoury had been raided; terrorists were among them. Suddenly the net lifted and fear was out in the open, waiting to attack, ready to defend.

Where were the marauding birds which must be repelled? Stones were grasped in defending hands. The guardians of precious fruit fell into two sections, some Hindus, some Sikhs, each seeing a different enemy. But the birds they could all see were right there, exposed like a bunch of jewels in the light on the dais. Those gathered on the dais had rapacious beaks which would take their heart's blood, draw hard-earned wealth away from fingers which now closed firmly around the stones or whatever other object of attack was available. The first stone, well-aimed, hit Sardarji's temple. The folds of his saffron turban saved him from certain death. Meanwhile police and officials tried to control the riot. They bunched around the dais, made a shield for the leaders and escorted them away. The rest were spaced out in the huge crowd, their *lathis* constrained and helpless. The audience, deprived of obvious targets for assault, turned against each other. Objects in everyday use suddenly became weapons: shoes, bottles of cold drink, all used with terrible effect at close quarters. The air was thick with the sound of ambulance cars and police sirens and the sharp bleeps of radio signals.

'You and your party must leave town immediately,' the District Commissioner told Sardarji urgently.

But there was no sign of the green Matador van which had been parked outside earlier. How would he collect his people so quickly? Besides, night had set in. 'First thing tomorrow morning,' Sardarji promised.

284

Meanwhile, Anita and Meera Aunty retrieved Gola, pouring ice-cold water on his face to bring him out of his faint. They would not leave him with Bhim Lal Whig.

Lines between the two camps were now firmly drawn. Sardarji's party had dwindled in number, many members having scattered to less exposed surroundings. Those that remained in the camp were grateful for the ring of encircling vehicles, though many were set on fire that night. Charred skeletons of buses and trucks still smoked from the night's destruction when the cavalcade assembled next morning. Meanwhile the green Matador van returned, slipped through the blazing ring of fire like a well-trained circus animal, and parked in front of Sardarji's quarters. It stood now, blinking innocuously, at the head of the battered assembly. The District Commissioner, his eyes weary and red from the long night of violence, was there to see them off. He still had to cope with the raid on the Armoury. Already journalists, politicians and officials were beginning to pour into Naoshera Doaba.

Sardarji's party left the town behind; they were out in the open now, with green fields on either side, some with peacocks picking at cotton leaves in the early light and occasionally a glimpse of a bare bottom squatting to relieve itself in low grass, a pitcher of water placed near by. Nevertheless, the inside of the van seemed to hold a piece of the town's ravaged air. It had the dry smell of pain, the greyness of ash.

Ram Adhikari's face waiting by the roadside seemed an extension of the atmosphere of disaster inside the van – they almost passed him by. Gola saw him and his whole body suddenly came alive. He stopped the driver.

But he could not ask immediately about Dr Sripal and the success of Ram Adhikari's mission to Dinga, as the others had turned to him with their own questions. The boy himself seemed determined to talk, as if he wanted to put down a weight.

'I was coming from Dinga with Baba Sampuran Singh, your old friend. We stopped at a village called Karwalian, in the house of Balmukand. He and Jagir Singh were there. They are political workers. They discussed with Baba Sampuran whether they should support this issue of taking Pledges in Amritsar on *Baisakhi* Day. They also spoke of your pilgrimage through Punjab.'

'My pilgrimage?' Sardarji said.

'Baba Sampuran loved you,' Ram Adhikari said, 'and now he is dead.'

'Dead?'

Ram Adhikari looked as if he would cry, then went on with the story. 'Baba Sampuran was to proceed to Taragarh for some work. I wanted to go with him. He said I should walk with Jagir Singh, whom he asked to follow him on his bicycle but to keep a hundred yards distance between them. We left Balmukand's house at about 4 pm. Baba was wearing a white *kurta* and pyjama. He carried a *khadi* towel in which he had tied some books. He carried nothing else, no arms.

'We reached the point where the main road meets the approach road to the village Khan Khanna. Baba turned on to the Khan Khanna road. He had barely done so when a police jeep sped past Jagir Singh and myself, overtook Baba, and came to an abrupt halt in front of him.

'Four or five policemen jumped out of the jeep, overpowered Baba and pushed him into the jeep. He resisted as best as he could. He kept yelling out that he was Baba Sampuran Singh of Basantpur and called out several times, "Revolution Zindabad! Long live the people!"

'Jagir Singh and I went back to Balmukand's house to wait. There was nothing else we could do. Early this morning some villagers came to take us to the canal. Baba's body was lying on the canal bank. There was not a single bloodmark on his white *kurta*-pyjama, and no blood around his body, which was beginning to stink. The death had taken place much earlier. Some people gathered a large amount of *neem* leaves and threw these over and around the body to cover the smell.'

Ram Adhikari was crying; sobs were wracking his body as if he had never cried before. He was looking at Sardarji for comfort; they were the only two who had known Baba Sampuran. So this was the end of Sampuran, Poonam's brother. Or he had once been her brother, as Satinder had been her husband. Until she died. The dead have no relatives. Sampuran had been faithful to his creed of violence all his life and in his death it clung to him. But Satinder had chopped and changed and now he was Sardarji, apostle of Non-Violence, at the end of his life. There was not much time left.

Sardarji said, 'Baba Sampuran Singh was an old nationalist, a fighter for the country's freedom, a leader of the extreme left parties in the Punjab. When the tiger is released, you cannot catch it by the tail. Violence brings more violence.' Gola turned away, looking out of the window.

286

Sampuran's existence had always helped Sardarji, though by choice he had not seen him for years. Now his last, tenuous link with Poonam had snapped. Her brother, Sampuran, had been killed last night. Poonam, his first wife, still the centre of his life though she was dead. He had hovered close to her as a man holds near a spot of heat in the middle of icy winter. He looked from the window of the green Matador at a rock leaning against a small hillock. Sampuran had been a thin lifeline, a web of fine, red veins, between himself and Poonam. Now he was dead and Satinder was truly alone. The deeds of his life, his age, his saffron turban, fell away from him. He heard nothing where he was, alone and empty, a man with little time left who had to create his whole life in that short space of time or else die in confusion.

Ram Adhikari did not go with them into Dinga. The van stopped just outside to let him off. 'I will meet you in Jullundur,' he said as he left. There was new authority in his voice, as if the few intervening days of grief had finally completed his shape. He was no longer a servant.

Gola got off with him when the van stopped. The fever had left him now, but his body was weak. His legs were unstable under him. The whole cavalcade had stopped. Their bodies emerged into the evening darkness behind trees and bushes as they got out to relieve themselves. In the ensuing, empty hush, Gola's voice was tight and breathless. 'Did you meet Dr Sripal?' he asked.

Despite his exhaustion, Ram Adhikari was fully alert. 'Hush!' he said. 'Don't say his name too loudly. I found out that these people travelling with you, Malik and his party, know him and hate his guts. It is because of him and Baba Sampuran that the leftist cadres have held out, not joined forces with them, and those cadres are strong and unified. Now Baba Sampuran is dead, there's only Dr Sripal left opposing them. Sharifa, leader of the radical edge of Malik's movement, has ordered Dr Sripal's death. You know that his *sheras* are especially well organised in this Doaba area, from here to Jullundur. They work under Sharifa's personal supervision. In fact, it could have been Sharifa's men, masquerading as the police in a police jeep, who picked up Baba Sampuran in front of my eyes. They've been wanting him dead for a long time.'

'Did Dr Sripal agree to go to Bombay?'

'I don't know. He didn't say. I gave him your message. He wants to talk to you first; he's expecting you here.'

'But how did you know I would come?'

'We guessed you would use your uncle's tour as cover to get here. His stops are well known. They've begun preparing for him in Dinga. The *shamianas* will be up already. Villagers are coming in from all the nearby areas. With the Armoury raid there will be a bigger crowd; everyone is frightened and excited and many will be foolhardy. Especially the *jathas* getting ready to leave the villages for the Pledge of Amritsar.'

'How will I find Sripal?' The line of vehicles was loaded once again, ready to move. Meera Aunty did not know that Ram Adhikari was leaving and called softly from the van for him to come back in.

He added hurriedly as he left, 'Dr Sripal has gone underground. You won't find him in the village. Tell the man in the *paan* and cigarette kiosk at the bus stop that Baba Sampuran has sent you and that you want to see Doctor Sahib. He will find you out on his own.'

Sardarji's tour was speeding up. Arrangements were almost complete even before they arrived, late at night. The meeting was to be the next evening. Tents had been set up for Sardarji and his family, and a separate one for Malik and Trikha.

The two men had an air of waiting for something. They were tense and irritable, impatient with the village elders and the big farmers who crowded their tent. Only Sudershan was perfectly at ease. His political debut at Naoshera Doaba had had a powerful effect on his personality which had flowered and expanded, finding its natural habitat. He was bubbling and exuberant, full of energy. The savage violence in Naoshera Doaba had not dampened his beliefs. It was obvious that he expected to speak that afternoon.

Sardarji was silent and brooding; he did not notice Meera Aunty hovering around him.

'Where is Ram Adhikari?' she kept asking Gola. 'I wish he had been here, he would have fixed all this.' She made a vague gesture towards the confusion in the tent.

Villagers had been pouring in all day. The crowd was much larger than before. Electricians and loudspeaker arrangements had been brought in all the way from Jullundur.

'Sharifa will reach Jullundur at the same time as you,' Malik told Sardarji. 'We are to assemble in Sheetal Chowk, before the offices of the *Punjabi Tej*. We have to make some symbolic gesture against Bhim Lal Whig who is its editor. Three Sikhs were killed in the riot in Naoshera Doaba.'

'They might burn his newspaper offices,' Gola warned. 'Even the people of our own party seem angry.'

Trikha shrugged. 'If that happens, it won't be our responsibility. Everyone knows that Sardarji is a man of Non-Violence. Everything he says in the meetings is about non-cooperation and inner strength.'

Sardarji was listening. 'But what about Sharifa?' he asked. 'There's nothing non-violent about him.'

'He is making no public statements,' Malik said. 'Just organising the *jathas*. You need not worry about him.'

Gola seated himself at a dark edge of the crowd under the *shamiana*, easily accessible to Dr Sripal. He hoped the *paan-wallah* had got the message to him. Sardarji's stiff voice had silenced the huge crowd. He was telling them about what had happened in Naoshera Doaba. Only Sudershan and Sardarji were on the dais. The atmosphere was tense and electric, quite different from the warm passions which had flowed out to the crowd in Ropar.

Gola was tapped on the shoulder. He turned to a tanned, bearded face with a turban above it, smiling at him. It was a moment before he recognised the creased brown eyes and wide, gentle mouth with its full underlip through the beard. Shalini had not told him that their comrade from Bombay was now Dr Sripal Singh with a *khalsa* identity of long hair and turban. Sripal saw Gola's surprise at his hairy cheeks and touched them lightly. 'It makes it easier to work here,' he whispered. 'Follow me at a distance. We'll go to my house. Nobody will notice us in this great overflow of people.'

They moved towards the village which lay behind the *shamiana*. Sripal's house was two small rooms with mud-plastered walls, and a tiny extension at the back which served as a bathroom. The front room had rows of shelves stocked with medicines along one wall, a table and a small desk with two chairs where they sat.

'I used to see patients here,' Sripal said, 'before I went underground.' He passed his hand over the dust which lay thick on the shelves.

Gola did not know how much time they had. Sripal had switched on a small shaded light at the corner of his desk. The door and small windows were shut and the room was heavy with heat. He went straight to the point.

'Ram Adhikari met you.'

'Yes.' Sripal looked at Gola. 'Do you know that Ram Adhikari was shot dead this morning?'

'What?' There was a great wrenching. The shock bought sweat flooding to his head and feet.

'He was killed at point-blank range within full view of a large number of villagers. It was within yards of the *phirni*, the road ringing Sampuran's village of Gyani Basantpur. He'd gone to Sampuran's house to collect his things for us. He's not recognised in the area and we thought he would escape notice.'

'What happened?' Gola asked.

Sripal went back, as if searching warily though layers of events to pull out the simplest outline. 'He stopped to have tea in Garashenkar Tehsil. It is at a short distance from Gyani Basantpur. One of our men, Kila Singh, was sitting on a box, on the bridge of the canal which passes near Madanhare. Around 3 pm he saw Ram Adhikari crossing the bridge and was about to call out to him when a police party consisting of an Assistant Sub-Inspector and four constables appeared on the scene. The policemen rushed towards Ram Adhikari, saying he was one of the terrorists who had raided the Armoury. Ram Adhikari tried to escape towards the village and the ASI fired at him. He realised the way was blocked by policemen, and jumped into the canal and swam across. The ASI continued to fire. He reached the further bank, but just as he was getting out of the canal a shot caught his foot. Injured as he was, he ran through the fields and took shelter in a garden. He waited there a while, then made his way to Sampuran's village. A number of neighbours saw him enter the village and reach the house of Bibi Chinti.'

'Who is Bibi Chinti?'

'No one knows much about her, except that she is a women of indeterminate age with huge heavy breasts who turns up everywhere, especially when people are in trouble. Baba Sampuran had told us that decades ago, when his sister Poonam was killed by the British police in a village outside Lahore, there was a woman on the scene who looked exactly like Bibi Chinti. She was crying over a dead buffalo when Baba Sampuran reached there to investigate his sister's death.'

'Why did Ram Adhikari go to her house?'

'Who knows? The time was now around 4 pm. Within a few minutes, the police reached Bibi Chinti's house. Ram Adhikari was dragged out, each arm held by a policeman. He was dragged for about twenty yards, then he tried to escape again and was shot dead.'

Darkness was piling up outside. All the power from the electric lines had been drawn to the *shamiana*. The light on Sripal's table was dim and flickering.

'Will you go to Bombay and testify for Shalini?' Gola asked.

'The police have registered a number of cases against me. They will arrest me the moment I come out of hiding. I will never be able to return to Punjab.'

'Never is too big a word.' Gola was desperate. 'The judges will see at what risk you've come. They will believe the alibi you give Shalini, especially as you're a doctor, a respectable, educated man. Please, Sripal. Do this for us.' It was a long moment.

'I'll go,' Sripal said.

'Meet me at Dagra, it's about five or six hours by bus from here. Please reach my father's house as soon as possible. We'll go together from there to Bombay, the next day.' Sripal nodded. Gola gave him his father's address in Dagra. He was floating with relief and hope. A thread had been drawn into the knot; there was some order now, a tough, fist-like centre from which time radiated forward to Shalini. He wanted to embrace Sripal. Instead he asked him, 'What do you think of the present situation in Punjab? What is going to happen?'

'I don't know; there are too many unpredictable factors.' Sripal did not want to talk – his voice was tired and reluctant – but Gola was anxious to hear his assessment. Until this point everything in him had been scooped up and directed towards the immediate objective of reaching Sripal. Now, the man having agreed to go, a space had been opened up in Gola's being; he became a political animal again. His uncle's drama had been thrust upon him, he had observed it through a fever-ridden haze. Now his mind was clear and vividly awake and his well-trained political instincts were back at work, like bunches of leaves unfolding at great speed. He asked Sripal again, insistently this time, 'What do you think of the demands which Malik and Trikha have been talking about? When I get back, our people will want an assessment.'

Sripal roused himself to talk, pulling his chair close to the table and resting his elbows on it. Shadows of old, dusty bottles of various shapes and flat layers of tablets secure in their nests of tin-foil, crowded the shelves.

'Malik's claim to represent the entire Sikh community is open to serious question. His party, with thirty-seven members, forms a minority group in the Punjab Assembly with its total strength of 117.'

'That's the whole point, isn't it? They want to be the majority group, to form the government?'

'Even among the Sikhs they are not a majority force. Their membership is not even half the total Sikh strength of eighty in the Assembly. True they are aggressive, but that is not reason enough for them to be treated as spokesmen for the Sikh community.'

'But their aggressiveness! They're fighters.'

Gola was eager to listen to Sripal. He had seen him only vaguely when he had been in Bombay, in passing, at trades union meetings. He had really been Shalini's contact. Now he had taken on a whole new identity, changed his name, to work in Punjab. His words were backed by solid experience.

'Many of their economic grievances are justified. But most other States have similar complaints. And the majority of the Indian population consists of Hindus. It's a result of laws and limitations of the capitalist path. Look at the arguments and demands recently put forward by some of their leaders, and you'll understand immediately the real nature and class basis of the problem. They produce wheat and have a large, marketable surplus. They want the right to sell it in the international market at the highest available price. Why should it be procured at prices fixed by the government of India? It is the same with paddy. Then they say they should have more cotton textile mills and more sugar mills. Punjab rivers should be the exclusive property of Punjab, despite the fact that they originate in Himachal, and that if there is hydro-power to spare it should be sold to neighbouring States.

'A breakthrough would require a radical change in the political power structure. The alternative we have to work for is based on a worker-peasant alliance coming to power, not this rag-tag lot of Malik and Trikha. And then there's Sharifa. He is carrying their politics beyond communal issues, which are dangerous enough, into areas which could destroy everything that people like your uncle stood for.'

Gola considered whether his brooding uncle stood for anything any longer. He said, 'Sharifa is meeting us in Jullundur. Maybe something's planned. Malik and Trikha seem to be waiting.'

'Is your uncle going to Jullundur?'

'Yes. I wish he wasn't. I wanted to go directly from here to

Dagra, after meeting you. But I'll have to go with him to Jullundur, now that Ram Adhikari is dead.'

'Ram Adhikari's dead?' Sudershan burst into the room, with an angry slamming. 'What are you doing here, Gola, talking to this man? Malik and I have been looking all over the village for you. Sardarji is asking for you. Someone told us she had seen you come in here. We know all about this fellow Sripal. A rabid Communist, that's what he is! My wife's own cousin, talking to such a man in the middle of the night! God knows what plots you were hatching.'

Gola wondered how long Sudershan had been listening outside the door. 'No plots at all,' he said. 'I came to him for a personal matter, nothing political.'

But Sudershan was not listening. He was peering at Sripal in the dim half-light of the room, obviously astonished. 'I recognise you,' he said finally. 'You are Ranjit Dhawan, surgeon in the Mombasa General Hospital, in Kenya. You operated on my father fifteen years ago for a prostate gland. You're not a Sikh at all, you're a Hindu, disguised to deceive good people.'

'I recognise you, too,' Sripal said quietly. 'But I live here now.'

'I can see that. Now you're a rabid Communist. I heard the things you were telling this boy against us. You wear a beard and long hair, a turban, and delude the poor peasants in the villages, filling their heads with your godless rubbish!'

'I ask them to keep religion and politics separate, to make religion a personal matter only, not to allow places of worship to be used for political purposes.'

'You don't understand us at all, you know nothing. How can you, you're not a Sikh by birth. And yet you dare to talk like this, and to take on the sacred symbols of a *khalsa* identity for your own devilish purposes. Wait, I'm going to expose you! I'll call the others in. Malik!' he yelled from the door. 'Come here, quickly!'

Before Sudershan turned back into the room the man whom Gola had always known as Dr Sripal had slipped out and disappeared into the night.

'Don't tell my uncle about Ram Adhikari's death,' Gola said to Sudershan, who was furious. 'It would greatly upset my aunt, she was very attached to him. She might fall sick.'

Sudershan was too angry to listen. He turned on Gola. 'How dare you talk to swine like this Ranjit Dhawan? A Hindu doctor from Mombasa lands up in a small village in Punjab and masquerades as a Sikh social worker. There must be some dark design, some plot or other, behind this. I don't care if you are a close relative of mine. My loyalty is to the cause of the Sikh community. You could be my own brother and I would not let you travel with us.' Malik and Trikha had arrived by then. 'This boy Gola is a leftist, a wretched Communist. He must leave our party right away,' he said solemnly. They seemed unimpressed.

Sardarji too dismissed Sudershan's wave of rhetorical abuse. He said to Gola, as if he had surfaced for a moment through a thick soup, 'You stay with me, I want you here.' There was no further argument.

The green Matador van took them to the compound of Khalsa College, just beyond a large railway crossing on the outskirts of Jullundur. Satinder had seen it the first time with Sampuran. Khalsa College had been a half-finished building, seen then from a bus bound for the village of Gyani Basantpur. Poonam's village. Poonam was still the meaning of his life. It was right that he had once more returned to Khalsa College, on the road to Gyani Basantpur, Bhai Dhian Singh, Colonel Fisher, a dynamite explosion and Poonam's death. Events going out in a wave and being thrown back, again and again, unselected.

Gola kept constantly in the room with him in Khalsa College. His son-in-law, Sudershan, was watching Gola. Satinder now found his presence irritating. It was definite, composed of undiluted enthusiasm and beliefs, and it intruded upon the deepening, shadowy landscape of Khalsa College. 'I am just a tired old man, my son,' he told Sudershan. 'Of no use in all this excitement. Why don't you go on into the city? Jullundur is waiting for you. Malik and Trikha left for Sheetal Chowk a long time ago.'

But Sudershan did not want to leave him alone with Gola. 'Why don't we all go in together? You would like to see Sheetal Chowk again. It is where the offices of the old Resettlement Board used to be, where you worked immediately after Partition. Anita showed them to me on our last visit.'

'I remember the offices, I'm not interested to see them again. They must be all changed now, anyway.'

The sense of suffocation and fear which had struck Satinder under the *shamiana* in Naoshera Doaba returned to touch him. 'No, I think I'll stay here for a while, at least for a day,' he said. 'There's no hurry; the demonstration is not until tomorrow.'

'Then I'll stay, too,' Sudershan said, casting a meaningful glance at Gola. But Malik and Trikha sent word that Sharifa and his men

294

had arrived already in Sheetal Chowk and that the speeches had begun. *Baisakhi* was only two days off and the crowds had to get to Amritsar for the Pledge. Sudershan could wait no longer; this was a good opportunity to further his political career. He left, giving firm instructions that the green Matador van was to bring Sardarji to Jullundur as soon as it showed up in Khalsa College. No one seemed to know where the van had gone.

A green-eyed, middle-aged man in army uniform, with the star of a Junior Commissioned Officer on the epaulettes, had been waiting for Sudershan's departure. He slipped into the room the moment his jeep sped off from the college courtyard.

'Sardarji, I have to tell you. You must not go to Sheetal Chowk.'

Satinder stared at the strange bright-eyed man who spoke so firmly. 'Why not?' he asked.

'I don't know. But please don't go.'

'Who are you?'

'The son of your aunt, Kailash Kaur. I was born in your house in Kohat. Your mother held me at my birth.'

His mother had told Satinder the story of his aunt, Kailash Kaur, and her green-eyed lover, Prakash. So this was their son. Kailash Kaur's husband, Palji, had taken Satinder into the mountains to meet the *dacoit* Garkal, to get guns for Bhaskar. Much later, someone had told Palji how his wife had been killed – in her lover's arms, by raiders who came across the border into Bhimbar. The old man had died of shock and grief in Srinagar.

'You saved my sister's life; you brought her with you from Kohat to Jullundur. Then she disappeared,' the green-eyed officer said.

'Was Gulshan your sister?' Satinder said. His heart was cold. 'What happened to her?' A young girl in a state of total shock had come from Bhimbar to Kohat with Bhagwana, and had travelled with Sardarji's family to Jullundur, part of a huge stream of refugees.

'She is a magician's assistant now and goes by the name of Miss Maitreyi Phillips. She swallows sword blades and broken glass and doesn't care about her life.'

'And you? What do you do?'

'I compose music for army bands. My head is full of little bits of music jangling around.'

The musician slipped behind a curtain when a driver entered the room and stood there in a bulky bundle, his large stomach pushing out the curtain, waiting.

295

'Malik Sahib has sent a jeep to take you to Sheetal Chowk immediately,' the driver said.

'Where is the Matador van?' Gola asked.

'I don't know. Maybe that is why they sent the jeep.'

'You go ahead. We will wait for the van. Don't worry, he'll drive me.' Sardarji gestured towards Gola.

The green Matador van was on a secret mission. No one saw who arrived in it when it drew up in Jullundur, on a narrow strip of tarmac between the offices of the *Punjabi Tej* and the central roundabout in Sheetal Chowk, where the speeches were being made. The crowd stood close together and a thousand deep at the *chowk*. It parted to let the van pass. There were detachments of armed police with strong bamboo shields, brass-bound *lathis* and small, shining black revolvers at their waistbands. Sharifa's men mingled in the crowd. It was difficult to distinguish them in the *jathas* which came in from the villages. The turbans of the villagers were loosely tied, perched on their heads, their bearded, open faces turned towards the speakers who, each in turn, climbed on top of the jeep parked in the centre of the *chowk*. Sharifa's men also mingled with men of Malik and Trikha's party who wore loose white shirts and pyjamas, their *kirpans* slung from leather straps which crossed firmly from one shoulder right across the chest to the waist on the opposite side. Sartorial distinctions were becoming difficult.

All parties had women members, dressed in *salwar-kameez* with *dupattas* wrapped tightly around their heads. That was how Bibi Chinti was dressed, too. Her leathery, ageless face looked out from folds of grey-white chiffon, the heavy outline of her hanging, old woman's breasts merged with the incline of her belly under its thin, muslin shirt. She had looked that way when Poonam had died and at the time of Ram Adhikari's death. Now she stood, waiting, behind the green van parked just beyond the front door of the *Tej* offices.

Its steel shutters had been drawn up. The sound of printing presses, still busily at work, came through as a rumbling undertone to the speeches. Bibi Chinti peered through empty spaces created by the Matador's rolled-down windows. There was a face beside hers, expressionless and stooping, which topped a spotless white *achkan* and *churidars*. It belonged to Chaman Bajaj. The jostling and gestures of enthusiastic, rapt supporters around them had disarranged his short, black-grey hair, tipped it boyishly over his

296

creaseless forehead and the tops of his square, black-framed spectacles.

On the opposite side of the *chowk*, perched on a high flight of stairs leading to the State Bank of India, looking out over a moving sea of heads, a thin woman huddled in a bright blue robe decorated with silver stars. This was Miss Maitreyi Phillips, the Magician's Assistant. She and Chaman Bajaj were the only two bare-headed people in the audience. Even Dr Zimbabwe, Master Magician, wore a gold-embroidered cap. He stood over her, resting on a tall stick and twirling a lazy blue flag which advertised his magic.

Higher than the heads were tips of naked swords, sharp heads of spears, round, brass knobs of *lathis* and the glint and shimmer of *kirpans*. They rose in serried ranks, radiating outwards from the central jeep from whose roof the speeches were being made. Then all the points seemed to come together.

Sharifa had climbed up on the jeep-top with Malik and Trikha, and stood between them, a tall figure with long, handsome eyes and clever bones. Sudershan had wanted to join them, but the bodyguard had pushed him back. He did not belong yet to the front rank of leadership. The three men there were silent, watching the progress of a shiny, black Ambassador car headed towards the entrance to the *Punjabi Tej*.

The crowd parted a second time, for the car. It moved slowly between lines of khaki-clad constables beside the path, then stopped behind a green Matador van which blocked its way. It had reached its destination. The front door of the *Punjabi Tej* was a few feet away. A back door of the Ambassador opened and Bhim Lal Whig got out. He was clearly amazed. The demonstration had been scheduled for the next day. He had dropped in ahead of time, just to ensure the safety of his property, and was not expecting these huge crowds.

As his bodyguard was getting out of the front door a hand rose and threw a grenade. It only half-exploded but its shards injured Bhim Lal Whig and killed a nine-year-old girl called Swaranjit Kaur who had joined the *jatha* from the village of Bhirnath with her mother and grandfather. The shards touched no one else. Though Bibi Chinti and Chaman Bajaj were nearby, they escaped uninjured. Then the same hand rose again and fired two shots from a carbine to finish the job. Bhim Lal Whig now lay sprawled on the tarmac, his body an untidy mess of blood.

No one knew when the green Matador van left the road, or how it got through so fast through the scattering groups of people fleeing from the police. The DSP arrested Sudershan and some others right away. The assassins could have been anywhere in the crowd and could have ducked back into its shelter after committing the crime. Only the three leaders, Malik, Trikha and Sharifa, standing exposed on the jeep-top, were spared. Obviously none of them, scrupulously watched throughout by the police, had committed the murder; their alibis were perfect.

Then everyone began to ask, 'Who was in the green Matador van? Who drove it away so fast through the crowd?'

It would have needed a magician to answer that. But Dr Zimbabwe, the Magician and his assistant, Miss Maitreyi Phillips, had already disappeared from the scene. Chaman Bajaj and Bibi Chinti had spread like water through the feet of running people. There was no one to pick up the questions.

They were asked again and again in the days which followed the murder and during the interrogations. 'Who was in the green Matador van?' they said.

Arson and violence broke out in Ludhiana, damaging over a dozen shops and five or six scooters, and night patrolling of its curfew-bound areas was intensified.

Again they asked the identity of the occupant of a vehicle resembling a Matador van, thought to be green in colour, when curfew was imposed on Adalat Bazar, Anardana Chowk, Tawakalli Chowk, Arya Samaj and other areas adjoining the *maidan* demarcated for the Pledging Ceremony on *Baisakhi* Day. Malik, Sharifa and Trikha, spruced and energetic, prepared to administer the Pledge to batches of the faithful collected in Guru-ka-Bagh on the outskirts of Amritsar. The venue had had to be shifted because of the murder of Bhim Lal Whig. The leaders denied all knowledge of the matter and, of course, condemned the killing, saying that violence had never been in their programme. That was quite clear. After all, Sardar Satinder Singh Chahal, well-known exponent of Non-Violence, had led their tour of Punjab. Naturally, then, violence was not part of their programme.

The question was asked again when Anil Sharma was killed outside his shop which sold radio parts in Lal Bazaar. He had heard firing in the area and had rushed to his shop with his mother and two friends. A bullet caught him in the eye. Even as people crowded round his dead body, anxious not to miss the drama, or dashed off to call the police, or comforted his distraught mother, the question going from mouth to mouth, picked up from the very air, spreading outwards in an ever-widening circle, was 'Who was in the van which stood in front of Bhim Lal Whig's black Ambassador, blocking its path, so that he was killed?' The police returned to the question again when they found the trussed up body of the Head Constable, who had been captured from the Armoury.

Much later, when the van finally drew up outside Khalsa College, the green-eyed musician had disappeared from behind the curtain.

Sardarji led Meera Aunty, who was confused and tired, to the van. 'Take us to Sheetal Chowk, Gola,' he said.

It was a long time before he realised that the van had left the city behind and that Gola was driving them through villages and little towns, along the Grand Trunk Road. He stopped Gola. 'You're not taking us to Jullundur. Did you believe that crazy man who walked into Khalsa College? Do you think I am afraid?'

Gola said, 'I didn't tell you before, but Ram Adhikari is dead. He was a suspect in the Armoury theft. They shot him as he tried to escape.'

'But he was nowhere near the Armoury!' Meera Aunty's voice was full of cracking pain. While Sardarji was taking care of her Gola drove on. The green Matador van was a prodigal son, returned after much merry-making in the Armoury, and with the Head Constable afterwards, then to the doings in Jullundur. The same green Matador van which had pursued the fleeing Brigadier in Kalidiggi until he shot out its tyres, like an animal in a green jungle. Now it took Sardarji and his clan over the low foothills of the Himalayas, then higher and higher, into the icy regions of Hemkund Sahib, a shrine at the end of a difficult road, 17,000 feet up into the mountains.

28

Arrivals and Departures in Dagra, 1984

Krishna heard her father's door bang shut behind him. Her mother had disappeared into the kitchen. She left them, each wrapped in a separate grief – a familiar scene in Dagra – and fled up the stairs to Sohail, her son.

A boy's clothes, some books, running shoes, all scattered round the room. No Sohail. Then sounds in the bathroom. He still had his old habit of bathing several times a day.

She went out to the verandah. An empty plot of land led off from the back wall of the house, bounded by a thick strip of trees. She thought of Mrs Kapur, who had travelled with her from Hardwar to Dagra, armed with new suitcases, and the power of Chaman Bajaj, who wanted Mrs Kapur's son, Dhiren, as his son-in-law. He had promised to get the tenants out of Mrs Kapur's house in Dagra. These were students who had established squatters' rights there. If Chaman Bajaj pleased Mrs Kapur, and he was a powerful man, his daughter would marry her beloved son, and Mona, who was Mr Surjit's daughter, Anjali's daughter, would not marry Dhiren, whom she loved. It was all very complicated. Krishna knew now which Mrs Kapur's house was. On the other side from her father's, hidden behind an orchard of *litchi* trees. And, of course, the tenants were her old friends, Chugh, Goyal, Bhisham and some others, all those had put up posters in Dagra and helped her stop the tree-auction.

There was no question about it. She knew what she had to do. She had to stop Chaman Bajaj in his tracks and hold him up forever. She went back into the room.

Sohail was emerging from the bathroom, rubbing at his hair. Once more she felt his smooth, fat cheeks against hers, the pressure of his broad stomach against her. She wanted to hold him

300

forever; it was such a sweet feeling, but you had to be careful with growing boys. 'You've put on weight again!' she said instead and he laughed happily, clearly delighted to see her.

'Your grandmother said you were home from school because you were sick. What's the matter?'

'Nothing, really. I just wanted to be here. Especially after Nanaji's heart attack two weeks ago. You were in London then. I really missed you, everybody here did. Gola Uncle kept saying, "I wish your mother were here". But how was your trip? Did you have a good time? What did you get me from London?'

Of course the suitcases had to be opened right away. She watched his eyes light up with joy, and the tenderness with which he held his new toys. 'Tell me about school,' she said. 'You wrote that you had met some relatives.'

'Yes, a peculiar woman called Miss Maitreyi Phillips, the Magician's Assistant. She said she was my aunt.'

'She is my cousin in a way. She is the daughter of my father's aunt, Kailash Kaur, who was killed in Bhimbar during the terrible riots which followed Partition in 1947, when the raiders came through into Kashmir. A servant called Bhagwana took the little girl to Kohat, to my uncle Satinder's house, and she came over with his family into India. She lived with them in Jullundur for a while, then disappeared. When she turned up again, years later, she was this Magician's Assistant.'

'She was really marvellous, the way she swallowed knives, a sword, pieces of broken glass.'

'They don't really swallow these things; just make you think they do.'

'She tried to tell me something afterwards, I couldn't understand – her language was odd. But she told such fantastic stories! Mainly about our family, how two children long, long ago set off on a journey from Sialkot and reached Kohat.'

The Magician's Assistant, Miss Maitreyi Phillips, hard lump of scar-tissue, mad survivor of the violence which had been Partition and Independence, had initiated Sohail into the rites and ceremonies of journey. Did he already know about the journey which goes on under the skin?

'Listen, Sohail. I need help for something that's going to happen in our neighbourhood. Mr Jaswant will be able to help, I'm sure. He's a senior government official, very nice, whom I met in London last month. He's definitely in Dagra now; he has an

301

important conference here. Can you locate him at the Circuit House and bring him over here?'

'Sure. It's only ten minutes from here on my bicycle. But what will Mr Jaswant do?'

'I'm not quite sure. We'll just have to wait and see.'

'But what's the problem?'

'Friends of mine, some students from Dagra, are in deep trouble. They have established themselves in the house behind the *litchi* trees, Mrs Kapur's house. And Chaman Bajaj, who is a powerful politician, will use every means, fair and foul, to get them out. It's against the law, to forcibly evict tenants. But Chaman Bajaj considers himself above the law. And I'm determined to stop him.'

'Why don't you just call the police?'

'It doesn't always work that way. I told you, he is a powerful man. They might need a push from the Police Commissioner. And Mr Jaswant is highly placed in Government, he can persuade the Police Commissioner.'

'Mummy, I didn't know all this, how things work. When did you learn?'

'As I went along. The *padyatra* taught me a great deal.'

'Your *padyatra* and the tree-auction afterwards, those were magnificent. They're still talking about it in school. Everybody thinks of you as a great leader in Tehri, all these Eastern Himalayan parts. They think you're going to fight the next elections.'

'Me, fight elections?'

'Why not? Miss Maitreyi Phillips told me a lot about the history of the family. Uncle Sardarji has been in politics. She said he was Minister in the Government even before Independence.'

'Yes, that's right. We're proud of him. I've still got a long way to go. And you, my dear, can begin by fetching Mr Jaswant. I don't know how much time we've got. Mrs Kapur said Chaman Bajaj was planning for today.'

'Yes Ma'am. I'm going right away.' He grinned, and she hugged him as he left. She wanted to touch him. Somehow, she longed to be held.

There were loud sounds of excitement from the front door. Her father's angry voice was calling out for the servant. Krishna just had time to send Sohail off.

Gola was emerging from the driver's seat of a green Matador

van, parked outside. Her uncle Satinder and Meera Aunty got out from beside him, their limbs slow with fatigue.

'We're on our way back from Hemkund Sahib, the Sikh shrine up in the Himalayas,' Sardarji said. 'We just dropped in to see you.'

Gola took Krishna aside. 'Did you read about Sardarji's political campaign through Punjab, persuading people to go to Amritsar for the Pledging Ceremony? But how could you, you were away in London. It's good to have you back. You know, there was no way of contacting you when Daddy had his heart attack.'

'Your telegram was waiting for me in my flat when I got in from the airport yesterday, Anu had come to pick me up. I left immediately, by the night train. I got in this morning. What's been happening?'

'A lot of excitement with this great journey through the Punjab. But I don't know about the last two to three days, I've been with Sardarji and Meera Aunty in that van, driving up and down in the mountains. But I must tell you why I've come from Bombay.'

'Why?'

'Shalini's been arrested, for murder. She's been framed. But I had to get proof. I was in Punjab, looking for the only man who could give her an authentic alibi. He's agreed to testify, though it's at great risk to himself. He should be here this evening. His name is Dr Sripal. Remember that, it's important – in case you meet him before I do. I'll take him with me to Bombay by the morning train.'

'What's your news, Krishna my dear?' Sardarji put his arm affectionately around her shoulders as he sat drinking beer in the cool shadows of the drawing-room.

'I got in from London last night. Anu was at the airport. You know that his father's been killed?'

'What! Bhim Lal Whig? But I was with him only a few days ago, in Naoshera Doaba.'

'Anu had just got back from Jullundur. His father was shot there.'

Krishna left Sardarji to rescue the Brigadier and Sonia. They were quarrelling in the kitchen. Neither of them knew what to do about lunch for the new arrivals.

'I'll get food from the Bazaar,' the Brigadier said.

'I'll drive you,' said Krishna. She wanted to get him out as soon as possible. 'We'll take the green van they arrived in.'

The Brigadier was sunk in a stupor, as if listening to sounds inside himself. It seemed impossible to communicate with him. She hadn't even told him yet about the murder of Bhim Lal Whig. He insisted on going into the shop alone. 'Not the place for a woman,' he said. 'It's full of truck-drivers and policemen.' She smiled; he knew so little of what she was now.

He came back balancing clay pots filled with various curries, mutton and chicken, and some oily vegetable.

'Is it good for a heart patient to eat this kind of food?' she asked. 'Do you do it often?'

'Every day, almost. Your mother refuses to cook for me. This makes her happy. She already imagines I'm a dead man. But I'll show her yet. Even if I don't outlive her, I've left my last will and testament. I've made sure she won't get a penny from my estate.'

'You haven't changed your will!' He had shown it to her on her last visit.

And to my wife, who will shed crocodile tears when I die, I leave nothing. It is enough that I brought her out of the small, backward island where she was born, to this great country, where she has lived a life of luxury at my expense, a queen in this beautiful house. And she did nothing for me except spoil my reputation, speak ill of me to everyone, and destroy me. She must get nothing. No house, no garden, no cow, no piece of furniture.

The will had made no mention of his daughter, Krishna; she was to get nothing. Everything had been left to her brother, Gola. 'But daughters and sons are equal,' she had said, no longer abashed about demanding what should be hers, 'you should treat us equally.'

'Nobody leaves property to his daughter. That's one of the rules of our society. She belongs to another family, once she gets married. You should have taken dowry when you got married. I offered it to you. Now you can't expect me to leave my house to you. Your husband's family is rich.'

'I'm no longer married. But even if I were, do you think my father-in-law would leave me a house? It's not that I need your property. It's your reason for dispossessing me that hurts, because I am a woman and so I don't belong anywhere. Neither does my mother. Patrimony and inheritance, that's all it means – that you're accepted, you belong with someone. But maybe it's better

304

this way, to do without property, not to be tied down to a particular piece of land, or to one father. Just to float, looking for fathers and other people to love, wherever you can find them. Then the whole world belongs to you.'

Now her father's mention of the will which she remembered so distinctly, called up a host of dispossessed women:– Sonia, Swaranjit Kaur, her niece Kailash, and the brave Poonam, shattered by a grenade. They were women who had pushed against the walls of dispossession.

She recognised her kinship with them. Once she had been different, she had treasured anonymity, hidden behind her skin. But meeting Ranjit and undertaking the *padyatra* through the Himalayas had changed everything.

She had begun to live, to touch reality, to change it. She could not be a watchful cipher again, sheltering behind her darkening skin which absorbed all the blows into its colour. And today she had to deal with Chaman Bajaj. He would come with Mrs Kapur, to help her get back her house next door.

Her father had settled the leaking pots into the green Matador – and was gesturing to her to start the van. 'I've changed my will. I'll show it to you as soon as we get back. What you said, what you have been doing in the last few years, has made me think a little. I've given you a lifetime share in the house and in the income from the mango trees. Equal with Gola.'

She looked at him, but he was staring straight ahead through the windscreen. 'So many things have happened to me, I wish I could tell you.' His voice was slow, like a sick man's. 'You remember that I went off to work in a hospital at the border during the 1970 war? I went there straight after Dhiraj Kumari committed suicide. I knew her well. She also used to say that women didn't get enough justice. Or love. I didn't want to keep it from you any more.'

Krishna was choking inside. She wanted to hold him carefully, tenderly, like the fragile gift of love he had made to her.

Once they got back into the house, everything was different. Within minutes he was quarrelling with Sardarji and with Sonia, through the maelstrom of lunch. It proved too much for him, Krishna heard his suppressed, spluttering voice from his room, and rushed in. She was shocked to see him, his arms doubled up across his chest, as if to hold in the great pain tearing up his insides. His face was ashen and his lips, fingers and skin were faintly blue. 'I'm

305

like you now. Blue, blue Krishna. Don't go, stay with me,' he was muttering incessantly.

'Hush. You mustn't talk. Just lie down. It's a heart attack, again. Damn this house, no telephones. I'll send Gola for a doctor.' She rushed out. He was still talking when she got back.

'Nobody. Just come here and sit with me. You see, your mother thinks I'm dead already, she's playing death music for me.'

'Daddy, you're not going to die.' But he was right about the music, it was coming over a radio – *bhajans* and mournful tunes, broken with eulogies and funeral bits. The Lion, Sheikh Abdullah, a national leader from the time of the Independence Movement, had died. 'That's for Sheikh Abdullah. It's coming over the radio. It's not for you; I won't let you die.' She leaned forwad and held him, as she had wanted to do for a long time. 'I love you, Daddy.'

She was rubbing his hands. The sounds of the green Matador had died away. Gola should be back soon with the doctors. She looked up and saw two faces at the window, their outlines rippling in hot waves of air. The woman's face was old and firmly creased; it was incongruous, set between two long, black braids plaited with silver thread which should have belonged to a young girl. Beside her was a green-eyed man waving a piece of paper. Krishna opened the window.

'I'm Maitreyi Phillips, Assistant to Dr Zimbabwe the Great Magician. I've come to meet Sohail,' the braided woman said.

The man said: 'I'm her brother. They called her Gulshan when she was born. I'm her half-brother, a bastard. Nobody acknowledges me or gives me a name. I am the love-child of Kailash Kaur, I make tunes for music, band tunes. Recently I warned Sardarji not to go to Jullundur. I have done my duty by my family.'

'Can you go through the front door and wait? I'll come out very soon. My father is very sick.'

'Don't worry. We'll wait right here.'

The Brigadier was agitated, asking about the people at the window.

'A brother and a sister – they're related to us,' she said. 'The woman has been meeting Sohail in school.'

'Ah yes. The brother and sister. So they've arrived at last, to take me. Manmohan Singh and Swaranjit Kaur, our first ancestors. They've been travelling from Sialkot to Kohat. Now they've arrived, to carry me off.'

'No, these are their descendants. Just like us. A crazy magician, and a green-eyed music-composer.'

He was struggling to sit up. She heard the ambulance arriving.

Sohail came in just then, leading Mr Jaswant, whose tall figure, with hair plastered down stylishly, appeared above the heads of the others. 'Hello Miss Chahal, nice to see you again. Some problems? You sent for me.'

'Yes, please. I think I'm going to need your help right away. What are those terrible sounds?' There was a chilling quiver of hounds, baying in a high-pitched, mournful tone, which rose above a clattering medley of slogans and ringing bells, like a religious procession. 'Those are Great Danes. Chaman Bajaj has arrived.'

'It's only an election procession,' said Mr Jaswant. 'We passed it at the end of the road. You're right. The posters are for Chaman Bajaj, and he's there in a white *achkan*.'

'They're going for your students,' Maitreyi Phillips said. 'Bibi Chinti is there, too, right beside him. Do you remember her, Krishna?'

Two jeeps came up the driveway, full of policemen. Gola, Sardarji and the others crowded round her at the front door. The DSP got out and came towards Sardarji with handcuffs. 'I've come to arrest you, on criminal charges, under Section 302, for murder, and for conspiracy under the Criminal Procedure Code, for the raid on the Armoury in Naoshera Doaba.'

Krishna stood between them. 'You don't need to use those. He's an old man. He won't run away. Anyway, I'm sure there's some mistake.'

The DSP was very polite, he recognised her as Krishna Chahal, leader of the *padyatra* through Himachal, Kashmir and Uttar Pradesh. Tomorrow she might be Minister, who knew? All kinds of young leaders were coming up, now that the old lot from the Independence Movement were dying off. He wiped the sweat from his forehead and put away the handcuffs. 'But you know that we usually do, when the charge is murder.'

'Murder? What do you mean, murder? Whose murder?' Sardarji was astonished.

'Bhim Lal Whig's murder.'

'But Krishna said he was killed in Jullundur! I didn't even go there.'

'Your green Matador was there. That same vehicle standing here. And it was also used in the raid on the Armoury, to carry away the guns.' The DSP was fast losing his politeness. 'And let me

307

tell you that in searching your house in Chandigarh, we found an illegal distillation unit under the staircase, in other words, a still for making alcohol. So we have to arrest the lady, too.' Poor Meera Aunty. Her beautiful, white liquid full of enchantment, her only success in life.

'And you, too.' The DSP told Gola. 'You've been driving the green Matador.'

'But my father is sick; he's dying inside the house. I've just brought the ambulance. We have to get him to hospital.'

'Someone else will have to take him. We are arresting you, because of the van. It's the same one, with a torn lace curtain at the back window. It was on the scene of various crimes. Guns were loaded into it when the Armoury in Naoshera Doaba was raided. In Jullundur it was stationed across the road, to block it while the assailants shot Mr Bhim Lal Whig.'

'Just one moment, then.' Gola took Krishna aside. His voice was breaking with urgency. 'This man I told you about. Sripal. From Punjab. He is to be in Dagra today. Please, you must get him on the train to Bombay, so he can give evidence in Shalini's case.'

'But how can I sit here waiting for him? I have to get Daddy to hospital.'

'Let Mummy take him. She'll be able to manage.' They could see Sonia in the Brigadier's bedroom, moving near his bed.

Sonia knew her husband was dying, and this fixed her firmly in the soil of India. For thirty-five years she had preserved the possibility of flight from him, from India. If he died there would be nothing to escape from.

A taxi drew up, and Aunty Anjali got out. 'I couldn't get to Mrs Kapur's house next door. She's inside, with the students. There's a huge crowd of political workers surrounding it, shouting, trying to get in. A man in a white *achkan* with a bunch of Great Danes leashed to his wrist is directing them.'

'Chaman Bajaj,' Krishna whispered. 'He's brought the Great Danes. Don't worry, Aunty Anjali, I'll go and find Mrs Kapur.'

'Then I'll go with your mother to the hospital,' Aunty Anjali said. Sonia was sobbing on her shoulder.

The DSP refused to help Krishna. 'There's no violence reported as yet. I don't know what you are saying, about this Mrs Kapur, her house, tenants, students, whatever. As far as we know, this is a peaceful election meeting; Mr Chaman Bajaj is an important politician.'

308

By then Mr Jaswant was beginning to understand the scenario. 'I don't want to mess around with this Chaman Bajaj,' he said frankly. 'He's a dangerous fellow. But the Police Commissioner is a friend of mine. I'll get him to send the police. Let Sohail go with me; he can bring them back.'

Everyone left at the same time, her sick father with two women hovering tenderly over him in the ambulance, the police jeeps with their three prisoners and, trailing after them, the captured green Matador van. A bewildered fury was possessing Krishna; there was just so much to do. She had to keep a lookout for Gola's contact, Dr Sripal; she had to find Mrs Kapur; and somehow she had to stop Chaman Bajaj. He must not be allowed to throw out the students from Mrs Kapur's house.

A figure detached itself from the shadows under the *litchi* trees and came towards her.

'Ranjit! It's Ranjit! She was holding him, clinging to him.

He said, after a while, 'Krishna, I'm Dr Sripal now, Gola might have told you about me. He wants me to go to Bombay to testify for Shalini.'

Does he know...about you and me?'

'No. He knew me only briefly, before Punjab, when I was hiding in Bombay.'

'Where have you been all these years? Why didn't you write to me, contact me, let me know where you were? It's been so difficult, not knowing anything about you. Why did you leave me alone?'

'There were things you had to do. And I ... well ... that's a long story too.'

'Do you know what's happening? The police have arrested Gola and Sardarji. For Bhim Lal Whig's murder.'

Don't worry, they'll get off. Malik, Trikha and the others from the extremist faction tried to frame Sardarji, to use him as cover for their own activities during his long journey through Punjab. But fortunately Sardarji didn't go to Jullundur at all, where the murder took place.'

'Oh Ranjit, you're back! I can hardly believe it. As if the gods had suddenly decided to be kind to me. But I knew you'd come, one day. It's been such a long, long time, I couldn't bear it.' She could hear her own voice, rolling in her ears. He was holding her, caressing her. 'Sometimes I thought you would never come.'

'Afterwards,' he said. 'Now you have things to do.' He was

gesturing towards Mrs Kapur's house.

'No,' she said, 'I don't want to go anywhere. Just to stay with you.' As if here she would find rest at last, peace. The intense loneliness of her body was a shell dropping away, she was soft and utterly tender.

'I have to go too,' Ranjit said, 'to Bombay.'

'But you've only just come back to me.'

'You know why I have to go.'

'I'll go with you.' But she knew that was only her desire, her strong movement towards him. There was no rest, no peace, not yet. She could not stop, or stay now, she had to go on.

'We'll come with you,' Miss Maitreyi Phillips said, bobbing up from nowhere, her plaits dark with sweat in the faint evening shadows. 'Krishna, you know the Lion is dead?'

She was puzzled by the intrusion, it took her a moment to get back to Maitreyi. She was intensely conscious of Ranjit's presence under the *litchi* trees, but already the brother and sister flanked her as she walked slowly towards Mrs Kapur's house.

'Sheikh Abdullah?' she said, 'yes. I heard the news and the mourning songs over the radio. My father saw his own death in it. All the old leaders are dying. Miss Pratibha Anand, Sheikh Abdullah...'

'And new ones are born. Krishna Chahal...' Maitreyi's voice was deep with laughter.

Krishna was quiet. She was impatient to get back to Ranjit, but the noise of shouting and commotion came to them in steady waves. She walked faster. Soon they were in a jungle of waving sticks and placards.

The ranks of the mob were tight around the house, lapping like an angry sea around its walls and barred door. Mrs Kapur was already inside; she must have gone in earlier to negotiate. Two of the students were struggling with her to prevent her from opening the front door to Chaman Bajaj and his men. Krishna and her two companions slid through the crowd, right to the front.

Chaman Bajaj was there, up against the front door. His huge dogs stood ranged beside him in a fleshy wall, still leashed to his wrist, their paws silent and bulbous, teeth bared, their bodies sparse and muscled and their hairless tails lashing behind them. More terrifying than their size and teeth were the high sounds of their fury which tore at her ears, churning her insides.

Chaman Bajaj turned savagely on her. 'What are you doing

310

here? There's no business for you, here. Leave at once, or I'll release these dogs on you.' She was full of fear, but she did not move.

Bibi Chinti was pressing up between them. She was dressed, as she always was, in a thin muslin shirt, her head wrapped in a *dupatta*, her breasts pressing out, flat under the white cloth like two full moons or shields.

'My daughter,' she said in a voice Krishna seemed to have been hearing for centuries, at burning and torture, at death by grenade and violence. 'Dear girl, leave all this fighting; it is for men. Chaman Bajaj will take care of everything.'

Krishna turned upon her, pushing away her fat, pulpy body with all her force. She was right beside Chaman Bajaj now. Somewhere in her mind she was waiting for the sounds of the police arriving.

He was hissing at her; his composure had vanished. 'The dogs will kill you. I'm going to put them on you!'

'They won't touch me; they're the dogs of Bhim Lal Whig; they won't touch me. Did you murder him? It's you that must leave now. Listen! I am not afraid of you any longer.'

Even as she said all this, she knew it was true. Chaman Bajaj's face changed in front of her like a dissolving map of fury. He unhooked the dogs.

Krishna pushed Maitreyi Phillips and her brother behind her and turned to face the dogs. Then she remembered their names. 'Down Brutus, down Shamin, down Sitara, down Bharti!' Maybe they smelled her lack of fear, maybe they remembered her from the years of her marriage, as family, and they did not attack, despite Chaman Bajaj's urging. Slowly they sank, grovelling, completely silent. Chaman Bajaj kicked out at them viciously in his anger and they turned upon him, leaping at his throat, oblivious to Krishna's loud commands.

Even as Chaman Bajaj's torn body sank between the dogs she heard the sound of police sirens. The crowd surged forward and broke open the door of the house. Mrs Kapur was thrown straight out into the mouths of the crazed dogs, now suddenly without a master. Sohail, leading the police, and Maitreyi were beside Krishna, moving to help Mrs Kapur.

Gunshots rang out, killing the dogs. Immediately, the tight bunch of the crowd fell apart and melted away, exposing the body of Chaman Bajaj, which someone had tried to cover with a short piece of cloth.

Mrs Kapur rushed up and embraced Krishna, her huge body trembling with relief. 'Krishna my dear, you saved my life.'

The students, released from the house, were swarming around her.

'Krishnaji, we need your help. Sanyukta is hurt. Not badly, but still, she needs medical attention.' Chugh, one of the student leaders from the tree-auction, was supporting a limping young girl whom Krishna had not seen before.

'Mrs Kapur, why don't you go with her to the hospital? I'll arrange for one of the police jeeps to take you. My mother and Aunty Anjali are there, with my father.'

She got them on the jeep, and gathered Sohail to her side. She wanted to get back to Ranjit. Now perhaps there would be time for them. The empty restlessness within her had settled down, vanished. She was ticking with an exciting harmony.

'Krishna, we've been waiting for you to get back to Dagra.' It was Chugh again. 'In fact, we were wondering where to contact you. It's so lucky for us to find you here today.'

'Why, what is it?' Soon, Ranjit would have to catch the train to Bombay. She understood that he must go.

'There is a by-election to the Tehri seat for Parliament, for the Lok Sabha. We want you to stand as our candidate and we're sure you'll win. Everybody in the area knows you now.'

'How can I stand for election? My work is different. I've just got money for an important river-project.'

'You can do all that so much better, if you're in Parliament. Please, you have to stand.' The others were crowding around her. She looked over their heads to Ranjit, waiting under the *litchi* trees.

'But we'll talk later. Perhaps tomorrow.' She watched Sohail walking off with Maitreyi Phillips and her green-eyed brother, in the middle of a knot of her new campaigners, all talking excitedly.

She felt no excitement now herself, just a full, tight wholeness, as she reached Ranjit. 'I suppose you'll have to go?'

'Yes. But this time I'll be back.'

'You must. You can't leave me again, I need you. My skin's got so dark, one day I'll disappear.'

'No,' he said, 'that is over, your darkening skin and all that. You won't darken any more. You don't need to.'

Her head was light, she was twirling in one place, like the

312

laburnum tree from her father's jungles, complete and whole, dense and yellow with silence.

Glossary of Hindustani Terms

achkan	long coat with a high, closed collar
Akal Takht	sanctum of a chief *gurudwara*
Akhbaar	newspaper
angwaltha	warm embrace
anna	old coin, no longer in use; 16 *annas* made one rupee
ASI	Assistant Sub-Inspector
ashoka tree	fairly tall tree with thick foliage and long, dark-green tapering leaves
ashram	a haven, usually a religious place, for those who have withdrawn from the world
babul tree	tree very particular to the Punjab, found in village lanes
badmash	bad character
bairagi	someone who has withdrawn into deep worship
Baisakhi	New Year in Punjab
bakain	Persian lilac
bambola	used as an epithet for anything very strong and effective
baoli	well
bar or bat	tree with small leaves
baraat	bridegroom's party
bara-singha	twelve-antlered deer
barrack	long, low shed, such as those where soldiers are housed
Bhaiji	Sikh priest
bhainji	sister
bhajans	devotional songs
bhuk-mari	dying of hunger
bukhari	wood- or coal-burning heater
burfi	sweetmeat

314

burqa	enveloping veil, like a tent
cannas	tall plants, with large red and yellow fleshy flowers
casuarina tree	flowering tree with beautiful pale pink and white blossoms
chabri-wallah	seller of grams, puffed rice, etc.
Chait	a month in the Hindu calendar
chappals	flat, open sandals
chappati	flat, thin wheat bread
chaprasi	peon, messenger
charpoy	string cot
chawl	tenement
chillum	pipe
chipko	to cling
chowk	crossroads
chowkidar	watchman
chunni	veil worn by Punjabi women with *salwar-kameez*, to cover their heads or just drape over their breasts and shoulders
churan	spicy powder eaten to help the digestive processes
churidar	tight pyjama
CMO	Chief Medical Officer
coolie	porter
daal	lentils
dacoit	bandit
dak-bunglow	house, built by the British administration, for its officers on tour in remote places
DAV college	a college in Lahore (one of a chain of colleges in India established by a nineteenth-century reformer)
deorhi	courtyard
Deva Bhumi	land of the gods
dhaba	roadside tea-shop
dhoti	loose, lower garment for men
DIG	Deputy Inspector General
DTC	Delhi Transport Corporation

315

dupatta	head covering
durries	cotton carpets
erl	bolt
fauji	military man
feringhee	foreigner
firman	proclamation
gauna	the time when a married girl reaches puberty and goes to her husband's house for the first time
ghazal	song, usually a love-song, with poignant sentiments
ghee	clarified butter
godown	warehouse or store
goonda	hit-man
gram	dried lentils
gul-mohor tree	tree with tiny leaves and masses of blossoms which are a flaming orange in summer
Gumbhira	the name of an important festival celebrated in East Bengal roundabout springtime
gur	unprocessed sugar
gurudwara	Sikh place of worship
Guru Granth Sahib	the Holy Book of the Sikhs, comparable to the Bible or Koran
guru ka Sikh	faithful follower of the gurus, the religious teachers of the Sikhs
halwai	man who makes sweetmeats
Hamam soap	cheap brand of toilet soap in use today in India
Hangu breeze	very cold wind which comes down periodically from the northern mountains in the Frontier Province
Harijan	the name given by Mahatma Gandhi to the untouchables or outcasts; literally means 'people of God'
haveli	sprawling mansion of older times

316

havildar	non-commissioned officer in the police or army
Heera Mandi	diamond market
hookah	pipe
ilex	small tree which grows in cold areas
Ittehadul-e-Mussalmeen	an organization set up by the Nizam of Hyderabad in the 1940s
jagir	estate
jalebi	crisp, fried sweetmeat filled with syrup
jamun	sweet, purple fruit
jatha	squad
jathedar	leader of a *jatha*
jawan	soldier
JCO	Junior Commissioned Officer
jonga	large, comfortable jeep
Jumna-par	the other side of the river Jumna
kabab	small, flat spicy meat cutlet
kacha and kara	long underwear and steel bracelet which Sikhs are required to wear
kameez	woman's shirt
kanungo	petty revenue official
karamchari	worker
karita	large bush with leafy branches
katal	fruit tree with large, bulbous fruit
karhai	wok-like vessel for deep frying
khadi, khaddar	hand-spun cloth
khalsa	a pure Sikh
khanda	curved weapon, double-edged sword
khes	woven sheet
khus-khus	woven grass panels hung against windows and doors in summer, watered for coolness
kikar tree	low thorny tree with sparse foliage, twisted, thin branches and dark-coloured wood
kirpan	short dagger
kohl	eye-black, cosmetic
kotwali	police station

317

kurta	long, loose shirt
laddoo	yellow, ball-shaped sweet
lakh	unit of one hundred thousand
lathi	big stick
litchi tree	low tree bearing *litchi* fruit, which orginated in China
lungi	long, loosely wrapped lower garment for men
lurgi	rice liquor
maidan	large, open space
mali	gardener
massak	goat skin sewn up to make a bag, used at one time to carry water
maund	weight measure, about 80lb
mela	fair or festival
miripiri	the double-edged sword of spiritual and physical valour, a Sikh symbol
MLA	Member of the Legislative Assembly, the State Parliament
morcha	political procession
mor pankh	large, ornamental bush, often used in Moghul gardens
mukti	freedom
mundu	young servant boy
Mushaira	an evening when poems are recited and sung
mutka	round, clay pot
naan	flat bread made of flour, baked in a clay oven
Nanaji	grandfather
neem tree	tree with bitter leaves, said to have medicinal properties; twigs from it are used to clean the teeth by chewing on them in lieu of toothbrush and paste
nipal	a kind of bamboo
NWFP	North-West Frontier Province

318

paan	betel-leaf
padyatra	significant journey performed entirely on foot
paise	small coin, a hundred to the rupee
pakora	savoury snack
pakur tree	short, sturdy tree
pallav	end of the sari
pashmina	very fine wool made from the softest hairs of special mountain goats, very expensive
patwari	village official
pathan	man from the Frontier region
peepul or pipal tree	tree connected with religious stories, which has broad leaves with long, elongated tips
pershad	offering to the gods
phirin	long, loose shirt
phulkari	heavily embroidered spread done in bright colours
pir	Mohammedan saint
puri	fried bread
ras-malais	sweet made from milk
Rasta Roko	barricade
raat-ki-rani	Queen of the Night, fragrant flowering bush
Razakars	para-military personnel
rickshaw-wallah	man who draws a rickshaw, a two-seated bicycle-drawn cart
rishis	holy men
riyasat	territory
Rustom	from the Persian story of Sohrab and Rustom, used as synonym for a brave warrior
saka	sacrifice
salwar-kameez	loose pyjamas, drawn in at the ankle and *kameez*, the loose shirt which goes with it, worn by Punjabi women
samadhi	place where a saint achieves enlightenment

samosa	thinly rolled out dough, stuffed with potatoes and deep fried
Sardar	usual prefix for a Sikh man. Used as a noun to denote 'leader' or 'Sikh'
Sarkar	government
satyagrahi	fighter for the truth
Seth	businessman
shamiana	canvas covering stretched on poles, erected as protection against the weather for marriages, meetings, etc
sheras	tigers, brave men
shikar	game shooting
shisham	tree with light-coloured wood, used in furniture-making
simul	tree with long, thin branches
solar topee	sun hat
tahsil	a division by area, for the purposes of administration
tandoori	food baked in a clay oven
toddy	date tree, whose sap is collected to make a strong liquor
tonga	horse-drawn covered buggy
topi	small, hard cap
Vaziri women	women belonging to a particular mountain tribe
Vilayat	England
yatra	journey, sometimes in the nature of a pilgrimage
zari	gold thread

Chronology of Events

The characters in *Yatra* are fictitious. This chronology is intended only as a historical background for the action of the novel, which deviates from history often and without scruple.

Early History of the Punjab

1839: Death of Maharajah Ranjit Singh, lion of Punjab.

1846: First Anglo-Sikh War

January 1849: Battle of Chillianwala

February 21 1849: Battle of Gujarat

March 29 1849: A proclamation published declaring the Kingdom of the Sikhs at an end. Maharajah Dalip Singh handed over the Koh-i-noor diamond to the British.

Early 19th Century: Sikh immigration into Canada and the U.S.A. Formation of the left-leaning Ghadr Party.

Guru-ka-Bagh

1914-1918: Sikh soldiers fought on all fronts of the war, in Europe, Turkey and Africa.

April 13, *Baisakhi* Day, 1919: Massacre by General Dyer at Jallianwala Bagh in Amritsar.

November 1920: Formation of the Shiromani Gurudwara Prabandhak Committee (SGPC), the central *gurudwara* management committee. More radical elements organised a semi-military army of volunteers known as the Akali Dal (army of immortals).

February 1921: A *jatha* led by Lachman Singh Dharovalia entered the *gurudwara* at Nankana Sahib, base of the corrupt Mahant Narain Das, who had them hacked and burned to death.

May 21, 1921: SGPC passed a resolution not to cooperate with the British government and exhorted Sikhs to boycott British goods.

August 1921: The Mahant, or Chief, of Guru-ka-Bagh (garden of the Guru), a small shrine about 13 miles from Amritsar, lodged a protest about Akalis cutting timber from the *gurudwara* land. *Jathas* of 100 Akali each took an oath at the Golden Temple in Amritsar to remain non-violent, and then proceeded to Guru-ka-Bagh, where they were beaten mercilessly by the British police. The Indian National Congress appointed a Committee of Inquiry. When C. F. Andrews visited the scene, he was deeply moved by the noble 'Christ-like' behaviour of the Akalis.

October 30 1921: Thousands of men and women laid themselves on the rail track at Panja Sahib in an attempt to stop the train, to give refreshment to the prisoners from Guru-ka-Bagh, who were being escorted to Naoshera goal. Two men were crushed to death before the engine driver could pull up.

1921-1923: The behaviour of the police at Guru-ka-Bagh induced some Sikhs to organise an underground terrorist movement, the Babbar Akali, drawn mainly from the Ghadr party and soldiers on leave. To get arms, the Babbars sent agents to the North West Frontier Province, and issued a bulletin, the *Babbar Akali Doaba Akhbar.*

August 31, 1923: Four Babbars led by Karam Singh, acting editor of the *Babbar Akali Doaba,* were betrayed and surrounded by police in the village of Babeli. Their hut was set on fire, the four emerged with drawn *kirpans* and fell under a hail of bullets.

October 25 1923: Dhanna Singh of Behbalpur was betrayed by one of his comrades and captured at night while asleep. With manacled hands he managed to explode a hand-grenade hidden in his armpit. The blast killed Dhanna Singh, nine policemen and a buffalo.

Partition

April 16 1932: Ramsay Macdonald made his award on communal representation: a bitter blow for the Sikhs, which gave Muslims permanent majority in the Punjab. Sikhs were awarded three of the fifty seats in the North West Frontier Province.

Third Round Table Conference: the Sikh nominee was Master Tara Singh of Ferozepur.

1939-1945: Sikh politicians struggled unsuccessfully against the movement for the formation of Pakistan.

March 22 1946: The Shiromani Akali Dal passed a resolution stating 'Sikhistan' to be its political objective, and claiming that 'the entity of the Sikhs is being threatened on account of the persistent demand of Pakistan by the Muslims on the one hand and of the danger of absorption by the Hindus on the other.' It demanded 'the preservation and protection of the religious, cultural and economic and political rights of the Sikh population, with provision for the transfer and exchange of population and property.'

March 1946: Civil strife in Punjab. Rioting in Amritsar, Rawalpindi, Gujarat, Multan and Cambellpur. The largest number of victims were Sikh.

April 13 *Baisakhi* Day, 1947: Master Tara Singh and 280 *jathedars* vowed at the Akal Takht (Golden Temple) to sacrifice their lives for the community.

August 15 1947: India gains Independence, and Pakistan is carved out of its territory. Much violence in Punjab, with Sikh violence attaining its peak in September 1947. In winter of 1946-47 Sikh refugees from the North West Frontier Province started trekking to the central provinces. Waves of hatred swept the Punjab: around 200,000 men, women and children were killed and some five million left their homes and crossed the border. Sikhs and Hindus of western Punjab migrated to India. A Resettlement Department with a staff of nearly 8,000 *patwaris* and rural officers was established at Jullundur. The government took over the houses and lands of Muslim evacuees, and gave them to Hindu and Sikh refugees.

Kashmir

July-October 1947: Maharajah Hari Singh, Hindu ruler of Kashmir which had a majority Muslim population, could not make up his mind about accession to India or to Pakistan.

24 October 1947: A large-scale invasion of tribesmen from the North West Frontier Province into Kashmir. Thereafter, the Maharajah acceded to India, and on 27 October the movement of Indian troops into Srinagar began. The raiders were repulsed.

Hyderabad

August 1947 – June 1948: V. P. Menon and Sardar Patel played a major role, as did Lord Mountbatten, in protracted and tortuous negotiations with the Nizam of Hyderabad, Muslim ruler of the state, with a majority Hindu population. A role was also played by the *Razakars*, the extreme Muslim organisation in Hyderabad, and their Chief, Qasim Razvi: every volunteer for the *Razakars*, the militant branch of the Ittehadul-e-Mussalmeen, had to take an oath which included the words: 'In the name of Allah, I hereby promise that I will fight to the last to maintain the supremacy of the Muslim power in the Deccan'. The Nizam and his advisers were convinced that India would be unable to take any action against Hyderabad because her hands were full with Kashmir and other problems.

October 1947: A delegation of Nawab of Chhatari, Sir Sultan Ahmed and Sir Walter Monckton arrived in Hyderabad. At 3 a.m. a crowd of 20,000 collected round the house where the delegation was staying. The Ittehadul-e-Mussalmeen publicly claimed credit for having organised this crowd in order to prevent by physical force the departure of the delegation to Delhi. The Nizam, fierce in denouncing the Ittehadul-e-Mussalmeen and its leader Qasim Razvi to members of the delegation, actually gave way to him.

29 November 1947: Standstill Agreement

May 22 1948: *Razakars* attack Hindus. K. M. Munshi was appointed as India's Representative in Hyderabad.

September 13 1948: Military action begun by Indian Government against Hyderabad State. The action lasted a week, then Hyderabad was integrated into India.

January 26 1950: India adopted a Constitution and became a Republic.

Bangladesh

March 1971: A military crackdown on East Pakistan began. Thousands of Bengali refugees fled over the border into India, and Mukti Bahini guerrilla camps were set up.

December 1971: Pakistan attacked India.

6 December: India recognised Bangladesh.

16 December: Lieutenant General A. A. K. Niazi, Chief of the Pakistan Army in Bangladesh, signed an instrument of surrender to Lieutenant General Jagjit Singh Aurora, General Officer Commanding-in-Chief, Eastern Command of India.